ROAD TO NOWHERE

USA TODAY BESTSELLING AUTHOR

M. ROBINSON

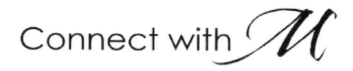

Connect with M

WEBSITE

FACEBOOK

INSTAGRAM

TWITTER

AMAZON PAGE

VIP READER GROUP

NEWSLETTER

EMAIL ADDRESS

MORE BOOKS BY M

All FREE WITH KINDLE UNLIMITED

EROTIC ROMANCE

VIP (The VIP Trilogy Book One)

THE MADAM (The VIP Trilogy Book Two)

MVP (The VIP Trilogy Book Three)

TEMPTING BAD (The VIP Spin-Off)

TWO SIDES GIANNA (Standalone)

CONTEMPORARY/NEW ADULT

THE GOOD OL' BOYS STANDALONE SERIES

COMPLICATE ME

FORBID ME

UNDO ME

CRAVE ME

EL DIABLO (THE DEVIL)

ROAD TO NOWHERE

ACKNOWLEDGMENTS

To ALL my readers and my VIPS!
Thank you for allowing me to do what I love every day of my life. I couldn't do this without you!

I LOVE YOU!!!

Boss man: Words cannot describe how much I love you. Thank you for ALWAYS being my best friend. I couldn't do this without you.

Dad: Thank you for always showing me what hard work is and what it can accomplish. For always telling me that I can do anything I put my mind to.

Mom: Thank you for ALWAYS being there for me no matter what. You are my best friend.

Julissa Rios: I love you and I am proud of you. Thank you for being a pain in my ass and for being my sister. I know you are always there for me when I need you.

Ysabelle & Gianna: Love you my babies.

Rebecca Marie: THANK YOU for an AMAZING cover. I wouldn't know what to do without you and your fabulous creativity.

Heather Moss: Thank you for everything that you do!! I wouldn't know what to do without you! You're. The. Best. PA. Ever!! You're NEVER leaving me!! XO

Silla Webb: Thank you so much for your edits and formatting! I love it and you!

Erin Noelle: Thank you for everything you do!

Michelle Tan: Best beta ever! **Argie Sokoli:** I couldn't do this without you. You're my chosen person. **Tammy McGowan:** Thank you for all your support, feedback, and boo boo's you find! I'm happy I made you cry. **Michele Henderson McMullen:** LOVE LOVE LOVE you!! **Dee Montoya:** I value our friendship more than anything. Thanks for always being honest.
Rebeka Christine Perales: You always make me smile. **Alison Evan-Maxwell:** Thank you for coming in last minute and getting it

done like a boss. **Mary Jo Toth:** Your boo-boos are always great! Thank you for everything you do in VIP! **Ella Gram:** You're such a sweet and amazing person! Thank you for your kindness. **Kimmie Lewis:** Your friendship means everything to me. **Tricia Bartley:** Your comments and voice always make me smile! **Kristi Lynn:** Thanks for all your honesty and for joining team M. **Pam Batchelor:** Thanks for all your suggestions. **Jenn Hazen:** Thank you for everything! **Laura Hansen:** I. Love. You. **Patti Correa:** You're amazing! Thank you for everything! **Jennifer Pon:** Thank you for all your feedback and suggestions! You're amazing! **Michelle Kubik Follis:** Welcome back! I missed you too! **Deborah E Shipuleski:** Thank you for all your quick honest feedback! **Kaye Blanchard:** Thank you for wanting to join team M! **Beth Morton Conley:** Thank you for everything! **KR Nadelson:** I love you! **Bri Partin:** Thank you for everything you do! **Mary Grzeszak:** Thanks for all the military info! You're amazing! **Patti McDaniel Adams:** Thanks for all the MC information! You're awesome! **Danielle Stewart:** Thanks for coming in late and helping! **Mel LuvstooRead:** Thank you so much for everything! You helped so much! **Lily Garcia:** I love you! **Allison East:** Thank you!

Michael Joseph: Thank you for all the MC and military knowledge!

Wander Aguiar: Thank you so much for doing a photo-shoot for me and being amazing. Wander Book Club

Marshall Perrin: Thank you for the amazing cover photo! You make the perfect Creed. Marshall Perrin

To all my author buddies:

Jettie Woodruff: You complete me.

Erin Noelle: I. Love. You!

To all the bloggers:

A HUGE THANK YOU for all the love and support you have shown me. I have made some amazing friendships with you that I hold dear to my heart. I know that without you I would be nothing!! I cannot THANK YOU enough!! Special thanks to Like A Boss Book Promotions for hosting my tours!

Last but not least.

YOU.

My readers.

THANK YOU!!

Without you…

I would be nothing.

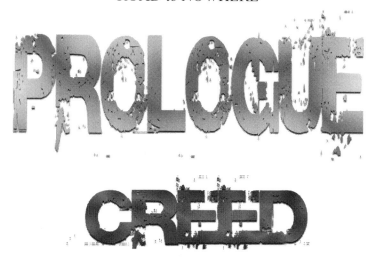

Mia Ryder.

Mia fuckin' Ryder.

I sat at the train tracks. Desperately trying not to think about her, but it was easier said than done. She came into my life like a fucking hurricane, destroying everything in her path. A girl from the right side of the tracks, which for some reason I couldn't ever fucking fathom.

Falling for a man like me.

I had made mistakes, too many to fucking count, but life didn't give you a do-over. All that was left for me to do was to accept them, even fucking embrace them. They became a part of me, as much as every tattoo that covered my body. Every one of them meant something to me. They were my battle scars. Far worse than the ones I got in war. In the eyes of others, they were just colorful, intricate art.

But to me...

They were my solace and my pain.

Nothing had changed since the last time I fucking lived in this godforsaken town. No welcome home party from family or friends, no thanks or parades from the town residents for serving our country.

Nothing.

Not one fucking thing.

Everything I had done, I had done for my family, for the MC, for her...

I fought for my fucking brothers.

I fought for my goddamn country.

I fought for my girl.

Never realizing…

I might fucking die for them too.

Ashes to ashes, dust to dust, and all that fucking shit. I once read that every warrior hoped a good death would find him. I always went looking for mine, but not even the Reaper wanted me. I thought fighting for something I believed in would make me a good man.

In the end, it never mattered. I would always be on the wrong side of the tracks, and they would always lead me to the wrong station. Changing my people, places, and things throughout the years didn't help change the outcome of the choices I'd made. Of the things I'd done.

At the end of the day…

I was already nailed to the cross.

I was fucking born on it.

"It ain't gonna suck itself, sweetheart," I stated with a predatory regard, eyeing the busty blonde up and down.

She was a new club whore with a banging body, huge tits, heart-shaped ass, and way too much fucking makeup on her mousy face. She'd been eye-fucking the shit out of me since she showed up at the clubhouse a few days ago. I was never much for dabbling in the club bunnies that bounced from one cock to another, but that didn't stop me from letting them suck my cock. After the day I'd had, I fucking earned it.

"Here? On your bike?" she coyly asked, gazing all around her. Trying to pretend like she'd never done this before.

We were tucked behind a row of trees on the club's property. My go-to spot for quickies, and the only place I could ride to on my bike. My pops gave me a sleek Harley Davidson Sportster for my sixteenth birthday almost two years ago. I'm pretty sure he didn't pay for it, but who was I to complain, it was a sick-looking bike. It had all matte black components, custom fenders, seat, and gas tank with the club logo painted on it. Not to mention the killer engine and exhaust system, visible on the sides. A set of shortened handlebars, and a massive front headlight that completed the badass machine.

The clubhouse was barely visible in the distance, making it impossible for anyone to see us. Not that I gave a flying fuck.

"You said you wanted to hang out."

"No, sweetheart," I chuckled. "What I said was I had somethin' hangin' for you." Gesturing to my cock.

Her eyes widened. Dark and dilated. Biting her pouty red lip that I couldn't wait to have wrapped around my dick.

"Can see how you would confuse that, though," I sarcastically added, grabbing a strand of her fake platinum blonde hair.

Women's place in an MC's life was always in the fucking background. The club came first no matter what. We all carried the same principles—honor, respect, and brotherhood. A family made up of ruthless motherfuckers right down to their goddamn bones. All led by the shadiest son of a bitch known to man.

My pops.

He was the president of the mother chapter, Devil's Rejects, in South Port, North Carolina. The first chapter established, making him the top fucking dog of the MC. Even though every chapter below had a president of their own, they couldn't make executive decisions without his final approval. Getting a visit from him only ended in death. He would only step in if he was fucking crossed or shit hit the fan in a catastrophic way.

Other than that, the chapters did whatever the fuck they wanted, it was a fucking free-for-all. My old man could do no wrong in everyone's eyes, when in reality that was all he ever fucking did. Cops' pockets were greased with dirty money to turn a blind eye to all our illegal activities. Everywhere we went, people looked the opposite direction and moved the fuck out of our way. Devil's Rejects were known to all, spread out all over the community, the state, even nation fucking wide.

Everywhere.

The only enemy we had was the law.

She smirked, cocking her head to the side, slowly licking her luscious lips as she casually reached for the front of my vest. Teasingly skimming her long red fingernails down the front of it, never taking her sinful eyes off mine.

"Creed," I murmured, wanting to hear my name fall from her lips.

"I know your name, Creed. Mine's—"

"Not fuckin' important, yeah?"

She arched an eyebrow, looking down at the rugged fabric of my cut.

Our black leather vests or cuts as we called them, were the MC's brand, our signature trademark recognized by everyone, especially women and civilians. They were each chapter's identification, who we were and what we stood for. On the back of our cuts were the club's colors, a badass looking tattooed pin-up girl with huge fucking tits sporting devil ears and a tail. Straddling a custom chopper, holding a skull with flames beating out of its eyes in one hand and an AK47 rifle in the other. Above the logo was a crescent-shaped red patch that read "Devil's Rejects" in black acidy lettering. Below the logo was another crescent-shaped patch with Southport, NC stitched on it.

On the front left of our cut was a "one-percent" patch that was worn with fucking pride, indicating we were outlaws. There were no rules to follow unless it came to the club or our brothers, fucking laws became obsolete. Devil's Rejects had been around since the forties and had more than proven their loyalty to the MC world. Quickly becoming one of the most feared clubs in society. One of the select few that was branded as a "one-percent" club. We were diehard bikers who would stop at nothing, even murder, to prove ourselves worthy.

Honorable fucking killers.

I've seen the brutality firsthand. It's not a pretty sight. Fucking Neanderthals, not to be fucked with, or else. Nothing happened in Southport without our knowledge or control.

Not one damn thing.

Our cuts were our holy grail.

Her fingers skimmed the right front panel of my cut, over my "MC" patch that only true motorcycle clubs sported. You'd never see this on a HOGS vest because let's face it, they were just a bunch of pussy-ass wannabe riders on expensive bikes, never willing to get their fucking hands dirty.

"Where are the rest of your patches, Creed?" she purred. "All the other bikers have years lined up under this MC patch, here. Haven't served much time, huh?"

I narrowed my eyes at her, growing more annoyed and irritated as the seconds passed. I was never one for fucking chit chat.

"You don't talk much, do you?"

I pointed to the name "Prospect" stitched on the right of my cut, where my name and rank would be as soon as I turned eighteen. The black leather was a blank canvas for now, but eventually, it would be filled with random duty patches scattered around. All representing what I had done and what I'd fucking do for the club and the brothers.

For now, I was at the bottom of the fucking chain, itching for my day to come. I couldn't really complain much, though, having my old man as Prez definitely had its fucking perks. Respect was one of them. Anyone fucking crossed me, they'd be crossing Pops, too. A fucking death wish you didn't want to sign up for.

I spent the last seventeen years of my life watching him rule with an iron fist, annihilating what so many Jameson men built before him. My future was sealed the day my parents found out I had a cock. I would follow in the long line of men in my family, taking over as MC Prez one day.

As of right now, I was just another fucking prospect doing the shit jobs that they didn't want to do. Making myself available at all hours, whether it was to dig a fucking grave, getting my hands dirty in more ways than one, or going on a fucking food run for the lazy bastards. I'd seen and done more shit than any mother would ever be proud of, but that never mattered. I was thrown in with the wolves too many goddamn times to count, just to see if I would come out alive. I did every fucking time, with a fat ass smile on my motherfucking face, just as ruthless as the rest of the brotherhood.

Always proving myself worthy to the club, but mostly to my father. He wouldn't just let me sign my life away. He wanted my fucking blood on it. Holding the shit I had done for the club over my head. Reminding me, if I ever stepped out of line, just how easy it would be for him to use the leverage he had to make me march right back in line where I belong. Following him, the Prez; his rules, his authority, his final word, once again. One day soon, I would patch in as a brother, whether I wanted to or not.

It wasn't a lifestyle. It was a way of life.

The only one I'd ever known.

I slipped my hand behind her neck, gripping tight and tugging her toward me not moving from the place I sat on my bike. Causing a gasp to escape from her lips at the sudden change in my demeanor. Patience was never one of my fucking virtues. It was a Jameson trait that ran deep in my blood. I determined the who, what, when, and where in life.

Anyone who didn't approve could go fuck themselves.

Bottom line, I lived and breathed for my mother and my baby brothers—Luke, who was fourteen years old, and Noah, who was eleven. Everything else was just a means to an end for me.

"I—"

"Shhh…" Silencing her with my index finger, I brought my mouth inches away from her lips. Her breathing hitched the closer I got, my warm breath assaulting her senses. "Only thing I want from this mouth," I paused, pecking her lips, "is for it to be wrapped around my cock," I rasped, emphasizing the last word as I guided my thumb into her pouty mouth.

She sucked it like a goddamn pro, eagerly reaching for my belt and unbuckling it.

"Good girl," I praised, removing my thumb with a pop. Guiding her closer to me by the nook of her neck. "Now pull out my cock," I groaned into her ear, causing her skin to immediately warm under my touch. She did as she was told with unsteady hands, never taking her eyes off mine.

I didn't know her fucking name. I didn't care to learn it either. None of these girls mattered. Besides, I was never any fucking good with names.

"Stroke it. Harder," I ordered as I continued to kiss down her neck to her tits that were on full display.

"Like this?" she breathed out.

I groaned, cupping her breasts and burying my face in them. "Yeah, babe. Just like that," I groaned, into her breasts. Jerking her head back by her hair, lowering her to the ground. Not letting go until she was on her fucking knees in front of me. She suddenly released my cock when I placed my own hand around my shaft, stroking myself up and down in front of her face.

She looked up at me with hooded eyes, craving to taste me. I continued to jerk myself off until she sucked the head of my cock into her greedy mouth. Moving down toward the base of my shaft, taking me in, inch by inch.

"Deeper," I demanded, gripping onto a fist full of her hair. She gagged as soon as I felt the back of her throat, but her hand never stopped working me over. Making it easy to quickly find a rhythm that had my head slightly leaning back, and my mouth parting.

My eyes remained focused on her as she sucked my cock like she had something to prove. Her hand followed the movements of her mouth, while her other hand tugged at my balls simultaneously. My breathing became erratic, fueling my need to rock my hips in the opposite direction of her heady movements. Wanting nothing more than to take full control and fuck her face.

"Gonna come," I growled.

I wasn't a complete asshole. I at least gave her a fucking warning.

She tried to remove her lips off my cock, but I gripped onto the back of her head, shoving it deeper. Moving my hips forward one last time and coming hard in the back of her throat. Shaking out my release, I pulled my dick from her mouth with a pop. "Swallow," I sternly ordered.

She peeked up at me through her lashes, immediately doing as she was told. Wiping the corners of her mouth, trying to fix her red lipstick that was now painted all over my cock. I tucked myself back into my pants and buckled my belt when she seductively glided her way up my body, going right for my mouth.

I jerked back. "If I wanted to taste my come I'd lick it off your face, sweetheart. Ya got a little somethin' right here." I gestured to the corner of my lip.

She pulled away, snarling, "Fuck you!"

I grinned, scoffing out, "No, thanks. Got requirements for that position, and you obviously don't fuckin' qualify, darlin'."

"You ass—"

"Creed!" I heard Luke's voice echo through the trees. "Ya out there?"

I revved my bike a few times, getting ready to take off.

"What the hell? You're just going to leave me out here?" She stomped her foot like a three-year-old, reminding me exactly why I never stayed around after my balls were empty.

"Use those legs for somethin' other than just spreadin' them open," I crudely mocked, riding off, hearing her scream something or another behind me. I sped up the path into the clearing, making

16

my way over to Luke, who had a shit-eating grin on his face when he came into sight.

He shook his head. "Another one? That's number three and it's only Friday," he called out over the rumbling noise of my bike.

"Mind your business, little brother."

He rolled his eyes, kicking some gravel beneath his shoes.

"What are you doin' here? Just get out of school? Where's Ma?" I questioned, pulling up right in front of him. Using the toe of my black combat boot to flip out the kickstand.

I should have been in school, too, instead, I was riding around all fucking day, getting everything in order for the club meeting. I was already falling behind in most of my classes from skipping all the damn time. I refused to sit in that hellhole and be told what to do by a bunch of teachers who didn't give a flying fuck about me. Not like I needed an education for my future.

"She's inside takin' care of business with Dad."

I chuckled, pointing to the clubhouse. "Christa is in there. He ain't gonna be happy she came uninvited, again."

"Is he ever happy?"

I laughed, knowing he was right.

Christa was one of Pops' main fucks. She was another whore barely off her momma's tit. I had witnessed my old man fucking club whores more times than I cared to fucking count. The bastard never bothered hiding the fact that he stuck his cock in every slut that spread her legs for him. I couldn't pinpoint a time when he wasn't cheating on my mother, and she wasn't crying herself to sleep over his infidelities. You'd think after so many acts of betrayals, she would wake the fuck up and leave him. Instead, she stuck right by his side, acting like nothing was wrong, giving him more sons. Probably hoping that was enough to prove her loyalty to him and the club.

Which was a crock of shit if you asked me.

Or maybe she just wanted to remind everyone that she was still his old lady. Except old ladies weren't allowed on the property unless invited, usually during big parties, when they were needed in the kitchen where they belonged, cooking for the members. On those days, it was a free for all. The rule allowed the brothers freedom to not worry about catfights that would break out due to their dicks getting wet by a pussy that wasn't their wives'. If the old ladies thought their men were keeping their cocks tucked in their pants, they deserved to be cheated on for being so fucking stupid. Ma already knew what Pops was up to, it wasn't a secret. He didn't give a fuck how it made her feel, he knew she had too much to lose by leaving him.

Leaning back, I killed the engine on my bike and grabbed the pack of smokes from the front of my cut. Placing the nicotine-fueled stick between my lips, lighting it up, and blowing the smoke into the air, away from Luke. He hated the smell of cigarettes, giving me shit for years on how I was killing myself slowly with every puff or some bullshit like that. He finally gave up recently, knowing I was a lost cause. Smoking was my vice, quickly becoming addicted to the nicotine that calmed me.

My refuge from the shit storm I lived in.

I was exposed to it all my life, everyone around me smoked like fucking fiends, one cigarette after another. I took my first drag when I was eleven, and shortly after that, I smoked my first joint with the brothers. It wasn't all that bad, I could've gotten into much worse shit. Drugs and booze were prevalent in my daily life, just as much as the women were. My body was already covered in ink.

Just another one of my vices.

"What's up?" I asked, setting the cigarette on the corner of my lips.

"Well… I kind of… I mean…" he stumbled over his words, shuffling his feet around. Looking everywhere but at me.

"Out with it, Luke."

He visibly took a deep breath, finally locking eyes with me and blurted, "I need some advice."

I cocked my head, curious.

"On… you know… life and stuff…"

"Pussy?" I stated with raised eyebrows, cutting to the chase.

"Never mind. Forget it." He abruptly turned to walk away from me, but I wasn't going to let him get away that easy. I got off my bike and grabbed him by the arm.

"Not so fast. Spill."

He turned back around to face me. "How do you know I want to talk about a girl?"

18

I grinned, letting go. "It's always about a girl. You hittin' it or you wanna hit it?"

"I got a girl, Creed."

"You got a dick, Luke. That's what you got. So stop pussyfootin' around and tell me what I can advise you on, other than whether or not you're gonna put it in. You sure as fuck better put it on," I reminded, referring to him wrapping it up.

"Yeah… yeah… I know."

"Gonna be fifteen soon. Balls got to drop any day now."

"I mean… when did you—"

"Eleven. Woke up in the middle of the night with my dick in her mouth. Lasted about twenty seconds once she started ridin' me," I laughed, remembering how much of a one-pump chump I was.

"Was she—"

"Couldn't tell you what she looked like in the dark. Pops needed to make sure his firstborn son loved pussy as much as he does and he wasn't raisin' a homo."

He jerked back, surprised by my revelation. Those were the exact words my father used the next morning. I reminded him that I was only eleven, which earned me a backhand to the face. Telling me I should be thanking him for what he provided, not mouthing off.

I shook off the memory. "It's okay, Luke. Can't rape the willin'." I smirked. "I'll always be honest with you. Not gonna sugarcoat shit, ain't got the time or patience for that. Had to learn things the hard way, don't want that for you. Everythin' I do is for Ma, you and Noah and don't you ever fuckin' forget it."

We were all in this life for the long run, left to deal with our shitty luck. It wasn't Luke or Noah's fault. They didn't ask to be born in this fucked up world any more than I did. I would die for my baby brothers and a part of me still held on to the hope that they wouldn't have to live this life forever. Deep down I knew I was a goddamn fool, just like my mother. She was holding onto the notion of a better husband and father while I was holding onto the notion of a better life.

Pops would give his last dying breath for his sons to follow in his footsteps. Come Hell or high water, we had no say in our destiny. It was already mapped out for us.

Especially mine.

"I know. I just... I really like her, you know? I don't want to mess it up."

"So, you're sayin' this isn't about pussy? It's about love?" I chuckled uncomfortably.

He nodded, placing his hands in his pockets, waiting for what, I wasn't sure.

I walked past him to sit on the top of the old wooden picnic table in the far back of the clubhouse. Resting my elbows on my knees, flicking the ashes from my cigarette down to the grass.

Trying like hell, to come up with some genuine advice for him. Thinking back to all the chick flicks my mother would watch with envy. The same shit over and over, boy meets girl, boy asks girl to marry him, and they live happily ever after with three kids, a dog, and a white picket fence. A bunch of fucking bullshit that wasn't real life, but there had to be something I could pull out of my ass to tell him.

"Look, Luke... don't think I'm the best person to be askin' love advice from. Love is... well, love is fuckin'..." I shrugged, taking another drag of my cigarette, not knowing what to say.

The sounds of motorcycle engines revving suddenly filled the air around us from the front of the clubhouse. Soon this place would be crawling with the elite of the fucking elite, and I was due inside at any second.

"It's fine, just go. I know you have obligations with Pops and the club," he sighed, disappointed. Watching me twist my watch around my wrist.

I ignored him. "You like her? Like, wanna date her and see where it goes, yeah?"

"Yes," he simply stated, hopping up onto the table next to me. "She's different, Creed. Not like the girls from around here, that's for sure," he admitted, rubbing the back of his neck. Trying to act like a man, when he was still such a kid.

I don't think I would ever be able to see my baby brothers for anything other than my responsibility. It had been that way since the day they were born. My mother wasn't a bad mom, she just had too much of her own shit to worry about. At the end of the day, she just didn't know any better. Raising three boys wasn't easy, and my dad was no help. All she did was fall for a guy from the wrong side of the tracks, getting knocked up young, with me. Trying to grow up ever since. She did love us, though, and tried to show us affection often, making up for my father's lack of.

He didn't give a shit about anything but the MC.

"She's just moved here from Dallas, Texas," Luke informed, pulling me away from my thoughts. I took another drag of my cigarette, flicking it out in front of me.

"Her daddy is in some kinda sales. Makes good money that's for sure. She wears nice clothes every day, has long brown hair, blue eyes, and smells so fuckin' good."

I smiled, glancing over at him, watching his face light up as he talked about his girl. I'd be lying if I said it didn't make me proud that he wanted to do right by her. That our upbringing hadn't jaded his thoughts about women and love like it had me.

"Anyway, we've been hangin' out at school. I haven't even kissed her yet. So, I just figured you have a lot of experience with girls... maybe you could give me some advice. I even wanted to ask you if maybe you could pick her up tomorrow night and drop us off at the movies? I'd ask Ma but..."

"She'd embarrass the shit out of you." We both laughed, knowing it was the truth. "Tell me if I'm followin'. You don't wanna just fuck her, but you want to play fuckin' house, yeah?"

He leaned forward, cocking his head to the side, and nodded.

"Feelin' okay?" I reached over, trying to feel his forehead. He jumped down from the table, out of my reach. "You know you're a Jameson, right?" I laughed.

"Fuck you! Forget about it. Forget I ever said anything. I'll figure this out on my own, douche bag." He shoved my shoulder and I immediately groaned in pain. Grabbing onto it, trying to deter the throbbing ache.

"Ah, hell, can't take a joke now, little brother? Man up," I let out, laughing it off.

"What happened to you?" he instantly asked, reaching over. Pulling my hand, cut, and shirt away from my shoulder. "Why is your shoulder all bandaged up?"

"Luke, I'm fine."

"Bullshit. Did you get shot at? Where is Dad sending—"

I pushed him away. "Don't need babyin', Luke. I'm fine. Promise," I reassured, holding three fingers in the air. "Scouts' honor."

"Since when are you a boy scout?"

"Since I ate a fuckin' brownie. Now get your skinny ass back over here and finish what you were sayin'."

He chuckled even though he was still worried, sitting back down next to me.

"She know how ya feel?" I questioned, changing the subject.

"I think so."

"Then go for her, Luke. You like her, you show her. Treat her with respect. Simple as that. Think and act with your brain and heart." I rested my hand on his chest. "Instead of your cock." Nudging his shoulder. "Ya feel me?"

He took a deep breath, contemplating what to say next. I narrowed my eyes at him.

"I also want to give her this. What do you think?" He reached up, unhooking the chain from around his neck.

I knew exactly what he was referring to before he even showed me. Pops had given all us boys a St. Columbanus, the patron saint of motorcyclists when we were born. A medallion on a silver chain. It was supposed to keep us safe, protected, and signify the life we were born into.

The MC life.

The back of each medallion had the time we were born engraved on it with the words "Ride or Die." When we were babies, Ma would pin the medallion to our onesies, but as we got older, we wore it around our necks.

"Luke, I don't think—"

"There you are, you piece of shit," Pops' voice bellowed from the back screen door, interrupting me. "You fuckin' deaf? You not hear the bikes pullin' up? Get your ass inside right now, before I think twice on lettin' you attend."

"Pops, it was my fault," Luke interfered.

"Don't." I put my hand up, silencing him.

"Did I tell ya to speak? You are just like your fuckin' ma, always speakin' when not spoken to. You're weak, and worthless like her too." He came through the door, down the three steps. Grabbing

Luke by his shirt and pulling him from the table. Knocking his necklace out of his hand, making it fall to the dirt below me. "Do I need to teach you another lesson, boy?"

I could see Luke's hands working into fists, his face flushed and his jaw clenched like he was about to say something he'd surely fucking regret.

"You're a Dick," Luke muttered under his breath.

"What was that?" Pops tugged him closer to his face.

I got up, stubbing my cigarette out on the wood. Immediately grabbing Luke by his arm, yanking him out of Dad's grasp. I stepped up, placing Luke securely behind me.

"Ain't his fault. My fuck up. Won't happen again," I gritted out, trying to remain calm. "Luke, walk away." I spun, shoving him back.

"Come on, boy, don't be a pussy. Spit it out, what did you say?" Dad antagonized further, needing to take out his aggression on someone.

Usually me.

I gave Luke a stern look, warning him to keep his goddamn mouth shut. The last thing I wanted was to go hand and fist with our father, but I would if he put his hands on my brothers or mother in front of me. I think a part of him knew not to cross that line with me. Which was why he never hit them in my presence, but that never stopped him from unleashing his wrath through his fists, nonetheless.

"Nothin', Sir," Luke replied, understanding my silent warning.

"Now run along, the real men have important business to take care of. When you grow a pair of fuckin' balls, you'll be able to play, too," he provoked, wanting to have the last word.

Pops watched Luke walk in the direction of Ma's car, where she was standing with nothing but pain and regret in her eyes. It was always worse when she tried to defend us, his anger would just turn to her. Furious that she was trying to raise us into a bunch of pussies, when all he was trying to do was make us into men.

I reached down, grabbing Luke's necklace. Shoving it in my pocket before Dad saw. Making a mental note to give it back to my brother later.

He nodded to me. "Get your ass inside." With that, he turned and walked up the back steps.

"Thanks, baby," Mom called out when he was back inside, bringing my attention to her.

I smiled, waving her off. Looking at Noah who was sitting in the passenger seat just shaking his head. She kissed Luke's cheek and whispered something in his ear I couldn't make out.

I took a long, deep, reassuring breath. Looking at the only thing that was ever truly important to me.

My family.

After I watched them drive off, my eyes went back to the clubhouse. The Prez had called in Church and I wasn't talking about the one where you sat in a chapel, praying to the lord above, asking forgiveness for your sins.

Because God didn't want us.

And Hell would spit us the fuck out.

I walked inside the old machine warehouse that was converted into the clubhouse decades ago. The run-down building was in the middle of nowhere, just outside of town with nothing but acres of open fields surrounding it. It was its own organization, governed by its own laws. The exterior was painted black with a massive mural of the club's logo on the front of the warehouse. Over the large steel door was the club's plaque that read Devil's Rejects MC, Southport, NC.

The building also housed several small loft apartments where club members would fuck the whores who were always hanging around, or use them for crashing occasionally. Some members even used them as their homes. Club whores were prevalent in the MC, fucking any brother at any given time. At times, we would get girls passing through town, just looking for a bad boy and a good fucking time. Knowing they'd find it here. There were a couple of girls who were nice, they just had a rough go at life and found shelter in this fucking place. The majority of them, though, were bouncing around from one cock to the next, hoping one of the brothers would be stupid enough to make them their old lady one day.

"You keep your fuckin' mouth shut. Understand me?" Dad threatened in a tone I was all too familiar with. Standing next to my post outside the door.

"Gonna let me in?" I replied, cocking my head to the side, referring to the meeting.

"After what you did for the club today. You fuckin' earned it."
He patted my back. "You'll be eighteen soon, we won't have
problems anymore. You'll stand where you're meant to be. By me,
son. By. Fuckin'. Me," he stated with pride.

I just nodded.

I took my position outside the door, standing guard, and
confiscating our guests' weapons and phones before they walked
into the room, an action necessary when civilians attended meetings.
All the patched in brothers took their places at the long rectangle
table where brothers sat on the right and guest attendees on the left.
My father always sat at the head of the table with his gavel in front
of him. Usually these meetings, church as we called them, were
always the same.

Alongside him was the Vice President, Striker, who had been
with the MC for over two decades. He was more than my father's
right-hand man. They were like blood brothers, having grown up
together. I grew up with his son, but really wasn't a fan of the
bastard. Personally, I always thought their friendship was all a crock
of shit.

Then there was Diesel, who went from being a nomad to the
Sergeant of Arms. Nomads were the Grim Reapers, they worked for
the club, killing anyone we said had to go without a second fucking
thought, or explanation. He took me to my first titty club when I was
fourteen, even bought me a fucking lap dance with a happy ending
from the young brunette with pouty lips, a luscious ass and tight
pussy. He was the brother I was the closest with.

Below his title was Stone, the Secretary. He transferred over
from the Arizona chapter and had been with us since last year. I'm
pretty sure he was responsible for "buying my bike," for Pops. He
was in his mid-twenties and never spoke much, but when he did, he
would have you laughing your ass off. He was the funniest son of a
bitch I ever met. Cracking jokes at the most inappropriate times. He
liked pussy as much as he liked making people laugh. The women
flocked to him for his sense of humor alone.

Last but not least was Phoenix, the treasurer of Devil's Rejects.
He counted our money as much as he did our goddamn drugs. I got
my first tattoo when I was ten years old by that cokehead, acquiring
several more pieces of ink from him since. I stopped counting how

many a few years ago. It was hard to say no when he offered all the damn time. He was a dope-ass artist, who was high as fuck all the time, but it only made him better at what he did.

Monthly meetings with just the patched-in brothers were less formal, compared to the ones when civilians attended. Pops preferred that church with business associates, be held on our turf, so he could still remain in control. In case shit ever hit the fan, which happened from time to time, the brothers would have direct shots from across the table. Not only were each of them loaded, there were guns rigged under the table where they sat, as well.

No one went in strapped other than the brothers.

No. One.

"Finish up here, there should only be a few more we are expectin'. Gonna start in about fifteen minutes, lock the artillery up, and come in. Stand in the back, pay attention, and keep your fuckin' mouth shut, ya hear?"

I nodded again, not really listening to a damn word he said, focusing on getting the guns checked. He walked into the meeting room and just as I was about to lock up shop, I saw a black limo with dark tinted windows pulling up to the front on the security screen above the door. I didn't have to fucking guess who it was, I knew exactly who sat behind the glass. His driver got out and opened the back passenger door, letting out several men including a tall man, with jet-black hair and tan skin. Only confirming what I already knew.

Alejandro Martinez.

He was a corrupt gangster straight out of New York City, who was feared by everyone that had ever crossed paths with him. They called him El Diablo or some shit. I didn't care for him. I never had. But he was the only man I ever saw my father somewhat cower down to, which probably should have meant something to me.

It didn't.

He'd show up from time to time unannounced. Stepping out of his chauffeured limo, wearing his fancy fucking suits and designer shoes. Not a hair out of place. Always rolling up deep with several bodyguards at his sides. All of them strapped and ready to kill, or be killed, for him. I couldn't figure out why my old man was wary of him. To me, he just seemed like a pussy hiding behind an expensive suit and his men. Pops couldn't figure out that Martinez worked for us, not the other way around. The MC was his supplier for guns and sometimes drugs.

He needed us. Plain and simple.

He buttoned his suit jacket, covering up the guns he had holstered underneath, and signaled for his men to stay put like fucking dogs, heeling behind their goddamn owner.

"Well if it isn't Creed Jameson," Martinez announced, walking through the steel door toward me. "Last time I saw you, you were still on your momma's tit," he paused, eyeing me up and down with a patronizing regard. "Very nice tits, if I remember correctly," he baited, standing tall in front of me with his hands in the pockets of his slacks. A smug look plastered on his fucking face. "Do you know who I am, son?"

I didn't falter. I didn't give a flying fuck who he was. No one came onto my turf, disrespecting my mother.

"Not your son." I nodded through a clenched jaw, crossing my arms over my chest, sizing him up.

I'd be lying if I said his solid muscular build, evident through his black three-piece suit, hadn't taken me back a little. We were the exact same size, 6'3, broad and stalky. Except I had fucking youth on my side, Martinez had to be in his late forties, but still had that pretty boy fucking face.

"I know exactly who you are," I stated, not backing down. Speaking my goddamn mind. "A pussy who hides behind his expensive fuckin' suits. Those goons suck your cock too?"

He let out a throaty laugh, his head falling back. "You have a set of real brass balls, *son*," he mocked, trying to brush past me, bumping into my shoulder. I stiff-armed him with my good arm right across his chest. Stopping him before he reached the door.

"Gonna need you to hand over all your guns." I peered down at him. "Includin' that Glock strapped to your leg."

"Aren't you cute." He grinned. "The fuck I am, you little shit. I'm already going in without my men. I'm not handing over my guns, especially to a hotheaded little Dick, whose fucking balls have barely dropped. You want to step up to me? I won't hesitate to put a fucking bullet in one of those balls," he spewed close to my face.

I didn't waver, grabbing onto the lapels of his suit, getting right up into his face. "Read the sign, motherfucker. No weapons beyond this point. You respect the club, or you get the fuck out." I smiled, releasing him, smoothing out the wrinkles I caused. Looking him straight in the eyes. "Let's try this again. Hand over your guns," I repeated in a cocky tone.

"What the fuck is goin' on out here?" Pops roared, barreling through the double doors, stopping when he was face to face with Martinez.

"I'm disappointed, Jameson. You should really teach your boy here some manners. Or should I teach him some for you?" Martinez snarled, arching an eyebrow, reaching into his suit jacket.

My father looked from him to me and back to him again.

"I suggest you tell this little ankle biter to shut the fuck up and let me pass. I'm your boss. I'm either coming in loaded, or I'm not coming in at all."

"I apologize for my son's behavior. I forgot to tell him you're the only exception. It won't happen again."

"Damn right it won't. He won't live to talk about it if it does," Martinez threatened, only glaring at me.

Dad eyed me. "Creed, stand down, boy. Martinez is a guest in this club. He doesn't need to check his weapons."

I jerked back. "Are you shittin' me?" I scoffed out, caught off guard by his response.

"Creed! Enough! I will deal with you later. Martinez, come on in, we were just about to start." He gestured toward the door.

Martinez walked past, body checking me in the shoulder, causing me to wince from the shooting pain radiating down my arm. I didn't sway, standing tall, resisting the urge to slam him up against the wall and fuck up his pretty boy face. My pissed-off old man, followed close behind him, shooting me a warning with his glare.

I backed away, shaking my head, surprised by the turn of events. I locked up the weapons, and followed them in, closing the door behind me. Taking my place by the far wall, right where I could keep an eye on the motherfucker, from across the room.

Martinez grinned like a fucking fool when he saw me, leaning back into his chair. Crossing his ankle over his leg, he unbuttoned his suit jacket, allowing the entire room to see that he was still locked and loaded. Fueling my anger.

He placed his hand on the table. "Since when do we let children attend the meetings?" he taunted.

"Since old fucks like you—"

Pops cleared his throat, bringing his attention back to him. If looks could kill, I'd be lying in a pool of my own blood at that moment.

Surrendering my hands, I shut my fucking mouth even though I had so much more to say.

The gavel sounded three times, announcing church was now in session. Silencing all the banter going on around the room, bringing everyone's focus to the Prez. It was the first time I was ever allowed in on church with other associates present, and I watched with a fascinated regard as my father took center stage. His demeanor read nothing but dominance and control, portraying the perfect image of the fearless, powerful, envied leader that he so desperately clung onto.

The older I got, the more my mother loved to remind me how I was the spitting image of him. From our deep-set gray eyes, narrow face, high cheekbones, square jaw, and pointed nose, to our stubborn, bullheaded personalities. With our dark brown hair that was always long on the top and shaved on the sides, reminding me of a military cut. Only Pops head was speckled with grays. We were both tall, slender, and had ripped tattooed bodies. He'd been having me work out with him since my voice changed and I was able to carry my own. Teaching me how to shoot everything from handguns to assault rifles, hitting targets at seventy-five yards out since I was fourteen.

"Let's just cut through the bullshit and get right to the problem at hand. Disagreements have arisen in the past few weeks, which led us to find out a group called Sinners Rejoice has stepped foot onto our territory. Tryin' to steal our business, our women, and actin' as if they are one of us. Goin' as far as usin' our goddamn name," he paused, looking around the room until his intense stare fell on Striker. "You wouldn't happen to know anythin' about these allegations, would you?"

All eyes went to Striker, our VP and probably one of the shadiest son of a bitch in Devil's Rejects.

He stood, adjusting his balls, shoving more chewing tobacco into his mouth, before replying, "Ain't heard shit, Prez, but tell me who I need to find and I will have the fucker in the ground before dawn."

Pops' laughter echoed through the room. "I beg to differ, motherfucker."

The lights dimmed and a picture illuminated on the far wall behind my father. I didn't have to look at the images to know what they were. I spent the last few weeks trailing his ass, taking those exact pictures. The same reason why my old man was so fucking proud of me.

"So, tell me, Striker, what the fuck do you think you're doin' in these pictures? Because you sure as shit ain't sellin' Girl Scout cookies."

"It ain't what it looks like, Prez," he stated, looking at the images of him with the rival gang members, leaning into each other, exchanging words.

"Is that right?" my father drawled out. "What about this one? It ain't what it looks like either?"

Another picture clicked over to Striker handing the same man an external USB stick. One picture after another, adding to the incriminating evidence that slowly brought down a trusted member.

Striker put his hands up in a surrendering gesture. "No, no, no, this is a misunderstanding. I... I... I—"

My father stood. "You... you... what? Gave the enemy intel? Betrayed every single person in this room? What, Striker?" He walked to the opposite side of the table, closest to me. "Cause to me that's exactly what it fuckin' looks like. And now, not only are you a fuckin' traitor. You're actin' like a fuckin' pussy." He suddenly slammed his fist down on the table, not making anyone jump, except Striker.

"You have till the count of three to come clean," Pops warned, never taking his fist off the table. One," he coaxed in a soft, calm voice.

"I... I..." Striker stammered, running his hands roughly through his silver hair, trying to find the words.

"Two..."

"Prez, please it's not what it looks like. We're fuckin' brothers! I love you. I love this fuckin' club. Please, you're my family! I... I..."

I looked from Striker back to my father. There was an eerie silence that filled the room. A quiet before the storm.

He narrowed his eyes at Striker, cocking his head to the side, and murmured, "Three." Before he even finished saying the number, he pulled out the semi-automatic from under the table, aiming directly at Striker's head. "Bang, bang, motherfucker!" Pops voice bellowed, followed by a deep chuckle. "Made ya flinch, didn't I?"

Striker lowered his hands, placing them on his chest, laughing along with my old man. "You had me there for a second, I'm not going to lie, asshole."

Pops swung the gun around his trigger finger a few times, stopping every time the barrel was aiming at Striker like a damn game of fucking roulette. Eyeing him with a menacing regard. "On second thought."

The gun went off, shooting Striker right in the shoulder. Then again in the groin, inches away from his cock, causing his body to jolt back from the unexpected blows. His back hit the wall hard as he shuddered to the ground, groaning in pain. He had one hand holding his shoulder, the other his leg with blood spewing from between his fingers.

I didn't know what was worse. That no one in the room batted a fucking eye, or that I didn't either. Not one of us was shocked by my father's actions. Not one of us was surprised by the consequences of betrayal. But most of all, not one of us stunned by the sight of a man bleeding out in front of us.

In four calculated strides, Pops was over to him, slowly crouching down in front of his wounded body. Getting close to his face, the gun inches away from Striker's heart.

"You got a cigarette?" he asked out of nowhere.

Striker leaned his head back against the wall, blood seeping from the corner of his chewing-tobacco-filled lips. As if he already knew his fate and the only thing he had left to do was to accept it. I always knew my father wasn't a man you'd ever want to fuck with, Striker knew that too. I would be lying if I said I didn't want to believe that maybe this was all one big misunderstanding. As much as I thought he was a crooked son of a bitch, he did love my father and the club. Proving his loyalty hand over fist, time and time again.

"No, why?" Striker bellowed.

Pop deviously grinned, leaning into his face. "Because I like to have a smoke after I get fucked."

"Prez, I didn't—"

He shoved the barrel of the gun into his heart. "Shhh... save your breath for the devil, we all know you're going to fuckin' Hell." He got closer, making the sign of the cross as he murmured, "Ashes to ashes. Dust to dust. And all that fucking shit." With that, he pulled the trigger.

One. Solid. Blow.

Killing his best friend without so much of a blink of an eye. Except this time, his blood was on my hands. I provided the evidence, sold his soul to the Prez, and signed his death certificate all in a matter of hours. My father may have pulled the trigger, but he would never have put him to ground.

If it wasn't for me.

"One down. Now, where were we?" Pops declared, sitting back down at the head of the table. Cracking his knuckles one by one.

Exercising his power and getting off on the fact that he just killed a man point blank. Thriving on the adrenaline that only taking someone's life always gave him.

No one gave a flying fuck that there was a dead body in the room. This wasn't the first time I saw someone murdered in cold blood, and it wouldn't be the last. I wish I could say I wasn't desensitized to the cruel brutality of the world, here one day and gone the next.

As fucked up as it was, we protected our own.

"Oh yes," Pops stated, pulling me away from my thoughts. Four faces projected up on the wall. "These cock suckers."

"This is all extremely entertaining, the shooting and all, bravo," Martinez interrupted, lighting his cigar and clapping his hands. "But what the fuck does this all have to do with me?" he questioned, blowing smoke out between his words. "I'm a very busy man, and as much as I like what you have going here, I don't have time for it. So, let's cut to the chase. I have other places to be."

"Creed spent the last few weeks followin' that fuckin' traitor over there around. Not only did he find the proof we needed. He also got the USB file back." He pulled it out of his pocket and threw it onto the middle of the table. "It contained orders, serial numbers, and shipment schedules for the next month. They could have intercepted all the gun and drug cartels from here to fuckin' Cuba. Creed saved our asses."

Martinez arched an eyebrow. "You called me in this meeting based on what a fucking child found?"

"Fu—"

"Creed," Dad gritted out, cutting me off. "I've had suspicions about Striker for a while now. Havin' Creed follow him around for the last few weeks. I sent him because Striker wouldn't suspect Creed, he also wouldn't be lookin' out for him like he would anyone else if he started gettin' suspicious. I found the opportunity to test my boy and I took it. A man of your stature could understand that, yeah?"

"I wouldn't send a boy to do a man's work," Martinez argued, shaking his head.

I didn't falter. "How can you let this piece of shit into our territory and talk to you like that? If it was anyone else, they'd be layin' on the goddamn floor bleedin' out next to Striker!" I interjected not giving a shit anymore.

"Enough, Creed!" Dad snarled.

"No, Jameson, the kid's right," Martinez chimed in, bringing our attention back to him. "Where are my manners?" He took a long puff of his cigar, snubbing it out, blowing a ring of smoke in the air. "Let's hear it, *son*. I dare you to fucking impress me," he added, gesturing for me to take the lead.

I glanced over at my father and he nodded. Pushing off the wall, I walked to the front of the room, feeling everyone's eyes on me. One pair, in particular, burning a hole right through my body.

I cleared my throat, making my presence known. "These four men." I pointed to each of them on the wall. "Hunter, Cross, Cruz, and Felix are the men Striker was in alliance with. They're from San Antonio, traffickin' women from across the border. Sellin' them off to the highest bidder. They wanted in our turf, seein' as though Southport has access to water, easier to transport not only the women but also the drugs and guns. They wanted in on the club's routes, to catch us with our fuckin' pants down and our cocks out. Striker was makin' it easier for them by handin' them that USB stick. I didn't know what was on there until this afternoon when Pops and I looked it over. After Striker left, I went in blind. I shoulda called in for backup, but I'd rather commit crimes by my fuckin' self, only way I know who's goin' to fuckin' snitch on me. Heat fell on me, but I got the USB. A bullet grazed my shoulder as I made a run for it. Didn't get followed, made sure of it."

"Unless you put them to ground," Martinez mimicked in a Southern tone. "You made sure of—"

I threw four grenade clips on the table in front of him. "Two would have done the job, but four is more my style."

He eyed the clips for a few seconds, then turned his attention back to me. "I personally would have tortured them until they gave up names. Instead, here we are with nothing but grenade clips. Rookie mistake."

"You givin' me shit?"

"I'm giving you a lesson, boy."

I narrowed my eyes at him. "I'll be sure to remember that. The next time I'm wipin' my fuckin' ass."

"On that note," Pops chimed in, hitting the gavel down on the table. "Score, Devil's Rejects four, Sinner's Rejoice zero. Meetin' adjourned. Diesel, get one of the other prospects to clean this fuckin' mess." He nodded toward Striker. "Time to get fucked up."

Banter filled the air as everyone stood, and headed out the door, stepping over Striker's limp body on the way out, like he was just taking a nap. I walked past Martinez, knocking into him like he had done to me earlier. Ignoring the shooting pain in my shoulder once again.

After everyone picked up their guns and headed out, leaving to get ready for the night, including Martinez who more than likely was too good to attend a party with a bunch of biker rednecks, I went and hung out with Luke and Noah to kill the time, mom must have come back sometime during the meeting. The boys were out back playing some ball, while she was in the kitchen with the other old ladies preparing for a night that promised to be nothing but a good fucking time, with booze, drugs, whores, and the occasional causalities.

The club always threw parties after business was taken care of in the meetings. Old ladies usually weren't allowed to attend, but my father must have made an exception this time, probably trying to play nice with my mother. Making up for the altercation I knew must have happened earlier with Christa. She happened to be nowhere to be found tonight, which was odd since she was on the property all the time. I'm sure my father had something to do with her absence.

On nights when both my parents were at the clubhouse, Luke and Noah would hang out in Dad's room. Playing video games and staying out of everyone's way. Neither one of them ever showed any interest in the MC life. After helping Ma get the boys situated in Pops' room at the back of the clubhouse, I joined some of the members outside for a few drinks. They congratulated me for my contribution to the clubs and brotherhoods well-being, wanting to hear how it all went down.

As the night progressed, people started scattering everywhere, the clubhouse was busting at the seams, inside and out. Everyone shooting the shit and getting fucked up. Colorful lights danced in sync to the music blaring through the speakers, filling the night air with a combination of rock, oldies, and blues.

People playing pool and darts for money. Snorting lines of coke, smoking weed and cigarettes while whores found brother's cocks to grind on to the beat of the music. I made my rounds, flirting up new girls, gaining potential pussy, all while avoiding the chicks that I already had the pleasure of pissing off.

I walked back inside, sifting through the crowd, going straight to the makeshift bar. Stopping dead in my tracks when I saw them. Wondering when the fuck he rolled back in.

"The fuck?" I said to myself, watching my mother and that motherfucker Martinez at the bar.

Standing too fucking close to each other, talking in an intimate way. I watched from afar, ignoring everyone around me, shocked as shit at what was happening in front of my very own eyes.

"Creed! Fuck, man, you are one badass son of a bitch," Phoenix greeted, patting me on the back.

I shrugged him off, focusing all my attention back at the fuckery going down before me.

"What the fuck, bro?" he asked, not understanding my sudden swing in mood.

I didn't pay him any mind, too consumed by Martinez and my mother enjoying themselves like they were on their first goddamn date. My vision tunneled, the music muffled in the background. All I could hear was my heart pounding out of my chest with every second that passed between them. It didn't matter that she was wearing her cut that read Property of Jameson, letting everyone know who she belonged to.

Including *him*.

He must have had a death wish coming in here and disrespecting my father, who I hadn't seen all night. My mother was fucking gorgeous, but she was also taken and not to be fucked with, especially the way he was eyeing her with a predatory regard.

He leaned forward, whispering something in her ear. Her head fell back in laughter, bringing her breasts inches away from his face. Exposing herself through the tight black tank she wore under her cut. His eyes shifted down, and a devilish grin marred his face, it was quick but I caught it.

His words, *"Very nice tits, if I remember correctly,"* played over and over in my head like a goddamn broken record.

I shook off the thought as my mother swung her long blonde hair to one shoulder, grabbing a piece and twirling it around her finger like she was a fucking school girl, as she continued to speak to him. His attention hanging on every word that fell from her lips as if she was telling him her life story.

When the bastard laughed or smiled, her eyes would light up like a goddamn Christmas tree, the way they used to for my old man. Clinking their bottles together, eyeing each other, more laughter, more touching, more banter. I wanted to look away, I wanted to fuck off and get another drink, but I couldn't. If it were anybody else's old lady, I wouldn't give a flying fuck. But the devil was seducing my mother, and that shit didn't fly with me.

I saw him reach over to brush a strand of blonde hair away from her face, and it took every ounce of my being not to lose my shit. He let his fingers linger there a little too long, caressing the side of her cheek with the back of his hand. It wasn't till he leaned in and kissed where his fingers had just been, that made me snap.

Before I realized what I was doing, I rolled up to Stone, who was on the opposite end of the bar. Without any hesitation, I pulled the Glock from the back of his jeans. Cocking the gun, making it over to them in three strides. Aiming the loaded pistol to the side of his pretty boy fucking face.

"You sorry ass motherfucker," I drawled out, pressing the gun into his temple.

"Creed!" my mother shrieked, taken back.

Stone came running over. "Creed! Back the fuck down, NOW! You don't know who you're fucking messin' with!" He grabbed ahold of my injured shoulder, trying to turn me so he could grab the pistol.

"Urrrrrgggg! Motherfucker!" I growled out in pain but didn't falter.

"We need to stop meeting like this, *son*," Martinez casually said. Not fazed by the loaded gun to his fucking head.

"I ain't your fuckin' son."

"Creed! Put the gun down, now!" Mom pleaded, reaching for my arm. I roughly pushed her hand away, causing her to stumble.

"You should really listen to your mother, boy. She's the only smart one in your family." He winked at her, only fueling my urge to splatter the walls with his fucking brains.

"Honey, listen this is all a huge misunderstandin'."

I chuckled. "That's exactly what it looked like, Ma, when his face was in your tits a few minutes ago!" I shouted, causing everyone around us to stop what they're doing and turn their attention to us.

Phoenix and Diesel came barreling through the crowd, pushing people out of the way to get to me. "Creed, be reasonable, bro. Don't wanna do this. Prez won't fuckin' like it. And Martinez won't think twice about putting a bullet in your head," Phoenix gritted out in my ear.

"Have that backward. Who's holdin' the gun to whose head?" I taunted not backing down.

"It is not what you think! Now put the gun down, Creed!" Mom ordered again.

"You stickin' up for this cocky ass motherfucker?"

"He was just keepin' me company while your father is off doin' God knows what."

"I know what, but that's neither here nor there," Martinez interrupted, baiting me with a snide smile.

"You got some brass fuckin' balls, steppin' in here, fuckin' around with the Prez's wife," I stated through a clenched jaw. Putting more force on his temple.

"Oh, is that what you think is going on here? Believe me, if I was fucking around with her, you'd hear her screaming my goddamn name."

"You cock suckin' son of a bitch!" I got up in his face, my finger itching to pull the trigger.

My mother screamed, "That is enough! Jameson!" Hollering at the top of her lungs for my father.

"He isn't going to hear you, sweetheart. Last I saw, he was riding off into the sunset with a brunette with huge tits on the back of his bike, heading up route sixty."

"Shut your fuckin' mouth!" I shoved the gun further into his head, causing him to sway. The look on her face alone caused the adrenaline that had been coursing through my veins to soar high, I couldn't fucking see straight.

"Have you ever shot a man? Have you had the pleasure of feeling what it's like to end someone's existence with a bullet? There is no feeling like it. Do it, son! Pull the fucking trigger! Here, I'll help you out," Martinez goaded, grabbing the barrel of the gun, moving it to the middle of his forehead. "Right here. Right here is the sweet spot."

I stilled my hand, squeezing the trigger ever so slightly.

"Do it! I don't have all fucking night to die! Come on, Creed! Show everyone in this room that you have the balls to shoot a man point blank like your daddy! Do it! You pussy, pull the fucking trigger!"

"Creed! Don't do this!" Phoenix pleaded, grabbing ahold of my shoulder.

"Creed! Creed! Creed! Creed!" All I could hear was my name being yelled in the distance. Echoing in my ears, driving me to the point of insanity.

So loud.

So unforgiving.

"Fuck you!" I yelled, my lungs burning from the anger I felt rising. Sweat pooled at my temples, my breathing becoming erratic. "Fuck!" I swiftly jerked my hand a few inches to the right of his face, pulling the fucking trigger.

Martinez didn't even flinch. The bullet flew past his head through the air, ricocheting off the rusted steel beam behind him, and into who was really yelling my name.

"NO!" My mother's ear-piercing scream resonated from deep within her lungs, echoing off the warehouse walls and through the room. Her body almost caved to the ground in unbearable pain.

I glanced over at her, narrowing my eyes. Searching deep into her petrified expression. I'd never seen that look on her face before. It immediately had my heart pounding against my ribcage, racing hard.

Her trembling hands covered her mouth. "What did you do?! Creed? What the fuck did you do?!" she bellowed in a quivering tone, shaking her head in fear.

Causing me to inadvertently stumble back as I slowly turned, trying to follow the sight of her horrified glare. My chest heaved, unable to hold back my hammering heart any longer. I could hear the drone in my ears loud and clear. Everything that followed happened in slow motion, like reels from a black and white movie, projecting out in front of me. The sound of the bullet replayed in the background.

I jerked back when the scene came into focus, the image that would forever haunt me for the rest of my sorry excuse of a fucking life.

I shuddered.

The gun fell from my grasp to the floor with a loud thud as all eyes went to the horrid mess before them. Chaos erupted, people running to and from the room one right after the other. Women screaming out in terror, brothers ushering bystanders out, pushing them to the doors, quickly. The music ceased, and the lights came on, only illuminating what I had done.

"Do somethin'! Don't just stand there!" Ma begged, looking around the room. Black-streaked tears ran down her cheeks, pooling on the floor beneath her.

My world was caving in on me, my walls crumbled down, and the floor felt like it was swallowing me whole. Bile rose in my throat, threatening to exit my body at the sickening display in front of me.

My life as I knew it…

Was over.

Luke's eyes widened as he lost his footing, trying to remain upright. "Cre-ed," he cautiously breathed out, looking at me with a gaze in his eyes that would forever be etched in my mind.

As if the man standing in front of him wasn't me, his brother.

As if the man standing in front of him wasn't his own flesh and blood.

As if the man standing in front of him hadn't protected and defended him all his life, but instead a stranger...

Who had just shot him in the chest.

I couldn't move.

I couldn't breathe.

I couldn't take my eyes off the antagonizing expression written across my baby brother's face. As his hands moved down toward his chest, so did my eyes, following the trail of blood that was seeping through his white shirt. He slowly lifted his shaking hand, placing it near his heart. Gasping for air, peering back up at me as blood trickled out of his mouth.

"He-ee-lllp m-ccc," he sputtered, reaching his now blood-soaked hand for me like we were the only two people in the room.

"NOOOOOOOO!!!" Mom fell apart. The terror in her voice ran deep in my being.

A mother's worst nightmare came to life.

Before I knew what was happening, she was lunging across the room, catching Luke's limp body as it collapsed to the ground. He was unable to hold himself up any longer.

"JAMESON!" she yelled, calling for my father. "DO SOMETHING, CREED! HELP! NOOOOOO! Please God, NOOOOOO!" she hysterically repeated, trying to stop the bleeding with her shaking hands on Luke's chest. Cradling her baby in her arms, rocking him uncontrollably.

I acted on pure impulse, my body moving on autopilot as I rushed to them, falling to my knees at the last second. Ignoring the instant sting the hard cement brought on. His body started to convulse, more blood spewed out of his trembling lips as he looked up at me with vacant eyes. I placed my hands over my mother's, trying to help her stop the blood from gushing out. Searching to find where the bullet hit him.

"EVERYONE OUT!" Phoenix ordered. "NOW!"

I heard people scattering around us, like a herd, leaving a path of destruction in their wake.

"Luke! Buddy, you stay with me, goddamn it. Do you hear me?" I demanded with tears sliding down my face onto his broken body, letting my eyes roam over what I had done. Quickly removing my cut, I pulled my t-shirt over my head, balling it up and pushing my ma's hands out of the way.

I gently laid him on the floor. My eyes blurred with nothing but tears, making it hard to see what I was doing. "Stay with me, Luke. Do you hear me? Stay with me!" I held his face in my hands, blood smearing on his cheeks. "Fight! Fucking fight!"

I ripped his shirt open and found where he had been hit. Discovering the gaping hole right above his heart. Hastily shoving my blood-soaked shirt on his wound.

"Hey! Look at me! I need you to put as much pressure as possible on this, Ma," I grabbed her hands, placing them back on the wound. She looked up at me with swollen eyes. "Now!"

Stumbling up to my knees, I tore off my belt. Immediately rolling him to his side to wrap the belt around his chest and pulled tight. More blood rolled from the corner of his mouth onto the floor.

"Luke, look at me. Come on! Open your eyes, stay with me." I slapped his cheeks.

Nothing.

Silence.

I was shaking so fucking bad. My heart thumped in my chest, vibrating throughout my entire core. Every last part of me was dying right along with him. I'd done some shady ass shit, been in some life or death situations, and never been so scared in my fucking life as I pulled Luke in my arms, checking to see if he was still breathing.

Checking to see if he was still alive.

"Creed…" Mom wept, her voice broken and torn. Looking up at me with pleading eyes to save him. "God, please take me instead," she pleaded over and over.

"Luke," I cried, cradling his frame against my chest. He was unresponsive.

"FUCK! We're losing him!"

I held my dying brother in my arms while I watched my mother slowly dying on the floor in front of me.

"SOMEONE call 9-1-1!" she urged, desperately looking around the room.

"SOMEBODY HELP! WHY IS NO ONE HELPING?! Why are you all standin' there, DO SOMETHIN'!" I screamed over and over again until my throat was burning and raw.

No one budged.

They all knew what calling 9-1-1 meant. Cops being called to the clubhouse was never allowed. It was a code of conduct no one would fucking break. Even if it meant innocent lives were lost.

"FUCKING CALL 9-1-1, YOU FUCKIN' PUSSIES!" I locked eyes with the brothers, silently pleading for them to break. "Oh my God! I'm so sorry! I'm so fuckin' sorry," I bawled, rocking Luke in my tight grasp.

Mom trembled, wrapping her arms around him, still putting pressure on the wound with a shaking hand. "Please God! Please help my baby! Please! I'll do anythin'! Don't take my baby! Please, not my baby! JAMESON!" She took him out of my arms, cradling his limp body, holding onto him for dear life. "Momma's here. Stay with me, I can't lose you. You hear me? Stay with me!" she whispered, still trying to get the blood to stop. "FUUUUCK. JAMESON! HELP! Where are you?!" she pleaded, pulling him closer, rocking him back and forth, blubbering incoherent words while trying to comfort him. Holding onto hope that this was all a horrible nightmare she'd wake up from soon. "Creed, they aren't doin' anything'! Call 9-1-1! NOW!"

I sprang into action. Running to the phone that was on the far wall. My hands shaking as I started to dial. Bloody fingerprints covered the numbers.

"Give me that!" I heard my father grit out, coming in out of nowhere. Yanking the receiver out of my grasp and hitting end. Quickly dialing another number. "Yeah, Joseph," he said calmly to the on-call doctor he had on payroll. "I need you here, stat." He hung up like this was normal, like he didn't fucking care that his son was lying in a pool of his own blood.

"Joseph?! Why aren't you callin—"

He peered back at my mother, rendering her speechless. "Jesus Christ! What the fuck happened?!" he snapped, running his hands through his hair. Taking in all the gore that lined the room. The rusty smell of blood assaulted his senses, potent in the air.

I peered around the room for the first time since the ricocheted bullet hit Luke's chest. Phoenix, Stone, and Diesel were the only ones left in the room, hanging their heads in remorse. Then my eyes landed on Martinez. His cold, dark, soulless eyes staring back at me, fueling my hatred for him.

"Your son here decided to fuck with the devil," Martinez stated, peering down at my mother, holding Luke's lifeless body. "He was trying to have a pissing contest with me tonight and clearly he lost. Teach him how to have better aim next time." The motherfucker turned and walked to the exit, turning at the last second, peering down at my mother. "My condolences, Diane," he added in a tone filled with sympathy. "I know what it's like to lose someone you love. My mother was brutally murdered right in front of me. She died in my arms." He bowed his head, turned and left.

I wanted to run after him and finish what I had started. I wanted him to pay for this, but I couldn't. An invisible force held me back. I was the one who pulled the trigger. I was the one who killed my baby brother.

This was no one's fault but mine.

I reached for the phone again but Pops shoved me back. "What the fuck did you do, boy?"

I couldn't help it. The fucking shame was eating me alive. "It was an accident! I swear to fuckin' God it was an accident!" I repeated, barely being able to get the words out.

"Momma? What's going on?" A sleepy-eyed Noah came walking in. "Where did Luke go?"

Diesel acted quick, scooping him up before he saw anything. Ma looked up, torn, as Noah was rushed out of the room.

"Let him call 9-1-1, Jameson! It was an accident! Where the fuck were you?!" Mom questioned, bringing our attention back to her. Her eyes still focused on the hall where Noah was escorted out.

"Accident or not, we can't call the cops! You want your son to go to prison?" he replied, ignoring her question. Not giving a fuck what Noah was about to walk into.

She shook her head violently, finally understanding. "No! Not Creed! I can't—"

"It was an accident!" I shouted back, reaching for the phone again.

He jerked it away, shoving me harder. Causing me to stumble from weakness, ready to pull a gun on me. "We will all go to prison over this!" he said, his eyes dancing from me over to the brothers.

She shook her head again, closing her eyes, trying to compose herself or possibly praying to God. "You fuckin' bastard," she wailed.

"I'm tryin' to save all our asses! Do you want to lose another son?"

I stepped away from him until my back hit the wall. The truth of his words was too much for me to bare. I slid down the wood paneling, slowly sinking further into the corner of my own mind. Into my own personal Hell, tuning them out. Pulling my knees close to my chest, letting tears fall down the sides of my face. I thought about all the happy memories I'd shared with Luke.

I remembered the first time he crawled.

His first words, the first time he said my name.

I opened my eyes, locking them with his. I willed myself to look away, but I couldn't. I forced myself to face what I had done.

Remembering the love those eyes once held. Every time I told him I loved him and the first time he said "I love you" back and every time since. Telling him how I would always be there for him no matter what. Promising to always protect him. How earlier that day, we were shooting the shit about girls and life. I reached into my pocket, pulling Luke's necklace out. Holding it up to my lips, clenching his protector in my hands, and bawling harder.

The irony wasn't lost on me.

All those memories were gone in a blink of an eye, now replaced with blood. So much fucking blood.

Blink.

Joseph hurried in with MC brothers behind him.

Blink.

Pulling my baby brother from my momma's arms.

Blink.
Performing CPR.
Blink.
Momma praying, sobbing, falling apart.
Blink.
Luke's lifeless eyes staring at me.
Blink.
Joseph filling syringes.
Blink.
An MC brother picking Momma up off the floor and taking her out the door as she kicked and screamed.
Blink.
The black bag being zipped. Swallowing Luke's bloody body.
Blink.
Chaos…
Blink.
More chaos…
Blink.
Nothing but chaos…
Blink.
An MC brother trying to stand me up.
Blink… Blink… Blink…
Blackness.

Luke was buried on Thursday, September twenty-sixth in the middle of the night. Four A.M. to be exact. Phoenix, Stone, and Diesel carried him in a black body bag to the furthest field beyond the woods, located behind the clubhouse. A few other MC brothers babysat my mother, who was sedated on the couch inside. Pops slipped a Xanax in her water a few hours before. It was the only way he could get away with burying Luke the way he did. He was going to let her come to the makeshift grave once the dirty work was over and there was no evidence left of my brother.

Only memories.

Every time I closed my eyes, all I could see was Luke's lifeless eyes staring back at me. I remember every step I took, following behind my father. I remember the thick suffocating fog in the night air that came after the rain we had gotten the day before. The way the wind blew a cool breeze through the trees, skimming the surface

48

of my overly heated skin. I remember the sounds of twigs cracking beneath our boots, the noises from the birds and owls along with whatever else lurked in the woods.

Most of all, I remember feeling so much fucking hatred for my father for not giving Luke, his son, a proper burial. Just wanting to throw him in a field along with countless other bodies the club had taken.

Luke deserved better.

He didn't fucking deserve that.

I watched Phoenix, Diesel, and Stone start digging his grave and I swear to God all I wanted to do was dig my own fucking grave beside him. I would take being buried alive over having to live with what I had done.

My father ordered them to stop digging, took the shovel right out of Stone's grasp. "You did this. He's dead because of you, boy. Now, I'm not going to make my brothers pay for your sins. You dig that grave and lay your brother to rest in it. I want you to remember that he's six feet under because of you. Next time you better keep your goddamn mouth shut. Mouthin' off to Martinez, you piece of shit. Coulda' cost a huge alliance." He threw the shovel at my face, daring me to defy him.

I didn't argue.

I didn't say a word.

He was right.

I gripped the shovel tight, welcoming the pain from the blisters forming on my palms, and dug Luke's grave while everyone watched. I could sense that the brothers didn't agree with what my old man was making me do, but they knew better than to open their fucking mouths. Not wanting to end up like Striker. I knew this was the real reason he drugged my mother. There was no way in hell she would allow him to punish me this way.

I kept my emotions in check, forcefully driving the blade into the hard ground over and over again. I didn't deserve to mourn the life I had taken. I deserved far fucking worse than what was happening to me.

The closer I got to finishing digging my brother's grave, the more pissed off I got. The thought of Luke's body rotting away in this black insect-infested hole without any barriers to protect him where he would just rot away.

A day.

A month.

A year from now…

All that would be left of him were his bones. I prayed to God he already took Luke's soul and he wasn't left to wander the world as a spirit. Unable to rest in peace. I tried to tell myself that the Lord couldn't be that cruel, but in the end what fuck had he done for me?

Not a goddamn thing.

"That's enough," Dad ordered, pulling me away from my thoughts. "Get your ass out of that hole and come get your brother. You're goin' to carry him into the ground by your damn self, and then you're goin' to bury him by your fuckin' self too."

"Prez, we can—"

"You can shut your fuckin' mouth! That's what you can do!" he cut Phoenix off, looking from me to him and back to me. "I'm not going to tell you again, Creed! Get your brother and lay his fuckin' ass to rest!" His large hands grabbed me by the front of my shirt and lifted me out, shoving me over by Luke's body.

I regained my footing before landing on him. Taking a deep breath, I did as I was told. It took everything inside me not to fall apart when I picked up Luke's body into my arms. Carrying him over to the hole, stalling, wanting to remember every last second before I gently placed him in his purgatory. I wanted to unzip the black bag, I wanted to see his face one last time, to properly say goodbye. There was so much I wanted to say, but no words would make things right. No amount of time would bring him back. So all I did was cradle his cold body as close as I could to my broken heart.

Wanting to at least remember the feel of him in my arms.

"I'm so fucking sorry, little brother," I whispered. My voice cracking with each word that left my lips.

"Let go of him, Creed! And get your ass out of that hole!" Pops gritted his teeth.

"Please… let me say goodbye. Just fuckin' allow me that…"

"I don't give a fuck what you're pleadin' for! The only thing you deserve is to be lyin' in the ground instead of him. Now get your ass up here so you can bury him!"

"Jesus Christ! Just let me—"

50

"Fuckin' Hell!" He jumped into the hole to pry Luke out of my arms. Ramming me back as hard as he could, making my back connect with the uneven earth. I winced in pain, welcoming the sting from my wounded shoulder, needing to feel anything other than the remorse and ache in my fucking heart.

He wrestled Luke's body from my grasp, and just threw him to the ground as if he were nothing. As if Luke meant nothing. He fell with a loud thump, landing in a contorted position that could be seen clear as day even though he was in a black fucking body bag.

I immediately stepped toward him, wanting to lay my brother in a more peaceful position. I didn't take a second step before my father punched me in the damn face. My head whooshed back as I stumbled. He gripped the front of my shirt, jerking me forward. Getting right up in my face.

"Prez, come on, that's enough," Stone coaxed.

"Yeah, Prez, leave him alone. He's been through enough," Diesel added.

"You listen and you listen good, boy," Dad clenched, ignoring the brother's pleas. "I don't give two shits about you, or what you're feeling. You're lucky I'm savin' your sorry ass from servin' a life sentence in prison for murder, you ungrateful dick. When I tell you to do somethin', you fuckin' do it. Do you understand me? I won't hesitate to remind you of your fuckin' place in my clubhouse."

He took one last look and pushed me back, stepping over Luke's body to climb out of the hole. He instantly turned to yank me up by my arm, throwing me to the dirt. I tried crawling to my feet, but he didn't falter, chucking the shovel right at my face. The rusty metal caught my mouth, causing me to spit out blood. I shook it off, getting up on unsteady legs, trying my hardest to stand up straight.

My shame.

My remorse.

My guilt.

Couldn't hold me up any longer.

I could have taken him, I could have fought back, defended myself, but I deserved everything he was dealing out and more.

I deserved it all.

I picked up the shovel once again, letting the dirt fall over Luke. I buried my brother that night with only the light of the moon shining above me. The next day, I watched my mother fall apart on the ground that her son lay beneath. I watched her once again being torn from the makeshift grave, kicking and screaming for God to give back her baby. I watched my father not give a fuck about the scene playing out in front of him, and the MC brothers shake their heads at the lack of sympathy he had for both his sons and his wife.

From that day forward, I carried the pain that I murdered my brother.

I carried the agony of not being able to say goodbye to him in the depths of my core.

Every day I found myself at the train tracks by the clubhouse, wanting nothing more than to just disappear. Finding myself in the middle of nowhere, relishing the freedom.

Waiting...

Thinking...

Contemplating...

The past. The present. The future.

Then. Now. Forever.

My fucking life.

Wishing I could get on the next train and never look back. But it was just that. A wish. A glimmer of hope outside of the bullshit that was my life. Except, I still had Noah to think about, more than ever before. Every time I looked in his eyes, I was reminded of Luke. Reminded of what I had done to him. Maybe that was my punishment. Being responsible for my brother in ways I had never been before. With each passing day, I felt the same guilt I did the day I took my brother's life.

Mistakes and regrets.

Choices and decisions.

Life and death.

It all blended together in an array of colors that painted a scary picture. There was no looking back...

I couldn't even bring myself to go where Luke was buried.

Knowing, that I was the only one to blame.

For putting him to ground.

ROAD to NOWHERE

I tilted my head and watched the storm clouds above, waiting for the heavens to unleash their fury upon me. Witnessing flashes of lightning strike in the distance, the smell of rain potent in the air as the wind brushed over my inked skin. Cooling me from the heat. Three loaded blasts filled my surroundings as a train rolled into town. Sounding its horn to make its presence known, tearing me away from my thoughts.

I watched as each massive steel car blurred by with hints of daylight shining through the gaps. I sat there contemplating jumping on until it was too late. The very last train car made its way out of my hellhole and onto the next. Taking the future I wanted so fucking badly with it. Leaving me behind to deal with everyone else's bullshit.

When all I wanted to do was drown in the storm.

While I was off pondering, leaving town on a daily basis since Luke's death sixth months ago, my mother regularly drowned herself in a pint of vodka. Letting death become her. Adding another life to my tally.

Hers.

My father's verbal abuse became worse toward her each day that passed, becoming more of a monster than he already was. She had paid the price of losing a child. She didn't deserve his goddamn hateful words too. He never even mourned his own flesh and blood.

As promised, a few days after I turned eighteen two months ago, I was patched in as a brother. The members went to Church that day, taking a vote on which prospects had earned the right to be patched in. The decision was unanimous. I signed my life away with my fucking blood, how my father always wanted it. Signifying my right into the Devil's Rejects. It was announced at the National Run that I was a fully patched in member. My father ripped off my Prospect patch and handed me my colors, which consisted of the club logo, the crescent-shaped red patch with "Devil's Rejects" on it, and the other crescent patch that read Southport.

Patching me in, a look of pride spread across his face. Eagerly awaiting my reaction.

I met his eyes, shook his hand, and just fucking nodded, showing him exactly what it meant to me.

Not one fucking thing.

The brothers all pulled me in for hugs, patting my back. Dousing me in beer, welcoming me with open arms, committing my life and loyalty to the club. Beginning a new chapter in my life when all I wanted was to end the last one. The moment I put Luke to ground was the last time any of the brothers, including Pops, spoke about what happened. About what I had done, as if Luke never even existed. The only reminder I ever had were my mother's tears and ramblings when she was shit-faced. Everyone who witnessed that night go down was sworn to silence. Threatened to keep their fucking mouths shut.

Using violence to cover up injustice by any means necessary.

After I received the official tat on my back, branding me as a member, it was official. I was a Devil's Reject. I had the logo etched into my skin for life to fucking prove it. The night went on with its usually festivities of drugs, booze, and whores, as I sat at the bar alone. Wanting nothing more than to get the fuck out of there. Still seeing Luke's lifeless body lying right beneath my feet. It didn't matter, nothing did anymore. I was stuck there whether I liked it or not. Pops even gave me the pick of the litter of whores, but I didn't give a fuck about that. No matter what I did or said, it wouldn't stop him from throwing pussy in my lap. Making sure I got my dick wet. I had my first threesome that night, two fucking chicks at once. I should have been on top of the world, not hoping I was buried under it.

ROAD to NOWHERE

After driving around aimlessly for hours, I decided to pull off the road, just after one o'clock in the afternoon. I knew of a small restaurant, on the water, in the heart of Oak Island, North Carolina, a small beach town just outside of Southport, where my kind never drifted. That never stopped me before, locals could judge me all they fucking wanted, and I wouldn't ever give a shit.

I pulled into the lot, parking a few spots from a black SUV, where a woman with long brown hair stepped out, arguing with someone in the back seat. Catching my attention. Suddenly the back door opened, revealing a little girl that couldn't have been more than eight or nine years old. Throwing her hands up in the air, mumbling under her breath, as her momma came around to get her.

I cut the engine on my bike, took off my helmet and grabbed the pack of smokes from my cut. Smacking the bottom of the new pack, I pulled out a cigarette and lit up. She was wearing a light yellow summer dress with bathing suit straps peeking out underneath it. Her hair was in braided pigtails, with matching yellow bows. What caught my attention the most, were the huge aviator sunglasses on her tiny face, sporting them like she was grown.

"Momma, why couldn't I just buy the pink bikini? I hate this stupid black, one-piece bathing suit, Daddy said I had to buy," the little girl whined. "I was perfectly happy with the bikini. It was pretty and cute, and now I just look like a boy. This isn't fair! Totally sucks balls."

"Mia Ryder! How many times do I have to tell you not to talk like that?" her momma reprimanded her.

"Apparently more than once. Mason says it all the time and you don't yell at him."

"Ugh, what am I going to do with you?"

"You can start by letting me buy that bikini. I'm not a baby anymore. Daddy needs to understand I'm going to be ten soon. That's almost two whole hands. Double digits," Mia emphasized, holding up her small fingers in the air.

Her momma chuckled, shaking her head. "You'll always be your Daddy's baby girl."

"He's never gonna let me grow up. He already scared off all the boys in my class. Even the cute ones, Momma. Uncle Dylan and Uncle Jacob aren't any better, telling my reading partner, Phil, I couldn't come to the phone cause I was poopin'!" She held her arms out to her sides. "I wasn't even poopin'! Who is the mature one here? Me. No one lets me do anything. It. Sucks. Balls," she sighed and I resisted the urge to laugh my ass off.

This kid is a spitfire.

"You are too young to be this boy crazy. Now stop your fussin'. We're short staffed today. Lori called in sick. Aunt Lily is even coming in early to wait tables."

Mia hopped out of the SUV, shutting the door behind her.

"Well, you going to go surf or stand here and pout all day?" her momma asked, cocking her head to the side.

"I'll think about it," she replied, sitting on the curb pouting.

Her momma just shook her head, ruffling up her hair as she walked inside.

I got off my bike, taking a few more drags off my cigarette before throwing it to the asphalt, using the toe of my boot to stub it out. When I looked up, I had two, big, bright blue eyes staring me down. Her head cocked to the side with her arms resting on her knees. Her sunglasses were now hanging in her hands.

"You some sort of celebrity?" Mia questioned.

I chuckled, shaking my head no.

"Wow, you look like one of those guys from a television show my daddy watches. Sons of a Bitches or something like that..."

I laughed so hard my head fell back. I couldn't remember the last time I laughed like that.

"Anyway." She shrugged me off. "He doesn't know I watch the show. I sneak down into the theater room and peek through the door crack. The guy with long blond hair is cute. I really like him."

I just nodded, trying like hell not to bust out laughing again. Thinking to myself, damn her parents have their hands full with this one.

"Do you have a voice? Or do you just do the shake and nod thing, like you're too cool?"

I grinned, walking over to her. She looked up at me, shielding her eyes from the sun. Waiting for my answer.

"I talk. I just don't talk to strangers, sweetie." I winked, walking past her, opening the door, leaving her there wide-eyed.

I found a table in the far corner, away from judgment. The place wasn't too busy yet, but I still had suspicious eyes on me.

"Hi, there," the waitress greeted. "I'm Lily. The entertainment turned waitress today. What can I get you to drink?" She eyed me up and down.

"Water."

"You're not from around these parts, are you?" she asked, tapping her pen on the order pad.

"What gave me away? The motorcycle out front, my cut, my tattoos, or is it just my overly rugged good looks?"

She laughed. "Actually, it was the Southport patch on your vest. Dead giveaway."

"Entertainment, huh? What sort of entertainment do you do? From the looks of the place, you ain't a stripper. Could be comedian... But I'm gonna go with musician, you're tappin' the hell out of that pen to the beat of the music playin' right now," I paused, arching an eyebrow. "Hot or cold?"

"Very hot."

"Why thank you."

She laughed again, throwing her head back. "You're good. Well played, Creed," she said, pointing her pen to my name patch. "You best contain that flirting around here, though. I'm a married woman, and this is my sister-in-law Alex's place. I'd hate for you to have a run in with the good ol' boys. My brother, Lucas, will lose his shit, and my husband won't be too far behind."

"Is that right? Thanks for the warnin', darlin', but I can hold my own."

She smiled. "I'll be right back with that water."

I spent the next hour eating, bullshitting with Lily, and watching the surfers come in and out the back. Wondering if the little girl, Mia, was out there. I wandered out the back, finding a place to sit. I removed my socks and boots, digging my toes into the sand, trying to remember the last time I was at the beach. It had been forever.

Ma used to take us all the time when we were little to play with Autumn. She was the daughter of my mom's best friend, Laura, and they lived in Southport, just a few miles away from us. My mother, Laura, and their other best friend, Stacey, were all originally from New York. Growing up together in Manhattan until Stacey moved to North Carolina her sophomore year of high school.

Autumn's parents' got a divorce a few years back. That's when Laura decided to move her and Autumn to Southport to be near my mom and Stacey, needing the support while going through a nasty divorce. Autumn's father, Carl was a chief for the New York Fire Department. He still lived there in Manhattan, so she went back to stay with him often. She had always been a daddy's girl, even though her parents' weren't together. That never changed.

I'd known Autumn all my life, we'd grown up together. Our birthdays only a few months apart. We spent family vacations, summers, and holidays with one another in North Carolina, or New York, every chance we got. It was the only time I ever felt somewhat like a normal kid. I always looked forward to hanging out with her. Ma wasn't the only one thrilled when they upped and moved here.

I sat there in the sand for I don't know how long, watching the waves crash on the shore. Spotting Mia, the little girl from the restaurant, fucking slaying the waves. I couldn't take my eyes off of her, mesmerized how something so small could ride the waves like she did and not be swallowed up by the ocean. She clearly had no fucking fear, beating grown ass men, stealing their waves, and cutting them off without blinking an eye.

Paddling way out beyond the safe points, owning the waves like they were her bitches. Falling and getting right back up. She had me grinning like a goddamn fool, laughing every time she'd fuck someone over, making them crash and burn. It was probably the first time in six months I'd felt something more than remorse, shame, and sadness.

That nine-year-old killing waves was the breath of fresh air I needed.

Even if it only lasted for a little while.

After about an hour of kicking ass, the short stack emerged from the water, dragging her huge-ass bright pink board that was easily twice her size under her arm. Pigtails bouncing in the breeze as she made her way up the beach headed in my direction. I couldn't help but laugh at the sight of her.

"What you laughing at, punk?" Mia stopped right in front of me, dropping her board to the sand as she placed her hands on her little hips, cocking her head to the side. Barely blocking the sun with her tininess.

I raised my hands in the air, surrendering them as I continued to laugh my ass off. "Not the shrimp that just carted an adult-sized board up the beach. Most likely not the little spitfire who is blockin' my sun, and definitely not the baby girl who has a sticker on her board that says 'Surfer bitch' with bright pink lips." I pointed to one of many stickers that covered her board. "Your momma know you have that?"

"Whoa! You do speak." She shifted her weight to her other hip, sassing me. "I guess we're not strangers anymore." Ignoring my question, plopping down in the sand next to me.

"How long you been surfin' like that?"

She tapped her index finger to her lips, thinking. "Since forever. It's in my blood. My daddy had me on a board as soon as I could walk. I'm better than both of my brothers. I'm better than all my cousins. I'm pretty sure I'm better than anyone in Oak Island. Maybe even the world."

I struggled, trying not to laugh again, nodding my response. Looking back out at the waves. I liked her confidence, cocky but in a sweet way. There wasn't enough of that in the world.

"Why are you so sad?" she questioned out of nowhere. Randomly shifting gears like most women did. Unable to focus on one subject at a time.

"Why you so nosey?" I glanced over at her.

"Duh... I'm a girl," she replied, rolling her eyes. "Do you collect patches?" She pointed to my cut, once again moving onto her next question.

"Not collect, I earn."

"Oh, like a Girl Scout! How cool! I have over one hundred on my sash. My momma says I have to stay in Girl Scouts because it will build me into a courageous, confident girl, even though I already have all that. I was born awesome. Plus, I don't know how sitting around a campfire, singing Kumbaya-whatever will give me anything but mosquito bites, but hell, what do I know?"

"You kiss your daddy with that mouth?" I chuckled.

She shrugged. "My brothers talk like that all the time. My first word was shit." She smiled, proud of herself. "Daddy yells at them, but they never listen. They get away with everything because they're boys. Personally, I think that's stupid. Girls are way better than boys. We're smarter. We smell nicer. And... if it weren't for girls, boys wouldn't even be here. So, boom," she exclaimed, making her hand explode. "Anyway, I'm a Brownie now so I have so many patches. I have the perfect one for your sash."

I threw my head back laughing. This kid was too much.

"What? You don't like brownies? I know for a fact, boys like brownies. My daddy loves them, my brothers love them, and my uncles love them, too. Even that boy who picks on me in class loves them. He's always trying to steal mine. Daddy says if I ever give him my brownie he will hurt him. He said he used to eat all kinds of brownies all the time, and Momma didn't like that very much. So then he started to eat just hers."

She had me laughing so damn hard my sides started to hurt. "Don't think he meant... nevermind. You always talk this much?"

"Oh! Let me get you my patch before I forget." She grabbed her pink backpack that was nestled in the sand next to her.

It didn't take much to realize that this baby girl liked pink. She rummaged around for a few seconds, finally finding what she wanted. Throwing her backpack to the side, she turned to fully face me.

"This is from me to you." She beamed. "So you can always remember me. I'll always remember you. Okay?" She handed me her patch. "That's my courage patch. You can have it since I already have enough of that to go around. Can you put it next to this one?" She pointed to my honor patch. "I think they'll look good together."

I was taken aback. I didn't know what to say, or what to fucking feel. No one had ever given me anything like this before. No one ever cared enough. I looked from her to the patch in my hands, fumbling it around and just nodded. Unable to form the words to express the sense of love I felt from this little girl I had only just met.

"You gonna answer my question?"

"Naw, you're a baby girl. Wouldn't understand."

"Who you callin'—"

"Creed?" A familiar voice interrupted Mia.

I looked up to see Autumn walking over to me. I stood, brushing the sand from my pants. "Damn, ain't you a sight for sore eyes," I greeted, pulling her into a hug.

I hadn't seen Autumn since before Luke died. I'd been avoiding her, not wanting the sympathy and compassion I knew she would provide.

I didn't fucking deserve it.

"I'm so sorry about Luke," she whispered in my ear, squeezing me tighter.

My happy mood quickly seeped into the sand between us. The mere mention of Luke's name threatened to bring me down, but I wouldn't let it. I quickly shook off the unease and pulled away, giving her a half smile.

Mia cleared her throat from behind me, bringing my attention back to her. She was giving Autumn the evil eye, a look I was more than familiar with when it came to women. She may have been just a kid, but that didn't stop the jealousy she may have been feeling. I winked at her, for a reason I couldn't explain. I wanted her to have the reassurance she needed.

Immediately feeling protective over her.

"MIA!" a voice yelled out, causing her to startle. "How many damn times do I need to tell you not to cut off other surfers?"

I turned, following the voice. Seeing Mason come running up behind Autumn.

"It isn't my fault y'all are slower than molasses," Mia responded, shrugging him off.

"You're lucky you're a little girl. Stealing waves like that could get your ass kicked."

"Well, lucky for me I can out run your asses."

"Watch your mouth!" Mason shouted, coming up to her. Turning his attention away from her when he saw me. "Creed, I didn't know you were heading down today." He dropped his board, pulling me in for a side hug, patting my back. "Been too long, brotha'. I see you met my baby sister, Mia," he said, nodding to a very pissed off little girl.

"She your baby sister? Makes sense now. Got a mouth on her, like you."

"Baby? Who are you all calling a baby?" Mia stood, placing her hands on her hips. "Creed, this is my big, but not better brother, Mason," she declared, rolling her eyes.

"Don't like your brother?" I chuckled.

"No, he is mean to me."

"Not mean, Mia. I'm just watching out for you like any big brother would."

"I don't need anyone looking out for me. I can take care of myself. Where's Giselle? Go find your girlfriend and let me be," she countered, only looking at Autumn.

I shook my head, stifling a laugh. I'd known Mason as long as I'd known Autumn. His mom was Stacey, my mother's other best friend. I'm not going to lie. At first, we fucking hated each other. Trying to prove who was the alpha dog before our fucking balls had even dropped. It was touch and go for the longest time, but as we got older we became close friends.

We went to the same school, that was, when we decided to actually go. Mason was the poster child for being a fucking rebel. A punk ass that did the opposite of everything his parents told him to. Other than school, Mason and I would hang out when he'd be at his mom's. Smoking weed, drinking, fucking around with girls, and getting into trouble. Autumn was never too far behind us, joining our festivities. Giselle, his girl, came into the picture a few years ago. She was the daughter of a narcotics detective who had more than a few run-ins with the MC. Her father was tight with Mason's old man, Lucas.

Which was why we never made our friendship known to his dad and stepmom, Alex. I'd never formally met either of them and probably never would. Mason's parents were never married. They had a complicated relationship. A rough start, but they found a way to co-parent and make it work. Stacey was like us, from the wrong side of the tracks, she passed no judgment. Alex and Lucas though were a different story. They would never approve of their boy hanging anywhere near someone like me. Especially, not with the son of Devil's Rejects' Prez.

"Mia, Daddy's here to get you! Grab your things, baby girl," her momma called out from the restaurant.

"I am not a baby," she mumbled under her breath, grabbing her board. Peering up at me. "See ya around?"

I nodded and a big smile spread across her face before she turned and left.

I would learn through the years that Mia Ryder…

Mia. Fuckin'. Ryder.

I would live and die…

62

ROAD to NOWHERE

For her.

Mia

"Happy birthday, dear Mia, happy birthday to you." Everyone finished singing, clapping their hands, hooting and hollering.

"Blow out your candles, baby girl," Dad said, swiping my hair back. Nodding toward my chocolate, surfer-themed cake. Complete with a girl riding a pink board like mine that Momma had specially made for my tenth birthday.

Shutting my eyes as tight as I could, I bit my bottom lip, placing my hands in prayer gesture out in front of me, concentrating really hard. Focusing all my efforts on my birthday wish, I blew out all the candles in front of my family, silently hoping it would come true.

"What did you wish for?" Aunt Lily asked.

"If I tell you, then it won't come true, and I really want it to come true." I blushed just thinking about it.

I opened my presents next while everyone ate a slice of cake on the back patio. My favorite present was the guitar Aunt Lily got me. She had been teaching me how to play for the last few years, and I was getting pretty good.

I told my parents I didn't want a birthday party, but Momma wasn't having that. She said it was my first birthday in the double digits, and we needed to celebrate. I just think it was another excuse for her to throw a party. She loved to entertain. If it were up to me, we would have just had my family over for a barbecue, but instead, our backyard was decked out with pink balloons, streamers, and a giant bouncy house.

ROAD to NOWHERE

I didn't have a lot of friends, but it never bothered me since I had so many cousins. Our ages were scattered all over the place, but that never mattered, we got along just fine. We were all born and raised together in Oak Island, just like our daddies and my momma, who were all best friends since they were in diapers. Everyone called them the Good Ol' Boys with their Half-Pint, my momma, following them around like she was a boy too. Looking at her now, I would never have guessed she wanted to be a boy.

My daddy and Aunt Lily were brother and sister. She was married to one of the boys, Uncle Jacob. They had two kids, Riley and Christian. Aunt Lily always told me that Daddy didn't like that Uncle Jacob fell in love with his baby sister. They kept their love a secret for a long time and when Daddy found out he was with Aunt Lily, he beat him up. Uncle Jacob says he let him win, but Daddy says he's just a pansy-ass lawyer who was just trying to save face, whatever that meant.

Uncle Dylan, another one of the boys, was married to Aunt Aubrey. He reminded me of a superhero, always carrying a gun and a badge, putting bad people behind bars. They had two daughters, Giselle and a newborn baby named Constance. Everyone says God blessed him with girls as punishment for being such a womanizing asshole. I don't know what that means either, but Momma says I'm not allowed to repeat that.

My brother Mason started dating Giselle, they had been boyfriend and girlfriend forever, and I really loved her. I caught them kissing in Mason's room a few times, but didn't tell on him because I'm not a snitch. I just made him take me places with him for a week to keep my lips sealed. Of course, he did.

Uncle Austin was the last good ol' boy. He was covered in tattoos just like Creed was, and he owned a local tattoo shop. His girlfriend was Briggs, who had bright purple hair and tattoos all over her body too. They were getting to know each other again. I guess Uncle Austin did some bad things, but he's better now and trying to win her back. I had a feeling he would. My daddy wasn't very happy when I asked if I could dye my hair my favorite color, bright pink. He looked at me like I had grown two heads, before saying no. When I told him I wanted to get my pink surfboard tattooed on my foot, he said not while he's alive and breathing.

Daddy didn't let me do anything.

Ever.

I didn't care that some of my cousins weren't blood-related, they were the only family I'd ever known. I loved each of them with all my heart.

"Daddy, can I go to the Southport Fourth of July festival with Mason next month?" I asked while helping Momma clean up after everyone had left.

"Mia, I already told you no," he replied, not looking up from the blueprint in front of him on the kitchen counter.

My daddy owned his own construction company and was the best damn contractor in the tri-state area. His words, not mine.

"Yeah, but I asked you when I was nine. Newsflash, I'm ten now."

"The answer is still no, Mia, and watch that lip, young lady."

"Why? It's not fair! You said Bo could go with Mason if he wanted. Last I checked, Bo is only two years older than I am," I argued, throwing the dishes into the sink a little harder than I should have.

"That's different," Dad simply stated, still focused on work.

"Why, because he has a wiener?"

"Mia Ryder! You cannot say stuff like that!" Momma shouted, walking back into the kitchen.

I could hear Mason and Bo laughing their butts off over the movie they were watching from the living room. I rolled my eyes, frustrated.

Daddy sighed, dropping his pencil, and finally looking up from his paperwork. "Mason! Bo! How many times do I have to tell you to stop talking like that around your baby sister!"

"I'm not a baby!" I yelled, stomping my foot.

Mason came strolling into the room, his hair all messy from Giselle scratching his head on the couch. "Dad, she's like a fuc—damn parrot." He caught himself. "Most of the time I don't even realize she's around until it's too late." He opened the fridge, grabbing the jug of milk and started drinking right from the carton.

"Mason Ryder! Where are your manners, boy?" Momma reprimanded.

"Oh, I'm sorry. Did you want some?" He held up the carton to her. She gave him a look that had him putting it right back in the fridge.

"Daddy, I could have said the word *dick* like he does, but I used wiener instead because I'm a lady."

Mason busted out laughing, quickly clearing his throat when Daddy gave him a stern look.

"And this is exactly why you're not going to the festival with Mason and his foul-mouthed friends," he justified.

"Lucas..." Momma coaxed.

"Half-Pint, don't start. My baby girl—"

"Our baby girl," she interrupted. Looking over at him as she loaded the dishwasher.

"I'm. Not. A. Baby!" I repeated much louder that time. Smacking my hand on the counter, needing to have my voice heard. "It's not fair, Daddy. You know all you are doing is pushing me away. I'm gonna start doing things without asking you first because you never let me do anything. I'm not always going to be your baby girl."

He cocked his head to the side. "Is that right?"

"Yes. That's right." I knew I was pushing his buttons, I knew I was crossing the line. I knew I was going to get in trouble...

I just didn't care anymore.

"Mia, go to your room," Momma ordered, looking from Daddy to me. Not only punishing me but saving me from my daddy's wrath.

"Dad, she can come with me," Mason chimed in. "I'll make sure everyone is on their best behavior."

My heart soared. Mason never stuck up for me before. That alone meant everything to me.

I smiled at him.

"Your mom and I will be out of town during the festival. Mia is staying with Lily and Jacob. She won't—"

"I don't want—"

"Time out!" Momma interrupted all of us. "Everyone out!"

"But—"

"Mia. Now!" Dad roared, bringing my attention back to him.

"Fine," I mumbled under my breath, turning to leave the room. Resisting the urge to slam my door once I walked into my bedroom.

I grabbed my notebook off my desk and made my way through the double doors out onto my balcony that overlooked the water. I spent the next few hours sitting in my lounger under the moon, listening to the soft lull of the waves crashing into the shore, welcoming the salty breeze coming off the ocean. The water always had a way of calming me, no matter what I was feeling or going through. It was my happy place, my own piece of Heaven, my escape. I should have been in bed sleeping like everyone else in my house, but it was summer break and I didn't have a bedtime. I was a night owl anyway, always had been.

I scribbled thoughts, lyrics, and doodles in my notebook for I don't know how long, finding myself writing Creed's name in bubble letters and practicing my cursive, over and over again. Surrounding his name with pink hearts on every page. Suddenly realizing I had my first crush.

I snuggled into my throw blanket, looking up at the stars, wondering if my birthday wish would magically come true. Wishing again that it would. I yawned, my eyes growing tired from the long day I'd had. I was about to go inside and go to bed when my window shook from Mason's bedroom door shutting. His room was next door to mine, and I could hear everything.

He must have just gotten home.

I picked up my notebook, looking back out at the water one last time when I saw him. He was walking away from my house toward the ocean, wearing the same vest he had on the last time I saw him. I immediately wondered if he was wearing the courage patch I gave him a few months ago. I giggled at the sight of him wearing his combat boots on the sand. He stopped at the shoreline, looking up at the sky, placing his hands in the pockets of his black jeans. He looked as huge and stocky as I remembered. Maybe even bigger.

Before I gave it a second thought, I ran into my room, grabbing my backpack and digging around in it. Grabbing what I was looking for, and my throw off my bed. It was chilly out on the water. I slipped out of my bedroom quietly, being extra careful not to wake anyone. I'd be in big trouble if my daddy woke since I wasn't allowed to leave the house by myself after dark. In my defense, I wasn't going to be alone, Creed was on the beach. I snuck out the back patio doors, closing them gently behind me. Walking down the steps onto our private piece of beach. No one would be able to see us without trespassing. He had to have come in with Mason.

"My wish came true!" I shouted over the noise of the waves.

"Ain't it past your bedtime?" he coldly said, not turning around to face me.

"Didn't you hear me?" I asked, wrapping the throw around my shoulders. "My wish came true, you're here."

He abruptly turned, narrowing his eyes at me. Taken back by my confession.

I continued on, "It was my birthday today, well yesterday seeing that it's after midnight. Anyway, before I blew my candles out, I got to make one wish. I closed my eyes tight, wishing I would see you again, and here you are."

"Shouldn't be wishin' for me, Pippin," he stated, turning his attention back to the water.

"Pippin?"

He suddenly turned back around, reached over, and tugged on the end of one of my braided pigtails.

"Oh! Like Pippy Longstocking! She was like Peter Pan for girls. Never wanting to grow up. She's kinda my idol, a playful, unpredictable, superhuman. A freak of nature like I am on a surfboard. And she had a rad pet monkey, Mr. Nilsson."

He nodded, still looking broody. I wanted to make him feel better. I wanted to see him laugh and smile like he did at the beach. For some reason, I felt as if he didn't do that very often. His eyes were still so sad, and I wanted to know why so badly. My momma always said I had the ability to make people happy. That there was something about my spunky personality that made people like me. I wanted Creed to like me more than anyone else ever had.

I spoke honestly, "But if I wouldn't have made that wish, I wouldn't be able to give this to you." I stepped forward, handing him another patch for his vest. "I saw it at a little shop in town when my momma and I were shopping a few weeks back. When she was in the dressing room, I grabbed it and bought it with my allowance. It reminded me of you."

He took it from me, murmuring, "Don't follow me. I'm lost too," he chuckled as he read it out loud. "Not lost, Pippin. Just haven't been found yet," he paused, looking down at the patch in his hand. "Thank you for this." A small smile played on his lips as he reached into his pocket, pulling something out. "I found this on the sidewalk today." He handed me a shiny penny. "Consider it my birthday present to ya."

I gave him a questioning glare. "Thank you... it's what I've always wanted," I sarcastically stated.

"No, smartass, the penny isn't the gift. The wish is. Do me a favor, yeah? Don't waste anymore wishes on me." With that he turned and walked away, leaving me alone and confused.

"But I already made—"

"Givin' you a do-over, Pippin. You'll thank me later," he called out over his shoulder.

I turned back toward the water, looking down at the penny in my open hand. Closing my fingers around it, placing it over my heart.

I didn't need a do-over. My first wish was perfect. My second wish to see him again.

Would be too.

"Creed... Creed... Creed... please help me... if you ever loved me... find me... please help me... I'm scared, Creed... I'm so scared..." Luke pleaded from a distance.

His voice sounded so far, yet so close. It echoed all around me, making it difficult to tell what direction it was coming from. Humming into the trees like the melody of an instrumental song, vibrating deep into my bones. I turned in a circle, whipping my head from north to south, east to west. Raking my hands through my hair, breathing profusely. Before I knew it, I ran. I ran as fast as I could through the endless woods with no direction whatsoever.

"Right here." I saw a figure out of the corner of my eye, but when I turned it was gone. "Run... run, faster, Creed! Help me!"

Every turn I took was the wrong one, always coming to a dead end. His pleas getting further and further away with each step I took. Pulling him into the black hole of the night.

The roads led me to nowhere.

"Creed... Creed... please help me... if you ever loved me... find me... please help me... I'm scared, Creed... I'm so scared..." Luke's voice repeated in a mantra, a never-ending cycle of nothing.

"Luke! Luke! Where are you? I'm comin', buddy. Where are you?" I yelled out into the dark night.

But it didn't echo, it didn't hum, there was no sound coming out of my mouth. Why couldn't I talk? Why couldn't he hear me? There was so much dense fog, so much fucking haze that suddenly rolled in, smothering me. Choking me. I couldn't see. I couldn't move. Was I running in place? My heart pounded against my chest, in my ears, through my mind, caving into my core.

I couldn't breathe.

I was suffocating.

"Creed... Creed... please help me... if you ever loved me... you would find me... please help me... I'm scared, Creed... I'm so scared..."

The train horn sounded, snapping my attention back. The rumbling on the tracks piercing my ears, as one by one, the cars rolled by. Circling all around me with no end in sight. Glimpses of my brother flashed through the gaps. Covered in blood, standing there with his hand over his chest, waiting.

"Creed... Creed... Creed... please help me... if you ever loved me... you would find me... please help me... I'm scared, Creed... I'm so scared..." His voice sounded closer and then further away with each word that droned out.

"Tell me where you are! Please, Luke! Just tell me where you are!" I placed my hands over my ears, trying to shut out the noises from the train, but they were just getting louder and louder and louder until all I could hear was a train and nothing else.

My mind spun.

My heart raced.

My body surrendered.

I fell to my knees, looking down at my blood-soaked hands; the Glock lay in between them.

"Creed... Creed... Creed... please help me... if you ever loved me... you would find me... please help me... I'm scared, Creed... I'm so scared..."

"I'm so sorry, Luke! I'm so fucking sorry!" I bawled uncontrollably. Lifting the gun up to my chin.

"Creed! Creed! It's okay! Wake up! It's okay!" Autumn's sweet voice coaxed, merging in with all the harshness. "Shhh... it's okay... I'm here, Creed! I'm here!"

I didn't hesitate. I never do.

I pulled the trigger.

BANG.

I shot straight up in my bed, gasping for air. Panting for my next breath, staring out in front of me. Sweat dripped from my pores, running down the sides of my face. I didn't move, trying to rationalize what was real and what was still a dream.

A fucking nightmare.

"Creed..." Autumn sympathized, reaching for my face.

I caught her wrist midair. "Don't," I crudely demanded, shoving her arm away.

It was the same dream I had every time I allowed myself to fall into a deep sleep. A moment of weakness my demons fed on. Regaining my composure, I abruptly stood before she could say anything else. I went out onto the back porch, letting the door shut behind me. Needing some fresh air. A goddamn minute to myself.

Something.

Anything.

Other than what I was fucking feeling.

I lit up a cigarette, taking in a deep drag. Letting the smoke linger in my mouth, trying to clear out the haze in my mind. The backdoor opened and then closed. I didn't have to turn around to know who it was. After I drove a drunk-ass Mason home last night, I called Autumn to come pick me up from his house. We were hanging out at the clubhouse with some brothers, shooting the shit, throwing back beers like they were fucking water. We were both pretty fucked up, but out of the two of us, I was the more sober one. I wasn't going to let him get behind the wheel in his state, so I drove his truck home for him.

Never thinking that Mia would come running out in the middle of the night to hand me another patch. Telling me her birthday wish to see me again came true. I hadn't seen her since the first time I met her on the beach, months ago. She was a sweet, innocent, little girl. I should have left it alone, but the last thing she needed was to be thinking about me, let alone making fucking wishes to see me again. I was nine years older than her.

By the time we got back to my place, it was close to two in the morning. There was no way in hell I was going to let Autumn drive back home, alone. She just ended up crashing in my bed with me. It was never a big deal. We'd been sharing a bed since we were kids. The only difference was that now we weren't fucking kids anymore, and she had the tits and ass to make my cock hard. Most likely giving her a morning wood surprise, but I didn't give a fuck.

I never thought of her as more than my best friend, even though our mothers wanted nothing more than for us to end up together. Sure, she was fucking beautiful, but her friendship meant more to me than her pussy. She deserved more than just being a piece of ass. And right now, that was the furthest thing from my mind.

"Those things are going to kill you," Autumn stated from behind me. The worry in her voice seared a hole in my heart.

"Well, lucky for me I'm already dying inside."

She knew all the shit I went through in my life. I confided in her often without worrying about being judged for my imperfections. For my fucking sins. No matter what I told her, I never feared she would walk away, or turn her back on me. There were times when I didn't have to say one fucking word, just listening to her breathe on the other end of the phone brought a sense of calm over me. Autumn was the only person that knew the truth about that night, about what I had done. I needed to tell someone the truth, needing to be honest about the whole thing.

My parents lied to everyone, saying Luke had accidentally shot himself. No one asked questions because what could you possibly say to that? Pops paid off the coroner, obtaining all the legitimate documents they needed, making it look like it was all an unfortunate accident. Telling everyone we had a private funeral for him with immediate family only, deciding to cremate him so they could always carry his ashes with them. He even went as far as posting an obituary in the local paper, keeping up the false pretenses of portraying the grieving loving father to the son I killed.

"Y-y-you alright?" she nervously stuttered when I remained silent. Taking a deep, reassuring breath, she walked over, leaning her back up against the railing of the patio, to face me. "How often does that happen? You know, the nightmares?"

I glanced over at her. "Who said they fuckin' stop?"

Her eyes widened. She reached out to place a hand on my shoulder. "Oh... Creed, I'm so—"

"Don't need your fuckin' pity, Autumn."

"You think I pity you? I care about you. I hate that you blame yourself for Luke's death. When are you going to realize it was an accident? You didn't mean—"

"Enough!" I pushed past her, taking another drag of my cigarette. Heading over to the seating area around the fire pit.

"Will you at least tell me what it was about? Your nightmare?" She walked up behind me. "It might help to talk about it. You can't keep that shit bottled up, Creed. I'm here for you. I have been for years, so stop trying to shut me out. Let me help you."

"Ain't gonna bring him back," I stated, letting the smoke seep out of my mouth as I spoke. I sat on one of the chairs, resting my elbows on my knees, holding my suddenly pounding head between my hands.

She sat next to me, grabbing my arm away from my face. "Tell me anyway."

I shook my head, scoffing out, "It's always the same goddamn dream. Hearin' Luke's voice in the woods. Beggin', pleadin' with me to come find him. Sayin' he's scared. Tellin' me if I ever loved him, I'd be able to find him."

She jerked back, surprised with my revelation.

"Can't find him, though. Never can. It's like I'm runnin' in circles, like one of them fuckin' hamsters on a spinnin' wheel. Then, out of nowhere, I'm at the train tracks over on McMullen. Except the train is spinnin' in circles around me. I see flashes of Luke through the cars. Again, pleadin' for me to come find him even though he's standin' right in front of me. It's not him. He's covered in blood. Holdin' the bullet wound over his heart."

"Jesus, Creed..."

I didn't hesitate. If she wanted to know exactly what I was going through, then I was going to tell her everything. "Always ends with me fallin' onto my knees in pain. My hands covered in blood, holdin' onto to the Glock. Just can't take anymore," I confessed for the first time, pausing to let my words sink in.

Her eyes filled with tears, knowing where my truths would lead.

74

"Luke's beggin', the sounds of the train, my conscience... I take the gun and aim it under my chin..." I peered deep into her eyes, stating, "Don't fuckin' hesitate to pull the trigger."

Tears fell down her pretty little face onto the pavers.

"Don't waste your tears on me, Autumn," I rasped, wiping one away. "Don't deserve them."

"It's obvious what you think you deserve, Creed." She wiped her cheeks with the back of her hand.

"Said you wanted to know. There ya go. Welcome to my fuckin' world."

"It was an accident. You love your brother more than anything in this world. I have seen it firsthand, Creed. I still see it every damn day. The way you still take care of Noah, even more so now than before. While your father doesn't have a care in the world besides that club, and your mother drowns herself in vodka, what do you do? Huh?"

I shook my head, not wanting to hear any more of this.

"You practically kill yourself every day, doing God knows what for that club. A club you don't even like or want to be a part of. Listening to every order your father barks at you. Doing everything he demands without so much of a blink of an eye. Who you doing that for? Sure as hell isn't for you. What happened was a terrible accident. I can't imagine what you're going through even after all these months. But you can't keep blaming yourself because you don't deserve that. Do you understand me? You don't fucking deserve it."

"Drive me over to get my bike, yeah? I'll buy you breakfast for not bitchin' about my cold ass room." I changed the subject.

She sighed, nodding even though she wanted to say so much more. I was tired of hearing her run her mouth. Nothing she could say would make it right, all it did was remind me how shitty my life really was. She definitely couldn't bring Luke back. I loved Autumn, I knew she meant well, but sometimes she didn't know when to just shut the fuck up.

I spent the next couple of days making runs for the club, driving for hours and getting home later than usual. I hadn't seen or talked to Autumn since that morning at breakfast, but it wasn't from the lack of trying. I'm sure she thought I was purposely avoiding her since I hadn't reached out. I was just too goddamn busy.

I walked into my house just after midnight, ready to crash for the night. I was fucking exhausted from dealing with bullshit all day, and all I wanted to do was fall on my bed and pass the fuck out. I hadn't been sleeping well, and even when I did, I woke up from the same recurring nightmare. My house was dark and quiet when I walked in. Laying my keys on the table, I walked into the dining room, shocked when I didn't find my mother passed out at the table. The empty bottles that usually littered the room were gone. As I made my way to my room, I noticed the light shining under my door, and out into the dark hallway.

I would be lying if I said I wasn't surprised when I opened my door to find Autumn sitting on my bed, waiting for me.

"Hey, I put your mom to bed. I made Noah some dinner and played video games with him all night. I came in here when I heard your bike pull up," she divulged as I closed the door behind me. "I don't want to fight anymore," she added, surrendering her hands.

"Wasn't aware we were fightin'." I walked over to the closet, kicking off my boots, and grabbing a fresh shirt from the hanger.

She smiled, her anxiety lessening. "I have something for you." She stood, walking over to me. Placing a white jewelry box in my hand.

I cocked an eyebrow, confused by the turn of events.

"I think this will help with your nightmares. I know you're struggling to stay above the surface, Creed. I know you feel all this guilt and remorse for what happened to Luke, but I know in my heart, you were his favorite person. Exactly how you are Noah's," she paused, letting her words sink in. "I know it's going to take time for you to find peace, but I'm hoping maybe this will help." She nodded toward the jewelry box in my hands. "Open it."

I did, pulling off the lid. Finding a picture of Luke staring back at me engraved in a dog tag. It hung off a silver chain that was fastened in the box. Autumn took the necklace out, turning it over for me to read the engraving.

"Death leaves a heartache no one can heal. Love leaves a memory no one can steal," she recited out loud to me. "I read that somewhere and it always stuck with me. I wasn't sure why, until now."

We locked eyes as she placed the dog tag over my heart. "Time heals all wounds, but your memory of Luke is forever. No one can steal that from you, do you hear me? Even though he is gone, he will always be with you here." She patted my heart, looking up at me through her lashes.

What happened next nearly dropped me on my fucking ass. She stood on the tips of her toes and shyly smiled, then leaned in and kissed my lips softly. Opening her mouth against mine, baiting me to move my lips in sync with hers.

I didn't.

She continued trying. Nudging her nose with mine, looking up at me through her lashes. Pressing her perfect tits firmly against my chest. She smelled so fucking good.

My cock twitched.

When she tenderly pecked my lips once again, this time running her tongue along my mouth, she moaned, a soft, sultry hum, luring me in. I couldn't take it anymore. I reached up holding her pretty, little, freckled face between my hands. Gently kissing her back, my walls crumbling down around me. All reservations I had about us, breaking apart with it.

As fast as it happened, it was over and I pulled away, leaning my forehead on hers and whispering, "This doesn't change anything, Autumn."

She closed her eyes tight for a second, taking in what I said. The hurt evident on her face. I would remember the next words that came out of her mouth for the rest of my life.

She slowly opened her eyes again, looking deep into mine, and spoke with conviction, "He won't rest in peace, Creed. Until you let him. It starts with you."

This was just the start of the sudden shift in our friendship. Already knowing in my fucking gut…

That no good could come of this.

"Winner! The young lady in the pink tank top, come on down. What can I get ya, darlin'?" the carnival worker's voice boomed over the crowd that started to gather around Uncle Jacob and me.

"Oh my God! I won again," I goaded, putting my hands up to my face, pretending to be shocked. "Take that, Uncle Jacob! What is that now? Zero wins for you and six for me? Boom!" I smiled, running over to the carney to claim another prize.

This time I picked out a big pink teddy bear with a tie-dyed shirt on, to go with my other prizes.

"You really are Lucas's kid," Uncle Jacob teased, ruffling my hair.

I pulled away from him, looking up at the side of his face as we walked side-by-side down the grassy field. "Did he use to kick your butt, too?"

He just laughed and shook his head, confirming I was right. "Let's go find your aunt and cousins, smartass."

The Fourth of July fair had been going on for decades in Southport. Always set up in the same field with the ocean as it's backdrop. People from all over came to town that weekend to join the festivities. The huge Ferris wheel could be seen for miles outside of town, lighting up the night with its neon-colored lights. There were beer tents, casino tents, games tents, any kind of attraction you could think of, it was there.

ROAD to NOWHERE

All of them surrounding the carnival-style rides and booths, like the one I had just schooled Uncle Jacob at. Music blasted through the speakers, bells rang out announcing winners and screams echoed off the rides. I loved the energy of the fair the most, people smiling and laughing without a care in the world. Oh, and the smell of the carnival food, just thinking about it made my tummy rumble.

My grandparents on daddy's side actually met at the fair. Papa had told me stories time and time again how love came to him on the merry-go-round. My grandma, who I had never met, was riding on one of the horses going up and down, laughing with her friends. He stood at the gate watching her being carefree and happy. Saying she had a smile that could light up anyone's life, and it had. She died from breast cancer when Mason was just a baby. My daddy said it was the hardest time of his and Aunt Lily's lives, the saddest too. But they keep her in their hearts and see a lot of her in me. I just wish I could have met her. It would have been nice to maybe have someone on my side.

After pleading with Daddy for over a month, he finally gave into letting me go to the Fourth of July Fair. Except, I had to go with Uncle Jacob, Aunt Lily, and their two kids, instead of with Mason, Bo, and their friends like I wanted to. Daddy and Momma were going out of town for the weekend for some romantic getaway, saying they needed some quiet time together. I told them they would have plenty of quiet time if Daddy would stop making Momma scream in their bedroom. He knew she didn't like to be tickled. I couldn't understand why he still tickled her all the time.

I was pissed when Daddy said I had to stay with my aunt and uncle all weekend. I wanted to stay home with Mason and Bo. There was no chance at winning that fight. Not even for one night. I was grateful to be going to the fair at least, but the last thing I wanted was to be treated like a baby again. I didn't want to go with my aunt and uncle, they wouldn't let me go on the big rides like Mason would. I went to go argue my case, but Momma gave me a stern look not to start with him again.

So I just dropped it, even though I hated losing. Nothing upset me more than not being right. Momma said I got that from my daddy, you would think that it would make him understand me better, but I think it only made it worse. All I could hope for was to run into Mason or Bo and be allowed to hang with them for a little while.

"Mia, if you win any more prizes, we're not going to be able to fit them in the car," Aunt Lily laughed, holding a giant monkey around her neck, hugging my dolphin, and carrying my goldfish I had won.

"I can't help that Uncle Jacob sucks," I replied, sticking my tongue out at him.

"Pssh... I wasn't even tryin', little girl."

"Alright you two, Riley wants to go on the Tilt-A-World again, and Christian is asleep in the stroller. Let's ride a few more and then go find a good spot for the nighttime parade, okay?"

"We just got here, Aunt Lily. I didn't get to go on any of the rollercoasters, especially The Scrambler. I haven't even eaten my funnel cake, you have to eat a funnel cake at the carnival." I cocked my head and put my hands on my hips.

"If we wait too long we won't be able to see the parade. Besides, you're too little to go on those rides."

"Says who? I'm tall enough," I argued, walking over to the cardboard clown holding a measuring tape. "See." I pointed up. "I'm plenty big. If Mason were here, he'd take me." I think since I was the first girl to be born in the family, everyone thought they had to baby me because of it. "Come on, Aunt Lily. What happened to you being fun?"

"Mia Ryder, you don't talk to your aunt that way," Uncle Jacob chastened.

I peered up at him through my lashes, resisting the urge to roll my eyes. Knowing it would only get me in more trouble.

I sighed, looking down at my feet. No one understood, no one ever took my side. Papa, my grandpa, tells me all the time that the good ol' boys, Momma, and aunt Lily never listened either. They were always causing trouble, but you'd never believe that now.

I kicked around the dirt, eating my funnel cake, following close behind them. Watching people get on and off the rides I wanted to go on, annoyed the entire time.

We went on a few more kiddy rides before Aunt Lily found an open spot next to one of the bars. I watched all the people gathering around, excited for the parade that would lead to fireworks. The

Southport festival had the best firework display in North Carolina, winning awards for years.

"Uncle Jacob, can I—" Bright headlights illuminated behind his tall frame, and the loud sound of motorcycle engines revving, broke my train of thought. I immediately peered behind him. Tons of Harleys came into view, there had to be at least twenty to twenty-five bikes filing into the parking lot next to the bar. Wearing vests exactly like Creed's.

"Un-fuckin'-believable," Uncle Jacob gritted out, turning his head toward the noise. "What are those pieces of shit doing here?"

"Jacob! How many times do I have to tell you to watch your mouth in front of the kids?" Aunt Lily reprimanded, holding her hands over Riley's ears like muffs.

"I know. It's just those heathens are no damn good. I should call Dylan and see if he wants to take out some trash tonight."

I frowned, lowering my eyebrows not understanding what he meant by that.

What was wrong with them?

I scanned the bikers, knowing he had to be with them, but it was hard to see with all the families suddenly picking up their kids and walking in the opposite direction. Whispering to look away. Crowds parted to get out of their way. Others just turned their heads, not making eye contact with the men.

I took a few steps in their direction, ignoring my uncle who started to pull on my hand, trying to tug me away.

"Mia, let's go. Now!" Aunt Lily shouted over the chaos. "Crap! Jacob, can you help me with this stroller? It's stuck."

That's when I saw him. Pulling off his helmet, shaking out his hair that looked longer now. I hadn't seen him since that night on the beach. The same night he granted me a second wish. A smile spread across my face, my heart fluttered in my chest, a feeling I had never felt before. My eyes were glued to the man in front of me. I wanted to run over to him to say hi, but after what Uncle Jacob said and how the people were acting, I figured it wasn't a good idea.

I watched from afar, waiting for him to turn and see me. I would have waited all night if that's what it took for him to look at me. I straightened out my light pink dress, fixing the bows in my pigtails, making sure I looked as pretty as I could. Waiting for him to walk this way.

He got off his bike, turning to put his helmet on the backrest when I caught a glimpse of long red hair behind him, a girl sitting on the back of his bike. Taking off her helmet, smiling up at him with loving eyes.

I jerked back, caught off guard.

It was the girl that came running up to him from the first time we met at the beach. I remembered she had chocolate brown eyes and thick black eyelashes that fluttered for him. Her long, messy, red hair was draped all over her face. He helped her off the bike, grabbing the helmet from her hands, and locking it next to his. Reaching up, he brushed the stray hairs away from her rosy cheeks. She was wearing tiny shorts, barely covering her long legs, with black combat boots like Creed's. Her tank top hardly covered her big boobs and skinny belly.

The way he looked at her hurt my stomach, hurt my heart, and I didn't understand why. I looked down at my girly dress, all of the sudden not feeling good enough. I wanted to look like her. I wanted to be her. If that's what it took for Creed to look at me the way he looked at her.

I could do that for him.

I waited for what felt like years, wanting him to glance my way, even if it was just for one second. All I wanted was a moment of his time. A flicker to feel a part of his life. All of a sudden as if he heard my thoughts, or felt my presence, he turned. Locking eyes with me from the distance between us.

I smiled big and wide, just so he could see my giddy face light up for him. He remained expressionless, looking right through me and not at me. Taking one last look in my direction, he turned back around, grabbed the girl's hand and walked toward the bar.

He didn't even acknowledge me. He acted like he didn't even know who I was. Like I meant nothing to him.

When he meant something to me.

I grinned, cocking my head to the side taking in the perfection of her creamy white skin as Autumn danced in front of me. Swaying her hips to the country music the live band was belting out. Running her hands up her banging body, through her hair, making every other man in the tent turn their heads to watch.

"You and Autumn, huh?" Mason asked, peering over at me. Bringing my attention away from her.

"She wanted to dance," I simply stated, shrugging, standing in the background. Leaning against the wood beam with my arms crossed over my chest, one leg over the other.

We rode in with the brothers, stopping to have a few beers at the bar my old man owned near the fairgrounds. I told Mason to grab Giselle, and meet us up there. The girls got a stick up their asses real quick, nagging us about how bored they were, and how they wanted to dance. The booze running warm through their bodies, getting to them faster than us. Autumn pulled me outside, smiling, laughing, not a care in the fucking world. Dragging my sorry ass out of the bar, causing the brothers to hoot and holler that I better be getting some of that ass for being a pussy and not putting my bitch in her place.

We ended up at one of the beer tents at the carnival, there was a big slab of cement in the middle of the tent, making up a makeshift dance floor. A small stage set up in the front where a live local band performed throughout the weekend. Twinkling white lights hung from the beams and tables surrounded the dance floor.

"I call bullshit. She's been coming onto you hard the last month, so somethin' must have happened between you."

"Ain't what it looks like." I didn't look at him, focusing on Autumn who was now dancing close with Giselle. Singing the lyrics of the song to each other with pretend microphones. Having the time of their lives.

"I don't see you turning her down."

"Not fuckin' her, Mason. Won't cross that line. Everythin' else is just fuckin' child's play."

"Does she know that?" he questioned, pointing to her, raising his eyebrows.

"She knows me."

Autumn had been throwing herself at me since that night in my bedroom. I would be lying if I said my cock wasn't interested. She was a fucking knockout with huge tits, a nice ass, and legs that went on for days. Pouty little lips that I used to think about being wrapped around my cock when I first started jacking off. Her loving, free-spirited personality alone was sexy as fuck to me. She turned me on in so many ways. But I knew better than to fuck around with her. It would only lead to her getting hurt. We'd been there for each other since we could walk. It was only natural for us to be drawn to one another, law of attraction and all that fucking shit.

Except things were different now.

I was different now.

Autumn needed a man that would always put her first. She was needy as all hell, always had been. I couldn't provide her with that anymore, it was an offer that would never be on my table for us. My priority was the club, Noah, and my mother. I didn't have the time to be the man she thought I was, the man she deserved. It fucking exhausted me just thinking about it, let alone being that person for her.

I didn't let that stop her from flirting with me, though. Needing the support only she could ever offer. No one else knew me the way she did. I needed the distraction from the Hell that had turned into my life. I may have been leading her on, but fuck it. I wasn't a goddamn saint, never claimed to be, and at the end of the day, she knew I wasn't.

As much she tried to pretend that I was.

"Come dance with me," Autumn interrupted, throwing her arms around my neck, faltering a little.

Giselle not far behind her, tugging Mason onto the dance floor without even asking first.

Pussy.

My arms naturally went around her waist. "Don't dance," I reminded her.

"Oh, come on... please." She pouted, deliberately swaying her hips against my cock. "I'll do everything, all you have to do is stand there and look like the badass you are."

"Tell that to my cock you're dry humpin'," I chuckled, enjoying the feel of her in my arms.

She rolled her eyes, stifling a smile. "I didn't know I needed his permission. Since when does your cock care?"

"Since I was eight. The day my cock realized he fuckin' liked you, that's when."

She giggled, turning around. Backing her ass up right to where her pussy had just been. Knowing I was an ass man. "Do you mind? Or are you just going to stand there?" she taunted, swaying her hips to the beat of the music.

I smiled, wide. Leaning into her ear, murmuring, "By all means, Autumn. Don't mind one fuckin' bit."

She shook her head. "You have no shame, Creed Jameson."

"Gonna take a lot more booze to get me to dance, darlin'," I rasped against her hair. "Ya feel me?"

"Oh, I feel you all right." She peered over her shoulder and winked.

"Oh, that ain't nothin', sweetheart."

"You may just need to show me then." She grabbed my hands, placing them on her thighs and ran them up her soft, silky legs to her hips.

That was my cue to get out of there. "Gonna get a drink, yeah?"

"Yeah." She spun, stumbling, throwing her arms around my neck again. "Bring me one of those girly umbrella drinks, okay?"

I cocked an eyebrow, looking at her like she couldn't be serious.

"Fine… bring me water," she added, pulling away.

I grabbed her hand at the last second and twirled her around in a circle. Showing her the only dance move I knew. "Don't fuckin' stray. Stay with Mason. Be right back." Smacking her ass.

She smiled, nodding.

I walked back inside the bar. It was a lot more packed than it was before. People crowded all together in the big open space, I could feel the desperation in the air, slutty fucking girls everywhere, and horny ass men following close behind them. The brothers sat in the same place I left them, lined with fresh pussy just champing at the bit. Fucking desperate bitches, beckoning for their attention, running their nails all over their cut. Or anywhere else they could.

I decided to take a piss before heading over to the bar, relieving myself before Autumn continued to dry- fuck the shit out of my cock. Leaving me with the worst case of fucking blue balls. I'm sure I could have pulled one of these eager bitches in a stall with me and had them suck my cock, but Autumn was waiting for me.

I was a dick, but I still had manners.

Skipping over all the people who were waiting to be served, I signaled Louie, the bartender, for two drinks.

He handed me a beer in a red solo cup and a bottle of water. Technically I wasn't supposed to be drinking since I was under twenty-one, but I was never one to follow rules. It helped that I looked way older than I was. I'd been drinking out in public since I could see behind the bar, especially at establishments that my father governed.

The crowd parted for me as I made my way back outside and over to the tent where Autumn was. The music had switched from the live band to a DJ spinning the latest hits. I walked inside the tent, trying to find her through the crowd of people who'd rushed in to see who was playing. People littered the whole tent, making it nearly impossible to see the dance floor. I searched for any sign of her red hair, finally spotting her on the opposite end.

Except she wasn't fucking alone.

Some pretty boy dipshit had his hands all over her body, working his cock into her ass, while she suddenly became a goddamn stripper on a pole. My beer dropped out of my hands and splashed to the ground, chucking her water bottle next. I hauled ass across the dance floor, shoving people out of the way. I was a ticking fucking time bomb about to explode the longer it took to get to her. Taking down anyone who was in my path of destruction, needing to get to her as fast as I could.

My fist was pulled back as I took my last step, and it connected with the motherfucker's jaw before he even saw me coming. His head snapped back, taking half of his now limp body with him. Autumn screamed as she was pulled to the ground by the fucker who didn't let her go. I leaned forward, grabbing her by the waist, saving her ass from meeting the concrete below. Pulling her up to my chest, snaking her body behind mine.

"Don't touch what fuckin' belongs to me!" I snarled, kicking him in the stomach while he was down. Squatting in front of his body, grabbing ahold of his fucking Polo shirt, getting right up in his bloody face. "You got any idea who the fuck you're dealin' with? Whose territory you're fuckin' pissin' on?" I cocked my fist back again, ramming it into his face. His head fell back on the ground with a thud.

"Come on, pussy! Get up!" I roared, lifting him from the ground again when I suddenly felt Autumn's hand on my shoulder. I shook her off, causing her to stumble back into Giselle. "Fucked with the wrong man!" I gritted out, close to his face.

I had a short fuse, my temper always getting the best of me. Seeing violence all my life didn't help my anger issues.

"Creed!" Mason yelled out, stepping his way through the crowd. Crouching down in between us. "Not here. Let's go!" he ordered, nodding behind me.

I turned around, seeing security heading in our direction. Immediately standing, I kicked the son of a bitch one last time. "Fuckin' welcome," I growled, grabbing Autumn's hand. Forcefully pulling her away from Giselle, through the tent and out to the lot.

"Thought she didn't mean anything," Mason whispered, bumping into my shoulder when we were outside and out of sight. "Come back to my house in case they call the cops. Won't take long for them to figure out who you are. My parents are out of town."

I nodded, practically throwing Autumn on the back of my bike.

"Creed—"

"Not one fuckin' word, Autumn." I shoved her helmet at her, and then threw on mine too.

Pissed as fuck…

That Mason was right.

"Thanks, Aunt Lily. See you later," I said, closing her car door behind me.

I ran up the stairs to the front door of my house, turning to wave at her one last time before unlocking the door and walking inside. I called Mason, waking him up around eight after I'd had breakfast. Letting him know Aunt Lily was dropping me off within the hour. I don't think he even paid me any mind, grumbling that he was home, sleeping, and not to wake him up again. I knew our parents would be home in a few hours, so he'd be up eventually. He must have been up late last night, doing whatever he wanted. Like always.

I dropped my key in the dish by the door and kicked off my sandals, not bothering to put them away. It was still early, and the house was completely silent, confirming my brothers were definitely passed out. I booked it up the stairs, taking two at a time, stopping by Mason's door. Debating on barging in and jumping on his bed to wake him, but I decided against it. The last time I barged into his room, he didn't have any clothes on, and let's just say that was when I learned how boys were different from girls. I ran down toward Bo's room and peeked in. He was sleeping too.

My brothers would sleep all day if you let them.

I continued down the hallway, abruptly stopping at my room. Caught off guard when I saw my bedroom door was closed. I never left it closed. I turned the knob, slowly pushing it open. Peeking my head around the door first.

ROAD to NOWHERE

My eyes widened as I took in the scene in front of me.

Creed was sleeping in my bed, my pink sheets pulled up to his waist. One muscular arm lying beneath my pillow, the other placed on his bare stomach. He had tattoos everywhere, colorful ink etched all over his skin, not a bare patch could be seen.

I stepped in, gently closing my door behind me, wanting to get a closer look. My fluffy pillows, stuffed animals, fuzzy throw blanket I loved were all scattered over the floor. Like he just threw them off my bed and passed out. His shirt, vest, and jeans were sitting on my desk. His black combat boots placed at the foot of my bed.

The closer I got to him, the more I realized how big he really was. Taking up my entire queen-sized bed. He had muscles everywhere on his body. I didn't know a person could look so scary and beautiful at the same time. I wanted to take a closer look at his tattoos. I wanted to know every design that was severed into his skin, and I wanted to trace them with my fingers, just to see if they felt as smooth as they appeared.

He looked so peaceful while he slept, I didn't want to wake him up even though I wanted to talk to him. Ask him why he was so mean to me the night before. Why he treated me like I didn't exist. Like he didn't even know me.

I shook off my questions, grabbing my notebook, a pen, and my guitar from my desk, instead. Quietly searching through my backpack to find the other thing I was looking for, shoving it in my pocket. I walked out onto my balcony, slightly closing the door behind me, not wanting to wake him. I placed my lounger where I could see my bed, wanting to wait for him to wake up. I didn't want him to leave without getting the chance to at least talk to him again. So, I sat there, softly strumming the strings of my new guitar, finding the right tune.

After a few minutes, he started to stir, I thought he was waking up, but his eyes started fluttering and his body shuddering. He started shaking his head side-to-side like he was having a bad dream. "Luke... Luke... tell me where you are..." he muttered, his voice laced with pure panic and desperation. A tone I'd never heard before.

I didn't know what to do, or how to help him, so I just started strumming a lullaby that Aunt Lily used to play for me when I was little. The soft, tranquil melody filled the air around us. Soothing and comforting him the same way it had for me. It only took a few minutes till his labored breathing soothed out, and he stopped panicking. Sleep had once again taken over, and I smiled, knowing I was able to ease him out of the darkness that plagued his mind, and stop his nightmare.

I finished playing the song, setting my guitar to the side of the lounger, out of sight. Getting up to close the balcony door to give him some privacy. Knowing I'd still be able to hear him shuffling around when he woke up. The last thing I wanted was for him to wake up to prying eyes. Thinking I was being some sort of creeper and watching him sleep, even though he was in my bed. Minutes seemed to drag into an hour or more that I sat out there, doodling Creed's name in my notebook. Waiting for what seemed like forever for him to wake up, thinking that maybe he was never going to.

I jumped out of my skin, slamming my notebook closed when the balcony door suddenly opened. It didn't matter I knew it was him, I hadn't even heard him get up. He must have been all stealth mode, or I might have just been distracted by my thoughts.

I immediately peered up at him, blocking the morning sun with my hand, taking in the fact that he still wasn't wearing a shirt. His jeans hung low on his hips, revealing his boxer's underneath. I couldn't help but realize how much more defined his body looked now that he wasn't lying down. He loomed over my small frame in a way I never recognized before. My heart started racing, I could feel it ringing in my ears. Feeling as though he could hear it too, but there was no expression on his face, making it hard to know what he was thinking.

Neither one of us spoke.

He shut the door, gesturing to the lounger in front of me, silently asking if he could take a seat. I nodded, pulling my knees to my chest, cradling my notebook. He set a cigarette on his lips, lighting up, blowing the smoke out through his nose. Looking over, eyeing me up and down with the same broody regard I had come to expect from him.

"You shouldn't smoke. It's bad for you," I blurted, breaking the uncomfortable silence between us.

"These are the least of my worries, Pippin," he groaned, his voice scratchy from just waking up.

Hearing his nickname for me caused butterflies to flutter in my tummy, again. I swallowed hard, hiding the smile that was threatening on my lips, remembering I was mad at him. At least I wanted him to think that I was.

"How many tattoos do you have?" I randomly asked, unable to take my wondering eyes off his art. The question alone made me blush.

He took another puff from his cigarette, letting it sit in the corner of his mouth. He leaned over, placing his elbows on his knees. Shielding his body from me, which only accentuated his big, bulky tattooed arms.

"Too many to count," he simply stated, looking out at the water.

"I can count them. I mean… if you wanted to know how many you had, I could count them for you," I nervously laughed.

He grinned. It was quick, but I saw it.

"I can't wait till I can get one. I want a—"

"Don't mar your skin. It's perfect the way it is," he interrupted, catching me off guard.

"Okay."

If somebody else would have said that to me, it would have made me furious. If there was one thing I hated, it was being bossed around, but it was different coming from Creed. I wanted to be perfect for him, like that girl on his bike was.

"Is she your girlfriend?" I questioned, unable to hold back any longer.

He cocked his head to the side, dragging the cigarette away from his mouth. Blowing the smoke straight up.

"Is that why you ignored me?" I added, nervously waiting for his reply. "That really hurt my feelings. I thought we were friends."

"I ignored you, cause I ain't no good. You're a baby girl, and I'm a grown-ass man. The list is endless for why I can't be your friend. So, do me a solid, forget about me, and go play with your dollies or some shit," he crudely replied.

I scowled, taken back. "That's the stupidest thing I've ever heard. I don't even like dolls. I like stuffed animals as you can clearly see in my room. And again, I'm not a baby. I'm around adults all the time. I have more friends that are your age or older, than are mine. Plus, I'm super mature and awesome all rolled into one. Everyone wants to be my friend. You're just being a big bully.

And you know what?" I paused, giving him the dirtiest look I could muster up. "I don't even know if I want to be your friend anymore, so there."

He shook his head, chuckling, meeting my eyes. "Don't know when to give up, do ya?"

"I'm a nice girl. You're lucky to have met me."

"Nice girls need to stay away from the likes of me," he breathed out, through the cigarette smoke.

"Mason is your friend. He's annoying and sometimes I want to punch him in the face, but he's a nice guy and he's your friend."

"That's different."

"Why does everyone always say that? I'm sick and tired of that being the only answer anyone can ever give me. Like it's supposed to make sense or something. Why is it different? Because he's a boy is not an answer, that's just a cop-out. Like when Momma says I can't eat any more ice cream because it will make my tummy hurt. How does she know it's going to make my tummy hurt until it happens? You think just because you're older and bigger than me, you know everything. Well, you don't know anything. Especially not what's good for me."

He narrowed his eyes at me, looking at me in a way he never had before, causing my belly to flutter again. I didn't understand how he could make me feel so many emotions, without even saying a word.

"You always throw a temper tantrum when you don't get your way?" he asked in a teasing tone.

"You always act like an asshole when you're trying to get yours?"

He didn't falter, spewing out, "Every time."

Usually adults yelled at me when I cussed, and I half expected him to do the same. I liked the fact that he didn't. Even though he was trying to boss me around, I knew it was coming from a good place. It just showed me I had to fight harder for our friendship. I didn't mind doing that, as long as it meant I could stay in his life.

"I don't have a lot of friends, Creed. I don't like to waste my time on people if I don't think they're worth it."

He abruptly stood, walking over to the railing, leaning forward. Placing his elbows on the wooden beam, taking one last puff of his cigarette as if he didn't know what to say. Opening his mouth to speak, but nothing came out. Uncomfortable silence filled the space between us again. He threw his cigarette to the ground, stubbing it out, before kicking it off the balcony.

I stood, pulling out a patch from my shorts that I'd bought for him a few weeks ago. Chucking it at him, watching it land by his feet. He looked down, picking it up.

"Asshole, not just a word, it's a lifestyle," he read aloud, a smile finally played on his lips.

"Fitting, ain't it?" I asked. Not giving him time to reply, I turned and left.

Hoping that he knew he wasn't going to get rid of me that easy.

I let the hot water run down my tense back muscles, leaning my hands and forehead on the cool tile. Standing under the showerhead in my bathroom, washing away the effect of last night. Flexing and releasing my fists, stretching out the soreness the motherfucker's jaw left behind. Trying to ignore the plaguing thoughts about a certain redhead that caused me to lose my shit. Seeing her practically fuck another guy on the dance floor pissed me off in a way I never saw coming. Never even expected.

I shouldn't have given a fuck.

I should have walked away.

But instead, I ended up beating a man's face in. Jumping over the invisible line from being a friend to being an enraged, jealous dick. Except, she wasn't mine to feel that way over. I had always been protective over Autumn, even when we were little, I was territorial. Last night proved that some things never changed. My biggest regret was feeding into her fantasy of us ending up together. I couldn't hate myself more for leading her on, even though I was just being myself. It was who I was. Somewhere along the line, the boundaries blurred.

Not knowing what was right or what was wrong anymore.

After we left the fair, I took her back to her house. She was off my bike before I even had the kickstand down, ripping her helmet off and throwing it at me.

"The fuck was that?" I snapped, catching the helmet before it hit my face. "What the hell is your problem?"

"You! You're my problem!" she yelled, turning to leave.

"Are you shittin' me?" I was off my bike and over to her in three strides, grabbing a hold of her arm. Turning her to face me.

She roughly pulled away, narrowing her eyes at me. "Don't touch me with another man's blood on your hands, Creed Jameson."

"Whose fuckin' fault it is that? Cuz it sure as hell ain't mine," I gritted out. "How 'bout a fuckin' thank you? Instead of givin' me lip for savin' your ass."

"Saving me? For going apeshit on a man I was just dancing with? I didn't ask you to do that! I don't want blood on your hands because of me. You do enough of that on your own."

I jerked back like she had hit me.

Her eyes instantly widened in realization of how I interpreted it. Immediately stepping toward me.

I moved back, stopping her.

"Creed, I didn't mean it like that. You know I didn't mean it like that."

I nodded toward her house. "Don't forget to lock the door." With that, I left, hearing her call out my name as I rode off.

Mason and I stayed up for a few more hours, passing a pint of whiskey back and forth between us. I bought it from one of the brother's liquor stores down the street from Autumn's. I was drunk as shit by the time I passed out. Waking up in a heap of pink sheets, confused as fuck as to where I was. It took me a minute to remember Mason told me to crash in Mia's room. She was at her aunt's.

I went out on her balcony to have a smoke, trying to clear the drunken haze before I got the hell out of there. Never thinking a bright-eyed, pigtail-wearing, Pippin would be staring back at me. Of course, I felt bad for ignoring her at the fair, she was just a kid. But the sooner she realized she needed to stay the hell away from me, the better.

Bottom line. Who the hell knows if she would...

My phone rang bringing me back to reality. I wrapped a towel around my waist and grabbed my cell, half expecting it to be Autumn, but the name 'Prez' lit up the screen.

"Yeah?" I answered.

"Get your ass to the club, now. I'm calling in Church." The line went dead.

"Good talk," I said to myself, throwing it on my bed.

I wasn't surprised Pops wasn't here when I got home. He never came home on most days, saying he was too busy with club shit, knowing he really meant he was too busy being balls deep in Christa or some other club whore.

I got dressed, stopping by Noah's room on the way to the living room, needing to check on him. He was already playing video games, shouting at the TV. Nodding his head in response to my questions. Not paying me any mind. Ma was in the dining room, cutting out coupons she'd never use. Already having a drink.

I shook my head, kissed her cheek and left, biting my tongue all the way out to my bike. She was getting worse with every day that passed. Slowly dying for the son who had died, not wanting to live for the two that were alive. I had no idea how to make it better, she was too far gone for any help. There were times she looked at me and I swear all I saw in her eyes was blame for killing Luke. The source of her drinking problem stared her in the face every single goddamn day.

Me.

I'd come home every night to find her at the dining room table passed out. I'd scoop her up into my arms and put her to bed. The few times Laura or Stacey tried to broach the subject, I shut it down real fucking quick. Letting them know my mother was not up for discussion. I refused to let anyone talk badly about her. I knew she was sick, I knew she was depressed I knew she neglected us, but she wasn't always a shitty mother. Deep down, I held onto the hope that she would one day come back to us. The light that was once in her eyes would shine again. Until then, I would take care of her. I would take care of Noah.

I would take care of everything.

I rolled up to the club just after twelve in the afternoon. I could hear Pops' voice roaring as soon as I stepped foot through the doors. I walked into the meeting room blind, never expecting what would come of today.

"Well, look who decided to grace us with his fuckin' presence," Dad greeted.

All eyes turned to me. Patched in brothers sat and stood around the room with expressions on their faces that I knew all too fucking well.

The Prez was holding something over their heads.

"I'm here, ain't I? Since when do you start church without everyone accounted for? What's this all about?" I nodded toward everyone.

"Since the meeting became about you. Today is your fuckin' lucky day, *VP*," he accentuated.

I cocked my head to the side, confused.

"We all voted in. It's unanimous. Congratu-fucking-lations," Pops stated with a snide grin.

I just stood there, looking all around the quiet room. Peering from one sullen face to the next, taking in all the brothers that had served way before me. Better equipped for such a high title. They should have been standing where I was, not sitting there being forced by the hand that feeds them. The air was so thick between us. It made it hard to breathe, hard to see, hard to even move.

For the first time in my life, there was nothing left to say. My father had me right where he wanted me.

Right under his fucking thumb.

I felt as though there was a bright, red target placed right over my heart.

Except I always knew my old man would be holding the loaded gun.

ROAD to NOWHERE

9
Mia

I watched Uncle Austin and my new aunt, Briggs, take the floor. Holding each other tight as they danced to their first song as husband and wife. The wedding reception was held at my parents' restaurant. They closed down for the day for the private party, transforming it into an elegant space for one of their best friends' special day. White linen tables surrounded the dance floor and stage where Aunt Lily always performed. Twinkling lights hung from the ceiling, adding the perfect touch to their romantic night.

A huge cake sat on the table in the corner, just waiting to be eaten, with a tattooed bride and groom on top. They'd gotten married on the dock at their house a few hours before, with family and friends surrounding them. She was the most beautiful bride I'd ever seen, glowing and radiant. Exuding happiness all around her. Her long, silky, white gown clung to her body, as her bright purple hair flowed with the breeze off the ocean.

The song "This Years Love" by David Grey played through the speakers while they moved across the floor. Reminding me of the way the Beast danced with Belle in *Beauty and the Beast*. A night straight out of a Disney fairytale, Aunt Briggs the perfect princess and Uncle Austin the handsome prince. He looked at her adoringly, dancing with the love of his life. The way they looked at each other in those moments were memories I'd always reflect back on. One day I'd meet my prince, and I'd have my perfect night too. Hoping that he would look at me the way Uncle Austin looked at her.

I was excited to be a part of their special day as their flower girl. Aunt Briggs even let me pick out my own light pink, flowy dress with matching strappy, heeled sandals. We spent that whole day shopping together, getting our nails done, eating ice cream, and talking about the latest gossip in Hollywood. Once I put the dress on, I knew it was the one. I never wanted to take it off. Daddy even said I looked like I had grown up overnight. He hadn't seen me wearing it until the morning of the wedding, and he said I took his breath away. Literally. He got choked up when I stepped out on the dock. It made him sad that I didn't look like his baby girl anymore, so I gave him a big squeeze hug to make him feel better.

It worked.

I spent most of the night tearing up the dance floor with my rowdy uncles. I even got Mason and Bo to dance with me a few times too, both of them looking so handsome in their tuxedos. Giselle couldn't take her eyes off Mason all night, more so than ever before. She was a little too excited when she caught the bouquet Aunt Briggs threw to all the single ladies attending the party. I nudged Mason, telling him he was next. He didn't like that very much.

A finger tapped my shoulder, drawing my attention away from my brother and Giselle who were lip-locked, dancing a little too close for Uncle Dylan's comfort. At one point, he casually moved aside his tux, showing Mason he had his gun on him. Mason surrendered his hands and laughed.

"Hey, Daddy. Why aren't you out there dancing with Momma?"

"I was hoping the prettiest girl in the room would want to dance with her daddy." He smiled, staring down at me.

I nodded. "I'd love to."

The song playing ended, smoothly transitioning into the next as we made our way onto the floor. "My Little Girl," by Tim McGraw started playing, as if on cue. He used to sing that song to me as a baby, comforting me instantly when I was fussing. At least that's what Momma told me.

"Oh my God, Daddy! They're playing our song," I rejoiced, grabbing his hand. He gave me a twirl before lifting me up, placing my bare feet on his shining black shoes.

98

"They must have known," he replied, winking at me. Leading us to the small space. Singing the lyrics about letting his little girl go.

A small crowd gathered around to watch us, including Momma who had a smile on her face, and tears in her eyes. She was always so emotional.

"Mia Pia?" Daddy pulled away, looking down at me, smiling.

"You haven't called me that in forever," I laughed.

"Can you promise me somethin'?"

"Depends. If it involves cleaning my room or taking out the trash, then no."

He chuckled, "Promise me you won't grow up. You will stay my baby girl for the rest of your life." He pulled me closer, hugging me tight.

"I promise, Daddy," I whispered.

Once the song had ended, Daddy gave me one more twirl and someone caught my eye.

"Thanks for the dance, Daddy."

He nodded, ruffling up my hair, walking out the back to join Momma and their friends on the beach. They were preparing to have a big bonfire after it was dark enough outside. When Daddy was out of sight, I put on my heeled sandals and ran out to the side door that led to the parking lot. A black motorcycle was parked a few spaces away from the door. My eyes searched all around to find him again, but I heard him before I saw him.

Creed.

It had been one year, two months, and three days since I last saw him. Not that I was tracking it. After I walked away from him on my balcony, he just seemed to have disappeared like he never even existed to begin with. I'm not going to lie.

It hurt.

I found myself looking for him everywhere I went, spending more time at the restaurant after school in hopes he'd show up one day.

He never did.

I wanted to ask Mason where he'd been, but he would've wonder why I cared. I was at a loss, so I kept busy with school, homework, and guitar lessons. Hitting the waves every chance I got, often sitting on my surfboard out in the water, looking at the shore, hoping he would appear.

Not once did he.

Days turned into months, the months turned into a year. Not a day went by that I didn't think of him. My four notebooks were proof.

Creed was having a pretty heated conversation with someone I couldn't see over by a black limousine.

"What's he doing here?" I asked myself, taking a few steps closer, trying to get a better view.

I ducked behind the newspaper stand in front of me when he looked in my direction. I peered over, getting a glimpse of whom he was talking to. I'd never seen Creed angry. It was weird seeing him like this. The man he was arguing with was Aunt Briggs' uncle, Alejandro. Uncle Austin called him Martinez. He had come into town from New York to watch his only niece get married, she said he was the only family she had.

When she introduced us, I couldn't help but stare, he was really handsome, but scary looking too. He carried guns on him like Uncle Dylan, but Aunt Briggs said he wasn't in the police force, so I didn't really understand why he had them. He didn't talk much, but when he did, he had somewhat of a Spanish accent. Aunt Briggs didn't seem to care for him very much, at least they didn't seem close.

Curiosity got the best of me. I couldn't hear what they were saying, so I ran and hid beside a nearby red car, peeking over the hood. I felt like I was in a Nancy Drew story, spying and looking for clues. They were in each other's face, yelling something I still couldn't make out. Both of them trying to stand bigger than the other. It reminded me of two Pitbull dogs, fighting over territory. Aunt Briggs' uncle reached into his jacket and pulled out something that looked like a stick, handing it to Creed. Looking around, making sure no one was watching them. I crouched down behind the car again, hiding. The last thing I wanted was to get caught snooping.

A loud noise sounded, making me jump up. Creed's hands connected with the roof of the limo, furious. Martinez was already gone, he must have walked back into the reception.

I don't know why, but there was something about the way Creed looked that scared me. Kind of like Aunt Briggs' uncle scared me. He had a certain glare in his eyes which was new and unfamiliar, making me extremely nervous and wary of him. Before I knew what I was doing, I turned, taking off toward the restaurant.

That's when I heard him yell, "Not so fast, Pippin." I immediately stopped.

I took a deep breath, spinning back around to face him. "I—"

"Was being nosey. Up to no good," Creed interrupted, making his way over to me. His shadow looming over my small frame.

How did he get so much bigger? Why did he look so different?

"No…" I murmured, loud enough for him to hear.

"No?" he repeated, folding his arms over his muscular chest, accentuating his stalky frame.

I acted fast, holding the skirt of my dress out, swaying side to side. Shuffling my heels on the pavement. Smiling wide, peeking up at him through my lashes, trying to act all cute.

I muttered in the sweetest voice, "Do you like my dress?"

He arched an eyebrow, nodding. "Think that's gonna work on me? May work wit' your daddy, but won't fly with me. What are you doin' out here?"

I sighed, rolling my eyes. Mostly disappointed that he didn't even acknowledge my dress when I looked so pretty. He was being so cold to me, nothing like the man I once knew. I couldn't tell if it was me he was mad at or what went down with Martinez, either way…

I didn't like this side of Creed.

"Not gonna ask again, Pippin," he sternly stated.

"I was just…" I shrugged. "I wasn't trying to eavesdrop. I mean not really… I didn't hear anything, I promise. Even if I did, I wouldn't tell anybody. I'm not a snitch. You can trust me," I rambled on.

He shook his head. "Could get hurt, standin' out here. Overhearin' conversations between men that don't concern you."

"Then maybe you shouldn't be having those kinds of conversations in public. Where anyone can walk out and overhear."

"That lip is gonna get you in trouble one day."

"I'm just saying…"

"I know what you're not sayin'. Why you came out here in the first place. Out with it, Pippin. Ain't got all day."

"I wanted to see you, okay?" I honestly admitted. "That's all. I saw you from the window inside. I haven't seen you in a really long time, over a year actually." I looked down at my sparkling pink toes, embarrassed. Fidgeting with the ribbon on my dress. "I missed you," I muttered, barely above a whisper.

He didn't say anything, if it wasn't for his combat boots being close to my feet, I'd think he took off. Nothing happened for what felt like a long time.

Then he suddenly reached over, placing his index finger under my chin. Making me look back up at him again. I blinked away some tears that started to form in my eyes. I think I may have stopped breathing. My belly fluttered, except this time, I felt it all over my body.

He looked deep into my eyes, in a comforting way, dropping his hand. Taking a few seconds to think about what he was going to say. I glanced down at his vest, his Creed patch was gone. Replaced with one that read Vice Prez instead. I couldn't help but notice any of my patches were on his vest either.

"You look cute as shit," he rasped out of nowhere.

I beamed, peering up at him instantly. My heart soaring once again.

"Gonna be fuckin' gorgeous one day, that's for damn sure. Slayin' hearts. Boys linin' up out the door for you. Your old man knows it, too. It's why he keeps you under lock and key. Doesn't want to end up behind bars for beatin' ass. Don't blame him either. You'll meet a cocky little shit who'll promise you the world," he paused, letting his words sink in. "You ain't even gonna remember me."

"I'll always remember you."

"May seem that way right now, Pippin. You're a baby girl. Got years of growin' up to do. Yeah?"

"Yeah," I simply stated.

He stepped back, looking at me one last time. "Best be stayin' out of trouble, ya hear? Stay little." With that, he turned and left.

Jumping on his bike, he threw on his helmet, and leaned forward, revving up the engine. The back of his vest rose up, as he took off, exposing a shiny black piece of metal.

I stopped smiling.

Unable to ignore the fact...

That Creed was now carrying a gun, too.

It had been a year and a half since I took over as Vice Prez. I was almost twenty-years-old and I'd put more people to ground than the average brother. It was the same ol' shit, just a different day. Marching to my father's fucking drum, paying the price when I stepped out of line, which I did often just to spite him. With my new title, came a newfound respect amongst the brothers. Not to mention the club whores that went out of their way to please me the only way they knew how.

I was second in command, meaning no one fucked with me. I stopped allowing myself to feel. I just did whatever was needed of me without a second thought. But my loyalty to the club cost me my morality, and without a conscience, a man was capable of anything. I didn't even recognize the man staring back at me in the mirror anymore.

Creed was gone.

Vice Prez was born.

"Think we wouldn't have fuckin' found out?" I interrogated the broker of the trucking company that moved our drug shipments across the state.

I tied them to a chair, ready to use any means of torture necessary to make him fucking talk. His two men in the same situation seated on the right and left of him, with duct tape over their mouths. Diesel and I had rolled up to the downtown warehouse, where all the loading docks for the trucks were stationed. Taking Jerico and his men by surprise, standing locked and loaded outside when they lifted the bay door to let us in. Diesel shot both men in the knees, bringing them down before Jerico even had a chance to blink his goddamn eyes.

Being the pussy ass motherfucker he was, he took off running. Making it about four steps when I nodded to Diesel to shoot him in the leg, too. He dropped to the cement, yelling obscenities in Spanish, trying to crawl away from us. I didn't hesitate. I grabbed him by his ponytail, dragged his ass over to an old rusty folding chair, leaving a trail of blood in his wake. Using cable ties, I secured his hands behind his back and his legs to the chair. Diesel did the same with his two men, duct taping their mouths shut. I needed to talk to Jerico, not his fucking henchmen.

"I don't know what you're talking about," Jerico spit out, shuddering in his seat. Suspiciously, looking around the dark warehouse, for I don't know what.

"Is that right?" I drawled out, slowly walking around where he sat, making him fucking nervous. Stopping to the left of him. "Blowin' smoke up my ass ain't gonna help your situation," I whispered over his shoulder. Sweat pooling at his temples.

"We've been doing business with Devil's Rejects for a long time. Why would I fuck that up?"

"Cuz you're a greedy fuck." Taking the barrel of my gun, I jabbed it into his good kneecap. "Don't appreciate bein' lied to, especially to my fuckin' face," I scoffed out, pulling the trigger.

"Argggggghhhh! Motherfucka'!" he screamed in pure agony, struggling to get his hands free.

"That's for lyin' to me. There are plenty more where that came from. I suggest you man the fuck up and tell me why you're traffickin' drugs over the border for those sons of bitches, Sinner's Rejoice. When you work for us," I reminded, crouching down to his level, getting right up in his face. "So, stop feedin' me your crock of bullshit before I decide I don't want to play fuckin' nice anymore."

"Listen," he coaxed with a quivering jaw. "I'll be honest with you. Sinner's did approach me, but I told them straight up, *ese*," he accentuated in a thick Spanish accent. "We only do business with you."

"Were you only doin' business with us last week, when Pedro here," I nodded to the other motherfucker in the chair beside him. "Moved twenty fuckin' kilos of blow on our route for them? It's our fuckin' territory, Jerico. Been our turf for a long fuckin' time. Think you could drive your trucks through our rounds and us not know about it? Thought you were smarter than that. Hate to be proved wrong."

"Creed, it's not what it looks like," he justified, looking me dead in the eyes.

"Ohhhhh, so you do know what I'm talkin' about, you fuck?"

He opened his mouth to say something, but I backhanded him with the butt of my gun, silencing him. "Give me a name," I ordered through a clenched jaw.

The grenades I used three years ago killed their Prez and Vice Prez. We thought the club was gone until recently they popped up out of nowhere, maybe stronger than before, but we had no intel on them. I needed to know who had taken over and was running the goddamn show. I needed names and I needed them right fucking now.

"Creed, it's—" I stood, grabbing him by the back of the head, slamming my knee his face several times, practically knocking him the fuck out. His head bobbled as he tried to blink through the haze. Jerico's bludgeoned face, becoming unrecognizable from all the blood.

A door slammed shut, and footsteps drew near. "Boss, you aiight?" a man questioned, appearing out of the darkness. "What the fuck is going on here?"

I turned around, looked him right in his eyes and shot him in the fucking head, clear across the room. His body fell to the ground with a thud. I didn't falter, aiming my gun at the center of Jerico's forehead next.

"Give me a name," I demanded, shoving my gun deeper into his skin. "Or you won't crawl out of here alive," I gritted out, losing the last bit of patience I had.

"My men will find you and kill you."

"Ain't that a bitch. Good thing I don't give a flyin' fuck if I die. Can you say the same, motherfucker?"

His eyes met mine, widening at the realization that I wasn't bluffing.

"Give me a reason," I breathed out. "Give me one fuckin' reason why I shouldn't pull the trigger, and lay you the fuck out for betrayin' us after everythin' we've done for you, you spic-ass son of a bitch."

His chest heaved and his nostrils flared, his mind reeled with uncertainty. I cocked the pistol deeper into his forehead, causing his head to jerk back. He swallowed hard, clearing his throat, holding his head up higher.

Mocking me.

"You got three fuckin' daughters," I spoke with conviction, catching him off guard. "Diesel, ever been with a Latina?"

"No, man. Haven't had the fuckin' pleasure."

"Veronica has the best cock suckin' lips on this side of the border." I snidely smiled, talking about his wife. "Jerico, how did an ugly fuck like you, bag some pussy like her?"

"Fuck you!"

"No thanks, already fucked your wife," I rasped, grinning.

"YOU SON OF A BITCH! YOU'RE A FUCKING LIAR!" he screamed at the top of his lungs, whipping around the chair, almost knocking it over.

We were used to the theatrics that came along with our interrogations. We didn't pay him any mind as he visibly struggled, trying to get loose. He wasn't going anywhere unless I wanted him to. I waited until he tired himself out, until there was no fight left in him and all he'd do was roll over and play fucking dead. Blood gushing out of him.

I crouched down again, leaning forward close to his face. Cocking my head to the side, I murmured, "Wonder if your baby girls wanna ride my cock as much as your wife did," I viciously spewed.

"You leave them alone, you motherfucker!"

I smiled wide, my eyes wild and brazen. "Can't do that. Give me a name or Diesel and I are gonna pay a little visit to your baby girls. Always wanted to run a train on your oldest daughter's culo," I mocked, saying ass in Spanish. "Don't worry, though. I'll make her deep-throat my cock before I take her up the ass. Wouldn't want to tear anythin'. Can't say the same for Diesel."

He jerked forward, wrestling to break free. "If you lay one finger on them—"

"I'm gonna count to three, and if I don't get a name, I'll fuckin' kill you, but not before I make you watch your daughters get fucked in the ass by my cock while Diesel has them deep throat his fuckin' Glock. Just to see which load gets off first."

"You—"

I suddenly raised my arm, aiming my gun to his boy tied to the chair on his right. "One," I counted, putting a bullet between his eyes. Blowing his fucking head off, blood and brains splattered behind him. "Give me a name," I repeated, aiming my gun over to the man in the same setup on his left. He was thrashing around, already knowing his fate.

I looked at Jerico.

"Please, enough. Don't—"

"Two." I pulled the trigger again, more blood, more brains.

More fucking death.

I was done playing games. I was never one for using women or loved ones as bait or collateral, but that didn't stop the brothers from letting it happen in the club. As much I didn't want to, I had to look the other way. Let it happen, whether I wanted it to or not.

It just is what it is.

I walked over to Jerico, placing the barrel of my gun under his chin. "Last chance, motherfucker. Or we're takin' a ride *home.*"

Cowering away from me, he closed his eyes tight.

"Thr—"

"Marcus!" he yelled out. "His name is fuckin' Marcus."

"He wit' Sinner's?"

"I don't know. He came here with some of them."

"He have a cut on?"

"A what?"

"A fuckin' cut. Like a vest, motherfucker, like a vest."

"I don't think so."

"You don't think so, or you don't know?"

"I don't know. I don't remember."

I didn't waver, I aimed the gun to his right inner thigh and pulled the trigger. He screamed out in pain, gasping for air. Convulsing right in front of me.

"Next bullet will go three inches to the left," I warned, gesturing to his cock.

With quivering lips, he trembled, "He had on a cut."

I grinned. "Thought that would jog your memory. Funny how that fuckin' works, yeah?"

He nodded, grinding his teeth.

I took one last look at him, growling, "Fuck you very much." Turning to leave. "On second thought." I spun back around, shoving my gun in his mouth and roared, "You don't fuck with the Devil's Rejects and live to see another day." I pulled the trigger, needing to end it once and for all. I got what I came for. End of story.

I nodded to Diesel and we got the hell out of there, expecting retaliation as soon as we got on our bikes. Ready to go to war, not giving a shit...

That more people would die.

There was no conscience left inside of me.

It died the day *Vice Prez* was stitched on my cut.

"Jesus Christ, Autumn. How many damn times do I have to tell ya that I don't want you here when I'm not around?" I snapped, pissed off she didn't listen to me.

Again.

The last thing I wanted was to worry about her too. I had enough shit on my mind. Between the club, Noah and Ma, my plate was fucking full. Noah would be starting high school in the fall, and God only knows what kind of trouble he was going to start getting into. He was already a little shit in middle school, having countless infractions sent home. Ma would get phone calls weekly, but she was too drunk to give a fuck. He barely had any supervision as it was. As much as I wished I could be in more places at one time, my priority was the club. Ma and Noah came in a close second. Noah was already starting to rebel, going toe-to-toe with me a few fucking times, wanting me to see him for the man he felt like he was.

Pops was no help when it came to him either. Proud as fuck that he was mouthing off in the first place, not taking shit from anyone. Except him. I didn't want Noah to grow up and be a troublemaker like I was. I wanted a better life for him, but there was only so much I could do. I wasn't around a lot, I had to travel all over the place to make sure other chapters under Devil's Rejects were running smoothly. Just when I thought things might slow down and I could find a balance, some goddamn normalcy, unexpected shit would happen, and I would be back on the road again. It had been two years since I became VP, and I was on the road more often than not.

Noah needed a role model in his life, someone to look up to. The scary thing was, I knew he wanted to be just like me.

"Why do you worry so much? All I do is walk into the clubhouse, go into your room, and wait for you. I barely see anyone on my way in and let's face it, no one's going to mess with me anyway, Creed. They know I'm yours," she said, pulling me away from my thoughts.

"You ain't mine, Autumn. You ain't my property. I haven't claimed you and ain't plannin' on doin' it either. Not gonna fight wit' you about this again. You're beatin' a dead fuckin' horse," I argued, taking off my cut, throwing it on the couch.

I had my own room at the clubhouse now, complete with a kitchenette and en suite bathroom. It wasn't much, but it was mine, even though most nights when I was in town, I went home. Wanting to see how Ma was coping, and check on Noah. It was pointless really. I didn't even recognize her anymore. She had aged at least ten years, her hair speckled with gray, wrinkles all along her once flawless face. She couldn't have weighed more than a hundred pounds.

There was nothing left of the mother I used to know.

Now she was just a drunk.

Adding to the guilt that was buried deep in my fucking heart. I hadn't walked back through the woods behind the clubhouse since the night that Luke was buried there so undignified. I couldn't bring myself to do it.

The dreams never stopped.

They became worse.

Only tallying all the lives, I had taken since.

Autumn walked over to where I stood by the counter, pressing her hands against my chest. Looking up at me. "That's only because you're so freaking stubborn. If you would just let us happen, you would see that we could make it work. I know your life story. I know what you do. I know exactly the kind of man you are, and I love you for it. Always have. I'll wait as long as I have to, Creed Jameson. You're worth it to me." She stood on the tips of her toes, pecking me on the lips. Beckoning my mouth to open for her. Sliding her hands down my chest, toward my cock, never taking her eyes off mine.

I caught her wrists, pushing her back. "Ain't gonna happen."

She scoffed out, rolling her eyes. "Right. I forgot. You don't need me for that. Do you?"

"I'm a man, Autumn," I simply stated, causing her to pull her wrists from my grasp, and take a few steps back. Not expecting my reply. "Made you no goddamn promises. Not one. Don't fuckin' try me. You won't win."

She grimaced, taking a deep visible breath. "You don't love those women."

"Don't need love to fuck, babe."

"You're being an asshole!"

"An honest one," I paused to let my words sink in. "What you want from me is somethin' I can never give you. Why can't you understand that? It's why I won't take you to bed. I respect you for more than what's between your legs. So stop fuckin' throwin' it at me. If I want pussy, all I have to do is step outside. Ya feel me?"

"Yeah, Creed... I feel ya. I feel the way you look at me sometimes when you think I can't see you. I feel the way you become calm when I'm around. I feel the way you worry about me when I'm not close by. I feel the way you need me to comfort you, support you, fucking love you. And I feel the way you love me too! Is that enough fucking feels for you?!"

"Always been my best friend, Autumn. Always will be."

She shook her head, disappointed with my response.

It was the truth. Every last word that fell from her lips was the goddamn truth, and I wasn't going to argue with that. So, I gave her the only answer that was as real to me, as she was. Even though I knew it would do nothing, but hurt her. She needed to realize that all I would do was cause pain.

I was no good for her.

"I sit around and wait for you. Do you know that? I wait for you to call, to tell me that you need me. To tell me you miss me. To tell me all the bullshit that comes out of your mouth when you're lonely! You're leading me on! And I'm the fool for letting it happen. I'm not doing that anymore, you dick! I'll go date. Sleep around. Be with other men, like you are with other women! How about that, huh? We will see who was right and who was wrong!"

"Don't fuckin' threaten me," I warned. "Not leadin' you on, you just keep comin' back," I blurted, regretting my words immediately.

She gasped. Her mouth dropped open, her eyes widened, instantly watering. Autumn was never much of a crier. She had tough skin, so I knew I fucked up.

I took a step in her direction. "Babe…"

She turned and left, slamming my bedroom door behind her, without another word.

"Fuck!" I yelled, pulling my hair in a frustrated gesture. Wanting to rip it the hell out. I didn't know what to do when it came to her. What to say, or how to handle her.

Not one damn thing.

I needed to figure out how to make it better, without making it worse. I paced around my room like I would suddenly find the answers written on my walls or some shit.

I was at a loss.

I grabbed a beer from the fridge, twisted off the cap, and threw it on the counter. Chugging it back as if it was water, needing something to calm me the fuck down. I slammed the empty bottle down onto the counter when I was done. Looking at the door where a huge piece of my life, had just walked out. A faint shadow caught my attention from the corner of my eyes, reflecting on the wall.

The rest played out in slow fucking motion.

I dropped to the ground, covering my head with my arms, ducking behind the counter. Using it as a shield, going in for cover as best as I could as bullets suddenly sprayed throughout my entire bedroom. Destroying everything its wake. Casings busted through the drywall, ricocheting off the metal appliances. Shattering windows everywhere, causing shards of glass to lodge into my skin.

I pulled out my gun from the back of my jeans, standing without a second thought, returning fire in the direction of the shooter. Hearing a hard thud seconds later. The motherfucker fell to the ground, dead. I ran over to my drawer, grabbing another Glock, and throwing extra clips in the pockets of my jeans. I hauled ass to my door, peering down the hallway before running out of my room. Brothers flew out of theirs, shooting in all directions. Ready to kill without a moment's notice. Acting on pure adrenaline and fury that someone was disrespecting us in our fucking home.

The warehouse was under fire.

ROAD to NOWHERE

The club was decorated with fucking bullet holes everywhere. An all-out war had broken out. Women were screaming bloody murder, running from rooms half-naked, trying to seek cover as best as they could. Some were not so fortunate.

"AUTUMN!" I shouted, stepping over bodies, searching around for her. Fear quickly taking over my body the longer it took to find her.

I sprinted down the hallway into the living room, trying to ignore all the bodies, gore, and blood surrounding me. Fucking praying to God I wouldn't find Autumn amongst them. Opening fire, shooting men I didn't even know or hadn't ever seen before. There was an endless stream of bullets coming at us from all directions. Our clubhouse unrecognizable from the mayhem, and the sons of bitches, who were bombarding our joint. Blood flying everywhere, not knowing if it was theirs or mine.

I was numb.

"AUTUMN!" I called out, again. "WHERE THE FUCK ARE YOU?!"

"Creed! Behind the bar! I saw her behind the bar!" Diesel yelled as he took out two more men. Nodding a silent gesture to go to her, that he was covering my back. He threw an assault rifle at me, knowing I was going to need it. Chucking one of my empty guns to the ground, I tucked the other one in the back of my jeans. Darting toward the fucking bar.

A rush of adrenaline coursed through my veins, throbbing into my bloodstream. Taking over every inch of my fucking body. My heart pounded against my chest as I tried to make my way over to her. Diesel and I took down every motherfucker who was in our way. No one was going to stop me, they could try, but they'd fucking lose.

"Fuck! They're swarming the club! Like fucking cockroaches! GET SOME!" Diesel seethed, bullet after bullet, after fucking bullet.

My vision tunneled, seeing nothing but red the closer I got to her. "AUTUMN!" I screamed over the bloodshed, turning the corner into the bar area.

She was sitting in the furthest corner behind a keg barrel as if she was trying to become part of the wall. Her head tucked in between her legs, her hands covering her ears. Rocking back and forth.

I'd never seen her look so fucking terrified.

It rocked my core.

I was over to her in two strides, crouching down in front of her as Diesel took position to lay out any motherfucker who came near.

"Babe," I coaxed, slowly reaching for her, needing her to see it was me.

I didn't care that the air was still filled with rapid fire. I needed to make sure she was responsive, and not going into fucking shock.

"Creed…" she bellowed, her eyes lighting up with fresh tears when she saw me. Grabbing my hand, she threw her arms around my neck. Holding me as tight as she could. "You're alive. I thought you were dead. I thought they killed you," she cried. Her body convulsed in my arms from the distress.

"Shhh…" I murmured to the side of her face. "Shhh… I'm here." Trying to get her to calm down as best as I could.

"Creed, come on! I got a prospect to guard her!" Diesel shouted from my right.

I pulled away, jerking out my gun from the back of my jeans, handing it to her. "Anyone not wearin' our colors comes near you, you fuckin' shoot. Point blank, in the goddamn head. You understand me?"

She fervently nodded, taking the gun into her shaking hand. Still clutching onto me like her life depended on it. I roughly tore her out of my arms.

"Creed!" she wept, scared for me.

"Be right back, babe. Right fuckin' back," I reassured, nodding to the prospect to come switch places with me. Threatening his life if he let anything happen to her.

Diesel and I held our guns high, waiting for the next string of fire to ring out. I looked around the corner to my left, while he did the same to his right, making sure the coast was clear before we left the safety of our spot behind the bar.

"See ya on the flip side, brother," he declared, taking off in the opposite direction.

I made my way over to the game room, the commotion getting louder with each step I took. Pausing at the door, I listened before kicking it in. Shot after shot erupted from my hands as I stepped into the room, bullet casings flying past my face, one right after another.

Ruthless and unforgiving.

Perpetrators falling to their deaths, all for the name of the fucking colors on their cuts.

Sinner's Rejoice were making their presence known, letting us experience that they weren't fucking around. Not only did they want our territory, they wanted our goddamn souls. Coming into our club, trying to show us who was boss, only to realize that their MC ain't got shit on us. I lost count of all the men I'd killed, put to ground that day. I wasn't any fucking better than they were. Fighting for my brothers with my last breath, if I had to.

Bottom line.

It was who I fucking was now.

Taking a deep breath for the first time since the first shots rang out, the smell of blood assaulted my senses. Nothing but the sounds of Harley's taking off in all directions could be heard, fire ceasing all around me. They were riding out from the hell and anarchy they brought to us. With fewer men than they walked in with. It didn't matter. This wasn't over.

It was far from fucking over.

It had only just begun.

I walked back into the living room, stopping at the doorway. Diesel, Pops, a few other brothers stood there with their weapons down, silently staring at a man that was lying in a pool of his own blood, in the center of the room. Pops turned around when he heard me, revealing it was one of our own.

Phoenix.

Memories of the first tattoo he ever gave me immediately played in my mind, and each one since then. My father crouched down, closing Phoenix's eyes.

He did the sign of the cross over his body, stating like always, "Ashes to ashes, dust to dust, and all that fucking shit."

I peered up, locking eyes with Autumn across the room, who was walking in with the prospect. A smile lit up her face when she saw I was alive, but it was quickly replaced with a frown when I didn't return the gesture. She followed my stare, taking in the sight of Phoenix's dead body. They had killed one of ours.

"I'm sorry," she mouthed from the distance between us.

A shadow appeared out of nowhere. I saw it before it actually happened. The man I knew in my fucking gut was Marcus, reached up behind Autumn.

Aimed his gun and pulled the trigger.

"NO!" I shouted, running as fast as I could. Images of Luke's death flashed in front of my eyes. The screaming, the blood, the chaos all coming back, hitting me like a ton of fucking bricks.

A blood-curdling scream snapped me out of one nightmare into the following.

The next thing I knew I was lying on the floor, the brothers all around me. Blinking away the throbbing pain. Realizing very fucking quickly that I just took a goddamn bullet...

For my father.

"Just fuckin' do it," I ordered, tossing back the bottle of whiskey. Sweating and shaking profusely from the bullet lodged in the right upper quadrant of my abdomen. I was lying on the right side of my bed, propped up with a few pillows.

"Creed, just let me numb the site, so I can extract the bullet, and stitch you up. You won't feel—"

"Won't feel shit with a few more swigs of this shit either. Do it," I interrupted Joseph, the doctor we had on payroll. Taking another drink from the already half-empty bottle.

"Goddamn it, Creed Jameson! Why are you being so stubborn? You're not Superman. Let him numb you up!" Autumn demanded, worry evident in her tone. Eyeing me up and down from the place she sat next to my bed.

"Don't need babyin'." I took three more swigs from the head. "Not gonna tell you again."

Joseph sighed, nodding before pouring rubbing alcohol on my open wound.

"Argggghhh!" I gritted out through clenched teeth, arching my back off the bed. "Motherfucker! Little warnin' next time."

"Diesel, I'm gonna need you to hold him down," Joseph ordered, ignoring me. "He can't move, or I won't be able to find the bullet."

Diesel grabbed the whiskey out of my hand, taking a few swigs himself, placing it on my bedside table when he was done. Joseph positioned my right arm across my chest, pushing me onto my left side for better access. Gesturing for him to get ready. Diesel knelt on the bed, hovering over me, putting one hand on the arm on my chest, securing it. The other on my waist, to hold me down.

"Here goes nothing," Joseph said before slicing the blade into my wounded skin.

I could hear my skin tearing as he reached in the wound, digging for the bullet. "Fuuuuccccckkkk," I groaned out.

The prospect in the room stood, rushing over. Grabbing the whiskey bottle off the nightstand and placed it to my lips, letting me chug the amber liquid down till there was nothing left.

"Ugh!" Autumn grumbled, standing up. "I can't watch this! You're fucking ridiculous! You all are! Unbelievable! I can't believe he's doing this. Such a fucking idiot. Thinks he's Tarzan..." she continued, hurrying out of the mess that was now my bedroom. Glass crunched beneath her feet. I could still hear her bitching down the hallway.

"Women," Diesel stated from above me. "Can't live with them. Can't live without 'em. I've tried. My hand gets too fuckin' tired."

I chuckled, the liquor finally taking over. Numbing the skin where the bullet went in.

"How ya feeling?"

I shrugged. Mostly hurting from the fact that Phoenix was gone. We didn't walk away unscathed, losing a few other good men as well.

"Took a bullet for your old man. Not gonna lie. Didn't see that shit comin'."

"Me and you both, brother. Can't even say it was a surprise. Knew it was comin'... didn't want him to die."

"Which is why we gotta talk, Creed."

"So fuckin' talk. Ain't goin' anywhere."

"Got it," Joseph chimed in, throwing the bloody bullet on my chest like a goddamn souvenir.

Diesel let me go, walking over to the kitchen.

"Clean hit, too. Didn't nick any nerves, sliced right through the muscle between the ribs. I'll stitch you up. Should close within a week. You're lucky. Could have been a few inches above." Joseph pointed to my heart. "I left my dressings in the car. Be right back."

Diesel nodded toward the door to the prospect, silently ordering him to leave too. Kicking the door closed behind him, and walked back over to the bed.

"Gonna need this after you hear what I gotta say," he advised, handing me a new bottle of whiskey.

"I'm listenin'," I muttered, taking back a few swigs.

He sighed, taking a deep breath. Sitting in the chair Autumn just vacated. "Been brothers along time. Even before you were patched in. Yeah?"

"Not a pussy. Don't need to make sure I'm wet, Diesel. Out with it."

"I wouldn't be sayin' anything if it weren't for what you did tonight. Taking a bullet for him. Putting your life on the line for his."

"For better or for worse. He's my old man," I simply stated, resting my head on the pillow. Looking up at the ceiling.

"He don't deserve it. Your loyalty. Your life."

"Ain't tellin' me nothin' I don't already know, Diesel."

"Striker was a good man. He may have been a grumpy old fuck, but he wasn't a traitor."

I narrowed my eyes at him, caught off guard.

"I think it was a setup, bro. I'm not the only one that suspects it either."

"My father lives and breathes this club, he wouldn't—"

"It got you to be Vice Prez, didn't it? Made you look like a goddamn hero. Look at the shit storm it started. How did they get on the compound? This place is Fort Fuckin' Knox. We've prided ourselves on making sure of it. Who do you think let those motherfuckers in? Cuz I hadn't ever heard of Sinners Rejoice before that meeting. I was a Nomad, been in the game for a long fuckin' time. There's somethin' more going on here than just a war over territory. It cost Striker and Phoenix their lives. Almost cost us yours too. This retaliation tonight…seems a little much, eh? For taking out Jerico and some of his men?"

My mind immediately started reeling with everything he just said, mainly because it made so much fucking sense. Every last bit of it.

"Think about it. We'll finish this later." He stood, walking over to the door. "Need anythin' before I go? More booze? Weed?

Pussy?" He winked. "I'll send someone up," he yelled over his shoulder.

I chuckled.

Joseph walked back in a few minutes later. He stitched and patched me up, wrapping an elastic bandage around my torso when he was finished. Wanting to keep as much pressure as possible on the wound. I drowned my sorrows to the bottom of the bottle. Numbing myself to the point of not giving a flying fuck about anything.

My mind was finally silent for the first time since I could remember.

When he was done, he placed a bottle of pain pills on the nightstand and left. I downed three of them, with whiskey as a chaser. I don't know how long I sat there, leaning my head against the headboard, fucked up to the point of exhaustion. Finally taking in the mess of my room. The bullet holes, the glass, the lampshades hanging sideways. It looked like a fucking hurricane tore through here.

Reflecting fucking life.

"You need to eat, or all that medication and liquor is going to tear up your already injured stomach, Creed," Autumn announced, walking back in the room with a plate of food in her hands. Shutting the door behind her.

"I'm fine," I replied, taking another swig. "It's late. Thought you went home."

"Like I could sleep." She took the bottle out of my hands, placing it on the nightstand next to the pills. Setting the food near it and took a seat beside me.

"Tryin' to kick me in the balls when I'm already fuckin' down, babe?"

"It's not your fault. You wouldn't ever let anything happen to me. At least not on purpose."

"Like I didn't let somethin' happen to Luke? Like that, Autumn?"

She frowned, knowing I was right.

I closed my eyes, wanting the darkness to take over. Between the shootout, Phoenix dying, putting Autumn's life in jeopardy, taking a bullet for my father—the man who could be responsible for all this to begin with—it was just too fucking much. It finally all caught up to me, taking me fucking under. The pills and booze no longer numbed me enough. Not even nearly enough. My heart started to race again just thinking about it.

"Earlier when I walked out of your room. I was so pissed at you."

I opened my eyes, locking gazes with her.

"I said some nasty things, you said some back. We were fighting. I walked past the bar to leave when all of a sudden I heard guns going off. Do you know what the first thing I thought was?" She shook her head like the mere memory hurt her.

I knew she would never be able to get rid of the images. It was now a part of her, just as much as I was.

"I thought... Creed is going to die and we're fighting. I hid behind the bar, hearing your voice in the back of my head, telling me to take cover. To stay safe. As much as I wanted to run back into your room, into your arms," she paused, letting her words sink in. "I stayed where I was. I did because of you. The more I sat there, the more I was sure you were dead. Making me want to die too. I don't think I could go on living. I don't know a life without you in it, Creed. You're all I've ever known," she honestly spoke, making me feel like a bigger piece of shit than I already was.

Her eyes started to water, she struggled to keep her tears at bay. I hated that I was the reason she was going to fucking cry again.

Knowing it wasn't in her character.

Breaking my heart in ways I didn't think were possible anymore.

Maybe it was the booze or the pills, but before I knew what I was doing, I grabbed her waist, pulling her toward me. She came willingly, crawling onto my lap. Straddling my thighs. Looking deep into my fucked-up eyes.

"I'm sorry, Autumn. I'm so fuckin' sorry for everythin'."

"Shhh..." She placed her index finger over my lips. "We've both been through a lot tonight. Let's be here for each other."

"Babe... Ain't gonna—"

"Please." She leaned forward, gently pressing her lips against mine. "Let me in. Please..." she pleaded, reaching down to grab the hem of her dress, not giving me a chance to protest. She pulled the cotton fabric over her head, freeing her perky tits. As if she knew I wouldn't be able to resist her if she was naked.

Vulnerable.

Exposed.

She was goddamn perfection.

Shaking out her red hair, she leaned in again. Kissing me softly, beckoning my lips to do the same while rocking her pussy on my cock simultaneously.

I roughly gripped her ass, groaning. No longer able to restrain myself, she felt too fucking good. The smell of her body engulfed me. Attacking my senses all at once.

My cock twitched, aching to be inside of her.

I kissed her back, pecking her lips softly at first. Teasing her with the tip of my tongue, running it all along the outline of her pouty mouth. The feel of her skin in that moment drove me over the edge, and all we were doing was fucking kissing. Our tongues moved in sync with one another, colliding, penetrating deep into my goddamn core. She started to sway her hips on my hard cock again, kissing me deeper, harder and more demanding than ever before.

I kissed her one last time, letting my lips linger for a few more seconds. Resting my forehead against hers, she was breathing profusely. Her eyes dark and dilated, luring me the fuck in. Her long, messy red hair draped all around her face, spreading out between us. I resisted the urge to tug it back just so I could kiss all along her neck, her collarbone, and all over her fucking breasts.

I slowly moved my rough, callused hands up her body. Feeling the softness of her silky white skin for the first time. Continuing my heated assault, causing her to squirm underneath my touch. Awaiting my next move.

Her breathing hitched when I cupped her tits, pushing them together, enjoying the feel of them in my grip. Her nipples were hard, begging to be sucked. Her round and perky breasts accentuated her slender waist and luscious fucking thighs.

"Please…" she begged, urging me to touch her in a way I never had before.

I grinned, sliding my hand into her panties, feeling her wetness on my fingers. Pulling them out almost immediately, I spread her juices along her mouth, just to get a taste of her sweet fucking pussy on her lips. Kneading her nipples with my other hand. She moaned loud, causing my cock to twitch from the sound of her. I plunged my tongue into her awaiting mouth, pulling her goddamn bottom lip between my teeth. Sucking off all her salty sweetness.

I slid my hand back in her panties, all along her pussy. Loving the feel of her heat against my fingers.

"So fuckin' wet," I growled into her mouth, manipulating her clit with the palm of my hand for a few minutes, watching her come apart.

I pushed my middle and ring fingers into her soaking wet cunt, aiming it directly toward her g-spot. I knew she wasn't a virgin anymore. I wouldn't have touched her if she still was. She lost it a while ago to a piece of shit that Mason and I put in the fucking hospital for taking advantage of her. The son of a bitch fed her alcohol one night, while I happened to be out of town, so she would spread her legs for him. Knowing he could get away with it since I wasn't around.

"I'm gonna come, Creed," she panted while I finger-fucked her sweet spot.

"Here, babe... Like it here...yeah?" I taunted, thrusting my finger harder and faster.

Her legs shook, her body trembled. She was close to losing control, shuddering, opening her legs wider, clawing her nails into my bare chest.

"Just like that... Fuck my fingers, ride them like you would my fuckin' cock."

Her pussy pulsated, squeezing my fingers so goddamn tight. Almost pushing them out. Come dripping down my hand.

She screamed out my fucking name.

There was no going back after this. I stepped on the line, now I was going to cross over it completely. I let her ride out her orgasm on my hand.

Her eyes immediately opened when she heard the zipper of my jeans, I maneuvered with my free hand. Reaching over to my bedside table, I pulled out a condom. Ripping it open with my teeth. She swiftly removed her panties while I pulled out my cock. Stroking it a few times while rolling the condom down.

Her eyes widened. "God, Creed," she breathed out when she took in my size.

I grinned, roughly gripping onto to her hips. Sliding her wet pussy all along my shaft, getting it nice and fucking wet for her to take me. Knowing I would hurt her if I didn't.

"Want my cock, Autumn? Gonna let me in?"

"Yes..." she purred, breathless. Getting off on the back and forth motion of her clit, sliding against my cock.

Getting fucking wetter.

Dripping down my balls.

I eased her up by her hips, holding the base of my cock for her to sit on. Positioning myself at her opening, she gradually moved her way down. Teasing the head of my cock, before choking the fuck out of my shaft with her tight goddamn pussy. Spreading her wetness, inching her way along, a little more each time. Her mouth parted, her eyes shut tightly as she took me in completely.

"Ride me, babe," I drawled out, claiming her lips. "Ride me fuckin' hard."

She slowly rocked her hips until she got used to the feeling of my cock deep inside of her. Placing her hands against the headboard for more leverage, swaying faster and harder. Causing her head to roll back, I took her nipple into my mouth, kneading the other one, unable to get enough of her. Another moan escaped deep down in her throat. All I could hear was desire, as I fondled her breasts and sucked on her nipples.

I moved one of my hands to her clit. Her breathing escalated as soon as she realized what I was about to do. She encouraged me, bucking her hips forward.

"Creed..."

"Yeah, babe. Just like that... Fuck me..." I growled from deep within my chest.

I could feel her pussy tighten, gripping my cock like a fucking vise. Vaguely feeling her shiver. Leaning in, she started kissing me more aggressively than before. I grabbed the back of her neck, wanting to bring her closer, needing her body to cover mine. Our lips moved on their own accord, no longer having control over our movements.

I kissed her jaw line, to her neck, and deliberately made my way back to her lips. Her delicate hands moved down my inked chest, wanting to feel my skin against her fingertips. Stopping at the edge of my bandage wrap, not wanting to hurt me.

"Fuck… you feel good," I groaned, thrusting my hips upward. Roughly gripping onto her hips once again. Moving her harder, faster, for her pleasure and mine. Feeling her g-spot on my tip.

My fucking sweet spot.

My pace increased as I made her fuck me as hard as she could, unable to get enough. I couldn't help it, I loved it fucking rough, and from the sounds escaping her, so did she. Both our mouths parted, breathless, riding the high, waiting to fall over the edge.

Pain fucking pounded through my abdomen from the impact, but I didn't care. I plunged my tongue into her mouth when I felt her pussy throb, pulsating long and fucking tight. Muffling her screams.

Her quivering was my undoing.

She was my undoing.

A groan escaped from deep within my core as I came so fucking hard.

We lay there for I don't know how long, both of us trying to catch our breaths. Until she shifted, lying next to me as I threw away the condom. Lazily tracing my tats. I pulled her into my embrace, kissing the top of her head.

"I love you," she sleepily said, coming down from her high. Falling asleep.

Bringing me back to reality.

That I just fucked up.

By. Fucking. Her.

My eyes fluttered open taking in the bright morning sun. Wondering where the fuck I was for a second. My head was pounding and my torso was fucking aching. All the previous night events immediately came to mind as if I was reliving them all over again. Realizing it wasn't a nightmare. Only adding to my splitting headache.

"Shit," I breathed out, looking down at Autumn, who was lying with her head on my chest. Her arm wrapped around my waist, her leg draped over mine, holding me tight.

I sunk back into the mattress, staring up the ceiling. Shaking my head back and forth, mentally kicking my own ass for what I had done. "I needed to add more fucking problems to my already full-of-shit life like I needed a fucking bullet in my head."

I had no one to blame but myself.

Autumn stirred, opening her eyes. Looking up at me adoringly with nothing but love in them. "Hey there," she greeted, snuggling deeper into my chest. Kissing it a few times. "I'm going to go wash up. Be right back." She kissed my chest one last time and rolled over, pulling the sheet with her. Reaching over to the chair, throwing on her dress and sandals. She got up, carefully walking through the fallen debris, making her way to my bathroom.

I sat up, groaning out in pain. Instantly grabbing two pain pills, taking them back dry. I pulled my drawer open, getting a pair of clean jeans and throwing them on. Shoving my bare feet in my boots. There was still glass everywhere. Pops was already on the phone last night, figuring out how long it would take to get this place fixed and cleaned up. I guess he said it wouldn't take too long, money could always buy you anything and everything.

Autumn walked back out, bright-eyed and fucking bushy-tailed. Practically skipping over to me. "I'll go see if I can find us some breakfast. Then I'll help you change your dressings, baby." She beamed, placing a kiss on my cheek.

I groaned in response, already fucking dreading what was to come. I took a piss, brushed my teeth, catching a glimpse of my sorry ass in the cracked mirror. Shards of glass shattered around the counter.

"You're a piece of shit," I gargled to my reflection, staring back at me. Spitting the toothpaste into the sink. Splashing some cold water on my face, I looked like death warmed over.

Autumn was sitting on the bed with a plate of fruit and some toast in front of her. "This was all I could find in the club kitchen. At least it's something to get in you. Come sit down so I can change your dressing, it's soaked in blood, Creed. You don't want it to get an infection."

"I'm fine."

"Creed..."

"Autumn, I'm fuckin' fine," I grumbled, grabbing my cigarettes, lighting one up. Needing the nicotine to shake off the haze.

She sighed, defeated. "Jesus, even when you get laid, you're still not a morning person. Good to know."

"We need to talk."

"About what?" she asked, throwing a strawberry in her mouth.

I walked over to her, sitting on the edge of the bed beside her. Not wanting to drag this out any longer.

"Listen, I fucked up. Last night, I was drunk, high, and just fuckin' hurtin'. Feelin' like shit that you were hurtin' too. Shouldn't have been here, Autumn. Coulda' been hurt. Really hurt," I hesitated, unable to say the words.

The thought of another life gone because of me was too much for me to bear. I took another drag of my cigarette, letting the smoke seep out through my nose. "Shouldn't have seen what you did. Puttin' your life in danger for me. Can't happen anymore." Glancing over at her, trying to be as kind as I could.

"I love you. It's that simple for me. I don't care."

I grimaced, swallowing hard, finally stating, "Last night was a mistake."

"What? Why? Was I not... I mean... was I not good?"

"Jesus Christ, babe. For fuck's sake, you were amazin'," I breathed out, leaning my elbows on my knees. Holding my pounding head. "But it ain't about that."

"I mean I know I'm not as experienced as you're used to, but I can—"

I looked back up at her. "I love you, Autumn. You fuckin' know that. But I ain't in love with you. And you know that, too."

She abruptly stood, hovering above me with her hands on her hips. "You're lying! You're just scared! I don't care. I just want to be with you! Why can't you open your eyes and see us for what we are? We're great together, and you know it. Last night only proved that to you, Creed. You're just trying to push me away! We're more than just best friends, and we always have been!"

"Don't make this harder than it already is."

Tears streamed down her face, driving a knife into my heart. I stood up, reaching over. "Stop wastin' those on me," I murmured, wiping away her sorrow. "Not fuckin' worth them."

She shoved my hand away. "Fuck you, Creed! After everything we've been through. You're going to treat me like just another piece of ass," she bellowed, stepping back away from me.

"If that were true, I would've told you to get the fuck out of my bed after I came. Wouldn't have slept in my goddamn arms last night."

She shook her head, disgusted. "Don't worry. I'll get the fuck out now." She turned, but I grabbed her arm, stopping her. "Don't touch me!" she snapped, shoving me away as hard as she could.

"Fuck!" I roared, hunching over. Wrapping my arm around my torso from the stinging pain.

She took one look at me, scoffing out, "Good, now we're both hurting." She turned again and left. Leaving me with the indisputable guilt of fucking her over.

I spent the rest of the day getting my room back in order, rejecting help from the countless whores that I knew Diesel kept sending up.

ROAD to NOWHERE

I wanted to be alone.

The next few days were much of the same thing. The brothers fixed what they could throughout the warehouse, while Pops kept calling in for some reinforcements. We were being extra cautious, identifying workers that were coming in and out. Spending all hours of the day and night, trying to get the compound back in working order. Pops didn't want the shootout to bring down the club's morale or the brotherhood in which we stood for. He wanted nothing to be jeopardized because some of our own were put to ground.

In true form.

He threw a fucking party.

The whores cleaned up the joint as best as they could, making sure the house was stocked with liquor, beer, and food. Diesel and Stone took care of getting an endless supply of fucking drugs. It was a free-for-all.

We were celebrating the life and death of our brothers.

"This is some good shit," Stone exclaimed, handing me a blunt.

We were sitting on one of the couches in the game room, shooting the shit. Acting like nothing had happened in that room days prior. Pretending to have a good ol' fucking time.

The coffee table in front of us was lined with rails of coke, brothers and whores stopping to get their fix of the free drugs. People were walking around everywhere, smoking weed, popping pills, fucking out in the open, and kicking back an obscene amount of booze. We were all on the same page, wanting nothing more than to just forget and have a good fucking time. Most of the women showed up half-naked, or not dressed at all. Dancing on poles, brothers, and each other.

I took the blunt to my mouth, sucking in long and hard, holding the smoke in. Trying to get as fucked up as I could. The guilt was eating me alive. As the night went on, so did the usual festivities. I was never much for doing drugs, only an occasional blunt here and there. I was always more of a drinker, been drinking ever since I could see over the damn bar.

I had never felt so empty and hollow in all my life, but as a VP I had to put on a good front. It was one thing after another lately. The club, my dad, and now Autumn. Everything was a fucking mess. The walls were closing in, and I had no way out. My life was leading me on a road to nowhere. The underlying demons never leaving me alone, my fucking companions, always sitting right next to me, waiting for the turmoil of more devastation to take over.

More lives.

More blood.

More fucking death.

For what?

For fucking nothing.

I blinked, finding myself on that same old couch. Except, this time I was snorting line after line of coke. Trying to forget, trying to go numb, trying to block out the last twenty years of my life. Nothing was working. The pain was still alive and bleeding out of me, leaving nothing but destruction in its wake.

I did another line, leaning back into the couch cushions, letting the blow take over. Watching the color lights dance around the room to the beat of the music. The distinct taste of the drip from the blow ran down the back of my throat, but I chased it down with a bottle of Jack Daniel's.

"Hey, Creed," some blonde with huge fucking tits purred, making herself at home on my lap. Bringing her brunette friend with her to sit down next to me. Just then realizing Stone had left.

"I'm Lola, and this is Candy," the blonde informed me, biting her lip in a seductive way. Twirling her finger in her hair. Grazing a long red manicured nail along her friend's breasts. "Candy forgot to put on a bra tonight." Slightly pulling down her friend's skintight white tank, she exposed a perfectly round nipple. Circling her finger around it, making it pebble even more. "She also forgot to wear panties," she added.

The brunette spread her legs open as on cue, propping her one stiletto heel on the table. Licking her finger before reaching between her legs, exposing her clit.

I cocked my head to the side, taking in her pink bare pussy. "Not complainin'," I rasped.

"How about Candy and I show you a good time tonight? She's new here, and I think you will really like her," she whispered in my ear, sucking my lobe into her mouth, flicking it with her tongue.

Her friend looked up at me with piercing bright blue eyes, licking her lips, slowly circling her clit.

Baiting me.

"What makes you think I ain't already havin' a good time?" I asked, never taking my eyes off the brunette, eye-fucking the shit out of me.

"You are sitting here all alone, figured you could use some company," the blonde responded, kissing along my jaw.

"Think y'all are worth my fuckin' time?"

She nodded, taking a vial out of her bra. Twisting off the cap, she tapped out blow on her tits. Instantly leaning back, brushing her blonde hair to the side. Waiting for my next move.

"Ladies first," I murmured, gesturing to her friend.

She nodded, leaning forward, snorting it right off her boobs. I followed suit.

I spent the next hour in a drug-induced blur. Watching the two whores dance for me on the poles in the corner of the room. Grinding on each other, taking turns hanging upside down with their legs out in splits, tongue fucking the shit out of each other's pussies. Brothers stood around hooting and hollering, throwing dollar bills at them. Enjoying the show as much as I was.

The blue-eyed brunette came strutting over to me, naked in all her glory. A green hue of light illuminated her curvy frame, reminding me of the redhead I had lost.

Autumn.

I quickly shook off the sentiment, trying to focus through my fog that was my mind while the whore straddled my lap backward. I didn't fucking hesitate, I pulled her back into my chest, nipping at her neck as she swayed her curvy hips to the sultry beat of the music. Grinding her ass into my cock, over and over again.

I reached down her stomach, slowly making a path to her pussy that I'd wanted to touch since the moment she spread her goddamn legs for me, giving me an instant hard on. I circled her clit with the palm of my hand, ramming my fingers into her wetness with my other one. Before I knew what was happening, the blonde was kneeling between her thighs, pushing my palm out of the way, lapping at her clit while I continued to fuck her with my fingers. Her pussy tightened around me, throbbing with her release. Muffled moans assaulted my senses, far away even though she was near.

Everything heightened from the blow.

I couldn't take it anymore. I need to be balls fucking deep in one of them.

We stumbled our way back to my bedroom laughing our asses off at nothing and everything all at once. I kicked the door shut behind me, leaning against it once it was closed. The music was blaring through the house, thumping against the walls, vibrating on my back. My room shifted around, coming in and out of focus as the girls walked backward toward the bed, swaying their hips, fucking me with their eyes.

Usually, guys in my current state of mind can't perform when they were as fucked up as I was, but I was a lucky bastard. Drugs and alcohol only made me hard as fuck.

"Fuck each other," I ordered in a low-pitched tone. "Get nice and wet for me."

They crawled their way onto my bed, sitting up on their knees in the center, devouring each other. Their tongues taking what the other wanted, as their hands glided in sync down their bodies, stopping when they reached the other's pussy. Moaning into one another's mouths causing my cock to twitch and throb against the zipper of my jeans.

I kicked off my boots and pulled off my shirt, walking over to my nightstand to grab condoms from the drawer. They never took their eyes off me, as they finger-fucked each other. I reached down, fumbling to unbuckle my pants, pulling out my cock, and jerking it off. Enjoying the goddamn show with hazy, hooded eyes. Stroking my cock harder the closer they got to coming undone.

"Come here," I demanded, nodding toward the brunette. Never letting up on stroking my dick. Already forgetting their goddamn names. I stood at the edge of the bed.

She happily obliged, leaving her friend. Crawling over to me, getting up on her knees on the mattress, leveling her face with mine. I gripped onto the back of her hair by the nook of her neck, forcefully tugging it back, when she leaned in to kiss my lips.

We weren't kissing.

We were fucking.

Plain and simple.

A moan escaped her mouth, confirming the bitch liked it rough. I dragged her down, moving her to face my cock, shoving it to the back of her throat until she gagged. She never stopped sucking. I grabbed on tighter, bobbing her head the way I fucking liked it.

"Arghhh…" I groaned out, nodding to the chick on my bed. "Put my balls in your fuckin' mouth. Show me how much you want to suck my cock too, and then maybe I'll give it to you."

She grinned, licking from my taint to my balls, sucking one into her mouth and humming, while the brunette sucked my dick like she had something to prove. Her sloppy wet mouth felt fucking amazing. The blonde stuck out her tongue and licked up my balls to my shaft, while the brunette sucked on the head of my cock. I gripped onto the sides of her face, thrusting my dick into the back of her throat.

Fucking her face for a few seconds, wanting to feel the back of her mouth

I pulled out my dick with a pop and she gasped for air. "Good girl," I growled in a low, rumbling tone. "Now fuckin' finish what you started."

They went back at it. I rolled on a condom, not trusting either of them to put it on me. Last thing I wanted was getting trapped by a club whore. This was a means to an end for me.

I wanted to come.

I didn't give a fuck about them.

Making my way onto the bed, I grabbed whoever was closer to me, it just happened to be the blonde.

"Eat her pussy," I ordered, gripping her hips. Roughly shoving her head down until she was on her hands and knees in front of me.

In one swift movement, I was balls deep inside her, taking her from behind. Smacking her fucking ass. Enjoying the feel of her cunt wrapped around my cock. Fucking her to the beat of the music still going strong outside my room. I smacked her ass again, causing her to buck her hips, backing her ass up on my cock. All while burying her face in her friend's pussy, caressing her tits at the same time.

Moans escaped both of their mouths. The brunette's back arched off the bed in ecstasy, riding out her orgasm on the blonde's fucking tongue. I twisted her hair in my hand, roughing pulling her up to her knees.

"I'm done wit' you," I groaned in her ear, releasing her, shoving her forward. "Your turn, sweetheart." I grabbed her friend's ankles, pulling her toward me.

The blonde grinned, kissing her friend's lips, savoring the taste of her own come. Before climbing on top of her to sit on her goddamn face. I placed the brunette's legs on my shoulder, rubbing my cock between her pussy lips. Positioning my dick at her opening, I thrust in. Fucking her hard, fast, and with much more determination. Hearing the slapping sound of my balls against her bare ass cheeks.

I pulled back out, nudging my cock into the pucker of her asshole, she moaned, wild and unashamed.

I chuckled to myself, "You like things up your ass, yeah?"

"Umm hmm..." she hummed, never letting up on eating her friend's pussy.

"Take my fuckin' cock then." I pushed in the head of my dick, teasing her. Causing her to shudder while she took every last inch of my cock. "Good girl," I growled loud and hard once I was fully inside her, she was so fucking tight it made my balls ache.

Her legs trembled as I thrust in and out of her. Matching every stroke, taking what wasn't mine. My head fell back, completely immersed in drugs, booze, and fucking her in the ass.

On the verge of coming.

"YOU SON OF A BITCH!"

The girls gasped, causing me to jerk back not grasping what the fuck was happening. I pulled my cock out of her ass, immediately looking over to my door where the voice came from. Narrowing my eyes, trying to blink away the drug-induced haze.

"Fuck..." I breathed out when Autumn came into focus. Standing in the doorway.

She shook her head, looking from me to the girls that were now jumping off the bed, scurrying around my room trying to find their shit and haul ass.

Autumn looked back at me again, seething, "You disgust me! I can't believe you! Four days! Four fucking days! That's all it took for you to fuck another whore! Jesus Christ, Creed! Making up for lost time, you had to fuck two of them at once?!"

She didn't pay them any mind as they ran past her, and out the room, the door slamming behind them. Autumn's sole focus was the fucked-up man in front of her.

Me.

I didn't know what to say, I didn't know what to do. Fuck, I barely knew how I was feeling. The drugs and booze had finally taken over. I just knelt there on the bed, looking into her eyes, fucking dumbfounded. Trying to shake away the fog. I rubbed my eyes, my brain fighting with my mouth to say something.

Anything.

I got off the bed instead, tearing off the condom and threw it away. Looking around the room for my jeans, rubbing the back of my head. Disoriented and confused as fuck.

Suddenly stumbling when Autumn chucked them at me, shaking her head in pure utter disbelief. I slipped them on, trying like hell to stay upright. Failing miserably to do so, almost falling to the bed that I just fucked two whores on.

"Who are you right now?" she scoffed out with an expression I'd never seen before.

I stepped toward her and she instantly stepped back, placing her hands out in front of her.

"Babe..."

"Don't *babe*, me. You don't get to call me that. I mean look at you! Your bandage is drenched in blood! Was it fucking worth it? Is this who you are when I'm not around, Creed? Huh? Is that why you don't want me here? Can't do your drugs? Can't drink yourself into a coma? Can't fuck your whores!" she yelled, grabbing the ashtray off the table and hurling it at me.

I barely moved out of the way, my reaction time lagging. "The fuck?! What do ya want me to say? You already know the answer!" I roared, pushing through the emotionless state. Rubbing the back of my head again. My mind unable to catch up with the bullshit happening right now.

"How could you do this to me? I came here to tell you I was sorry. I came here to tell you how much I love you! I'm not your fucking doormat! You may treat these women like the whores they are, but it's nothing compared to the way you just treated me. Showing me I mean nothing to you!" she yelled, her eyes watering with tears.

"You weren't supposed to be here, Autumn. Weren't supposed to see that."

"And that makes it okay? That changes things? No! It doesn't change one fucking thing! Not what you did. Not how I feel. NOTHING!"

I tried to step toward her again, but the look on her face was enough to stop me. I sat on the edge of the bed no longer able to stand on my own two feet. Holding my head in my hands, resting my elbows on my knees.

"Shoulda' never taken you to bed. That was my fuck up. Caused you pain and for that I'm fuckin' sorry," I stated in a sincere tone, hoping she would understand. "But this is who I am." Cocking my head to look at her. "This is who I've always been, babe. Never lied to you, and you know that."

Tears fell down her beautiful face, her lip quivering. She wiped them all away. The look on her face in that moment nearly brought to my fucking knees.

She stepped back, shaking her head. As if we already didn't have enough space between us. "I hate you," she breathed out. "Do you hear me? I fucking hate you, Creed Jameson! I wish I never met you! You finally got what you wanted. I want nothing to do with you! EVER! You're dead to me!"

I abruptly stood. "Autumn, you don't mean that. You don't fuckin' mean that," I gritted out, sobering the fuck up real fast.

She walked toward me, each step precise and calculated. Grabbing my face between her hands, looking deep into my eyes long and hard for what felt like forever as if she was trying to remember my face. She whispered, "Luke wouldn't have wanted this for you. He would have of been so disappointed in the man you've become."

I grimaced, her words searing my skin. It was a pain far worse than taking a fucking bullet for my old man.

"I hate you," she repeated with much more conviction in her tone. "You just lost the last good thing in your life." With that she turned, never once looking back.

Walking out of my life.

Knowing everything she said.
Was true.

I missed her.

I fucking missed her.

But most of all...

I missed us.

Depression wasn't something to fuck with. I hated what I did to her, what it did to us, but mostly I just hated my goddamn self for being such a goddamn bastard. I couldn't take it anymore. She had been on my mind constantly for the last month.

I rode to her house ready to give her whatever she wanted, as long as it kept her in my life.

Knocking on her door, waiting anxiously for her to answer.

"Hey, sweetie," her mom greeted, opening the door. Pulling me in for a hug.

"Hey, how are you doin'?"

"I'm great. How are you?"

I sighed, pulling away. "Been better." Placing my hands in my pockets, I stood on their porch, looking down at my boots. The guilt consuming me. I couldn't even bring myself to look at her mother, the woman who treated me like her own son.

I glanced at her and she knowingly smiled, cocking her head to the side.

"She around?"

"No, honey, she's not."

I nodded. "Listen, I know she don't wanna see me. I don't blame her, either. But I gotta talk to her, Laura. Can't go on like this anymore. I miss the hell out of her."

"I know. She misses you too, Creed."

I smiled, needing to hear that. "Can I see her? Please."

She shook her head. "Honey, she's not here."

"Where is she? I'll go find her. Just tell me where she is. Need to make things right, Laura."

"She's in New York."

I jerked back not expecting her to say that. "New York? What she doin' there?"

"She's living with her daddy now."

"*Livin'*?" I questioned, feeling as if she kicked me in the balls.

The news hitting me fucking hard.

She nodded, muttering, "She moved there about two weeks ago. She just... she just needs some time, Creed," she paused, letting her words sink in. "You really hurt her. Broke her heart, she wanted a fresh start. Her daddy has been begging her to come back to New York for years. You know that."

Shaking my head, I scoffed out, "She wanted away from me. I did this."

Laura didn't say a word, knowing I was right. I didn't think twice about it. My mind was made up the second she said Autumn was in New York.

"He still live in lower Manhattan, off of Parks?" I asked, stepping back. Making my way back over to my bike.

"Yes."

I spoke with execution, "You tell her I'm comin' for her."

I spent the rest of day, getting everything in order with the club. Letting them know I was taking a much-needed vacation. Pops wasn't happy about it, but what could he do...

I was a grown-ass man.

I took a redeye flight, wanting to get to her, as fast as possible. I was going to fight for her and if that didn't work, I was ready to drag her ass back home, kicking and screaming if I had to. Using any means necessary.

She didn't belong in New York.

She belonged by my side.

ROAD to NOWHERE

By the time I landed, I was fucking exhausted. Almost passing out on the cab ride to my hotel. The Residence Inn Downtown Manhattan wasn't far from where she lived. I knew this part of New York pretty well, having spent a lot of summers and holidays with her family. Autumn loved showing me everything and anything she could, even the shit that bored the absolute hell out of me.

After I checked in just after three in the morning, I took a shower. Cleaning up from the late flight. Before hitting the sack, I sat out on the balcony, smoking a cigarette. Looking at the bright lights of the city that never sleeps. I always loved New York at night. There was something about the scenic view only Manhattan could provide. Breathing in a deep drag off my cigarette, I could physically feel the energy all around.

Wanting to get a few hours of sleep before seeing Autumn, I finally passed out about an hour later. My phone rang, waking me up early the next morning.

I reached over, grabbing it off the nightstand not bothering to see who it was.

"Yeah?" I groggily answered, wiping the sleep away from my eyes.

"Creed! Creed! Oh my God! Are you here in New York?" Autumn hysterically wailed into the phone.

I shot up out of bed, feeling as if my heart was in my fucking throat. All I could hear were emergency sirens all around her, cars honking their horns, and people screaming.

"Autumn! What's goin' on? You all right? Where are you?" I frantically asked, throwing on clothes and my boots. Hurrying around the room, grabbing my wallet and room key, ready to head out the door. Needing to get to wherever she was.

"My mom told me you were coming. I didn't believe her. I can't believe you're here. You're really here?"

"I'm here, babe. Now tell me where you are?" I asked, trying to remain calm.

"Oh God, Creed... Turn on the news! Just turn on the news, right now! I'm in the car with my dad. We were going to breakfast. They just radioed him for an emergency. We're on our way over! Just... please! Turn on the news! It will explain it better than I can. I can't believe this is—"

"Calm down. I can barely hear you. What the fuck is goin'—"

"Just turn on the damn news, Creed!"

I turned around, grabbing the remote off the nightstand. Clicking on the television and turning it to the first news station I could find.

My eyes widened at the scene playing out before me.

"The fuck…" I murmured to myself.

"We have unconfirmed reports that a plane has crashed into the North Twin Tower moments ago. We are affording more information on the subject as it becomes available," the broadcaster declared. I flipped a few more channels, all reporting the same thing.

"You are watching LIVE coverage of the North Twin Tower clearly on fire."

"Something devastating has happened. Again, unconfirmed reports that a plane has crashed into the North Twin Tower."

"A two-engine jet has crashed into one of the Twin Towers. More information as it become available."

"A plane has crashed into the World Trade Center."

"What a catastrophic day for New York City. A plane has flown directly into the World Trade Center."

"Holy shit," I breathed out, taking in the live images of the smoke billowing out of the sides of the North Tower of the World Trade Center. Flames licked the side of the building, producing dark gray clouds that blanketed the bright blue morning skies. A gaping hole marred the side of the tower, where a plane crashed, lodging itself into the steel frame. Taking out several floors in its destruction.

My eyes searched out the time, eleven minutes to nine. An uneasiness I hadn't felt in years washed over me, picturing how many innocent lives were taken. And how many more would perish in the coming hours.

My goddamn humanity that I turned off came back full force, seeing the horrific scene in front of me.

Autumn's panicked voice brought me back to reality. "Creed, are you there? Did you see?"

I shook my head as if she could see me, running out the room. Heading for the stairway. "Where are you?!"

"We're heading to the Towers! We're almost there!" she shouted over the noise.

"Autumn, you listen to me! You stay on the phone! Do you understand me?! You stay on the fuckin' phone until I get to you!"

ROAD to NOWHERE

"Okay," she whimpered.

I ran out of the hotel building, searching the streets left and right, taking in the calm before the storm.

"Chief, are you en route? We need you here, now! It's anarchy. All shit is breaking lose and we have no correspondence on what the fuck just happened," I heard a man's voice yell over the radio, through the phone.

"I'm on my way. I have my daughter with me, but I'm on my way. My ETA is about five minutes. I'm turning down the road now. Get the crew assembled, I'll meet you in the front lobby of the North Tower," her dad, Carl, replied in a steady tone.

"Autumn! Autumn! Can you hear me?!"

I took off running down the street in the direction of the East River, toward the Twin Towers. Trying to decide the fastest route to get to her. Busting a left on Liberty Street, I came face to face with mayhem. Flashing lights, sirens echoing off the skyscrapers that were a part of the Manhattan skyline.

There was so much noise, so many fucking screams coming from every direction. Debris falling from the heavens, like snow. Covering everything in its wake. All I saw was chaos and disorder erupting all around me. Local business alarms sounding from the impact of the explosion. People stampeded the streets and sidewalks, abandoning their fucking cars to run to safety. Trying like hell to get to and from the building as I tried to make my way through. The closer I got the more debris floated through the air, and my visibility started to fog.

I ran faster, pounding my feet into the pavement, ignoring the burn in my lungs. The stinging at my sides. Making my way through the streets, plowing through everything and everyone that stood in my fucking way. Shoving reporters out of my face, hounding me, asking me if I saw what happened. If I could describe what I had seen to them, what I was feeling, what I thought was happening, but all I could think about was getting to her.

Getting to fucking, Autumn.

"Creed! I'm so scared! I'm really scared! Where are you?!" she bellowed through the noise, into the phone on the verge of hysterics.

"On my way to you! Just stay on the line with me! No matter what, you stay on the fuckin' line with me!"

"Chief!" I heard someone shout from a distance on the phone.

"Autumn, you guys there? Where are you? Tell me exactly where you are?!" I shouted into the phone, running as fast as I fucking could down the street. Pulling my t-shirt up over my mouth and nose, the smog becoming too much. My boots pounded against the pavement with nothing but adrenaline keeping me going.

"We're in front of the lobby of the North Tower. I'm in my dad's car. We're right out in front!" she yelled back.

"The plane crashed into the North Tower, Chief," I heard someone say over the phone again. "Floors ninety through ninety-nine are covered in smoke and engulfed in flames. We can't get in there, though. The main stairwell has collapsed between those floors. We're going to try the other emergency exits."

"Do we know how many are trapped?"

"No, Chief! We need to move fast. The fire is out of control. People are starting to hang out the windows up there."

"Okay, get me the floor plans for the North Tower now! Suit up, we're going in!" I heard him order.

"Autumn, what's goin' on?"

She didn't answer. All I could hear was her cries. "Dad, don't do this! Why are you putting on a uniform?! Why are you going in there?! You're the chief! You don't have to go in there! What are you doing?!" Autumn panicked, screaming to her father.

I ran fucking faster, dodging police cars, ambulances, and people running in the opposite directions. Shoving them out of the way.

"Baby girl, I need to go in there. I need to lead my men. This is my job, what I'm trained for. This is what I do. You stay in this car, do you understand me, Autumn! You do not get out of this car!" Carl ordered to his daughter.

"NO! Don't go in there! Please! Please! Please don't go in there! Please!" she pleaded in a desperate tone I could make out clear as day, even with all the madness around me.

"Creed, you there?"

"Yes, Sir!" I responded to her father. I hadn't spoken to him in years, but he still sounded the same. "On my way! Almost there! About five minutes if I can get through."

"You make sure she stays in the car. She does not go into that building. You both stay out of that building!"

"You have my word," I swore, meaning it with every last fucking fiber in my being.

"Daddy! Don't do this to me! You can help! Just stay right here with me! You can still help! Please!"

"Autumn, I'll be right back. I promise. Creed is almost here. You do not get out of this car!"

I heard a door slam shut and then Autumn broke down. Crying uncontrollably, beating her hands on the window. Pleading for him to come back.

"Babe, almost there! Shhh… I'm almost there! Calm down!"

"He can't go in there! It's bad, Creed! It's so fucking bad! I don't want to lose him! He's my father! Creed, I can't do this! I can't just sit here—"

"Babe, I love you. I fuckin' love you," I declared, without a second thought. Trying to distract her before I made it to her.

She sniffled, "Do you mean that?"

I missed the hell out of her. Finally understanding the meaning of absence makes the heart grow fonder.

This last month was fucking brutal without seeing or hearing from her. After that night she'd walked in on me, I kept to myself, focusing on my Vice Prez duties. Turning down every piece of ass thrown my way. Spending every fucking night staring at my ceiling, wondering what she was doing, what she was thinking, and most of all, praying she didn't really fucking hate me. I did love Autumn, and maybe with time, I could grow to be in love with her, but I would tell her anything she needed to hear in that moment to keep her fucking safe.

Even if it meant I was lying.

"I missed you. I missed you so fuckin' much. Need you in my life. By my side. On the back of my fuckin' bike, yeah?"

"Yeah," she wept like it was all she ever wanted to hear as I dodged more and more people, evacuating the area.

"Almost there. I can see the buildin'!"

"Oka—" Suddenly a piercing boom sounded from the building, causing me to pull the phone away from my ear.

"Autumn!" I shouted back into the receiver, checking my screen to see if there was still a connection. "Babe! Autumn!"

"Oh my God!" she faintly muttered.

"You okay? What was that? What's goin' on?" The building was right in my sight. And so was the cause of the noise. People fell to their deaths, making the choice to jump. Knowing there was no other way out. I swallowed the bile that rose in my throat and pushed myself harder to get to her.

I'd seen some fucked-up shit in life but nothing compared to this. "Autumn, answer me goddamnit!"

"I can't just sit here. I have to go inside. I have to go find my dad!" she rattled. "I can't just stand back and let him go. People are—"

"Autumn! Autumn! Do not get out of that fuckin' car. Stay there! Ya hear me?! Promise me you'll stay there! Autumn! Autumn! Fuckin' say somethin'!"

All I could hear over the screams was heavy breathing and sobs. "I'm sorry, Creed. I have my dad's radio. In case—" I heard the car door slam shut and more commotion take the place of her sobs over the phone.

Sirens blasted louder and louder.

"Autumn, stay in the fuckin' car!"

Beep, beep, beep. The line went dead.

"Fuck!" I yelled out, frustrated that she never fucking listened.

Not thinking twice about it, I hauled ass over a car, sprinting down the street, needing to get to her. Praying I would find her before she got up the nerve to enter the Tower. Knocking people down, not giving a fuck anymore. Real fucking fear coursed through my veins for the third time in my life, throbbing through my bloodstream. Taking over every last inch of my body. My heart pounded against my chest as I tried to cross the street and make my way over to the building.

Over to Autumn.

My vision tunneled, seeing nothing but Luke staring back at me. Flashes of Autumn's face intermixed with his. I tried to shake them away, but they were merciless and unforgiving. I spotted her dad's car confirming my worst nightmare.

She was gone.

I darted toward the front of building, dreading that I wouldn't be able to find her. There were people everywhere covered in ash and blood, stumbling out of the entry where the doors used to be.

ROAD to NOWHERE

As soon as I got close enough, all I could see were fire trucks and emergency vehicles, all lined up on the streets. Emergency personnel grabbed the injured, running them to safety. If such a place, even existed anymore. There wasn't an inch of space that wasn't surrounded by something or someone. I searched the area for any sign of her, jumping up on an abandoned car to my right. Desperately trying to find Autumn in all the goddamn mayhem.

"Autumn! Autumn!" I screamed as loud as I could when I spotted a girl near the entrance that was Autumn's build. "Autumn! No! Stay there!" I took off running, dodging people left and right, when a strong arm came out of nowhere, stopping me cold.

"Sir, you can't go in there!" a firefighter shouted, blocking my way with a few others.

"Need to find Autumn! I need to get in there! Get the fuck out of my way!" I roared, shoving my way through.

"Sir, I understand. But you need to let us do our job!"

"Some fuckin' job you're doin'! You let her go in there. Where the fuck were ya a few minutes ago?!" I seethed, grabbing him by his uniform, getting right up in his face. "You let me by, or I will fuck you up! You have no idea who you're messing with." I shoved him away from me, getting ready to cock my fist back.

"Creed?"

I agitatedly turned around, coming face to face with Carl's ex-partner. His family and him used to come on vacations with us. Fuck, I hadn't seen him in years either, but I never thought I'd be so happy to see him again in that moment.

"Troy! Autumn went in there! She went in the fuckin' buildin'!"

He jerked back, stunned. "Shit," he breathed out.

"Need to get in there, Troy. Need to find her. She has her dad's radio—" he abruptly turned, cutting me off. Gesturing for me to follow him.

I did. Running behind him toward his fire truck. He grabbed his radio, turning the frequency on. Putting his mouth up to the walkie, he pressed the side button, stating, "Come in, Autumn. Are you there? It's Troy. Can you hear me?"

The static noise of the radio faded in and out, screams and chaos rang through the receiver. She was inside. I swear I stopped fucking breathing as I waited to hear Autumn's voice or some indication that she was okay.

She was alive.

"Troy?" the radio crackled, more screaming. "I'm here. Can you hear me?"

My heart soared back to life, roughly snatching the radio out of his hand, visibly taking a deep breath. Stressing out, "Babe, where are ya?"

"Creed... Creed... is that you? People are on fire! Oh my God, Creed! I can't find my dad!"

More crackling.

More loud booms.

More chaos and cries.

"Where. Are. You?" I demanded on the verge of fucking losing it. Hanging on by a goddamn thread.

Nothing but static radiated from my hand. I peered all around me looking for an opening to bust through, taking matters into my own hands and getting her the fuck out of there. Taking down anyone who fucking stood in my way. Praying to God that this would soon be over, ready to get on my hands and knees and beg for mercy for Autumn's safety. For Carl's. Pleading for his forgiveness for all my sins. A loud noise caused me to look up at the sky.

It was then that I knew my nightmare had only just begun.

It was then that I knew the life I'd been living was over.

A passenger plane appeared out of nowhere, disappearing into the South Tower, crashing into the other side of the building. As more minutes passed, thicker black smoke flew out of the windows. Glass shattered into the air, raining down on the streets of Manhattan. More chaos erupted and bystanders started to scream and run for cover all around me. Another explosion hit the building causing me to duck, throwing my arms over my head. Falling to the ground onto my shoulder, dislocating it. Grabbing my throbbing arm, I peered up from the ground to see people running out of the building making the sign of the cross, praying for the people who were stuck and couldn't get out. Or who had already fucking died.

I put the radio up to my mouth. "Autumn," I coughed out. "Autumn! Please answer me! Autumn!"

I spent almost the next hour trying the radio, looking through the masses of people for some sight of her. Refusing medical treatment for my arm. I would endure the pain the rest of my life, just to see my girls face again. To know she was alright and not lying somewhere hurt, scared, and alone. Praying she'd found Carl and they were safe.

Praying the Reaper, that I always wanted to take me, didn't fucking take her instead.

I was about to give up all hope. I could physically feel her slipping away from my existence, exactly like I felt Luke so many years before. Firefighters, cops, ambulances, health professionals, all stepped up that day, trying to help. Giving their lives for others. Complete strangers. Nothing could even come close to describing what I saw.

What would forever be engrained in my mind till my fucking time was up.

The radio clicked over. "Creed," Autumn whimpered through the receiver.

"Babe… babe, where are you?" I urged, running toward the building, ignoring every fucking person who got in my way.

"I'm hurt, I hurt everywhere… please… please… help me…"

"Baby," I wept, unable to hold back the tears any longer. "Just tell me where ya are, Autumn."

"I can't… I can't move… I'm sorry, Creed…" Her voice was barely audible.

"Autumn, listen to me. I'm comin', babe. Need you to fight… please, I love you so fuckin' much. So damn much. I'm sorry… I'm so fuckin' sorry for everythin'," I confessed.

"I… love… you… always. I'm so—"

BOOM!

The loudest sound spread over Manhattan, breaking the sound barrier. Traveling from the Towers to the streets in waves, like a bomb went off. Jerking me back with an unexplainable force. The buildings started to explode, as the rescue team was pulling me away. Panic and pandemonium surrounded me, engulfing me in nothing, but sorrow and desperation of what just happened. Debris falling everywhere.

A dark plume of smoke billowed out of the buildings as if Hell had officially taken over.

Swallowing the eleventh day of September and everything thing down into the black abyss.

It was an endless stream of havoc and destruction.

The tower started collapsing like a fucking game of dominos, floor after floor to the ground in flames.
The tragedy.
The devastation.
The loss of faith in humanity.
And my fucking world...
As I knew it.

"The day that changed America," President Bush declared during his speech from Ellis Island, commencing the one-year anniversary of the terrorist's attacks on the World Trade Center. *"For those who lost loved ones, it has been a year of sorrow, of empty places, of newborn children who will never know their father's here on earth. For members of our military, it's been a year of sacrifice and service far from their homes. For all Americans, it has been a year of adjustment, of coming to terms with the difficult knowledge that our nation has determined enemies, and that we are not invulnerable to their attacks."*

I had been walking the streets, surrounding Ground Zero all day, since I landed early that morning, reflecting on my life. Remembering those who had fallen under the hands of terrorists, including my best fucking friend. The sight of the once thriving towers was nothing but a pit in the ground. Across the street, there was a wall lined with victims' pictures, some who were found in the rubble, others who weren't so fortunate. A makeshift memorial of letters to loved ones, flowers, stuffed animals, candles all filled the space, acting as a place to grieve for those who lost a huge part of their lives in seconds. Watching families break down even after a year of loss on that tragic day of September eleventh was like reliving it all over again.

Both towers came down that day, collapsing into a heap of marred steel. Later finding out the temperature of the fires melted the steel, causing floor after floor to fall upon the next till the towers were no longer upright. There was zero visibility for the longest time. Everything for miles covered in white ash, emergency vehicles, cars, and buses crushed beneath, barely sticking up through the mayhem.

I spent the three days following the attacks searching for Autumn and Carl. Praying I'd find them among the ashes and debris, dead or alive. I remembered it as if it were yesterday, reliving it every goddamn day since. Diesel and some of the other brothers rode in the next morning, riding out all fucking night. Just so they could help me search for the woman I knew was gone. Mayor Giuliani, along with thousands of other citizens of New York City, rummaged through the two-thousand tons of steel for days, forgoing sleep to try to save lives that were hanging on by a fucking thread.

Death was all around me.

It had been around me all my fucking life.

Now here I was a year later standing by the pit of the worst nightmare America had ever lived through, trying to get my feet to move. To take the steps across the street, to add pictures of Autumn and Carl to the Memorial. To feel as if they weren't just figments of my imagination, to know that they were truly real. It took me all fucking day to walk across the street to do just that. I lit a candle for their souls, praying they were resting in peace.

I never found their bodies under all the mangled metal. I never found any sign that they actually existed. Just dust and ashes. All I had left was my tarnished memory of them. Like a broken mirror that was nothing but shards of glass.

I never slept anymore. Hearing Autumn's voice play over and over in my head like a broken record I couldn't stop, I couldn't pause, I couldn't fucking forget.

"I... love... you... always. I'm so—"

The BOOM jolting me awake every fucking time.

Sometimes I felt like I had died right along with them.

Sometimes I wish I had.

"September 11th, 2001 will always be a fixed point in the life of America. The loss of so many lives left us to examine our own. Each of us were reminded that we were only here for a time. These counted days should be filled with things that matter. Love for our families. Love for our neighbors. And for our Country."

ROAD to NOWHERE

I spent the last year aimlessly wandering around through daily life. Fighting for a cause I felt like I was always fucking losing. Didn't matter how many lives I took, for whatever reason, good or bad. I protected my brothers, I fought and killed for the club, I did everything that was expected of me, all in the name of the colors on my cut. Making me realize I was no better than those goddamn terrorists.

Autumn was right. She was the last bit of good left in my life. The last piece of the man she wished I could be, died right along with her. She was gone, and I felt like there was only so much I could do to try to make it right. If there was one thing I learned about living and breathing the MC, it was vengeance wasn't a way of life, it was life.

An eye for an eye.

Was all I'd ever fucking known.

My mind had been struggling with the decision, going back forth an endless amount of times, contemplating what was right or what was wrong. The thoughts consumed me until there was no doubt left inside of me. Knowing the only good that could come of it.

Was my own peace of mind.

I checked in on Laura often, hoping it would drown out the remorse, alleviate some of my guilty conscience. Making sure she was alright. Helping her any way I could, being responsible for her only daughter's death stemmed from me. Autumn would have never been in New York if I hadn't pushed her away. Her mother was coping as best as she could, but each day seemed like a struggle, some better than others. I swear there were times she looked at me the same way my mother did.

Blaming me for another innocent life I had taken.

I walked around aimlessly, needing the distraction. The sidewalks filled with endless amounts of people. Civilians, police, first responders, and military. Men and women dressed in fatigues, there to honor the fallen. Including their own who lost their lives fighting for our country.

All gathered together to remember another day that will forever fucking haunt me.

My flight landed back in North Carolina just after nine o'clock at night. I walked up to the front door of my house, placing my hand on the door knob. Pausing before walking into my broken fucking household. Considering when to break the news to my mother, to Noah, to the goddamn Prez.

I flipped on the light as I walked in, throwing my keys on the entry shelf, before making my way to the kitchen, not surprised to find her passed out at the dining room table. I stood there taking in her appearance for what seemed like an eternity.

Her bony right hand wrapped around an empty bottle of vodka, while the other one clutched onto a framed picture of Luke. Pulling out the chair adjacent to her, I sat down, leaning back and placing my boots on the table. Giving her arm a little shove.

"Wake up, Ma. Need to talk to you."

She stirred, groaning, "Not now, baby. I'm so tired," she yawned. "It's been a really long day. We can talk tomorrow." She placed her head back down on the table, completely dismissing me.

I abruptly stood, my chair hitting the wall behind me with a thud. "Tired my ass," I gritted out, hovering above her, working my hands in fists at my sides.

My patience was wearing very fucking thin, there was only so much more I could take. My temper looming, I could feel myself at the tipping point of surrendering to my anger.

Losing all fucking control.

She groggily looked up at me, squinting from the bright light. "What do you want from me?" she mumbled, her head swayed and her eyes flickered shut. Before I knew what I was doing, my hands connected with the table, slamming down onto the wood.

Causing her to jerk back. "What the he—" I grabbed a hold of her chair, roughly spinning her to look me in the eyes.

"This is how it's gonna go down," I snapped through a clenched jaw, close to her face. The smell of booze immediately assaulted my senses. Fueling the rage I felt deep in my core. "You're gonna listen to everythin' I gotta say, whether you like it or not. I've had enough of your fuckin' bullshit!"

Her head rolled back, then upright again. "I said not tonight, Creed, and don't you dare talk to me like that! I'm still your momma!"

Without warning, I lifted her out of her chair, throwing her over my shoulder like she weighed nothing. Barreling down the hallway, past Noah's room to the bathroom, as she pounded her fists weakly into my back.

"Put me down, Creed! What are you doing?! Put me down!" she belligerently screamed.

I didn't falter, tearing back the shower curtain. I turned on the faucet, cranking the lever to cold water.

"Don't you dare! You put me down right now!"

"Not a fuckin' problem!" I slammed her ass down into the tub with her clothes on. Grabbing the showerhead from the cradle, dousing her body with the spray.

"Ahhh! That's freezing! STOP!"

I didn't let up, making sure I drenched every last inch of her. She needed to be fucking sober to try to have a normal conversation with her.

"Stop! Now! Who do you think you are?"

I shut off the water, throwing the sprayer into the tub next to her.

"What is so important that it couldn't wait till tomorrow?" she spat, looking down at her soaking wet body with her arms out to her sides.

I crouched down, leaning close to her face. Gazing deep into her drunken, vacant eyes for the first time in years. Looking past her demons, needing to see the real woman staring back at me. The mother I still had and wanted in my mind. The same one I still knew lived inside of her, buried under all the hurt and pain. Hidden behind all the happy memories that had become her worst nightmares.

The realization hit me right then and there. I needed to calm the fuck down, there was no use screaming at a drunk. It wouldn't get me anywhere except more pissed off than I already was. At the end of the day, she would always be my mother, the woman who gave me life. The one I loved more than anything in my fucked-up life. I needed to rationalize with her. Make her see the big picture. Make her understand what I saw. What Noah saw.

How there was nothing fucking left of her, but the memories in our minds.

"Do you even care anymore, Ma? Do you have any idea how hard it's been seein' you like this? How bad it fuckin' hurts that I'm lookin' at you right now, and I have no idea who this woman is starin' back at me. She ain't my mother," I confessed, leaning back on the heels of my boots, shaking my head.

Her eyes quickly glazed over. My words hitting her hard, breaking through the alcohol-induced blur.

"Luke died, Ma. I know it fuckin' hurts. I know that more than anyone, yeah?" I breathed out, cocking my head to the side. Taking her in. "I'm the one that pulled the trigger, remember? I'm the one that put him to ground. Me." Hitting my chest, needing to get through to her. "I know there are some days it hurts so fuckin' bad that you can't breathe. Suffocatin' cuz the pain won't let you go. I get it... I understand cuz I feel it too, and there hasn't been a day that's gone by that I haven't."

She winced, biting her bottom lip to control the trembling, allowing her emotions to seep through. Finally permitting herself to mourn the death of her son.

"Autumn died, Ma. She fuckin' died..."

Her eyes watered with tears, nodding, "I know."

"Coulda' fooled me. Haven't said a word about it. You were barely coherent through her funeral," I reminded, remembering how I put her belligerent ass in a cab after the service. Ordering a prospect to follow and put her to bed, since she could barely stand on her own.

I rubbed the back of my head, peering down at the ground, lost in my own thoughts. "I'm tryin'... I'm tryin' so fuckin' hard to keep it together. Pushin' through all the bullshit, all the hurt and pain. Keepin' my emotions in check by throwin' myself into the club, into bein' VP. This is my life, Ma, violence and death. There is no turnin' back for me," I spoke sincerely, taking a deep breath before continuing.

"I keep makin' excuses for you, enablin' you, and I can't fuckin' do it anymore, Ma. It ain't right," I scoffed out, pausing to let my words sink in. Looking up at her tear-soaked face, we locked eyes. "You're nothin' but a drunk and a sorry-ass excuse for a mother. Noah deserves better." With that, I stood, grabbing the towel off the rack, throwing it at her. Immediately feeling like shit that I just said that to her, knowing it was my fault to begin with.

She caught it mid-air. Her chest rising and falling, contemplating what to say. I could see her mind spinning out of control. Opening her mouth to say something, but nothing came out. I couldn't look at her any longer without saying something I would fucking regret. So I just turned around, leaving her to battle her own demons.

I couldn't protect her anymore.

I walked onto the back porch, leaving the door open. Needing to get some fresh air, to clear my head. Listening to her sobs wreak havoc on her frail body through the bathroom window. I sat on the steps, resting my elbows on my knees as I pulled out a cigarette. Bringing it to the corner of my mouth, I flicked back the lighter, inhaling long and hard, searing the filter. Allowing the nicotine to burn its way through my lungs before blowing out a wad of smoke.

"Creed, I..." Ma whispered, crying from behind me.

I didn't bother to turn around, her fucking shame was already burning a hole in my back.

"I just... I don't know how to stop..." she bellowed, sucking in air, trying to find her breath. "I was his momma for God's sake. My only job was to protect him. I failed. You may have pulled the trigger, baby... but he was only there because of me. He should have been home, in bed. What kind of momma, am I? I don't deserve you or Noah... I don't deserve anything."

I closed my eyes, leaning my head back against the porch railing. Needing a minute. I always knew she felt responsible for Luke's death, but hearing her actually say the goddamn words was almost too much for me to take.

Heavy footsteps filled the silence, coming up the driveway, echoing through my thoughts. I didn't have to wonder who it was. Neither one of us did. I took one last drag of my cigarette, waiting until the footsteps stopped out in front of me. Already fucking dreading the outcome of what I was about to say.

I took a deep breath, speaking with conviction, "Gonna enlist in the Army," I divulged, opening my eyes and looking up, meeting my father's stare.

"The fuck you are, Creed!" he instantly drawled out.

I immediately stood, flicking out my cigarette not backing down. Coming face to face with him.

"Jameson..." Ma coaxed, slowly stepping up beside me. Fixing her wet dress and wiping away her tears.

"Don't wanna hear your shit tonight, woman! Do you hear your son? Where the fuck did this come from? What bullshit are you tellin' him?"

"Nothing. I haven't told him anything. Leave him alone! He wants to do some good in his life. He's your son! Start treating him like one!"

"I give my boys everything. The fuck you talkin' about?"

"And Luke—"

"Jesus Christ… back to this shit again," he viciously spewed, eyeing her up and down. "It's been one less mouth to fuckin' feed. I ain't even sure that little shit was mine."

My mother never reacted to my father's abuse, but there was something about the look in her eyes in that moment that showed me this wasn't going to fucking end well.

"You son of a bitch! You piece of shit!" she screamed, lunging at him off the porch, using all her strength to scratch, punch, and kick him. Doing anything and everything she could in her power to physically hurt him.

Her fist connected with his temple, stunning him for a second. I sprang into action, stepping in before he regained his composure, and was able to really hurt her. Grabbing ahold of her waist, I roughly jerked her flailing body off of him. Holding her in my arms.

"It's your fault! It's your fault he's fucking dead! Your godforsaken club is just violence and death! You did this, and I hope you burn in Hell for it!" she seethed, trying to fight me off.

"Ma, enough! Enough!" I yelled, trying to calm her down. Locking my arms tighter around her.

"You stupid bitch! Look around. I have given you everythin' because of that godforsaken club! This is how you treat me? After everythin' I've done for you! After taking you back, after you—"

"I wish I would have stayed! I wish I had never come back to you! That was the worst decision of my life!" She wrestled her way out of my grasp, getting right up to his face. "You aren't half the man you think you are. You're nothing like he—"

The barrel of his gun was right under her chin, rendering her speechless. The cool metal didn't faze her one bit. She didn't back down. The alcohol and fury running through her veins was all the liquid courage she needed.

I didn't falter, moving fast.

Getting over to them in two strides, forcefully pushing her body out of the line of fire. Her tiny frame fell to the ground, but all that mattered to me was that she wasn't on the other end of that fucking barrel.

When I turned back around, the gun was now pointed at my chest.

"Creed, no! Let—" I shoved her back down.

"Do it! Wanna kill someone? Then fuckin' do it, *Prez*," I mocked, gritting my teeth. "Pull the trigger. It don't matter to me anymore." Grabbing the barrel of the gun, I held it firmly in place over my heart.

His eyes glazed over at the sincerity of my words. It was quick, but I saw it. I knew he wouldn't do it, his finger didn't move from the trigger, though. I secretly wished he would take the shot. He never even thanked me for taking a bullet for him, never even said one goddamn word about it.

I saved his life, and he still wanted to own mine.

I saw Noah from the corner of my eye, standing by the door. Watching it all go down. I didn't know how long he'd been standing there, but by the look on his face, he had seen enough.

Pops took a long, deep breath, stepping back. Lowering his gun. "She died, Creed. Autumn fuckin' died. Wanna go fight for your country? Be G.I. Fucking Joe. That ain't gonna bring her back."

"You don't know shit about shit," I spit out.

"Turnin' your back on your brothers? On your fuckin' family?" He pushed me, but I didn't waver. "Don't deserve to wear that fuckin' cut."

His fist collided with my face before he got the last word out. My head whooshed back, taking half of my body with me. Ma screamed as Noah witnessed Pops' assault. She rushed over to him and took him inside.

I stumbled, shaking it off. "This how it's gonna go down?" I asked, spitting blood onto the lawn.

He growled, charging me, ramming his shoulder into my torso. Taking me to the ground, my back skidded into the rough grass beneath me, but I was prepared for it now and instantly fought back. We wrestled around for a few minutes, each of us trying to gain the upper hand on the other. Elbows, fists, and legs flew everywhere, intermingling together as we threw down. I was able to get on top of him and get a few hits to his fucking face.

Taking out all the years of pent-up anger and resentment toward him for Luke and the way he buried him.

"Don't wanna fuckin' fight you! You old fuck! Calm down and let me explain!"

He hit me in the gut, causing me to fall to the side. Using the momentum of his punch, to flip me over, locking me in with his weight. I immediately guarded my face, but it didn't matter. He punched me in the ribs, the stomach, getting a few good hits to the side of my face, too.

"Goddamn it!" I roared, blocking another blow. "Not takin' off my cut! Don't want outta the club. I earned these fuckin' colors! You dick! I just need this! Not just for her, for me! I'm fuckin' losin' myself, old man!"

He abruptly stopped with his fist mid-air, both of us panting heavily, sweating profusely. Our eyes remained wild and brazen as we took in each other. A few moments later he lowered his fist, shoving off me, never taking our intense, crazed stares away from one another.

I stood up, needing to take a few steps back to collect myself. "All my life, all I've done is follow your fuckin' orders, never asked you for a damn thing in return. Need you to be my father this one fuckin' time," I breathed out, breaking the silence between us. "Need to make this right and take those motherfuckers out. You can understand that more than anyone, *Prez.*" Cocking my head to the side. "Just need a leave of absence, ain't no different if I was locked up, my loyalty is still to the club when I get discharged. I just need this," I repeated.

His face was void of any emotion. For the first time in my life, I couldn't read him at all.

"Don't make me beg…" I found myself saying.

He stepped back, wiping the blood from the corner of his mouth with the back of his hand. His thoughts clearly raged war in his mind, in regards to what he was going to do. He turned to leave, stopping at the last second. Looking at me with nothing but disgust in his eyes, he finally said, "Callin' church. Your ass better be there at noon tomorrow." He left, never once turning back to look at me.

I staggered my way inside, grabbing a dish towel for my bloody nose and lip before heading into the living room. Ma came running up to me as soon as she saw me walking in. "I'm fine," I groaned, wrapping my arm around my ribs. Hissing through the pain. I took a seat on the couch.

"Let me get the first aid kit." She hurried out of the room before I could refuse.

I sank further into the couch, placing my legs on the coffee table, closing my eyes and breathing through the pain. And I wasn't talking about the aches on my body.

"You really leavin' us?" Noah murmured from behind me, just loud enough for me to hear.

It seemed like it was one fucking thing after another. Feeling his disappointment stabbing into my skin with a jagged blade. "Noah, I—"

"You're gonna leave me with them? You're all I got, Creed," he lamented, his voice breaking. "What if you die? Like Luke? What if someone accidentally pulls the trigger on you, Creed? What happens then?"

I opened my mouth to say something but quickly shut it. Realizing Noah knew more than I ever gave him credit for. I didn't know how to make him understand my reasoning for a decision I had never taken lightly. I spent the last year contemplating this life-altering choice and today only confirmed what I already knew I had to fucking do.

He walked over, standing in front of me. "Joe's dad never came back from war. I don't want to lose another brother."

"I gotta do this, Noah. Not only for Autumn but for myself. Don't expect you to understand, but I do need you to respect my decision and know, this is for you too."

"I call bullshit."

I shrugged. "Don't know what you want me to say, Noah."

"Just go, Creed! Don't worry about me. I'll figure shit out on my own."

"I love you, Noah. You're my brother. You're in my blood. Nothin' gonna change that."

He slowly backed away. "Whatever you have to tell yourself. Go die for your fuckin' country." He took one last look at me, shook his head, and left.

I didn't sleep at all that night, listening to the voices inside my head. Praying to God I was making the right choice.

Knowing in the end it didn't fucking matter.

I rode out to the clubhouse early next the morning. Sat in on Church as if I was a man waiting for his execution.

The vote was unanimous.

I left the club that afternoon and enlisted into the U.S. Army.

My family had been fighting for weeks. My momma in tears, my daddy constantly yelling, I hated seeing everyone so upset. My family wasn't perfect, we had our disagreements, arguments even broke out from time to time, but they never lasted longer than a few hours, maybe a day.

This was different.

It didn't stop.

The same thing every day.

Mason enlisted in the Army without even discussing it with anyone, including my parents. He'd be leaving in a few days for boot camp, saying he needed to do something for the greater good. Make a difference. My parents didn't understand nor agree with the way he decided to go about it. All they saw was that he was putting his life in danger.

There were plenty of opportunities to do good right here in North Carolina. We all knew he wanted to go into the military someday, he'd been saying it ever since I could remember. I didn't take him seriously.

No one did.

It had been a year since some terror guys took down the World Trade Center in New York. I didn't understand what that meant, or why anyone would want to hurt people they didn't know. Why we couldn't all just get along and spread love, not hate. Daddy said the world wasn't made like that, but people like me are what made it better.

Everyone kept saying it was a day America would never forget, especially my brother. His friend, Autumn, the girl Creed was always around, was killed in the North Tower that day. The news took a toll on Mason, giving him the excuse he needed to enlist. Fighting for our country was his calling. Protecting the ones, he loved was his mission. The tension was on high alert in my house, making it become our own war zone since he told them.

Giselle wouldn't even speak to him. From what I gathered eavesdropping at his door, he didn't discuss this life-changing decision with her either. Aunt Aubrey and Giselle came over one night to hang out, and all she did was cry to my momma about Mason. I felt so bad for her, but my brother had always been an asshole. This behavior was nothing new, I wasn't allowed to say that about him, but it didn't change the truth. Giselle thought they were going to get married, start having babies and be a family together.

And then he enlisted.

See... asshole.

My other brother Bo started working at the restaurant after school and on the weekends, bussing tables and helping in the back. The day he turned fourteen, he asked Momma for a job, so she gave him one. I started hanging out at the restaurant more too, riding to work alongside him on our bikes. Daddy said since I would be twelve in a few months, he would let me go with Bo. I think it was more because he didn't want me in the house, hearing them fight all the time.

I took all my sadness out on the waves, spending all my free time in the water. Being able to relish in the free feeling of being pushed along by nature's force. Riding the perfect waves, and be one with the ocean. There was no feeling in the world that could describe it.

The ocean had always been my happy place.

I sat on the beach, watching the sunset not paying attention to anyone around me. Enjoying the peacefulness before having to go home to the madness.

I glanced over when I felt someone sit beside me.

"Hey, Pippin," Creed greeted, grinning from ear-to-ear. Making me instantly smile back.

I hadn't seen him in what felt like forever. He looked older and bigger if that was even possible.

"I haven't seen you in a while. You're lucky you always wear the same clothes or else I wouldn't have even recognized you," I teased. "Do you have any other clothes?" I smirked, unable to help myself. Gesturing to his vest. I'd never seen him wearing anything but jeans, a shirt, and that vest. I was starting to think he didn't own any real clothes.

"It's called a cut."

"Yeah… well, that. I guess it's a good thing. What else would I get you if you didn't wear it anymore."

He chuckled, looking back out toward the water. "Don't need to get me anythin'."

"Too late. I have more patches for you. Look." I grabbed my backpack, reaching around until I found them. Gesturing for him to put his hand out. "I guess you can put them wherever you put the other ones," I suggested, wanting him to know, I noticed they weren't on his cut the last time I saw him.

He grabbed them out of my hand, reading the first one out loud, "Ain't Nobody Got Time for That."

When I saw it, I thought it was perfect. He was always in a rush. Telling me to hurry up. That he had places to be. Whatever that meant.

He read the next one. "Do I look like a people person." Cocking his head to the side, giving me a knowing look.

I laughed. I thought that one was pretty self-explanatory.

He went on, reciting, "Here I am. What are your other two wishes?" Smiling, remembering why I got him that one. He moved onto the next, reading, "Bad example." Smiling again, knowing it was because he kept telling me he was no good.

I finally handed him the last one I kept clutched in my hand. "This one's for your girlfriend, Autumn," I stated as he took in the 'In Memory of 911. Our Fallen Angels' patch. "I'm really sorry, Creed."

He nodded, holding back his emotions. "Thanks for these." Placing them in his pocket, he grabbed his cigarettes and lit one up. Blowing out the smoke to the side of him, away from me. Resting his elbows on his knees, bowing his head, deep in thought.

I resisted the urge to tell him those were bad for him again, feeling as though he was trying to comfort himself the only way he knew how.

"Not gonna see me for a while, Pippin," he said out of nowhere. Shuffling the sand around with his boot.

"Longer than this last time?" I asked, confused.

"Gonna go fight the bad guys," he confessed, nodding his head to me.

My mouth parted, and my stomach dropped. Now I would have two people to worry about. "You're going with Mason," I breathed out, my heart in my throat. Already knowing the answer.

"Got your brother's back. Don't worry about him," he whispered as if reading my mind.

"What about you?"

"Been takin' care of myself for a long time. Don't need to worry about me either."

I had so much to say...

But mostly, I just wanted him to know I'd miss him. More than I already had.

"Pinky promise me you'll stay safe. That you won't be reckless, and if you get scared... you'll run. You won't try to be a hero. Promise me, soldier," I urged, holding my little finger out in front of his face.

Waiting.

He hooked his pinky with mine, looking deep into my eyes with a lopsided grin. Making my belly flutter like he always did. I wrapped my other arm around my tummy, hoping he wouldn't notice I was trying to calm myself. Trying to focus my attention on the roughness of his hand, the scars etched into his skin, noticing how much bigger it was than mine. He could easily swallow it in his whole fist and still have space.

I leaned in and kissed our pinkies for good measure. He never said the words, but it didn't matter. A pinky promise was legit business and not to be messed with.

"Gotta go. Meetin' Mason. Just saw you sittin' out here and wanted to say goodbye." He started to stand.

"Can I write you?"

He sat back down, giving me a puzzling expression. "Write me?"

"You know, with a pen and paper. Like pen pals. I'll write you. You write me back. So you know you have a friend waiting for you when you come back home."

He scoffed out, taken aback, "We'll see, yeah?"

"Yeah," I replied, trying to hide my disappointment.

He stood, brushing the sand from his black jeans. I followed suit, needing to head back inside. Without giving it any thought, I threw my arms around his waist, laying my head on his rock-solid stomach. Feeling the hard metal tucked in the back of his jeans, digging into my skin. I didn't care, I just wanted to remember how he smelt, how he felt. Most of all, I wanted to give him a hug before he left.

Scared I would never see him again.

He froze, caught off guard by my sentiment, but I didn't care. I just hugged him harder, squeezing him tight. He finally relaxed after a few seconds, placing his arm around me, lightly hugging me back.

I smiled through the tears that threatened in my eyes. I couldn't help it, I was getting through his icy, broody demeanor, and that was something to be happy about.

He pulled away first, tugging on the end of my pigtail. "Stay little. Ya feel me?"

"I feel ya."

He nodded one last time and turned to leave.

"Creed!" I called out, stopping him. He looked back at me. "It's not goodbye. It's just an I'll see you later." I saluted him.

He smiled, nodding. Saluting me back.

I watched him leave with a heavy heart. Silently praying for him and Mason to come home…

Safe.

I walked onto the bus around six in the morning on a Sunday, waiting for Mason. They were transporting us seven-and-a-half hours away to Fort Benning, Georgia for nineteen weeks of hell. Then onto Fort Bragg to begin our job training for at least a year. My recruiter helped me get my GED so I was able to enlist. We didn't want to be just any soldiers. We wanted to be special operation soldiers. I wanted to be a weapons specialist, already knowing so much about guns, while Mason wanted to be an engineer.

I watched from the window as his whole family hugged him goodbye, including Pippin who had tears streaming down her little face. His mom Stacey, and stepmom, Alex, stood behind her trying like hell to keep it together but failing miserably. No one showed up to see me off, not giving a fuck I was leaving.

Mia's eyes found mine as if she could sense my stare. Immediately wiping away her tears, not wanting me to see her cry. Proving to me that she really was just a baby girl. Her eyes held so much worry, so much sincerity in that moment, not only for Mason.

For me too.

A kid I had only seen a handful of times in the last three years, cared more about me than my own blood. In ways I'd never seen or felt before. The emotion showing in her bright blue, glossy eyes heightened a connection between us that I hadn't ever realized before.

ROAD to NOWHERE

I reached into my pocket and pulled out the first patch she ever gave me. Placing the word 'courage' on the window for her to see. She instantly smiled, and it lit up her entire face. I couldn't help but smile back.

She was just too fucking adorable not to.

Basic training-AKA Boot Camp was an adjustment to say the fucking least. I went from doing whatever the hell I wanted in Devil's Rejects, to beyond strict, no bullshit, daily regimens in the military. As soon as we stepped foot on that fucking base, we were no longer civilians, but soldiers. Getting stripped of our normal clothes and thrown into a chair for a military buzz cut.

The further we got into training, the more brutal it became. We went from the classroom learning the ropes of being an Army soldier, to the field where our drill sergeants pushed us to the breaking point. Testing our strength, endurance, and most importantly, our fucking sanity. Pulling us out of bunks at all hours of the night, in the shittiest conditions possible, running drills and crawling obstacles. Digging holes just for the hell of it, being belittled to the extreme of wanting to fucking hang yourself.

I learned quickly not to speak unless spoken to.

"What the fuck," we all groaned out. Being woken up at two in the morning to bright lights and yelling.

"Come on, you pansy-ass sons of bitches! Get the fuck out of bed and suit up!" Drill Sergeant Emery's voice boomed through our sleeping quarters. "I ain't got all day. Move! Move! Move!"

Everyone was half-asleep but still managed to hop off their beds, throw on clothes and boots, and line up in front of their bunks.

"Your fucking grandma moves faster than that Paulsen, you lazy ass motherfucker!" he spewed in the private's face.

"My mema is dead, Drill Sergeant."

"Did she die waiting on your sorry ass to get her to the goddamn hospital?"

"No, Drill Sergeant!"

"Drop and give your mema twenty, Private! And count um'."

Paulsen fell to the linoleum and started counting out loud.

"Nice of you to fucking join us, Private Jameson," he called me out, not even looking in my direction. "Why you dragging ass? Don't tell me it's because you needed your beauty sleep!" He walked over to me, getting right in my face. "You are one bulldog looking cocksucker!" he yelled inches away from my mouth, the veins in his neck working overtime.

I didn't back down. "I needed to piss, Drill Sergeant!" I shouted, standing up taller. Looking over his head.

"You piss when I tell you to piss! Did I tell you to fuckin' piss?"

I hesitated, working my fists at my sides. I never liked being told what I could and couldn't do. This motherfucker was pushing my goddamn buttons.

"No... Drill Sergeant."

"Drop and give me fifty for pissing."

"Yes, Drill Sergeant."

I got down in a plank position, the dog tag Autumn gave me with Luke's face on it, slipped out of my t-shirt, catching the Sergeant's eye.

"What do we have here?" he questioned, crouching down in front of me, ripping the chain from my neck in one swift motion.

Before giving it any thought, I jumped to my feet, shoving my superior hard in the chest. "Don't fuckin' touch those!" I roared.

"Creed, stand down," Mason gritted out in a low tone only I heard. Knowing shit was about to hit the fan.

"You have some brass balls, Private. This your son?" He held up the necklace.

I shook my head no.

"I asked you a fucking question, Private Jameson! When I ask you a question, I expect a fucking answer. Now! Is this your son?"

"My little brother, Drill Sergeant," I replied through a clenched jaw.

"Awe, ain't that sweet. You can get this back after you earn it. No personal effects wore on your body. Already breaking fucking rules, Private. Trust me, you'll pay for this today. Now drop and give me hundred. You got five minutes. You go over one second, you'll start again. Let's see how long it takes you to be a real fucking man."

I completed them in three. And I swear the son of a bitch grinned as he walked away from me.

Mason and I completed basic and job infantry training with flying colors. Moving onto airborne training in which we'd be learning to jump out of planes and shit. Becoming paratroopers, and gaining our wings.

ROAD to NOWHERE

I couldn't fucking wait to make that jump.

That's where we met Owen, a ruthless motherfucker from Arkansas. He happened to be the same fucker I had a run in with at the Oak Island fair tent, because of Autumn a few years back. He was there, vacationing with his family. It didn't take long for me to realize how fucking small the world truly was. We were unpacking our shit at our new headquarters when a picture of Autumn fell to the floor.

"This your girlfriend?" Owen asked, holding up the Polaroid.

"Somethin' like that." I tore it from his grasp, throwing it on the dresser. Not wanting to explain or get into that with a complete goddamn stranger.

"Wait, let me see that again." He helped himself, reaching over to take a closer look. "Where did you say you're from?"

"I didn't."

"Oh man, I'd recognize these tits and ass anywhere. She's the feisty redhead I met in Oak Island awhile back. I would have fucked her if it weren't for—"

I had him pinned up against the wall by his throat before he got the last word out.

"Me?! Beatin' your fuckin' face in. I suggest you choose your words wisely, or I won't hesitate to fuck you up again." I released him with a shove, going back to unpacking.

"That was you. I knew you looked vaguely familiar. You put me in the damn hospital for days. You broke my fucking jaw. My mouth was wired shut for weeks."

"Not even sorry." I walked out of the room.

Owen and I eventually put our differences behind us, both wanting to make our country proud and take down the fuckers who took so much away from us.

Especially me.

I wasn't fighting just for the United States. I was fighting for Autumn.

My men had my fucking back, and I had theirs.

When our nineteen weeks at Fort Benning was completed, we got stationed at Fort Bragg, North Carolina together for Special Forces job training. I was top in my fucking class when it came to speed. I could draw my gun in the matter of seconds, taking out anyone who stood in my fucking way. All those years of handling guns for the wrong reasons with the MC came in handy. I had the eye of a sniper with a quick hand. Knowing military-issued guns like the back of my hand brought me to where I was now, my job.

No one fucking crossed me.

Upon completion, we were all assigned to the same barracks, the building that housed us.

We got orders for our first deployment to Afghanistan right after we finished training. At the time I thought I was a badass motherfucker who was invincible. I was on top of the fucking world, ready to go in with guns fucking blazing, killing the fuckers who took so much away from me, from us.

I was trained to kill.

I was trained to not ask questions.

I was trained to turn off the last bit of my humanity.

But no amount of training prepared me for the things I was forced to witness. The things they don't tell you about before you enlist and devote your life for the greater fucking good. The things they don't show you on the news or read about in newspapers.

They don't show you the fucking bad.

Only the good.

I thought I had seen it all, but I couldn't have been more fucking wrong. Watching the aftermath of women and children being raped, beaten, and shot by their own insurgents because the men wouldn't join their cause. The devastation brought on by their own fucking kind. There was no telling the difference between the innocent and corrupt overseas. It all blended together. You quickly realized that every time you suited up. Every time you threw on those army fatigues, it was life or death.

It was their lives or yours.

Special Ops were trained fucking killers. Every mission we were assigned to was top secret. We didn't even know what we were being dragged in for until we got there. Being deployed on any given day without warning. Couldn't say shit about anything either, especially when we came back. Our main mission that never changed was to fucking find them before they killed us.

Kill... or be killed.

Exactly like the fucking MC.

ROAD to NOWHERE

Being in Special Forces, meant being deployed more often, but for shorter increments. Typically, they only lasted anywhere from four-to-six months, depending on the unit, location, and need.

I had been back at Fort Bragg in North Carolina for a month. I was stationed about an hour and a half from home. I didn't know when I would be shipped out again, so I was planning on taking advantage of the little freedom I had as best as I could. As I sat in my barracks though, my mind replayed scenes I wish I could erase for good.

I lit a cigarette, inhaling the nicotine. Immediately feeling the rush of the toxins course through my lungs. Leaning my head back, blowing a puff of smoke into the stale air. Thinking of all these memories that plagued my soul.

My unit was called out to a small, run-down village to search out insurgents, and collect intel on Osama Bin Laden's whereabouts. It was pouring rain, God unleashing his wrath upon the battlegrounds. When a group of kids, came sneaking out of an abandon, concrete building.

"Two boys, dressed in uniform, and three elders about two yards out. Heading north," Owen's voice rasped over the radio.

"I got a visual," I replied, talking into my shoulder. Never taking my eyes off them.

"Creed, it's your call. They look like they're holding something, bro. It's not a good time to be a fucking pussy. Pull out your damn tampon, grow a pair of fucking balls, and take them the fuck out!"

"Motherfucker!" I seethed, making my way closer, my eye trained on them through the scope of my gun.

They stopped dead in their tracks, exchanging some words, looking all around them, searching for I don't know what. Then the elders suddenly pulled out grenades from their jackets, handing them to the boys.

I jerked back. "Fuck," I breathed out, knowing what I had to do. I didn't hesitate, pulling the trigger till they were no longer little boys in school uniforms, but the enemy I was trained to take out.

Here one minute.

Gone the next.

The casualties of war.

That was the first kill under my belt on my first deployment to Afghanistan.

The military desensitized me, more so than I was before, or maybe I had already been numb to it all. I had new nightmares, new ghosts of men, women, and sometimes children I had killed for my country, haunting me. Kids as young as Noah, some even younger.

All of them engrained to hate the red, white, and blue.

I caught a glimpse of myself in the floor-length mirror hanging from my closet door. Taking in all the ink I had collected over the years. Between the MC and the military tattoos, each and every piece I had etched in my skin had a story to tell, a memory to hold onto, till the day I fucking died. Most soldiers collected something important to them. I collected tattoos, branding my skin every chance I fucking got.

It was the same thing day in and day out.

Nights in the military were some of the loneliest times of my life. I had nothing to distract myself with, it didn't matter how exhausted I was. How much I pushed my body physically and mentally, sleep never came easily.

My memories were always there.

The bad and brutal ones outweighed the good.

The good memories never lasted. My mind only programmed to bring back the bad. It was instinctual for me, seeing the images of my goddamn life rotating around me like the moon rotated around the earth. Reminding me of the life I'd only known as fucking hell. There were times when I couldn't shake it off, as much as I tried they wouldn't let me go, tightening around my neck. The weaving of a tight rope of memories, strangling me until I couldn't fucking breathe. Like a noose, sucking the life right out of me.

I welcomed that feeling.

At least then I knew I was still fucking alive.

Being a special operations weapon specialist, I was allowed thirty days leave a calendar year. I spent most of my free time on the weekends when I wasn't working or when I was on leave, at the club. Diesel had stepped in as acting Vice Prez until I could return. I still paid my dues and was involved as much as I could be, and they kept me informed and up to date on everything that was going down.

I tried to see Noah every chance I got, except he never wanted to fucking see me. In the event I did see him, he refused to talk, letting me do all the talking. I could feel the resentment oozing off his pores. He was sixteen, acting as if he was a grown-ass man. Spending more and more time at the clubhouse, against my wishes. I went from one fucked up situation to another.

My mother seemed like she was trying to get her shit together. She had kept me in the loop when I was away, writing me letters often, telling me about her journey to sobriety. Telling me she was attending meetings and had found a sponsor. Busying herself with Stacey and Laura, too. Barely ever mentioning my old man, as if he didn't exist in her life anymore.

I saw Mia more often than I saw Noah. Driving in with Mason so he could kiss Giselle's ass, who hadn't forgiven him for enlisting in the first place. Pippin was still the smart-ass baby girl, wise beyond her fucking years. I found myself looking forward to the next time I saw the now fourteen-year-old spitfire. One morning a few weeks after I left, they said my name during mail call. It shocked the shit out of me, I never expected to receive mail from her, not in a million years. But when Mia set her mind on something, come hell or high water, she was going to make it happen.

There was an envelope with pink handwriting from Mia Ryder, AKA Pippin. She wrote me letters every so often, each time sending a new patch. Telling me all about what was happening back in the states, what was going on with her life, how her daddy still didn't let her do anything. How surfing was her only source of freedom. Telling me she had placed first in a local surfing contest, taking down some of the best. Kicking their asses. And how much she prayed for Mason and me, missing us both.

I actually started looking forward to her letters. Taking in the little bit of happiness and fucking sunshine she brought into my life. She was a breath of fresh air in this death-infested land. But on most days, I was just left alone with only my thoughts and memories.

Fighting my demons, as I protected my country.

There was a small manmade lake just off Pepperbush Drive in Woodland Parks. I'd ride my bike there often, just to have some peace and quiet. A secluded place I could be alone with my thoughts. Away from the busy beaches of Oak Island. I had discovered it after Uncle Austin bought his house on the property, exploring the area one day when we were there for a barbecue.

I took the dirt road down to my special spot at the lake, parking my bike near the willow tree. I grabbed my sunglasses, radio, and headphones from my backpack, and headed down to the water's edge. Slipping off my sandals near the shoreline, I waded through the tall grass into the murky warm water. Letting the hot sun beam down on me as I listened to the crickets chirp.

Finding peace amongst the world's chaos.

I climbed up onto the rope swing that hung just above the water off a willow branch. Put my headphones on, scrolled through my songs, and found what I was looking for. I started to swing to the soft melody of "Broken" by Seether. Watching the ground beneath me blur into one. Singing at the top of my lungs when the song hit my favorite part.

When all of a sudden the swing jerked back, almost sending me into the water. I let out a scream, turning back to see who was behind me. Never expecting to see him.

Creed.

"Got some set of lungs on ya," he chuckled, letting go of the swing.

"What the hell? You scared the shit out of me!" I exclaimed, immediately hopping off the swing. Kicking water up, splashing him.

He grinned in that Creed, smartass sort of way. Cocking his head to the side, he challenged, "Don't start a war you can't win, Pippin."

"Oh yeah, soldier?" I never took my eyes off his as I tossed all my stuff next to my sandals on the shoreline, so it wouldn't get wet.

With a shit-eating grin on my face, I leaned forward, building up the anticipation of what I was about to do. Pushing my hands through the water, I shoved a huge wave into his face.

He stepped back, his eyes widening in shock of what I'd done. "Don't try me," he dared, hiding back a smile.

"I thought I already did." I splashed him again, this time with much more water in my hands. Not caring he was wearing his cut, which still didn't have any of my patches on it. "Do it one more time and watch what happens, baby girl."

"Hmmm…" I contemplated, placing my finger on the corner of my lips. "I'm not a baby, I'm almost fifteen! And the name's Pippin! Get it straight!"

I didn't give him a chance to reply before I went full force, splashing him as much as I could. Laughing my ass off the entire time, never letting up. Throwing heaps of water at him.

I vaguely heard him say, "Can't bitch, I warned ya."

"Wha—" He threw me over his shoulder as if I weighed nothing. Catching me by surprise. Holding the back of my knees to keep me locked in place.

"Wait! What are you doing? This isn't fair! You're bigger than me!" I shouted, pressing my hands on his back to look up and see where we were going.

He walked deeper into the lake, not caring he was getting his jeans completely soaked.

"NO! I don't want to go in there, Creed! I'm wearing a pretty dress! Please!" I pleaded, kicking and screaming. His hands shifted to grip onto my waist, getting ready to do the unthinkable. I held onto him tighter, even though I knew it didn't matter, he was stronger than me.

"Beggin' won't work in this situation, Pippin. Shoulda' thought of that before you decided you wanted to go to war with a soldier. I don't lose."

"I'm sorry! I was just playing! Put me down! Please!"

"Alright, only cuz you asked so nicely."

I smiled, thinking I'd won. I couldn't have been more wrong. All of a sudden he lifted me up by my waist, tearing my arms off of him, and hurling me into the air. I landed in the lake, submerged in water. My whole body going under.

"You asshole!" I shouted, coming up from under the water, swimming back over to him. Stumbling to my feet, once I was standing in knee-deep water. I looked down with my hands out at my sides. "Look! Look what you did to my pretty white dress! It's ruined now!"

I peered up, glaring, ready to give him hell, but the expression on his face rendered me speechless. His eyes roamed my soaking wet body. Starting from my hips to my chest and up to my face with a predatory regard. Our eyes locked for a split second, and he reached up, wiping a droplet of water from my cheek. His warm thumb stirred emotions deep inside of me, causing my lips to part and my body to shudder. I swear I could see his walls slowly crumbling down, revealing a look I had never seen from him before.

As fast as it happened, it was gone. He shook it off, clearing his throat, stepping back and looking away from me. Lost in his own thoughts. He rubbed the back of his head while an uncomfortable silence filled the air between us.

I didn't understand what had just happened, or what earned me that look, all I knew was…

I liked it.

A lot.

I followed the wake of his stare, looking down at my dress again. Finally realizing the white flowy cotton clung to my body like a second skin. Accentuating my curves and breasts. The outline of my cream bra and panties showed through the very see-through fabric.

I swallowed hard.

Suddenly feeling exposed and vulnerable, but I didn't move to cover myself up. For the first time in my life, I felt as though someone was looking at me as the woman I was becoming, and not the baby girl everyone kept saying I still was.

It wasn't just anyone…

It was Creed.

And I loved that more than anything.

"My dress—" He took off his cut, throwing it on the shore beside my things. Reaching for the hem of his white shirt next, pulling it over his head and taking it off.

"Here," he interrupted, throwing it at me. Still looking away.

I grinned. Bringing it up to my nose for a second before slipping it on. Wanting to memorize his scent. Giggling as I took in my appearance, "I look like I'm wearing a potato sack."

He turned, facing me again, crossing his arms over his chest. Just when I thought it couldn't get any more uncomfortable, this added a whole new spin on the awkwardness.

My mouth almost dropped open at the sight of the man standing in front of me. His body was so tense from what just happened between us, showing off every sleek muscle and tattoo. He was covered in ink, from his sculpted chest, down to his carved abs, emphasizing his eight-pack.

His boots were submerged in the lake, soaking the bottom of his jeans. The heaviness of the water dragged them down his slender waist, showing off a V right above his happy trail. Which, that in itself, did all sorts of things to me. His tattooed arms were defined, toned, and bulky, only adding to his tall, husky frame.

He was a real life bad boy.

I. Couldn't. Breathe.

He followed my stare down to his exposed body, exactly the way I just did moments ago when he was peering at me. Looking back up to my face, he pursed his lips, trying not to grin. It was my turn to look away from him, even though I didn't want to. My cheeks were flushed, my heart raced, rapidly beating hard against my chest, making me weak in the knees. His silence only made things more awkward between us.

I hated it as much as I loved it.

"Don't look bad wearin' my shirt, potato sack and all," he remarked, finally breaking the silence.

I blushed, looking back over at him. Smirking, I replied, "You make it a habit of following girls out to the lake?"

"Not since I was twelve," he drawled out, placing his hands in his pockets, accentuating his strong build.

It was baffling how a grown man could look bigger every time he came around. I didn't see him or my brother very often, even though they were only stationed in Fort Bragg, two hours away from Oak Island. Both of them held high positions in the army which had them deployed on missions or in training a lot. Creed was Mason's sergeant in their special forces unit. He was a weapons specialist, and Mason was an engineer who blew shit up.

I would always count down the days for their return, even if I only saw them for a few hours. Mason would come home on leave for a few weeks, but I never saw Creed when he did.

Things hadn't been the same since Mason left over two-and-a-half years ago. My momma and Stacey were a nervous wreck on most days, worrying if their baby boy was okay. Especially when they were off on missions or deployed. Momma jumped every time the phone rang, thinking bad news was waiting for her on the other end.

Dad busied himself with work and acted like nothing had changed. But we all knew he was just as worried, he was good about keeping his emotions in check. Momma, on the other hand, was not. Life at home just wasn't the same without Mason. It was definitely quieter, though.

We all missed him and prayed every night he was safe. Looking forward to his next letter he'd send monthly, whenever he could.

Not much had changed with me, except my body, which only had my dad implementing more rules. Adding to the never-ending list of things I couldn't do. I was suffocating in my own home, more so than ever before. No one understood where I was coming from, it was a battle I'd never win, but I refused to stop fighting. I drowned myself in school, work, and surfing, when all I really wanted was to feel like I belonged.

"I didn't know you were coming to visit with Mason. When did you guys get in? Wait... how did you know I was down here?" I asked, putting my hands on my hips, cocking my head to the side. Giving him a questioning glare.

He cleared his throat again, rasping in a hoarse tone, "Was sittin' up at the diner, saw you rollin' by."

"Ah, so you did follow me."

"Why the sad song, Pippin'?" he asked, ignoring my question. "Boy break your heart? I'll break his fuckin' legs."

I laughed for what felt like the first time in months. "You need boys to talk to you before they can break your heart," I confessed, walking to my stuff by the shoreline.

I sat down, leaning back on my hands, leaving my feet dangling in the lake. Creed followed, sitting beside me, putting his cut back on. He pulled out his cigarettes.

"Look what you did." He nodded, throwing the wet pack of smokes in between us.

"Serves you right. They're bad for you anyway."

"Is that right?" he drawled out, sarcastically. "Never heard that one before."

"Fine." I shrugged. "I'll start smoking too then."

"The fuck you are," he scoffed out, chuckling. "So what's this about boys not talkin' to ya?" Staring at the side of my face.

I shrugged again not knowing what to say.

"Don't need boys to talk to ya anyway. Got enough men in your life to make up for those little shits."

I rolled my eyes. "You sound like my dad. Between him and my uncles, no guys have even made it to the front door. I'm almost fifteen, Creed, and I've never even been kissed. Do you know what it's like to be the only girl in ninth grade who's never been on a date or been kissed?" I questioned, looking up at him. "All my friends have, it's all they talk about when we hang out, which isn't often anymore. Most of them already have boyfriends who they spend every waking moment with." Sighing, I took a deep breath.

"Never said a thing about it in your letters."

"You want to hear about my love life or lack thereof?" I arched an eyebrow. "You know how my dad is… you think that's changed? Hell no. It's only gotten worse, especially since Mason took off. Bo doesn't cause half of the trouble he did. They have nothing to do but focus on me."

"You're a baby girl," he simply stated.

"Is that why you never write me back?"

He placed his hands on his knees. "Don't think your daddy would appreciate that."

"Ugh!" I blurted, knowing he was right. He would lose his shit if a letter from Creed came addressed to me. "It's so frustrating. I can't date. I can barely leave my house without my dad on my ass, asking me where I'm going. He's never going to let me grow up. There's a dance at school next week and I didn't even get asked, nor am I allowed to go. I'm going to end up alone with twenty cats, wearing shirts that say 'Meow's it going.'"

He let out a throaty laugh from deep within his chest.

My eyes widened, caught off guard by his reaction. "It's not funny! I'm gonna be the cat lady, and you're laughing!"

"I'll lay it out for you, Pippin," he muttered through his laughter, shaking his head. "Boys your age just wanna get laid. Shit... men in general just wanna piece of ass. They don't care about anythin' but your legs spreadin', especially when their balls just dropped. And the bullshit they feed is just so you'll let 'em in."

"Oh..." I jerked back, glancing over at him. "Were you... I mean... you know... did you... do stuff... you know, like that too?"

"Naw, sweetheart. I'm an honest asshole."

"What about Autumn? I thought she was your girlfriend. I mean... she was... gorgeous. I wish I looked like her."

He narrowed his eyes at me, contemplating what he was going to say. "Don't ever try to be somethin' you ain't. You're perfect the way you are, yeah?"

My belly fluttered, but I warily nodded, looking back out at the water.

"To hell with those little shits who won't stand up for you. You'll meet a man one day who'll love ya and show ya. Takin' names for whoever steps in his fuckin' way. And he'll be one lucky bastard to have you as his woman by his side."

"You really think so?"

"I know so. You're only gonna be fifteen, sweetheart, got your whole life ahead of ya."

I smiled, big and wide.

I knew I was still young. I knew Creed was a lot older than I was, always would be. I knew we were from opposite sides of the tracks, always had been. Probably always would be. But I also knew right then and there, I wanted him to be that man in my life. The one he just described with so much sincerity and love in his voice.

ROAD to NOWHERE

Knowing with every last beat of my still young heart…

I always had.

I walked into the debriefing tent just after zero-four-hundred in the morning to receive instructions on our next mission. It was the tail-end of my third deployment to Afghanistan since entering the military for over three years prior. I hadn't been home in six months.

The debriefing tents were like classrooms, with rows of desks and folding chairs. All situated around white boards with instructions and notes. Pictures of enemies, territories, and intelligence projected up on a screen. Who needed to be found and taken down.

Dead or fucking alive.

The last four months of this deployment had been pure Hell on earth.

The same old bullshit every single day on repeat. Embarking on endless foot-patrol missions that would last for two to three weeks at a time. Literally eating shit, having no clue what it really was. It was either choke it down or fucking starve. We took turns sleeping in ditches or in the mud with one eye open, waiting for the insurgents to emerge from the goddamn hills. Always feeling like we were being watched. Our finger on the trigger of our guns at all times, ready to unleash on the enemies at any given moment.

Days were long and the nights even longer.

We climbed every fucking mountain. Searching every cave for a man I started to believe didn't fucking exist to begin with. Raiding villages, gaining intel that led us nowhere but chasing our own fucking asses. Sniffing out insurgents like fucking rabid dogs. Using any measures necessary to get the cocksuckers to fucking talk.

The crazy part about all of it was being back in Afghanistan, almost felt like home. We all felt that way. Being a civilian was much harder than being a solider. War will fuck you up to the point where nothing would make sense when you came back to the states. Our minds always on the battlefield along with the souls we'd fucking taken. That was another thing the military didn't prepare you for.

Real life.

Readjusting to normal life was the hardest fucking pill to swallow. It was so fucking difficult to switch your normalcy back on, and turn off the 'kill or be killed' mentality at all times of the day. The littlest things like a lawn mower starting, or a ceiling fan spinning around could trigger things in my mind that I didn't even fucking know were there. A momentary lapse in judgment would occur between not knowing where you were, or how you should react.

I lived and breathed war for months at a time. We were under constant attack—car bombs, suicide bombers, roadside bombs, mortars, motherfuckers looking at you like they fucking hated you, day in and day out.

I killed enemies.

I lost brothers.

Exactly like the MC.

The long periods of violence were a psychological beating. In the real world, I was suspicious, tightly wound, and easily angered. If I thought my temper was bad before, well I couldn't have been more wrong about that. I'd wake up several times throughout the night, freaking the fuck out that I couldn't find my gun. The fight or flight mentality I had, became just fight.

It now became my life.

Always waiting for the other shoe to fucking drop, always on alert, always waiting to kill what I couldn't fucking see.

These missions all required the same thing, finesse and stealth-like abilities, which only a hand full of special operations teams could pull off. My team, the one I was in charge of, was the best of the fucking best, a group of ruthless motherfuckers who feared nothing. Dropped into the shittiest conditions imaginable, enduring the worst possible situations known to man.

And coming back for more.

We headed into the drop zone that day, active combat duty. About fifteen miles out we were informed to get ready. A group of assholes was already spotted heading in our direction by another U.S. team of soldiers. My unit bunked down in a wooded area about two miles from some local villages and started scouting the area. Rifles loaded and fucking ready to shoot, stepping one foot in front of the other, listening all around for any sign of the fuckers.

I put my left hand up, signaling to continue. "All clear," I informed through my radio.

Looking through my scope, turning right and left. We trucked through the woods, trying to be as invisible as possible. Blending in with nature. Not even my breathing could get out of sync. The more treacherous the situation, the calmer I was.

See, my worst nightmares had already come true, there was nothing left for me to fear but fear itself.

My adrenaline worked overtime, knowing the enemy was close, but I had no visual at all. All my actions and orders needed to be calculated and precise. My hearing only heightened with every step I took toward the direction of danger.

Suddenly, screams echoed in the distance, halting our descent. I signaled my team to stop, pointing to my ear and then out front of me. More commotion just outside the village we were approaching filled the wooded area. A whizzing noise sounded to my right, instantly followed by a hard thud. My initial instinct was to fall to the ground, but I ignored that feeling.

"Fuck! Get down!" I bellowed through my radio. Looking over to find Andrews, laying on his back a few feet away, not moving. Blood ran down his face, into the earth. My team took cover, ducking behind trees, lying on their stomachs in the mud. Scoping the area to find the motherfucker who opened fire. Four or five Afghani militants were coming upon us fast.

There was no time to think.

No time to breathe.

No time to get the fuck out of there.

"Take those motherfuckers out! Now!" I shouted over the noise of bullets flying inches away from taking my life. Women screaming, shots blaring with open fire all around as I made my way to him.

"Andrews! You stay with us! Do you hear me? Fight. Motherfucker! Today is not your day to die!" I screamed, wading through the mud, ducking left and right. Dodging the copper rounds from the enemies and my own men, trying to get over to him. Another bullet flew past me, this time grazing my left shoulder.

"Ughhhhh…Fuck!" I gritted, bringing my right hand up to the wound, feeling how bad I was hit. Blood came oozing out of my arm onto my fingers. "Fucking cocksucker!"

Grabbing my rifle, I aimed right at the asshole responsible, shooting his ass down dead in his tracks. Falling to my knees next to Andrews who was still unresponsive. I didn't have to check for a pulse, I knew by the gaping hole in his forehead he was gone. I stripped him of his gun and ammo, grabbing his helmet that had a picture of his wife Deb and their brand-new baby girl secured in it. A letter peeking out through his pocket.

I did the sign of the cross over his body, muttering, "Ashes to ashes, dust to dust, and all that fucking shit."

The first time we lost one of our own in the line of duty I didn't know how to send off the soldier, so I found myself doing the exact same sentiment I had seen my father do too many goddamn times to count. I was never a religious man, and that seemed better than saying nothing at all.

"I'm so sorry, brother… we will take every last one of these bastards down."

"Creed!" Mason yelled, bringing my attention to him, pointing north.

I looked up through the clearing, revealing a scene of complete horror unfolding in the village. Insurgents dragging girls out of the village school by their hair, kicking and screaming. I knew what was in the cards for these girls, and it took every last fiber of my being not to rush in there and take down every last son of a bitch.

Mason came running over, dodging bullets and falling next to us. Breaking me away from the scene. "Creed, you hit?"

"You seein' this?" I seethed, nodding over to them.

Ignoring my question, he asked again. "Are you hit?"

"For fuck's sake, I'm fine, just a graze. We need to do somethin' before those bastards rape and then murder them all. Help me get Andrews over to that fallen tree."

I nodded toward the massive log, laying just a few feet away. Slipping his pictures and letter into my pocket. Wanting to make sure I personally delivered them to his wife, if and when we got out of here. Owen covered us as we lifted Andrews' limp body by his pack and dragged him to the tree.

The first rule of fucking war.

No soldier was left behind.

None of us had time to reflect on another stolen life. On another solider not returning home to his wife and kids. On another innocent life taken.

"Sergeant Jameson to headquarters, do ya copy?" I radioed as Owen took some gauze from his pack and started wrapping my arm tight like a tourniquet. He was our medic.

"Copy, Jameson. This is Major Douglas from headquarters."

"We got one soldier dead and several wounded," I informed, cupping my ear to muffle out the sound all around us. Searching the area. "We're near Hesarak, located 33° 59' 49" North, 69° 2' 23" east of Lowgar. We have a visual on the village, several Taliban men are raidin' an all-girls schoolhouse. Fuckin' pullin' them out by their goddamn hair, beatin' them and doin' God knows what else. We're going in. I repeat… we're going in."

"Stand down, soldier!"

"What?" I jerked back, holding the receiver closer to my ear, thinking I didn't hear him correctly.

"You heard me! You stand the fuck down!" Major Douglas's voice screeched through the radio. "That village is none of the U.S. Government's concern. It is not part of your mission, Sergeant. Do you hear me? You stand the fuck down. That's an order! Do you copy?"

"You shittin' me right now? We're not gonna sit back and watch innocent little girls get fuckin' raped and killed when we can help them. We got visual of another U.S. Army Troop right outside the premises. We can take these motherfuckers down, complete our missions and be back by dinner. We're going in!"

Once the coast was clear, I stood, ignoring the surge of pain radiating down my arm, and the blood dripping from my fingers.

"Creed! You heard him! Stand down!" Owen yelled after me.

"If you want those baby girls' lives on your conscience, then you're one fucked-up soldier! Grab your shit and let's go, you fuckin' pussy! Won't tell you again. That's an order."

Major Douglas's voice came back over the radio again. "The fuck you are, soldier! Stand down! They have orders not to return fire, not to engage in any way. You go in there, you are dead! We must pick and choose our battles, and this is not our battle to fight. Now stand the fuck down, Jameson."

I didn't hesitate, I ran as fast as I fucking could, but not fast enough. A little girl's agonizing screams filled my ears as I watched her take punch after punch to her tiny frame. Her face nearly unrecognizable from the distance between us. Covered in her own blood and dirt. Muffled by the impact of his fists. My vision tunneled the closer I got. Another rush of adrenaline coursed through me as my heart pumped in my ears at a rapid speed as if I was having a goddamn heart attack.

All I saw was red.

All I wanted was to save them.

Even if it would cost my life.

Another Taliban towered over the girl, ripping her panties off, letting his artillery belt fall to the dirt as he unzipped his pants and pulled out his cock.

"That's an order!" I heard the major's voice echo through the woods from the radio.

"You can take your order and shove it up your fuckin' ass!" I barely got the last word out when a bullet struck my thigh, tripping me up. Time seemed to pick that moment to suddenly slow down.

Everything happened in slow motion.

I fell forward, screaming, "Nooooooo!" As another bullet blurred past my face, an AK47 from behind me struck an Afghani running toward me right between the eyes as I hit the ground.

Mason may have saved my life, but what I was forced to witness in the coming minutes nearly fucking killed me in itself.

"Soldier down! I repeat… Sergeant Jameson is down," Mason's muffled voice announced over the radio.

"Fuck! Goddamn it! I have a helicopter en route. ETA—fifteen minutes."

"Copy that," Mason stated, suddenly lifting me over his shoulder, walking us back to the unit where they took cover.

We were all forced to witness the deaths of the little girls. None of us made a sound as we watched the brutal violence unfolding in front of us. I swear you could hear their screams miles from the village.

The last bit of our morality was taken from all of us that day as we sat there, allowing the motherfuckers to rip away their innocence. Thrusting in and out of them, beating them until they were no longer screaming, laughing and fucking enjoying themselves the entire time.

Their horrid screams filled the air, bringing my squad to their goddamn knees. Helplessly covering their ears, silently breaking down.

They silently prayed to the Lord above to forgive them for their sins. I fucking cursed him for allowing it to begin with. This wasn't the first, and it wouldn't be the last we were told to stand down.

Only fueling my hatred for our government.

I went to school that day never expecting what was to come. Rick was in a bunch of my classes that semester at school. Most of my classes were advanced. I was only a Sophomore, but he was in Junior classes. He was the only boy who paid me any mind. Taking every opportunity to flirt with me, asking to borrow a pencil, or questions about math he didn't understand. I knew it was a ploy. I saw all his tests and assignments were A's when our math teacher handed them back.

After the final bell rang at school, I went to my locker to put my books away, and a piece of paper fell to my feet. I picked it up, turned it over and it said, "You and me, Friday night? - Rick."

My stomach dropped, my cheeks warmed, and my hands suddenly became clammy. I peeked around my locker door and locked eyes with him.

Grinning, he mouthed, "So?" from down the hall.

I looked from him to the paper and back, nodding a little too excitedly. Happy on the outside, but flipping the fuck out on the inside. My dad was not going to approve.

Later that day, we had it out to say the least. Hands were flying, feet were stomping, trying to talk some sense into his stupid head.

"Dad! I am fifteen years old! You can't keep treating me like a baby!" I yelled from the kitchen island. He was helping Momma prepare dinner.

"Mia Alexandra Ryder, you're not going out with that boy. End of story."

"You just full-named me?! And no! The story has just begun! Dad, he's a good kid. Smart, athletic, loves fast cars. Did I mention smart?"

"I don't care if he is the president of the chess club, has braces and zits. You're not going on a date."

"Come on, Daddy! You were fifteen once. Give me a break! I'm not asking to get married! I'm asking to go hang out. Be a normal teenager. Don't you trust me?"

"It's him I don't trust, Mia. And yes, I was fifteen once, not a good example to compare yourself to by any means, baby girl." He gave me a smug look, causing Momma to chuckle under her breath.

Papa once told me that Dad was an asshole to Mom when they were kids, and he was surprised she even forgave him for all the stuff he put her through. I bit my tongue, wanting to blurt this tidbit of information out, so he could see that he wasn't perfect. That I deserved a chance to make mistakes and learn from them like he did, but I decided against it.

Instead, I played the girl-card and went for Momma.

"Mom, you know what it's like to be a girl. Talk some sense into your husband. Enlighten him, please!"

"Lucas, I have met this boy's parents. He's a good seed. I say she goes."

"He better not do anything with his seed, especially plant it."

"Are we still talking about Rick? Or gardening?" I looked at them, dumbfounded. "So, I can go?"

"Fine. But on one condition." He set down the knife he was using to chop up potatoes. "Mason will be home on leave in a few days. If you want to go on this… date," he said, struggling to say the last word. "Your brother will have to agree to go along."

I jumped off my chair and ran over to him, giving him a big squeeze hug. Almost knocking him to the floor. "Thank you! Thank you! Thank you!"

"Don't thank me yet. Your brother hasn't said yes."

Mason came home a few days later like Dad said. I tackled him at the door, hugging him tight, telling him how much I missed him. Right to asking him if he'd come on my date with me that Friday night. He looked at me like I had two heads, but Giselle agreed immediately, and he wasn't in the right position to say no to her.

Much like my dad…
Mason was putting Giselle through shit, too.

I spent two weeks recovering in the military hospital on base, after being shot up in the woods. I should have embraced the fucking down-time, but I hated knowing my men were out on missions without me. I passed the time flirting with the nurses, seeing how many I could get to suck my cock after hours.

Playing the I'm-a-wounded-soldier card.

I got more pussy in those two weeks than I had in months. You'd be surprised how many women were willing to serve their country on their knees.

Getting a slap on the wrist, so to speak, for my actions of not standing down like I was ordered to do by my major. My only saving grace from being fucking demoted was that I was really good at what I did. We were our own entity, and most of the time we did whatever the fuck we wanted, anyway. But once I was discharged, my major handled it with me behind closed doors, man to fucking man.

Meaning he punched me in the goddamn face a few times, rendering me to the ground, and getting another few good hits on my chest, face, and stomach. Threatening me if I ever disobeyed him again, he wouldn't think twice about taking away my fucking rank. For once in my life, I took every last hit like a fucking man, even though I could have taken him the fuck out. I was just grateful it was only my body that was taking the brunt of his punishment.

We were back in the states, on leave for two weeks. Owen was heading home to Arkansas to see his family and new baby girl. His wife gave birth to their first kid while we were footing the hills. I had never seen a grown man cry like he did when we returned to base. His wife sent him a video recording from the delivery room her mom had taken for him.

"Want to head out with us tonight?" Mason asked as I walked through the door of Giselle's apartment.

I'd spent most of the day with Diesel, throwing back some beers at a local bar and shooting the shit. Bringing me up to speed on what'd been happening at the club in my absence. Everything from official business down to how many new whores he had fucked.

We talked about how my old man pretty much made the clubhouse his permanent residence. Officially abandoning Ma, but still giving her money to live on. Adding to what I sent her every month. Like that made things right.

He still hadn't changed, he was still shady as fuck.

"You can help me scare the shit out of him," Mason added as I sat down in the armchair next to them, throwing my keys on the coffee table. Wondering who the fuck they were talking about.

"I think it's cute," Giselle chimed in, bringing my attention to her. "I don't mind chaperoning at all. You're just pissed your baby sister is going on her first date. Get over it, Mason, she's fifteen now. It's about damn time your dad let her do something normal. Do you know what I had to go through just to go take her to get her nails done and to shop for a new outfit today? That poor girl is stuck at home all the time. Much like me waiting for you," she emphasized, pushing her finger into his chest.

I leaned forward, resting my elbows on my knees. Arching an eyebrow, I asked, "Mia's goin' on a date?" Caught off guard.

Mason sighed, "Yeah."

"With who?"

"Some fucking ass-clown at her school, who's been on her ass to go out with him for the last month. I don't fuckin' know, probably some fucking douche who pops his collar, wearing polos and khakis. I guess my mom laid into my dad's ass to let her go on a date. He only agreed to let her go if I would go with them. Mia begged me as soon as we walked through the door last night," he stated, nodding to Giselle. "And this one being the hopeless romantic she is, champed at the fuckin' bit."

Giselle smiled, wide. "What if they end up getting married?" She clapped her hands together enthusiastically. "We can say we were there on their first date! Oh my god, she showed me a picture of him, and he's so cute! They're going to make pretty babies."

"The fuck?" I snapped at her exaggerated bullshit.

"No shit," he agreed. "You in?"

"Meet ya there. Got some business to take care of."

I quickly showered at Giselle's, putting on a clean pair of jeans, a white shirt I had packed with me, and my cut. Sliding my gun in the back of my jeans before throwing on my leather jacket. I jumped on my bike and sped off toward the warehouse where my meeting was taking place. All I could think about was handling business and getting the fuck out. Feeling the need to put that little shit in his place if he laid one hand on Mia.

I pulled into the lot, parking beside Martinez's limo. Taking off my helmet, I nodded to his fucking welcoming party of five armed men wearing black suits. One of them opened the back door, gesturing for me to step inside.

I did, taking a seat across from the arrogant motherfucker in a black three-piece suit.

"You're late."

Eyeing him up and down with a cocky grin. "Just gettin' all pretty for you," I snidely replied. Locking eyes with Martinez.

"I don't wait for anyone. Don't let it happen again."

"I'll remember that the next time I decide to actually give a fuck. Now, gonna handle business, or just sit here and waste my fuckin' time."

He pulled out a disk from inside his suit jacket, handing it to me.

I cocked my head to the side, flipping it around in my hand to read the inscription: "Truths."

"This it?"

"Were you expecting a goddamn pony? It has everything you need. Now get the fuck out."

I opened the door. "As always... it was a fuckin' pleasure."

I didn't give him or the disk anymore thought. Sticking it inside the pocket of my leather jacket, I jumped back on my bike, revved the engine, and took off. Parking my bike near the back entrance of the bowling alley just after eight, I removed my leather jacket and securely fastened it to the back of my bike. Placing my helmet on top of it.

The place was crowded with kids running all over, screaming, laughing, and already annoying the hell out of me as I tried to make my way through the adolescent chaos. I spotted Mia before anyone else. She wasn't hard to fucking miss, showing more skin than I'd ever seen before. She was wearing a cream-colored dress that was

M. ROBINSON

way too fucking short and hung low on her chest. Her cowboy boots only added to her cutesy goddamn outfit.

The cocky little shit standing in front of her couldn't have been taller than five-feet-ten, weighing no more than a buck-seventy. Wearing a salmon-colored polo shirt, dark jeans, and Nike's.

The kid definitely came from money.

He wasn't staring at her face while she was yapping away. His eyes never left her cleavage that was on full display. She just stood there twirling the ends of her hair, as her body softly swayed to the shitty pop music playing through the speakers. He reached up, brushing a stray piece of hair behind her ear, grinning.

She gave the bastard a look I knew far too fucking well.

Mason and Giselle were nowhere to be found, and I instantly knew that was Giselle's doing. Probably saying some bullshit like they needed to be left alone.

The fuck they did.

I made my way toward them, grabbing her jean jacket off the table, and shoving it in front of her. Stepping in between them.

"A little cold in here, yeah?" I announced, turning my back to her date, nodding to her tits.

She jerked back, caught off guard, narrowing her eyes at me. Following it up with a questioning glare.

"I didn't know you slummed, Mia. Who's the guy in the vest?" the little shit behind me asked, making his presence known. I looked over my shoulder to lay into the motherfucker for his comment but was stopped when I felt a hand on my chest. Bringing my attention back to her.

Mia shoved her jacket into my chest. "Don't ruin this for me," she mouthed.

I crossed my heart with my index fingers, giving her a shit-eating grin. She sighed, rolling her eyes, then stepped around me and started to talk to her date again.

I turned, putting my arm around her, placing the jean jacket on her shoulders.

"What are you doing here?" she questioned, slipping it off her shoulders and draping it over her arm. Knowing better than to put it back down on the table.

"Aren't ya gonna introduce me to the boy?"

194

ROAD to NOWHERE

"Oh, where are my manners," she sassed, shaking her head. "Creed, this is Rick. Rick, this is Creed, one of my brother's best friends. Happy? Now what are you doing here?"

"Nice to meet ya, Dick."

"Rick," he corrected.

"That's what I said. Didn't Mason tell you he invited me? I wouldn't miss this," I paused, gesturing between her and Dick, "for the world."

She shot me a warning look.

"Said you needed babysittin'. Where the fuck is he anyway?" I backed away, looking around the arcade.

"Over there, finding us a table to eat while we wait for the lanes to open up. Giving *Rick* and I some space to talk and hang out, you know the things you do on a date," she stated, emphasizing the last word. "Maybe you should go help them out."

"Naw, I'm good."

She rolled her eyes again, trying to initiate conversation with the fucking pretty boy standing in front of her. Talking about some bullshit that didn't matter. Mason waved us over to the table after a few minutes of her pretending like I wasn't even there.

"Ladies first," I insisted, gesturing for Mia to lead the way, stepping in close behind her so I could cut off her pretty-boy date.

I could hear him grumbling under his breath as we walked over to the table. At the last second, I decided to stop at the bar, grabbing Mason, Giselle, and myself had a beer, Mia a sweet tea, and Dick a chocolate milk in a fucking kiddie cup. Mia scowled when I handed it to him, but Mason chuckled under his breath, I thought it was pretty fucking funny.

"Just tryin' to be polite," I murmured into the side of her face, taking a seat beside her.

Dinner carried on. Mason and Giselle talked about what they were doing during our leave, not paying any attention to anyone else at the table. While Mia hung on every word that left Dick's fucking mouth. I just sat there like the odd man out, sipping my beer. Taking in all the bullshit he was spouting to her.

"My dad owns a blue 1968 Plymouth Roadrunner with a 340 six-pack that's 500 horsepower. When I turn seventeen next month, it's all mine. Maybe you and I can head up the coast, take a drive or something," he suggested, winking, causing her cheeks to turn bright red.

"Oh my God, that is so awesome. My uncles are into fast cars," Mia replied, leaning over the table, twirling her hair around her finger. Acting like she really knew what the little shit was talking about.

"Do you like fast things?" he implied, cocking a smile, brushing his thumb over her hand on top of the table. I resisted the urge to break his fucking fingers.

"Damn... at least know your shit when tryin' to impress your girl. A 1968 Plymouth Roadrunner with a 340 six pack can only have 290 horsepower. That's like sayin' you gotta ten-inch cock when it's really five," I chimed in, shrugging. Taking another swig of my beer, eying him over the rim.

Mia choked on her drink, clearing her throat, bringing his attention back to her. "I'd love to take a drive with you one day." She smiled.

"Good luck with that, *Dick*. Her daddy is like a rabid guard dog, just waitin' to rip a boy to shreds. Why do ya think this is her first—" Mia's foot connected with my shin, kicking me under the table.

I grinned. "Goin' to the bar." Pushing out my stool, I headed over to get another beer. Keeping my eye on the table while I waited. Watching Mia toss her hair, taking animatedly with her hands.

All while the cocksucker's eyes strayed to her cleavage.

I decided to stay at the bar, trying to play nice. Mason and Giselle eventually made their way over, giving the couple some space. They downed some beers with me and then took off. Saying their lane opened up or some shit. I kept my eyes on Mia and her date, knowing where they were at all times. Roaming around before stopping to play a couple games of bowling. Taking a lane a few rows down from Mason and Giselle's. I would catch her glancing my way from time to time, flashing her contagious fucking smile at me. Looking so goddamn grown.

Where did the baby girl with pigtails go?

It was like she grew up overnight. Wearing makeup, highlighting her bright blue eyes and plump pouty lips that were almost too big for her tiny face. Her dark brown hair long and straight, cascading down her slender back.

Smelling so fucking good.

I shook off the thoughts that could only bring trouble, throwing back some more beers. Trying to ignore the fact that Mia wasn't a baby girl anymore, but a fifteen-year-old turning into a young woman.

One I couldn't keep my damn eyes off of.

Five beers later, I got off my stool at the bar and headed to the bathroom to take a piss. When I came out, Mason and Giselle were back at the table, looking over to the far wall where a row of carnival-style games filled the space. The one that caught my eye was a red booth, lined with stuffed animals and a bright neon sign that said "Shooting Gallery." Mia and Dick were waiting in line to play. It was one of those games where targets would pop up and you had a few seconds to shoot them down.

Looked easier than it really fucking was.

Dick stepped up to the booth, grabbing the rifle while Mia stood back, excited to watch her pretty boy try to win her a prize. I took a seat with Mason and watched what this kid could do. He positioned the rifle at his shoulder and looked through the scope, waiting for the bell to ring.

It did. One target after another started popping up as he took shots to get them to fall. Mia was jumping up and down like a fucking cheerleader, clapping her hands, rooting him on.

Ping, ping, ping.

The BB's hit the metal targets, missing about ten when all was said and done.

"That was so good!" Mia shouted, practically fucking bouncing over to him.

The little shit handed her a small pink stuffed teddy bear, and she threw her arms around his neck. Hugging him a little too close and long for my fucking comfort.

"Creed, no," Giselle warned before I even got out of my chair. The expression on my face must have given me away.

"What? A little friendly competition won't hurt anyone, boy's gotta grow some balls sometime," I said, looking over at her.

"He needs to be pegged down a few steps. I don't like the way he's looking at her. Mia will give me shit if I do it. I don't want to hear it. Go fucking show him up," Mason agreed, nodding to me.

"Ugh!" Giselle scoffed out. "You both are terrible."

I stood, making my way over to the booth. Walking up behind Mia, who was still hugging the little shit, I whispered near her ear, "Watch this."

She jerked back, pulling away from him. Caught off guard by my voice coming up behind her. I grinned, picking up the rifle Dick had just used, and positioned myself in place.

"Ready. Set. Shoot!" the game attendant shouted. The bell rang once again.

Each target popped up and fell before it was even fully upright. I shot at every angle from where I stood, never moving my goddamn feet. One target right after the other fell over without so much as a blink of an eye. Catching the next target before it barely had a chance to move, tracking it with my gun.

A buzzer sounded over the shooting gallery, and the announcer came over the PA System, "We have a hot shooter ladies and gentleman! Let's see if he can survive the bonus round! No one ever has!"

A crowd began to gather, including Mason and Giselle. Wanting to get a glimpse of the excitement. I looked over at Mia and winked. Dick stood there with his arms crossed over his chest, pouting like the pansy ass pussy he was.

I cocked the rifle, waiting for the signal to go.

"Ready. Set. Shoot!"

This time the targets were moving, flipping up faster but falling down just as quick as before. I moved with stealth precision, white-knuckling the gun, taking out the targets like they were the fucking enemies of war. Having flashbacks of being on the battleground, killing everything that fucking moved.

The lights and buzzers echoed all around me, bringing me back to the now.

"Sir," the game attendant interrupted, bring my attention to him. I tried to shake off the haze and haunting memories.

"I have been running this game for over three years, and you are the first to kick its ass! That was awesome to watch, man! How do you know how to shoot like that?"

I set the rifle down, pulling out my dog tags from under my shirt. "You're a soldier."

"I'm a Sergeant," I corrected him.

His eyes widened. "Damn, man. Thank you for your service."

I nodded, locking eyes with Mia who was looking at me with an expression I couldn't read. As if she knew where my mind had wandered off to. Staring from me to the attendant and back to me again, taking in what he just said.

With our connection feeling stronger than it ever had before.

"Choose your prize, man. You can get anything from the top. They're the best prizes," he added.

I smiled, breaking the sudden tension between us. "Choose your prize, Pippin."

She smirked, looking away from me. Realizing it was the first time I was getting her something for a change. She pointed to the huge bear wearing camouflage, holding an American flag.

I chuckled, narrowing my eyes in on Dick. "That's how real men do it, boy." Walking past him to the other side where Mason and Giselle were standing with the rest of the bystanders.

It didn't take long for Giselle lay into me. "Wow, Creed, you are something else. You got into a pissing contest with a sixteen-year-old boy. Congrats, asshole. Poor Mia… If it's not her daddy, it's her brothers. Today it's you. I'm not going to stay around while you two terrorize her date. I'm going over to the movie theater." She abruptly turned, walking toward the doors.

"Giselle! Come on, baby, it was all in fun!" Mason called out behind her. "Fuck! Not spending the next ten day's fucking fighting with her, we do that shit enough. Do me a favor, bro. Keep an eye on Mia. Make sure the little fucker doesn't overstep. I need to go take care of that." He gestured toward the doors Giselle left out of.

I nodded.

"Thanks, man. I owe you one."

I watched him leave, chasing after Giselle. I couldn't give him too much shit. They did fight a lot. Anyone could see he loved her, but they didn't want the same things, they were so fucking different. Sometimes I wondered how much longer they could make it work.

A pissed-off Dick caught my attention from the corner of my eye. Rushing toward the exit in the back of the building where I was parked, with a concerned Mia following close behind him, hugging her bears to her chest.

They were standing by the curb when I walked out, talking. I went over to my bike, grabbed my smokes, lighting one up. Leaning against the metal frame, listening from afar.

"I'm going to call it a night," he asserted, opening his car door.

"I'm so sorry, Rick. I'm so embarrassed. I didn't know my brother would call in reinforcements," Mia apologized when she didn't fucking have to.

The little shit was leaving her there.

"Maybe next date you can leave your bodyguards at home?"

She sighed. "I don't know about that one. My dad's… I mean… maybe with time it will happen. But I'm just really happy to be out with you tonight. I mean, maybe next time—"

"How many times will you need a babysitter?" He cut her off with a look I wanted to wipe off his sorry ass fucking face.

Mia jerked back, not knowing what to say.

I didn't falter. The little shit hurt her feelings. "As many times it takes for you to realize she ain't gonna spread her legs for you, motherfucker!" I chimed in from a distance.

"CREED!" Mia turned, realizing I was there. Glaring at me.

"Sorry, Mia. I didn't sign up for this. Call me when you're allowed to grow up," he spoke over his shoulder, getting in his car. She turned back around to stop him, but he slammed the door in her face.

It took everything inside me not to go over there and teach him some goddamn manners. A little fucking respect.

He backed out of his spot, looking in his rearview mirror, watching Mia raise one of her arms up in the air, the other holding the stuffed animals we'd won for her. Not giving a fuck, he still took off.

She shook her head, dropping it in defeat once he was gone. "Why? Why, God? What have I done to deserve this," she said to herself, looking up at the sky.

"Pippin, don't be so damn dramatic," I blew out with a wad of smoke.

She slowly turned around, coming face to face with me from across the parking lot. With nothing but fury in her bright blue eyes.

She seethed, "YOU!" Marching over to me like she was going to do something.

I eyed her up and down, bringing my cigarette back up to my mouth. Struggling to hold in a laugh as she stood in front of me. All five feet nothing of her.

"How could you do that to me?!" Stomping her foot on the ground, she pointed at me. "You know how my daddy treats me, you know how my brothers do, and you know all I wanted was to experience something real. Something true! How could you ruin that for me?" she snapped, chucking one bear, then the other, at my head. I ducked, only pissing her off more.

"Only thing you were goin' to learn, sweetheart, was how to get to second base," I rasped, speaking the truth. Taking her in, nodding toward her chest. "Surprised your old man let you leave the house dressed like that. Just cuz he's wearin' a collared shirt don't mean shit. Doesn't mean he's a nice fuckin' guy."

"Well, wearin' that cut don't either!"

I never expected what would happen next.

Or maybe... I fucking did.

I always pictured my first date to be like a fairy tale. Boy meets girl, boy falls in love with girl, boy asks girl to get married. My first date didn't even make it till the end, because of a highhanded, stubborn-ass man, covered in tattoos.

Creed Jameson.

"I can't believe you did this to me! Not only did you embarrass me, you scared off the one boy who paid attention to me!" I shouted, jabbing my long index finger into his chest as hard as I could. "Who do you think you are?"

He just stood there, leaning up against his bike. One leg over the other, with his arms crossed over his broad chest. His cigarette sat on the corner of his lips while a look of amusement played on his face. A face I wanted to punch so bad. I thought my dad and brothers were horrible, but Creed took the cake. I had never been so embarrassed in my entire life.

Everything was going great until he showed up. I felt him before I even saw him walk up behind me. I'd be lying if I said I wasn't shocked as shit that he was there. The bowling alley wasn't exactly the place a man of his stature hung out at. I knew as soon as he opened his mouth my fairy-tale night would turn out a nightmare. He made a point to make Rick feel unwelcomed, uncomfortable, and unapproved of. Taking every chance he got to make my life a living hell.

I didn't falter, continuing on, "You of all people knew how important tonight was for me! How long I've waited for this! And what do you do? You ruin everything!"

"Not ruined. Protected," he simply stated, taking a drag of his cigarette.

"I don't need your protection! You're about to need some, though!" I shoved his chest as hard as I could.

He didn't waver. "Is that right?" he drawled out, smoke seeping from his lips.

"Yes, that's right! I wouldn't have said it if it weren't!" I didn't know what was worse. Him standing there all cool and collected, or the fact I couldn't get a reaction out of him.

The whole evening was an embarrassment. From him correcting Rick at dinner, insulting the size of his manhood, to showing him up at the shooting game. And all the endless jabs in between. Mason was no help either. He played along with Creed. Giselle was the only one having any sympathy for me. In the matter of a few hours, Creed drove Rick away, making him leave me on the curb with nothing but insults. All I wanted was to feel normal. To feel like a girl. Wanting a cute boy in the eleventh grade to like me.

Most of all I wanted to experience his lips on mine.

My first kiss.

I guess you couldn't always get what you wanted. Life wasn't all hearts, flowers, and unicorns. Especially when a tall, broody man rolled into your life. What he put me through all night was unacceptable, but I couldn't help notice the look in his eyes. They spoke volumes over the chaos of the bowling alley. He watched over me like a big brother, but his eyes held something more. Something that made my stomach flutter like it did all the time when he was around and my heart race out of my chest.

His penetrating glare could be felt deep within my soul from across the room. Roping me in, taking a hold of my heart and not letting go. I was conflicted. My mind and heart raged a war on each other all night.

My mind hated him for his actions, but my heart loved that he really did care.

He was just jealous.

I was over to Creed in three strides, standing on my tip-toes, getting right in his face. I was beyond pissed with him. His behavior was shitty.

I wasn't his by any means.

"Rick's going to go to school on Monday and tell everyone! I'm going to be the laughing stock of the tenth grade! I'll never get asked to go out on another date!" I yelled, shoving him even harder than before.

"Good. Let 'em run his mouth. He's no good for you. Will keep other little shits away, too."

"Ohhh… just like you're not good for me. So, tell me, Creed, will anyone ever be good enough for me in your eyes? Will I ever be good enough for you?" I threw his words back at him not giving him a chance to respond. "He was nothing but a gentleman to me! You don't get it! Tonight was supposed to be perfect!" I shoved harder.

He still didn't budge. "Pippin, he spent the whole fuckin' night starin' at your tits. All he wanted from ya was your pussy," he vulgarly blurted out.

Before I knew what I was doing, my palm connected with his cheek. Smacking him right across the face. "You don't get to talk to me like that!"

His head cocked back from the impact. I ignored the stinging pain that radiated through my hand. Pounding my fists into his chest.

Finally losing all resolve. Not caring who was watching us outside the building.

He took it all.

"All I wanted was for him to kiss me! To experience what every other girl has already done! You took that away from me, you asshole! You had no right! You ruined my fairy-tale ending!" I didn't let up on his chest, hitting him harder and harder again.

Finally, over the fact that I wasn't getting anywhere with him, I stopped. Glaring deep into his amused gaze.

He nonchalantly brought his cigarette up to his lips, took a long drag, blew the smoke above my head and flicked it to the ground.

I never expected what happened next.

Never in a million years...

He stepped forward, closing the small distance between us. His rough hands reached up and grabbed ahold of my cheeks. The smell of cigarettes, beer, and mint immediately assaulted my senses as he pulled me up to his level. Leaning in, laying his lips on mine.

He. Kissed. Me.

My eyes shut tightly, my breathing hitched, and my arms fell to my sides in defeat. All the fight in me was gone. I had no clue what to do, but stand there and feel what I had wanted for so long. His lips were rough but smooth against mine. My heart drummed so fast, I swear he could hear it. My knees went weak the longer his lips stayed on me. It was the most overwhelming, mind blowing, consuming feeling I'd ever felt in my entire life. There would be no coming back from this. Ruining me for every other boy that may come along.

As if reading my mind, he slowly parted his lips, pulling me in closer. Placing my shaking hands on his chest, I parted mine, following his lead. Matching the same rhythm he set.

His tongue touched my lips, leaving the craziest sensation in its wake. I pulled back my tongue, and he took it as an open invitation to gently push his into my awaiting mouth. His tongue sought out mine, turning the kiss into something more than I knew he intended it to be.

As if he was getting lost in me as well.

No words could come close to describing what was happening in that moment between us. The feelings he stirred deep within my core matched my emotions with each stroke of his tongue. Feelings I didn't think were possible to experience. That I didn't even think existed.

I never wanted him to stop kissing me.

A soft moan escaped my mouth as he pecked my lips one last time, gradually pulling away from me. Leaving me breathless and wanting more. Incoherent thoughts ran rapidly in my mind.

When my eyes fluttered open, he was grinning down at me, not removing his hands from the sides of my face. His amused stare hadn't changed, if anything it was worse.

He murmured against my lips, "Gave you your first kiss, now stop fuckin' bitchin'." Softly pecking me again before pulling away.

Taking everything I ever wanted.

Him.

"Are you okay? You haven't been yourself since your date. Spill," Giselle insisted, walking back into the living room at her apartment. Having a seat next to me on the couch with popcorn and the remote control in hand.

She invited me over for a much needed girls' night, full of chick flicks, mani and pedis, and popcorn. Mason was going to be out for the night, he was leaving in a few days to go back to base and wanted to see some of his old friends.

"I'm fine. I promise," I lied.

"You know, just because I'm your brother's girlfriend doesn't mean you can't talk to me, Mia. Maybe I can help." She looked over at me.

"I know. It's just… well… I'm a little confused," was all I could get out.

"Is this about your date?"

I nodded, biting my lip.

"What happened? When we came out from the movie, Rick was gone, and you and Creed looked like you were… I don't even know. Fighting? I don't blame you if you laid into him. What an asshole. It was almost like he—"

Her phone rang from the table, Mason's face flashed on the screen, interrupting her train of thought. Stopping her from saying what I knew she was about to say. I had never been so grateful for my brother as I was in that second. She picked it up and walked into the kitchen, leaving me alone with my thoughts.

"Your brother is drunkity-drunk-drunk," she chuckled, walking back into the room. Throwing her phone back on the coffee table. "Speaking of the devil, I guess Creed met up with him at the bar. He's coming home with Mason. Going to crash in the other guest room. No worries, it won't interrupt our girl time. Who knows what hour of the night they'll crawl in. They're both shameless."

I nodded again, not knowing what to say. Shocked at the fact that I would get to see him again. I hadn't seen him since he kissed me. I couldn't tell if he was avoiding me on purpose or if he was just being Creed. Going long absences before I saw him again had been our relationship since day one.

"Anyway, what was I saying?" she asked, cocking her head to the side. "Oh yes! The date. I'm so sorry, Mia. I tried really hard not to let that go down. I had no idea they'd turn into complete assholes and terrorize the kid. But you know your brother. He does what he wants and doesn't give two shits about what other people think."

"I know. How are you guys?" I replied, trying to change the subject and take the heat off me.

She sighed, "It depends on what day you ask me. Today, we are great. Yesterday, I wanted to kill him."

"Yeah..."

"I love Mason. I love him with all my heart. I've loved him ever since the first time I laid eyes on him. I wanted to marry—"

"Wanted to?" I interrupted, narrowing my eyes.

"What?"

"You just said you *wanted* to marry him. Not *want*."

She frowned. "I did?"

"Yeah..."

She looked around the room like she would find the answers written on the walls or something. "I... wow..." she breathed out, looking at me embarrassed. "I'm just... I guess... I mean... I'm tired of putting my life on hold for him."

I jerked back, surprised by her revelation.

"I feel like I have given so much of myself to him, and it's never been mutual. I'm still bitter that he enlisted in the damn Army without even talking to me first. I feel like he constantly puts me in second place. We haven't even talked about his discharge. What's going to happen when he's done serving? He has less than a year left. I have a feeling in my gut, Mia… he wants to re-enlist, and that's why we haven't talked about what's next. If he's going to battle for the United States again, he's going to have a battle with me."

I wouldn't be surprised if my brother became a permanent soldier. I had overheard some conversations he had with our parents, and I could tell he really loved his military life. He had no regrets and this wasn't some phase for him.

"If he goes. I don't think I can sit around and wait for him anymore," she confessed, looking down at her hands. "Please don't tell him I—"

"I promise. He won't hear it from me."

Looking back up at me, she smiled. Her worry immediately subsided. "So, back to you. What happened that night?"

"I don't even know," I blurted, speaking the truth.

"I liked Rick, he seemed like a nice kid. Has he tried to talk to you at school or anything?"

"Not really, but I've been avoiding him. Too embarrassed to show my face."

"Do you like him? You know… like really like him? Butterflies in the stomach, makes your heart skip a beat, sweaty palms?"

I shrugged. "I've felt that before." *Just not with Rick*, I wanted to say.

"Listen, I'm only telling you this stuff because I'd rather you hear it from me and not some teenage hussies. Boys—men in general—are stupid, Mia. Their bottom head monopolizes their thoughts. I think you're old enough now to realize that. It's not like what you see in the movies by any means. I got lucky with Mason. But for a lot of my girlfriends, the first time they had sex it was awful for them. Most guys don't know what they're doing, especially at your age. It's all about them. Totally selfish."

"But older guys do? They have experience right?" I found myself asking, turning beet red.

She grinned. "Rick's older, right?"

"He'll be seventeen next month," I answered, even though Rick was the furthest guy from my mind.

"Do you want to do any of those things, Mia? You can tell me."

My eyes widened.

"Oh my God! You do!" She got on her knees all excited. "With Rick?"

"Maybe," I lied, just to see where she was going with this.

"I would never tell you to throw yourself at a guy, that's just slutty. But if he likes you and you like him and you feel like he's a good guy, then date him. Have fun and take your time."

"Is sex and doing things... that important in a relationship? If I didn't do things, would an experienced guy bother with me?" I questioned, needing to know.

It's not like I could talk to anyone else about these things. Especially my mom, she was a saint. Of course, we talked about sex and stuff, but she just said I should wait until I was married. I guess that was every mom's advice to their daughters.

Giselle was only twenty-four. She was closer to my age and knew more about the way things happened now, compared to when my parents were growing up. It was nice to have someone to finally understand what I was going through and feel as though they weren't trying to baby me by telling me what I could and couldn't do.

I appreciated her honesty. She felt like the big sister I never had.

"I wouldn't say it was the most important thing but it's a big part of a relationship. It can be scary, but if it's the right person then it could be amazing. Sharing yourself with someone you love, it's a bond that nothing could come close to. It's a way to show someone you love them without having to say the words out loud. That being said, having sex with someone for the first time is a big deal, so before you make that leap make sure it's for you, not them. Make sense?"

"Yes. Actually, that really does make a lot of sense."

I needed to show a certain someone my love.

She beamed. "You better tell me if something happens, Mia. And if it leads to something else then you always use protection. I don't care if he says his cock will shrivel up and die if he uses a condom. You make him wrap it up," she demanded in a stern tone.

I laughed. "Okay. I promise."

"Good. Now let's watch this movie."

We spent the rest of the night immersing ourselves in romance movies that only fueled my desire for a certain tattooed, broody, handsome man. We started watching *Pearl Harbor*, one of Giselle's favorite movies. She said she loved the love story, but I knew she had a secret crush on Josh Harnett, a handsome soldier fighting for the love of his life.

The irony was not lost on me.

The further we got into the movie, the more it really resonated with me. I always knew Creed could get hurt, but I always imagined he was made of steel and nothing could bring him down. I couldn't have been more wrong, realizing very quickly that life could change in an instant, and he would never truly know how I felt if he left in a few days and never came back.

Making everything Giselle said that much more real for me.

We went to bed a little after three in the morning. I brushed my teeth and combed my hair, taking a good look at myself in the mirror. Debating if I was honestly going to do what I had been thinking about all night.

I jumped when I heard the front door open and some commotion. Peeking into the hall to see what was going on.

"Where's my girl?!" Mason called out, stumbling around, barely remaining upright. "There she is…"

"Oh, God! How much did you guys drink? You reek of nothing but booze and cigarettes," Giselle asked, walking into the foyer.

"I'm gonna make you feel so good," Mason rasped, pulling her into his arms. Causing her to smile and laugh.

"Okay, Romeo, let me take you to bed. Goodnight, Creed. You know where the guestroom is."

I peered over at Creed who was looking at them the same way I was. Maybe it was the alcohol, but for the first time, I saw him look at them as though something was missing in his life, too.

Love.

I slowly backed away so he wouldn't see me. Leaving all the doubt and hesitation at the door.

I walked into his room.

After loverboy and his girl said goodnight and made their way to Giselle's room, I went in the opposite direction toward the guest room on the other end of the apartment. I'd spent many nights in that room. Her apartment was huge for living there by herself, but her daddy could fucking afford it.

I walked into the bedroom, not bothering with the lights. The moon gave off a soft glow from the balcony doors. I stripped down and threw my cut and clothes on the armchair and headed for the en-suite bathroom. I took a quick shower, needing to wash away the night. I hated going to bed stinking of bar stench, and cheap perfume. I'd spent too many nights going to sleep in God-knows-what covering my fucking uniform when I was in Afghanistan. I found myself showering several times a day when I was on leave, needing to feel clean at all hours of the day.

I threw my boxer briefs back on, opening the bathroom door to walk onto the balcony and smoke a cigarette. Taking in the view of the ocean, questioning life. Remembering how many soldiers' lives had fallen at the hands of the enemy. Wondering which one of those bullets was really meant for me. Why good men like Andrews with a wife and kid were ripped from this world, when scum like me was left to roam free? Question after question plagued my thoughts as I stood there smoking.

Every thought more unforgiving than the last.

I took a deep breath, finishing off my cigarette, flicking it off the balcony. Opening the slider, I walked back into the room. Deciding at the last second to close the drapes, hoping to make it dark enough so I could make myself sleep in tomorrow. Enjoying the last bit of freedom I still had. My body was so used to being up at the crack of dawn that I never slept for more than a few hours a night.

I pulled back the covers, getting into bed. Hoping sleep would come fast, but knowing it wouldn't, it never did. Propping my head up on a few pillows, I laid there for a few seconds, allowing my mind to process what the fuck was going on, to prepare myself for the shit-storm that was about to go down. I switched on the soft recess lighting right above my head.

Still gazing up at the ceiling, I murmured, "What are you doin' in my bed, Pippin?"

I knew she had been lying there the entire time. I was trying to avoid the inevitable of having this conversation with her.

As soon as she pulled back the covers, I jumped out of the bed. Resisting the urge to look in her direction, knowing exactly what I'd fucking see. Throwing my jeans on, not bothering to button them, I sat on the armchair in the dark corner of the room. My face void of any emotion as I finally looked her way. Taking in the fucking vixen sitting in front of me on the center of the bed for the first time. Only dressed in her pink bra and panties. Leaving very little to the imagination.

She looked fucking sinful with her creamy white skin glowing in the moonlight, her long, brown, wavy hair that framed her beautiful face cascading down her back. Making her look much more mature than the pigtail-wearing Pippin I'd grown to adore. With a predatory regard, my gaze continued to travel down, my eyes roaming over her tits that were popping out of the lacy fabric of her bra. Slightly showing the outline of her nipples. To her slender, hourglass waist, down to the top of her matching panties that barely covered her pussy.

"Fucking A," I drawled out, locking eyes with her. "Not gonna ask again."

"I wanted to see you," she coaxed, peering up at me through her lashes. Gazing at me in a way I knew all too fucking well.

"Coulda' seen me in the mornin'. Ain't right for you to be waitin' in a man's bed. Especially *mine*. If your bro—"

"He's busy with Giselle, and he's never checked on me a day in his life. I don't see him starting tonight. Plus, they can't hear us. They're on the other side of the apartment. You have nothing to worry about," she reasoned.

"Find that hard to believe," I scoffed out, shaking my head.

"Did you know I was spending the night, too?"

"No."

"Then how did you know I was in here?"

"I'm trained to," I simply stated, trying like hell to keep my eyes focused on her face and not her tempting fucking body.

"Like you could feel me?"

"Somethin' like that."

She opened her mouth to say something, but quickly shut it. I could physically feel her conflicting emotions radiating off her in waves as we sat there in silence. Knowing deep down she was up to no good.

I wish I could tell you I didn't expect what would happen next.

But I'd be lying.

Though nothing could have prepared me for this moment.

I should have stopped her.

I should have told her no.

I should have done something, anything...

Except allow her to close the distance between us. She slowly, provocatively, slid off the bed. Making her way toward me, each step precise and calculated while her luscious hips swayed, never missing a fucking beat. Only stopping when she was a foot in front of me, yearning for me to truly take her in. When my stare didn't leave her face, I didn't have to fight the internal battle for very long.

She smirked, boldly leaning in. Her delicate hands moved down my chest in a slow, agonizing motion, causing my breath to hitch. Her fingers traced my pecs, moving down to the contours of my abs, stopping to trace all my tattoos along the way. As if she'd been wanting to since the first time she saw me shirtless on her balcony, all those years ago. Countless women had touched me the way she was right in that moment, more times than I cared to fucking count.

This was different.

This was so meaningful, so emotional, so goddamn loving.

This was Mia.

My Pippin.

When her hands started moving lower beneath my jeans, toward my cock, I roughly shoved them away.

She smiled.

Gently placing her hands on my shoulders, she gradually started to climb onto my lap, straddling my thighs. Just waiting for me to stop her.

I didn't.

She sat up in my lap, tossing her hair over her shoulder. Using her arms to pull us closer together so our faces were now only inches apart. Her ample tits pressed against my chest, making my cock twitch from the simple delicate feeling. She wanted me to see her as a confident woman, showing me she was grown and no longer looking like a baby girl. But all the confidence in the world couldn't take away the nervousness exuding off of her. The awkward way she was sitting on my thighs, the way she was anxiously anticipating my response and awaiting my next move.

But then...

She bit her lip, fucking baiting me.

"What do ya think is gonna go down here, Pippin?" I questioned, arching an eyebrow. My hands craved to grip her waist and show her exactly what to do with her pussy which was settled on my cock.

My fingers begging me to touch her, to feel her up against me. Aching for something I shouldn't, knowing it would only lead to fucking trouble.

"You're leaving," she purred as if that answered everything.

"No shit."

"What if you don't come back? What if something happens to you? Then you'll never know how I feel. How I've always felt. About you."

"Jesus Christ," I breathed out. "Pippin, you don't—"

"Please," she interrupted with the sincerest expression on her pretty little face that I've ever seen. "Don't tell me what I can feel." Grabbing my hand, she placed it over her racing heart. "You do this to me every time I'm around you. You're the one person in my life who's never made me feel like a child. I've known you since I was nine-years-old, Creed. And from the first moment I saw you, I've thought about you every day since. Please…"

"What do you want from me, Mia?" I asked, letting my hand slip from her chest and down her waist. Unable to handle the feel of her smooth, silky skin under my calloused palms.

I could see all the build up, months of anticipation, longing, and desire in her eyes as she hesitantly leaned forward, placing her hands back on my chest. Slowly bringing her lips to meet mine. It started off with just a peck until she opened her mouth seeking out my tongue.

This kiss was so much different from our last.

It was all her now, showing me everything *I* had fucking taught her, just to shut her up. I let it go on. I enabled her, allowing her to feel like she was in control for a few seconds. Carelessly letting my walls and reserve come crumbling down. She kissed me with all the passion she could muster, exploring my mouth in ways no one else ever had. Bringing me to the verge of fucking losing myself, getting lost in the moment.

Getting lost in her.

Forgetting who the fuck was straddling me. My hands gripped onto her thighs, itching to move up to the seam of her panties.

Fighting the battle between right and wrong.

But she smelled so fucking good...

A man could only take so much, and I was at my tipping point. I no longer had any control over my movements as she was sitting in my arms for the first time. Sliding my hands along her smooth thighs to feel her soft skin against my fingers. Gliding them up toward her waist, my thumbs pressing higher on the wire of her bra.

"You're the prettiest thing I've ever laid eyes on," I rasped against her lips, kissing her, claiming her, fucking devouring her.

She smiled, rotating her hips against my cock in approval. I gripped her waist hard like I wanted to do the second she straddled my lap. She gasped when I stood in one swift motion. Wrapping her legs around my waist from the sudden shift in power. I never stopped kissing her as I made my way back to the bed. Laying her down on the mattress, hovering above her heady frame, causing her breathing to escalate when she realized she was now beneath me.

"For fuck's sake, what are ya doin' to me?" I whispered, resting my forehead on hers, looking down at her swollen lips.

She was so beautiful.

So loving.

So fucking innocent.

The way she was looking at me as if I was everything she ever wanted.

Only encouraging me to keep going, I couldn't help myself. I kissed her more aggressively than before, crashing our lips together as I hovered over her small body. Chastising myself mentally the entire time I continued to consume her mouth. Her hands went to the back of my neck, pulling me closer, but not nearly close enough. The kiss turned urgent and demanding, as she met each and every pull. It was full of emotion, mixed with pure lust and something else I'd never felt before.

My hands continued to roam over her body. Knowing I was the only man to have ever touched her this way was doing all sorts of things to my mind.

Especially my goddamn cock.

It was conflicting.

It was a struggle.

It was the first war I was willing to lose.

She tilted her head back, giving my lips more access to her flushed skin. I'd never been like this with any other woman, taking my time, wanting to explore every last inch of her body.

Needing her…

Wanting her…

In a way I never had with anyone else.

My mouth moved, kissing from her neck down to her collarbone, stopping just above her breasts that were rising and falling with every movement of my lips. I ran my tongue along the seam of her bra, leaving goose bumps in its wake. Looking up at her with hooded eyes, lightly blowing her aroused skin, watching her come undone. Wanting nothing more than to tear her bra off and take her perky tits into my eager mouth.

I resisted, flicking her hard nipple through the fabric instead before continuing down to her stomach. Slowly savoring the elevated heat of her body pressed up against mine. Getting hotter with each caress of my lips, touching her skin as I made my way to where I wanted to kiss her the most.

A moan escaped her lips.

And that was my undoing. Like a fucking rubber band snapping some sense into me. My brain taking over my cock, realizing what I was doing, what I was about to fucking do. I jumped off the bed, leaving her there panting and exposed. Breathless and aroused.

Because. Of. Me.

I tried to shake off all the bullshit she stirred inside of me. Holding my head between my hands, pacing around the room.

Knowing I'd just fucked up royally.

The first time I kissed her was mostly to shut her up. This time…

It was an entirely whole other reason, one that I would put a bullet in someone's head for.

I took a deep breath. Grabbing my shirt off the chair and throwing it at her. "Put some goddamn clothes on," I snapped, mostly pissed at myself for letting it go this far.

The last thing I wanted to do was hurt her feelings.

I walked out onto the balcony, leaving the slider open behind me. Lighting up a cigarette, leaning over the railing, needing to calm the fuck down. She stepped out shortly after, wearing nothing but my shirt and her panties. Closing the slider behind her.

"Hey…" She grabbed my arm, turning me to face her. "It's okay, Creed."

"It's far from fuckin' okay, Pippin."

"I love you," she said out of nowhere, almost knocking me on my ass. "I've always loved you."

"You don't even know what that means, sweetheart. This is my fault. I shoulda never kissed you. I shoulda never crossed the line wit' you. But throwin' yourself at me… ain't right."

"Throwing myself? What the hell is that supposed to mean? I wasn't throwing myself at you, asshole! I can't believe you just said that to me! I love you!"

"Shit… Mia, you don't know what you're sayin'. You're a kid. A goddamn virgin. Who just got her first kiss a week ago, and now you think you're in love with me and want to fuck? Cuz that's what I do. That's who I am. Ain't your boyfriend. Ain't ever gonna be the man from your fairy-tales, darlin'. I'm barely even your fuckin' friend." I regretted the words as soon as they came out of my mouth.

She jerked back like I had slapped her in the face, and I guess in a way I just had.

"Pippin…" I reached for her, but she stepped back.

"Barely your friend?" she repeated, frowning. "So we're not friends. I'm just some kid who's a virgin and just threw herself at you. Yeah?" she mocked in a hurt tone.

"You're fifteen," I honestly spoke.

"I was still fifteen when I made your dick hard!"

"I'm a man, Mia. Doesn't take much to get my cock hard. Especially when your dry fuckin' the shit out of it with your pussy."

She stood taller, eyeing me up and down. "You're not fooling anyone but yourself, Creed. You're using that as a cop-out, pushing me away because you're scared. You've been my friend since the moment you waited for me on the beach, watching me surf. Smiling for the first time in who knows how long. As much as you want to fight it, I know you love me too! I can feel it in here." She placed her hand over her heart.

"If you didn't, you wouldn't have stayed in my life for the last six years. Looking for me! Coming to see me! Telling me goodbye before you left for the military when you didn't have to. Taking my courage patch with you! So you would still have a part of me with you even when you're thousands of miles away. Reading all my letters I've sent you! Following me to the lake. Listening to me when you don't listen to anyone. Caring about how I feel when you don't even give a shit about how you're feeling!" she argued, pausing to let her words sink in. She stepped toward me, getting right up in my face.

"Was that enough for you?" Cocking her head to the side. "No? How about… going to such extreme lengths to chase Rick away. My first date. Acting all jealous that I was out with someone who wasn't you! Pretty much pissing on me, marking your territory as soon as you shoved my jacket against my chest. Not wanting any other guy's eyes on me except yours! And if that wasn't enough, you kissed me. Making damn sure your lips were the first ones I ever felt, not giving a shit that we were in a parking lot for anyone to see! Especially my brother! You had way more of a chance to get caught that night than we did here." She took a deep breath, contemplating what she was going to say next.

"But most of all, you wouldn't have let what just went down in there happen in the first place. As much as you think you're no good for me, using the excuse I'm only fifteen! You want to make sure I only remember your touch. Your scent… your lips… your hands all over me. You want me to be yours, and that fucking scares you more than anything, because you've never wanted that from anyone else. Not any of the women you've slept with. Not even Autumn. So cut the fucking bullshit, soldier, and man the fuck up! You're not hurting me… you're only hurting yourself."

I arched an eyebrow, grinning. Hating myself for what I was about to do, but she needed to get it through her head that we weren't going to happen.

Not now.

Not ever.

I crossed over the line. I fucked everything up. She was right. I needed to man up, pushing her away the only way I knew how.

"Think you got me all figured out, yeah? You haven't even scratched the fuckin' surface, darlin'. I don't love you. Not in love with you. When you flaunt your tits and pussy around, I'm gonna try to take it. I already told ya, I'm a man, I fuck. Don't make you my fuckin' girlfriend, sweetheart. Just makes ya another one of my whores."

She shook her head, her eyes immediately watering with tears. "You've said enough. Can't you see... are you that blind... my heart is bleeding out for you, Creed... you might have hurt me right now, but when you're ready to admit it I won't be there anymore."

I spoke with conviction, even though it killed me inside. "Truth hurts. You're a kid, Mia. I'm a grown-ass man who shoulda fuckin' known better. End of story. Now take your ass back inside, you don't belong in my fuckin' bed." With that, I left her there, knowing I'd just broke her heart.

Walking away from the only other person who had always been there for me.

Never expecting anything in return but for me to love her.

I was almost twenty-five years old and on my fourth deployment to Afghanistan. In a few short months, I would be honorably discharged from the Army for serving my country the last four years.

One thing I knew to be true…

I was more fucked up now than I was when I enlisted, that was for damn sure.

My unit had been overseas for the last six months, surviving the only way we knew how. Taking more lives, adding more deaths to the notches on our belts and losing ourselves a little more each day. It didn't help that Mia stopped writing me, I hadn't heard from her since I left her on the balcony of Giselle's apartment eight months ago. I spent the last few days of my leave keeping my distance. Busying myself with the club and brothers. Giving her space. Feeling like the worst piece of shit for hurting her in the first place.

I didn't expect her to stop writing me, not that I could blame her. But it fucking pissed me off nonetheless.

I missed her.

I missed her smart ass mouth, her wit, and the way she always caught me up on her life, making me feel like I was a part of it even when I was overseas. Always writing her letters in pink ink, signing it—Pippin XOXO.

Most of all, I missed the patches she sent me. Not just the funny ones which always made me laugh my ass off, but also the ones that had only one word of encouragement written on them. Sending them at times when I really need it, as if she knew. Sensing my despair like she felt me from the millions of miles between us. The last letter she sent me had her school picture in it. For some reason the day we left on deployment, I brought it back with me. Starting to carry it around with me everywhere.

Realizing for the first time how much I needed her in my life. How she had been the only constant blessing I had since the moment I met her.

"Seriously, man. Think about it. Had I not been forced to bend over and take it up the ass again, I'd either be eating steak or pussy right now," Owen stated, pulling me away from my thoughts.

I chuckled, needing to laugh. Even though I was on full alert, glancing around the empty streets with him following behind me. Mason and the rest of our unit were in the opposite alley, surrounding the building we were patrolling. An eerie feeling I knew all too well crept up my spine. I shuddered with a chill, protectively moving out in front of Owen.

For a second I thought I saw movement out of the corner of my eye, but then a gust of wind blinded me with a fine, powdery dust from the dirt in the stale, dry air.

"Shhh… did you hear that?" I murmured, loud enough for him to hear me.

"Fuck no, I didn't hear that. We've been here for seven fucking days, patrolling the same fucking area, over and over and over, and I haven't heard a goddamn thing. Stupid motherfuckers. They don't give a fuck about you, me, or anyone else. It's all about the almighty dollar, Creed. You know it, and so do I. Three more weeks, my friend. Three more weeks and they all can suck my cock."

I turned and pushed Owen, trying to give him a look, ordering him to post. "Shut the fuck up, Owen."

He didn't listen.

Owen had been fired up since they fucked up our orders to go home a little more than a month ago. Or so they said. We all knew why we were here, and it had nothing to do with paperwork. It didn't take too many fucking brain cells to figure it out, but it didn't matter. We hadn't seen another soul on this mission for the last seven days. Making it easy for him to let his guard slip a little when he should have been on-point. Owen fucking knew better. He was just pissed about being there when we shouldn't have been, letting it consume him to the point of carelessness.

I understood his frustrations. I wanted to go home, too. I was exhausted, game fucking over, but I was too close to getting us the fuck out of there to fuck it up now.

Owen cughed up fine dust, hacking up half a lung before continuing to be a goddamn idiot. "Chill, man. The whole unit has our back. Nobody's fucking here. You know the first thing I'm doing when I get home, Creed? I'm taking a fucking bubble bath with my wife's fancy-ass soap. I don't care if it makes me a pussy. I don't care if I smell like the poop fragrance she sprays after I take a shit in the bathroom. I'm fucking sitting in there, knowing, marinating in the fact that I never have to come back over here again. Breathing in this fucking shit that who the fuck knows if it will cause us fucking cancer one day. Or the whiff of rotting dead bodies every time the wind shifts." He nodded behind him. "Did you see that shit?"

I did see it.

I saw everything, but I didn't need to turn my head to see where the foul stench had come from. Just like everything I learned in all my years of service, my peripheral vision was sharper than most. With my eyes focused on the corner building, I avoided glancing to the pile of dead bodies.

From that point forward it all became a blur and not from the gust of wind filling my eyes with dry sand. It happened so fast, yet it seemed so fucking slow. I pulled my gun on a dog, running from an alley at the exact same time I caught the sniper out of the corner of my eye, aiming right for Owen. Quickly realizing the dog was a goddamn distraction ploy.

I took action, shoving him back as hard as I could, with my gun out in front of me. A bullet whistled through the desert air, just missing the back of my head. If I hadn't shoved him, if I hadn't moved him out of the way things could have been different, but they weren't.

I regained my balance and ran several feet forward, taking out the sniper before he had the chance to try to take out Owen. Shooting a bullet in the center of his forehead like it was just another motherfucking day.

"Shit," Owen called out. "You just saved my life, Creed." He stepped forward at the exact same time I looked back.

BOOM!

At first, I didn't even know what happened. My body jolted back from the impact of the land mine, roughly being thrown into a pile of rubble and rocks. Sharp pain radiated throughout my entire core, reaching places I didn't even know you could possibly feel pain. The wind knocked out of me with so much fucking force that I felt like my lungs had collapsed and I was suffocating to death.

Coughing, wheezing, gasping for my next breath.

When I opened my eyes, I couldn't fucking see anything but bright white all around me. My head throbbed with a sudden splitting headache. The loud ringing in my ears blocked out all the chaos surrounding me. Piercing pain at my temples made me think my brain had just exploded. Clouding my judgment, my strength, and my will to keep fucking going.

"Creed! Fuck man! Creed! You hit?!" I heard Mason shouting from above me. "Bro, don't do this to me! Don't you fucking do this to me!" He patted my chest, down my arms and my legs. Trying to feel if I was hit.

"Fine..." I sputtered, my throat raw and burning, making it extremely difficult to get any words out. I carefully turned over to my stomach, struggling to catch my bearings. Fighting a war with my body to do what it was trained to.

"I'm fine... Owen... where is—"

"Shit! I'll be right back! We're getting raided! Gonna go get these motherfuckers! Don't. Fucking. Move! Do you understand me?! Stay right here! I'll be right fucking back!"

I weakly nodded, staring blindly in the direction of Mason's voice. My eyes readjusted, slightly coming back into focus. I sat up, pressing my hand hard against my chest, trying to breathe through the excruciating pain from the impact. Applying pressure on my sternum, wanting to alleviate some of the tension, some of the buildup. Feeling as though I was internally bleeding, my body was giving out on me. I slouched against the wall, looking down at the ground, gasping for the air that wasn't available for the taking. The sunlight and the dirty air were almost as blinding as the bomb that just went off in front of me.

ROAD to NOWHERE

My eyes felt like they were bleeding, burning from the chemicals that radiated from the explosive. I reached up wanting to wipe away the debris, knowing it was fucking pointless, my hands were covered in God-knows-what. I blinked a few times, gradually looking up. Adjusting to the light, looking all around me. Needing to find Owen. Desperately pushing through the disorientation and confusion of our location from where we were and where his body could have been tossed.

Several explosions sounded nearby, and it felt like the seconds turned into minutes and minutes turned into hours. I was frantically trying to see who else had been hit, if it was more of my men.

I pushed off the wall, stumbling to stand on my own. Placing one foot in front of the other, mind over fucking matter, I kept telling myself as my body started going into shock. The more I moved, the closer I got, maneuvering on autopilot as I hurried down the alleyway. Making my way toward the guy who had become a brother to me. Not giving a fuck about anything else but getting to him.

Guns blazing.

Bullets firing in all directions.

War was all around me.

It didn't fucking faze me anymore.

Not knowing if anything ever could, till I came upon his broken form. There was so much fucking blood coming out of what was left of his body as he convulsed, shaking uncontrollably, as I watched him fucking dying right in front of my eyes. I didn't think twice about it. I grabbed him, dragging his limp body into the building next to us. Leaving a trail of blood staining the dirt. I didn't have the strength to carry him, to throw him over my shoulder like I had done for so many soldiers prior, to get us the fuck out of there.

I dragged his contorted body, ignoring his pleas of desperation to not move him, urgently begging me to just leave him there. That everything hurt. That he couldn't take the pain. Crying, groaning, sounds of pure agony and misery fell from his lips in a way I'd never heard before. I stopped once we were far enough inside the concrete walls, away from any broken windows or points of entry, hiding us as best as I could, given the shitty fucking circumstances. Knowing one of my men would find us. Disregarding all the rotting dead bodies that were already in there, lives that were taken for good or for evil.

It all blended together.

"Ahh, shit, Creed," he continued in a tone that wasn't his. As if he had already given up on life.

"You're okay, man. You're okay. I got ya." I laid him by the wall, leaning over and covering his body with mine like a shield.

Kneeling beside his mangled frame, looking up at the ceiling, keeping my emotions in check. Ignoring the active rounds of fire happening just on the other side of the concrete. Where I should have been fighting with my men. But I couldn't leave my brother.

"Creed…"

I swallowed hard, shutting my eyes for a few seconds, needing a minute to get my shit together to look down at him.

Not for me.

For him.

Mentally preparing myself for what I would see, for what would happen, for what I knew he was going to ask of me.

Because I would ask for the same fucking thing.

I peered down at the soldier I'd known for what felt like a lifetime, taking in what was left of his body, a gruesome scene right out of a war movie. Except this was a reality.

My fucking reality.

Nothing of the man that would risk his life for me was left. Anything that made him human had just been blown off, and I was damn certain it didn't stop there.

"I'm here, brother. I'm here," I gritted out, my lips trembling.

"Creed… It's bad, man… it's fucking bad…" he lamented, struggling to get the words out. "I'm gonna die… Please… please… don't let me die, Creed. I want to go home…" bawling, his voice breaking.

I reached over and grabbed his hand on the only arm he had left, squeezing it, providing any comfort I could. Letting him know I was there with him.

He wasn't alone.

"I want to see my family… my girl, Creed…" he groaned, gargling over the blood coming out of his mouth.

"You're goin' home, buddy. You're goin' fuckin' home! You hear me? You're not gonna fuckin' die. You're not! Not here, not now! Fight, motherfucker, fight!" I yelled, unsure of who I was trying to convince.

He started to cough up clots of blood. I tried to sit him up but he screamed in agony, so I laid him back down. Grabbing his hand again, waiting.

"Fuck... man..." he whispered, looking up at me with half his face disfigured and covered in blood. "Tell my girl... I fucking love her... Creed. Tell my baby girl... I died with honor... I died a man... a goddamn soldier... fighting to keep her safe..." he let out, gasping through the despair. For his next breath. "Tell my mom not to be sad... tell her I died a happy man... with her on my mind... You... tell them... I did not suffer... You make sure... they know that... please... fucking... please... promise me... swear to me... they will know... it was quick and I did not fucking suuufffeeerrr..."

I nodded, unable to form words. "I'm sorry, man. I'm so fuckin' sorry. I shoulda seen it. It's my job to fuckin' protect my unit. My men. This is my fault. I'm so fuckin' sorry, brother." Bowing my head in shame.

His body started to convulse again, this time worse than before. "Creed! I can't do this! Don't make me suffer, man! I don't want to go out like this!" he roared, crying uncontrollably through the pain. The agony, the future he would never have.

"Don't ask me to do that... please..." I begged, knowing what he was asking me to do.

"Do it! Cut the cord! I'm not going home! It could be over in a split second! And... you know it! Bullet to the head! Let me die with fucking honor! Let me die a fucking soldier with my fucking dignity, not this pitiful man bleeding out!" He spit out more blood, forcing his body to yell at me. Telling me what he needed.

Another gasp of air gurgled in his lungs. His end was near. I knew my worst fucking nightmare was about to come true. Visualizing my friend suffocating in his own blood until his lungs gave out, exploding in his fucking chest. His eyes rolling to the back of his head, the terrified expression on his face, fearing the next phase of his soul was too real.

I couldn't do that.

Pulling him into my arms, I laid his head on my bicep. Holding him close, rocking his shaking body back and forth, it immediately brought back memories of when I did this with Luke.

"Shhh... shhh... shhh... Owen... watching your baby girl be born on that video your wife sent was one of the most beautiful things I've ever seen, man. Shhh..." I repeated, reminiscing of happier times. Wanting him to go out with good memories, a sedated heart, a clear fucking conscience.

"Yeah, Creed..." he gasped for air. "She's... beautiful... most... beautiful... thing in... the world."

"I promise I will tell her all about you. She will know who her daddy was and what he did for our country." My eyes watered with tears, but I blinked them away, wanting to be strong for him.

Allowing his mind and body to calm down.

Waiting until he felt some peace.

"Thank... you... Creed..." he murmured, trying to smile, looking up at me.

"I love you, man. Thanks for being my friend," I softly said, hugging him closer. Reaching over, jolting my arm, hearing one very loud pop.

Snapping his neck.

Putting him out of his goddamn misery.

I broke down, holding Owen's lifeless body in my arms. Bawling, tears ran down my face, heaving in and out, crying like a little girl. He was so fucking close to never looking back.

Freedom.

And just like that.

Owen was gone, and his blood was on my hands.

Mia

"Finally! Took you long enough," Jill said as I got in her car, shutting the door behind me,

Jill was a junior from my AP English class. We hit it off after being paired together on our last assignment. She was a wild child to say the least, telling me all about the parties she would go to, drinking and fooling around with boys all the time. Her parents' were divorced and didn't really care what she did as long as she got good grades.

I wish my parents' were more like that.

"I know! Sorry! My brother's girlfriend needed to remind me again that she was covering for my ass with my parents'. Giving me a lecture on having fun but being safe and to text her every hour. Using Giselle was the only way I could come out with you tonight. They trust her."

"Your parents' are ridic. You'll be sixteen in like two months," she replied, driving out of Giselle's apartment complex. "You're one of the smartest girls in our grade, they should learn to trust you more."

"It's not really my mom, it's my dad. But whatever, I don't want to talk about them anymore. Where are we going?"

"To one of the best parties you will ever go to. They have them all the time. So buckle in, biotch, you're in for a hell of a night."

It didn't take too long for us to get there, even though we had to drive through the woods. It was hard to see where we were going, branches scraped the top of the car as she made her way down a dark and narrow road. The headlights only illuminated so far in front of us, making the night creepy as hell. For a second I thought she may have gotten lost, but suddenly a huge warehouse appeared in the middle of nowhere. Rows of motorcycles lined the grass and gravel along with scattered cars in between. I could hear the rock music blaring through their sound system, beating against the windows of her car.

There were people everywhere, most of the women dressed in skimpy outfits, while others were dressed in leather. It was then that I realized most of the men were wearing cuts exactly like Creed's with the Devil's Rejects logo.

"Where are we?" I asked as she pulled into an empty parking spot in the back and killed the engine.

"Mia, my sweet, innocent friend, we're at an MC clubhouse."

"MC?"

She laughed, looking at herself in the visor mirror before opening her door. "Wow, you really are sheltered. It's a motorcycle club, girl. They have the best parties with the hottest guys. I'm actually meeting one of them. I bet he will have a hot friend for you, too." She wiggled her perfectly sculpted eyebrows at me, closing the door the behind her.

I nodded to myself. Coming to the realization that Creed was a biker and a part of this club. Remembering his cut said 'Vice Prez' on it. After all these years, I'd never associated him with this lifestyle, but now it made so much sense.

I hadn't seen him since that horrible night several months ago. Mason and he left to go back to war. I stopped writing him, I stopped sending him patches, but I never stopped thinking about him.

What if he was here?

I shook off the thoughts, wanting to have a good time tonight. For once I was about to experience what everyone else my age did every weekend, while I was at home thinking about all I was missing.

Praying for *him* to return home safely.

We walked up to the front of the warehouse, and it was almost like I was walking up to a different world. I felt like a fish out of water. The smell of smoke and weed instantly assaulted my senses as we made our way through a swarm of people by the entrance. They were all drinking heavily and swearing up a storm. Jill grabbed my hand and pulled me through the crowd, and into the clubhouse where there were just as many partygoers, if not more.

Drugs were everywhere, lining every open surface. Some women were lying on the tables while men snorted white powder off their bodies, which I assumed was cocaine. While other women sat on men's laps, dancing for them naked, for all to see. Couples were kissing in the corners, starting to go at it. It was like a train wreck you couldn't look away from.

I couldn't help but think about Creed…

Was this the life he led?

Was this why he told me he was no good?

Was he one of these men?

No wonder he thought of me as a baby girl if this was what he was used to. I never stood a chance.

The more I took in the scene playing out in front of me, the more uncomfortable I became. I'd never been around anything like this in my entire life. This was definitely not my kind of party. The chaos all around made me wish Creed was there. One group of bikers with women who weren't acting like animals caught my eye. The women had actual clothes on, wearing cuts that said property of so and so on them. It seemed like they were on a different level than the rest of the party.

I was about to tell Jill I was going to call Giselle to come pick me up, but when I turned to find her, she was gone.

"Shit…" I whispered to myself, remembering I left my cell phone in her car.

I started to roam around other rooms, each one more graphic than the last. Trying to find Jill amongst the crowds of people and chaos. I must have gotten lost, ending up in what looked like a basement.

"Well, lookie what we have here, fresh meat," someone whispered from behind me, causing me to stumble back against the wall. He cornered me in with his arms on the sides of my head. "Ain't ever seen you before. I would remember such a pretty little face and bangin' fuckin' body," he rasped too close to my face, smelling like liquor and weed. "You got a name?"

"Mia," I replied, feeling much more vulnerable than before.

"Pretty name, for a pretty girl. What are ya doin' here?"

"I came with a friend."

"A friend?" he questioned, cocking his head to the side. Smirking, "Don't see a friend anywhere. All I see is you. Maybe you and I can become friends. In my room alone. Yeah?"

My eyes widened. "Umm... I don't—"

"Jesus Christ, Jigsaw! Leave her the fuck alone! She look interested to you?" a man's voice echoed through the basement, interrupting him.

I had never been more relieved to hear a stranger's voice than I did in that moment. I released the breath I had been holding when Jigsaw backed away, turning around. We both looked in the direction of where the voice came from. A tall guy with dark brown hair that hung low around his eyes was standing by the door, wearing a cut that read 'Prospect' on it. I looked back at the guy he called Jigsaw, and he was wearing the same cut with the same word patched on it.

"Mind your business, Rebel. You don't know shit!"

He grinned, looking in my direction again. Nodding to Jigsaw. "You wanna suck his cock?"

I peered back and forth between them, sputtering, "Umm... no thank you."

Rebel laughed, smirking wide. Making me smile back, I couldn't help but notice how cute he was. The light shade of blue in his eyes was so damn enticing, luring me into his smile. He was covered in tattoos, wearing jeans, a cut, and combat boots. I was starting to think it was standard biker attire.

When he caught me staring at his defined arms and broad chest, I blushed looking back at Jigsaw.

"Oh, there's some sort of love connection here, I see," Jigsaw sneered, pointing between us. "Rebel don't like to be held down, pretty girl. He also don't like to be told what to do. I'm looking for an ol' lady. He ain't. Choose your battles wisely. Pretty boy over there just thinks with his cock."

"Thanks for the introduction, Jigsaw. Now get the fuck out."

Jigsaw shook his head, taking the steel steps two at a time, body-checking my rescuer in the shoulder before slamming the door behind him.

"His bark is bigger than his bite. He comes on a little strong," Rebel chimed in, walking down the stairs toward me.

"Yeah... can see that. But umm... thanks. You kinda saved me there."

"No worries. Ain't ever seen you around here. Got a name?" he asked, towering over me and letting his eyes wander all over my body.

"Mia, but you can call me Pippin," I answered without thinking.

"Pippin," he repeated, nodding.

It was weird hearing him call me that when only one other person ever did. The way it rolled off his tongue was doing things to me, making me feel familiar flutters in my stomach. I found myself liking it, waiting for him to say it again. I didn't know if it was from the way he said it or from who gave me the nickname in the first place, but it brought a sense of calm over me, making me feel safe for some reason.

"How old are you?" he questioned, pulling me away from my thoughts.

"Why do you ask?"

He chuckled, "Right... girls don't like sayin' their age. Yeah?"

"I'm eighteen," I lied.

"Ah, the only reason I asked was cuz you look too sweet and innocent to be hangin' around these parts. Doesn't seem like your scene."

"Is it because I'm not dressed like a whore?" I blurted, unable to help myself.

He grinned, eyeing me up and down again. Taking in my black flowy dress and cowboy boots. Stopping just above my cleavage, he murmured, "I like what you're wearin'. Nice change of pace."

I swallowed hard, locking eyes with him.

"Besides everythin' you're showin' are just the parts I really like."

I beamed, my face turning beet red. It was the first time a guy had talked to me that way.

"Wanna beer?"

"Sure."

"Come on." He gestured with a nod to follow him.

When we walked back inside to grab a few beers, it was even more packed than before. Leaving very little room to shift through the crowd. Husky men towered above me making it nearly impossible to see over everyone's heads. I tried my best to keep up with Rebel but lost him for a second in the madness. Before I could panic, his strong hands gripped my waist, pulling me back into his hard body. He smiled down at me with a look of reassurance, making my belly flutter and my heart beat faster. Whispering in my ear to stay close, he grabbed my hand that time and led the way.

We stopped by the bar and he grabbed a bottle of vodka from the cooler instead of beer, taking a cup and a few club sodas, too. I followed him outside, walking past the partygoers, going to the field where most of the cars were parked. He never let go of my hand, which I was grateful for. I still wasn't completely comfortable with the whole situation. Though he made things better.

"You're gonna need some help," Rebel said, glancing back at me with the same grin I'd come to expect. He pulled down the tailgate to his massive souped-up Chevy truck, patting the metal for me to take a seat. "I'm used to handlin' big things." Winking at me, he grabbed a hold of my waist as if I weighed nothing, gently setting me down on the tailgate. Stepping between my thighs and still holding my waist when he was done, he stated, "You feel good in my arms, Pippin."

My breathing hitched. "Wow... you need better lines, buddy. You sure you're getting laid as much as your friend said?"

He laughed from deep within his chest, throwing his head back. "I fuckin' like you." Pulling away, hopping up on the truck bed to sit beside me. "Never brought a girl out to my truck."

"Yeah... yeah... yeah..."

Grinning, he reached behind me to grab a cup. Filling it more than half way with vodka, mixing in a dash of the club soda. "Even brought ya some girly shit to drink," he responded, handing it to me.

I took a sip. Immediately clearing my throat from the strong taste burning its way down my chest. Trying to act like it wasn't the first time I drank this.

He knowingly smiled, placing the bottle between his legs. He started to rub my back. "Sorry... I got a loose hand."

"What about you?" I asked, suddenly feeling all warm inside. I didn't know if it was from his hand touching me again or the liquor.

Maybe it was a little of both.

He brought the bottle up to his lips, taking a swig. Setting it back between his legs again. Taking it down like a pro. "What about me?"

"You drink a lot?" I sarcastically questioned.

"Enough."

"I see that. How old are you?"

"Almost nineteen."

I was relieved he was only three years older than me, even though he didn't have to know that.

"Ya live around here?"

"Not far. Oak Island. How about you?"

He shook his head, taking another swig from the bottle. "Don't wanna talk about me. I know all about this motherfucker, wanna learn about you," he informed, bumping my shoulder with his.

"Not much to tell. What you see is what you get," I countered, twirling my hair around my finger, biting my lip.

"Well, then... I'm fuckin' liking every inch of what I see."

He reached over, rubbing his rough, calloused fingers back and forth on my thigh, igniting something familiar in my body. Bringing back memories of Creed touching me the exact same way not too long ago. Making me wish he was here to see that I wasn't the baby girl he claimed I was. To see that I was a grown-ass woman too, having the time of her life. My mind drifted wondering if I wasn't a virgin would he still have stopped that night? If I went to him in a week or a month not a virgin anymore, would he have me?

I quickly shook off the plaguing thoughts before they ruined my night. Chastising myself for thinking of him in the first place.

I was there with Rebel.

Not Creed.

Even though... I wanted Creed.

I brought my red Solo cup to my lips, drinking back way more than I had been. Wanting to get rid of the thoughts and memories of the guy who hurt me on purpose. Stifling a grin when I saw Rebel eyeing me over the rim of his bottle. Looking at me with nothing but mischief in his eyes.

I wanted to forget.

And I knew Rebel was the perfect guy I could do that with. He was trouble in the best possible way.

We sat there for I don't know how long, exchanging flirty banter. Throwing drink after drink back like they were water, till the bottle of vodka was almost gone. My lips tingled, my face was on fire, and my body was numb. It was the first time in forever I felt so carefree, throwing my head back laughing, enjoying the way he made me feel. Having a great time with a guy who was just along for the ride, like me.

At one point the song "American Pie" by Don McLean came on from the clubhouse. I hopped off the tailgate and stumbled a bit, realizing just how drunk I really was. Rebel caught me around the waist before I face-planted to the ground, laughing his ass off along with me. Giggling as I was trying to regain my balance.

"You're just like a savior, huh? You my own Prince Charming?" I chuckled, standing upright in his arms.

He caressed the side of my cheek, rubbing his thumb over my lips in a back and forth motion. "Been called worse things."

I smiled, pushing off of him, dancing all around and twirling in circles with my arms out. Singing at the top of my lungs, not giving a shit who was watching the drunken performance of my lifetime. Rebel leaned against his truck, folding his arms over his chest and watching me make a fool out of myself but liking every second of it. As if it was the first time someone was being real around him.

The alcohol acting as the liquid courage I needed for what I was about to do. Relishing in the way he was looking at me, I started to dance for him. Seductively working my hands up my sides, bringing my dress up a little with them. Peeking over at him, swaying my body to the beat of the music, provocatively looking into his eyes as the song continued to blare in the night. I spun around with my back now facing him, shutting my eyes, lifting my hair up off the nook of my neck as I continued to move my hips in a slow, steady rhythm.

Until I felt a strong hand grab my stomach, tugging me back against his hard chest. Swaying us slowly together to the melody. He gripped my chin, tilting my head back and making me look up through my lashes into his dilated, dark blue eyes. His expression had turned heady, matching my own. I licked my lips, my mouth suddenly becoming dry. His eyes followed the movement of my tongue as he leaned in, softly pecking my lips. Turning me back around so his warm body was flush with mine as our mouths danced against one another. Starting off slow but quickly escalating to the point where his hands started to roam down my back, reaching my ass. Gripping it hard, causing me to moan into his mouth.

"Woooweee! Rebel, git'er done, boy!" someone yelled from the clubhouse.

I jolted, immediately trying to pull away, but he held me firmer, not allowing me to move an inch.

"Walk along! You fuck! Ain't nothin' to see!" he yelled back, flipping him off. Focusing his attention back on me.

"So…" I breathed out, wrapping my arms around his neck. Still trying to govern my breaths. Pretending like we weren't just interrupted. "Are you going to show me your room?"

He grinned without another word, crashing his mouth on mine as he lifted me in his arms and carried me toward the clubhouse. Placing me down on my feet once we reached the partygoers. He took me by the hand and led me inside toward a long, narrow hallway. I made a mental note to remember where the front door was from his room. He opened the door into the dim lighting of the room, instantly kicking it shut and backing me up against it with a loud thud as if he couldn't get enough of me. Kissing me exactly the same way he had been all night.

Our greedy hands never left each other's bodies as we stumbled our way toward his bed. Knocking shit over, making things shatter to the ground.

The only thing I knew to be true was in that moment I wanted him. I wanted his kiss, his touch, his taste, and his hands all over me.

Specifically, his dick.

I reached for his cut, and he helped me pull it off of him, throwing it out of the way. Continuing the assault on our mouths like we were glued together and couldn't come apart not even for a second. I'd never felt anything like this before. I didn't have any control over my actions, my body desperately wanting something I'd never experienced. At the same time, it felt like I knew what I was doing, my movements instinctual like they had been programmed inside me since birth.

For the first time, I understood how my friends could have meaningless sex, how you could want to give yourself to someone, give into the moment that just felt really good. No emotions, no I love yous, just primal yearning for some sort of relief.

My stomach clenched.

My sex throbbed.

I reached for the buckle of his belt.

"Hey... hey... hey... calm down... I'm not goin' anywhere," he groaned, smiling against my lips and reaching for the hem of my dress.

I let him take it off, leaving me in nothing but my bra and panties. Promptly pulling away, leaning back to admire my body. His eyes devouring me in ways I remembered all too well.

I closed my eyes, shaking off the sentiment of the guy I couldn't stop thinking about, leaning in to kiss Rebel instead. Needing the passion and desire to cloud my thoughts. I reached for his belt buckle again, this time he allowed me to undo it.

"You smell so fucking good," he groaned against my lips, moving us onto the bed. "Anyone ever tell you that?"

I chuckled, shaking my head no as he gently laid me down on the mattress, hovering above me. Continuing his assault down the side of my neck, placing soft kisses down to my cleavage. In one sudden movement he removed my bra, tossing it aside, caressing and sucking my other breast, leaving me breathless beneath him. I could feel his erection on my sex, purposely moving his hips, creating an insane tingling I felt all over.

He looked up at me with hooded eyes, working his way down my body, pulling at the seam of my panties, tossing them aside, too. When I realized what he was going to do, I grabbed onto the sides of his face. Bringing him back up to kiss me. It brought back too many memories of Creed, and he was the last person I wanted to think about in that moment...

There with Rebel.

His hand slid in between my thighs. It didn't take long for my breathing to become heavy, feeling my chest rising and my back arching as he moved his fingers all around my core. My legs started to shake. I couldn't keep my eyes open, and I felt like I was going to explode. I couldn't take it anymore, the room started to spin and my breathing faltered.

Falling over the edge.

"Ah..." I gasped over and over again. Not wanting the feeling to ever end.

ROAD to NOWHERE

I rode the high for as long as I could until I heard a rustling of some sort to my right. Fluttering my eyes open, I realized he was tearing open a condom. Pulling his shirt over his head and kicking off his boots and jeans. He half-smiled as I tried to hide the surprised look on my face when I saw his hard dick spring free. Deciding to look the other way as he was sliding the condom down his length.

He crawled back over to my naked body, locking me in with his arms. Kissing me again, placing his dick at my opening. I let myself get lost in the feel of his body on top of mine, of his lips against mine, of the way everything felt so damn good.

All those emotions were gone in an instant.

In one swift movement, he was deep inside me. Tearing through my innocence in a way I never expected it would feel before. My back jolted off the bed as I yelping loud from the sudden intrusion and pain of it all.

He immediately stopped, looking down at me, bewildered. I tightly shut my eyes, not wanting to look at him, even though I could still feel his penetrating stare on me.

"You're a fuckin' virgin?" he stated as a question in a shocked and pissed off tone.

I nodded, still not opening my eyes. Mostly because I didn't want him to see how embarrassed I was.

"Fuck..." he scoffed out, starting to remove himself from me.

"No!" I opened my eyes, grabbing onto his shoulders, holding him in place. "It's fine... I swear. Don't stop."

He jerked back, arching an eyebrow. Peering down at me, confused. "What the fuck? Don't girls want their first time to be special or some shit?" he paused, contemplating what he was going to say next. Rendering him speechless. His conflicting emotions getting in the way of what I still wanted to happen between us.

Taking a deep breath, he let on, "Mia, I'm not that guy. I mean I like ya... but fuck... I'm not... you know... I don't... Shit this is hard..." He shook his head, thinking he was hurting my feelings, but I understood what he was trying to say.

"I'm not that girl, okay? You have nothing to worry about. I know this is just... whatever it is. I don't expect anything from you. All I want is to have some fun, you're fun," I honestly spoke, hoping he would understand but not knowing how much I could tell him to where he would.

He sighed with wide eyes, tugging the hair back away from his face with his right hand. Peering down at me with a look of concern. "Jesus... did I... I mean... fuck, are you okay... I didn't know... I would have never... I mean... you're the first virgin... I've ever... fuck..." he breathed out. "How bad did I hurt you?"

I reassuringly smiled. "I'm fine," I whispered, grabbing the back of his neck, kissing him again. The alcohol still coursing through me.

He kissed me with uncertainty as I moved my hips, beckoning him to keep going. He still didn't move, and I started to worry that he was going to stop and get off of me, but then I felt his hand move lower toward my core. I started to relax. Appreciating he was trying to make this better for me. Seconds later, he began to move in and out as he worked my sweet spot. The sensations of his fingers replaced the uncomfortable feeling of his thrusts.

"Better? That feel good?" he grunted into my mouth.

"Yeah... don't stop..."

It didn't take long for some of the tension and friction to reside and for the heat to return. His fingers never stopped moving against me, controlling me as he continued to take what I so desperately wanted to save for someone else.

I may have lost my virginity to Rebel that night, but my mind never strayed far from...

Creed.

Mia

"Thanks for bringing me back over here, Jill. I really appreciate it. I know it's really early," I said as she pulled into the clubhouse.

"No problem. Gotta see your man, right?"

I smiled.

"Besides I told Tank I was stopping by, waking him up, you know… to talk and stuff." She grinned. "Just text me when you're ready. I know you got that christening."

I nodded, opening the door. Stepping out onto the grass, fixing my dress before we went up to the clubhouse. A huge guy with honey-colored eyes and blonde hair recognized Jill and let us in. Nodding a hello to her, he had the name 'Sergeant of Arms' stitched on his cut. I couldn't help but look around, expecting to see Creed coming out of the rooms with a girl on his arm. I still hadn't seen him since that night at Giselle's.

It didn't matter, he wasn't why I was here.

Jill and I walked down the hallway together until she walked into Tank's room, closing the door behind her. I made my way toward Rebel's room, knocking on the door but no one answered.

I pushed it open slightly. "Rebel? You here? It's Mia." Peeking my head in, I saw that no one was in there. I was about to turn around and leave, but I heard the shower running.

I walked inside, closing the door behind me. Moving my way through his room, I sat on the edge of his bed, deciding to wait for him. Looking around the open space.

The bathroom door opened moments later, startling me.

"Pippin?"

We locked eyes.

"What are you doing in Rebel's room?" I blurted, not knowing what else to say.

There *he* was...

Fresh out of the shower with a towel hanging low around his waist. Another one of my wishes coming true. He opened his mouth to reply but was cut off when the bedroom door opened. In walked Rebel who instantly stopped, looking from me to him, back to me again.

"Creed?" Rebel announced, caught off guard. "When the hell did you get back?"

"An hour ago," he simply replied, never taking his eyes off me.

"You on leave?"

"I was discharged this morning, Noah. Woulda' known if you read my fuckin' letters. I served my four years. I'm done."

"Noah?" I chimed in, looking over at him. "I thought your name was Rebel?"

"It is. No one calls me Noah but him." He nodded toward Creed. "Pippin, what—"

"Pippin?" Creed interrupted, looking over at him. "Her name's Mia." He shook his head. "The fuck?" Trying to control his temper. Not only was another man calling me Pippin, it confirmed why I was there. Narrowing his eyes at me, he spewed, "Are you shittin' me?"

I abruptly stood, getting right up in his face, shoving his bare chest. He didn't waver. I couldn't believe he thought he had any right to be pissed at me when he was the one who pushed me away in the first place.

"I can do whatever the hell I want. You don't own me, Creed!"

His eyes widened, arching an eyebrow. Cocking his head to the side, he scoffed out, "So you decided to fuck my brother? For what, to prove a point?"

My mouth dropped open. I jerked back from the unexpected revelation, almost being knocked on my ass. Immediately feeling sick to my stomach.

"You're lying."

"I look like I'm lyin'?"

I peered back and forth between them not knowing who to settle my eyes on. "You guys are brothers?"

"This ain't his room. It's mine. That's my bed you were sittin' on. Tell me, sweetheart, did you fuck on it, too?" he viciously remarked, making his way to his dresser. Pulling out a pair of jeans.

"Creed, Jesus Christ... you haven't been sleepin' in here for more than a week at a time for the past four years. It's been my fuckin' room more than yours," Rebel argued, not backing down. "What the fuck is goin' on, anyway?" He locked eyes with me. "How do you know her?"

"Don't worry about it. The question is how the fuck do you know her?" He threw his jeans on under his towel, ripping it off and throwing it on the bed.

"She came here one night for a party. I woke up the next mornin' and she was gone."

He slowly nodded, the recognition crept across his face. The next thing I knew, a large hand shoved me out of the way, causing me to fall back on the bed. Creed was over to his brother in three strides pinning him to the wall by his throat.

"So you did fuck her, you little shit!"

"Stop saying it like that! Let him go!" I yelled, bringing their attention back to me.

He released Noah. "Consider yourself lucky. If she weren't here, you'd be fuckin' hurtin'." Shoving him into the wall again.

"This is ridiculous! Can't you use your words instead of fists?" I remarked.

"Fuck you, Creed! I'm not scared of you!" Rebel countered, pushing him off.

Creed ignored his brother, walking back over to me. "You givin' me shit now, Pippin? Un-fucking-believable."

"I didn't know he was your brother. I swear. I would never do that to you. And you know it."

"So that makes it okay? You fucked my little brother! Knowin' or not, his cock was inside you," he gritted out. "Can't even fuckin' look at you right now." He backed away and stormed out of the room, slamming the door behind him hard enough to shake the walls. Making me jump.

I sat back down on the edge of the bed, unable to hold myself up any longer. Crouching forward, holding my stomach, trying to swallow back the bile rising in my throat.

This was all just too much.

"Are you his girl?" Rebel asked what I knew he had been thinking since the second he saw his brother go all ape shit.

I shook my head. "No."

He gave me a curt nod. "What are you doin' here? You left me hanging that morning. I thought maybe I imagined you or some shit. Never been used like that before. Can't say I liked it, either."

"I'm sorry about that. I didn't use you, Rebel... Noah... whatever the hell your name is. I had a great time that entire night. With *you*. But obviously, you know I've never done anything like that before. It's not who I am. I guess... I just didn't know what would happened next. So I left, making it easier for both of us."

He walked toward me, pulling up a chair in front of me and sitting on it backward. Looking me straight in the eyes, he asked, "How do you know Creed?"

"Long story."

"I got time."

I took a deep breath, considering what I wanted to say and how to say it. "I don't want to talk about Creed. I came here to talk to you."

It was now or never, I needed to do this before I lost the courage. I would have to deal with Creed and him being brothers and all that brought about later. Right now it was the least of my worries. I grabbed my purse, pulling out what I needed and handed it to him.

He narrowed his eyes at me as soon as he realized what it was, reading the one word I'd been staring at for the last three days.

Positive.

Raising his eyebrows, he breathed out, "You're fuckin' pregnant?" Like he didn't want to believe it.

I nodded, biting my lip. Waiting for wherever this would lead to.

"How... how did this happen? We used a condom. I fuckin' used a condom." He pointed to himself. "This is bullshit. How do I even know it's mine?"

I grimaced, closing my eyes. Hearing him say those words was a wake-up call. I really was a baby girl. A stupid, naive kid. Exactly what Creed had been saying I was all along.

How could I let this happen?

"Look, Mia, I don't know you. Not tryin' to be a dick here. But you show up weeks late tellin' me you're pregnant. Claiming I'm the one who knocked you up? Yeah, I may have taken your fuckin' virginity but it don't mean you haven't spread your legs for anyone else since then."

I didn't hesitate, opening my eyes. Gazing right into his. "I guess being a fucking asshole runs in your family."

I hastily grabbed my purse, sensing that he immediately regretted his words. I didn't give him a chance to apologize, running out the same door Creed had moments before with Rebel calling out my name behind me.

There was no looking back. The damage was done, and I had no one to blame but myself.

"Jesus Christ, man. Relax."

"Fuck you, Diesel!" I seethed, punching the bag in the weight room. Trying like hell not to picture my brother's fucking face as I delivered blow upon blow to the leather. Failing miserably in doing so.

"I knew she looked familiar. I thought I saw them together that—"

I shot him a warning glare, shutting him up real fucking quick.

"Damn…" He stepped back, surrendering his hands. "This girl has really gotten under your skin. Never thought I'd see the day. How did an ugly fuck like you bag a young one? Her pussy must be tight as fuck."

"Talk about her pussy one more time, motherfucker, and watch what happens," I growled, meaning every word.

Diesel chuckled, backing away and leaving me alone.

I received my DD 214 discharge papers at zero-six-hundred that morning, releasing me from the Army. Never in a million years did I think I'd walk out of *my* bathroom and see Pippin sitting on *my* bed in *my* room.

In the fucking clubhouse.

Waiting for my little brother to fuck her…

Again.

I punched the bag harder, almost knocking it off the goddamn chain. I was so pissed I could barely fucking see straight. Not believing one goddamn word she said, knowing she did this to get back at me for rejecting her. For pushing her away. I couldn't believe she didn't know that she was in my club. As soon as she saw the cuts on the men, it should have clicked, especially my fucking brother's. She knew what she was doing here. That fact alone had me seeing red. My mind was reeling, spinning out of control.

What if something would have happened to her?

An unclaimed woman at club parties is free for all.

Pushing her into my brother's arms was never my fucking intention.

I walked back into my room an hour later, my blood boiling and my temper searing to the point of fucking pain. Finding Noah sitting on a chair with his back toward me like he hadn't moved from the place he sat.

"Where is she, you little shit?" I asked through a clenched jaw, looking around the room. Holding back the urge to break his face in, I grabbed a beer out of the fridge instead, chugging it. Grabbing another one and doing the same.

He got up, throwing something in the trash. Turning back around to face me, leaning on the counter with his arms crossed over his chest. He simply stated, "She left." Nodding. "Listen, Creed, I don't know what's going on between you two or how you even know each other. You may not be my favorite fuckin' person, but you're still my brother. I never would have touched her if I knew she was your girl. I just asked her point blank, and she confirmed she isn't. That said… I like her, bro. She's different. Never met anyone like her before. Nice change of pace from the whores all around here."

"She ain't right for you, Noah. Stay the fuck away from her. Do you understand me?"

"Don't think I can do that anymore," he implied, looking down at the trash.

"The fuck is that supposed to mean?"

He shrugged. "I guess we'll find out." Pushing off the counter, he walked past me to leave.

"She's fifteen. She's a fuckin' minor. You know that?"

He abruptly stopped dead in his tracks, turning to look at me again. I knew by the expression on his face he didn't know that little fact.

"She told me she was eighteen. What do you mean she's only fifteen?"

I scoffed out, cocking my head, "She lied."

"Well, shit…" He shook his head, wide-eyed. Without saying another word, he backed away from me and left.

"Fuck," I said to myself, finishing off my beer. Chucking it at the trash so hard it knocked it over.

I sighed, rubbing the back of my head from the sudden splitting headache. Pissed as hell that I'd only been home for two hours and was already knee deep in a shit- storm. I had a feeling war was far from fucking over. I just never imagined it would be over Mia. I don't know how long I stood there before finally getting my feet to move. Crouching down in front of the mess to pick the garbage up off the floor. A few beer bottles, paper towels, and a paper bag that a white stick fell out of onto the floor by my feet.

I reached down and picked it up. "The fuck?" I said out loud, almost knocked on my ass seeing the positive pregnancy stick in my hands.

I threw on a shirt, my cut, and boots, hauling ass out of my room. "Noah! Where the fuck are ya?!" I screamed so loud it echoed off the walls.

Walking outside to see that his truck was gone, I didn't think twice about it. Jumping on my bike, I took off like a bat out of hell. I went to Mia's parents' house first, not giving a fuck if they found out about me.

No one was home.

I headed to their restaurant next, looking for her there with no luck. Asking the waitress if she knew where she was or if she'd seen her. She said she was over at some party for a christening, dismissing me. I used my charm to get what I wanted until she finally gave me the address.

I sped the entire way there, not giving a shit I was going way over the speed limit. My heart pounded the closer I got, but I unable to get to her fast enough. There were cars everywhere lining the small private drive. I parked my bike right on the street, barely getting the kickstand down before rushing toward the house.

Rage took over as I slammed the front door open, not bothering to knock.

"Where is she? Mia! Where the fuck are you?! I know you're here!" I hollered, barreling through the door.

My eyes couldn't move fast enough, intently peering around the room full of preppy, uptight people. Giving them all a threatening look to not intervene. A few seconds later, I spotted Mia in the corner, shocked as shit to see me there.

I was over to her in four strides, getting right up in her face. Her bright blue eyes wide and anxious.

"Creed!" she screeched, trying to back away.

I didn't waver, grabbing her arm and holding her in place. It was the first time I ever manhandled her this way, but the moment I read positive on the white pregnancy stick my patience was long fucking gone. I loomed over her small frame with a menacing glare, causing her to cower back.

Afraid of me.

"I found this in the trash," I gritted out through a clenched jaw, throwing the stick at her. "You did this on purpose, didn't you?! You wanted this!" I snarled, pulling her closer to me by her arm.

"I... no... I didn't! I swear!" she stuttered, fervently shaking her head.

"Look me in the goddamn eyes and tell me you didn't plan this."

"No! Of cour—"

I saw him from the corner of my eye before he came right between us without thinking of the consequences.

I knew right then and there.

This was her fucking daddy.

"Back the fuck up if you know what's good for you. And get the fuck out of this house," he ordered, eyeing me up and down with a threatening regard.

I scoffed, matching his stare. "Fuck you! Now you want to be all protective? You're too late. Your fifteen-year-old daughter went and got herself knocked up. Congratu-fucking-lations, Grandpa." I shoved him, wanting him out of my fucking face. He barely wavered, ready to strike back.

"Creed! Enough!"

I recognized that voice. My eyes flew to Martinez who was casually walking over to us. I jerked back, stunned that he was there.

"This isn't the time or the place. There are women and children present."

I scowled. "Since when the fuck do you care about any of that?"

"Since this is my niece's home. And her kids are my blood. Me and your club have never had any problems. If you want to keep it that way, I suggest you take your ass outside and walk away."

I took a look around, finally realizing Martinez was right. Pissed that my temper outweighed anything else, I stepped back, looking over at Mia again.

"This ain't over." I nodded at her.

And it wasn't.

It was far from fucking over.

It had only just begun.

The rumbling of his motorcycle as it roared to life shook the entire living room. Driving away, taking my heart with him. It hurt like hell when he ripped out the pregnancy stick in front of everyone, including my parents. Throwing me under the bus and leaving me there to face the wrath that he unleashed. It didn't bother me half as bad as him thinking I'd done this intentionally to hurt him. I could swear on everyone's lives staring at me in the room, I didn't know Rebel was his brother. I didn't even know he had a brother! It wasn't like he talked about his life all those times we saw each other.

For the first time since I'd met him all those years ago, I was terrified of him. I'd never seen him that angry, that cruel or vicious. Making me question if I ever really knew the man behind the cut.

The real Creed.

I couldn't blame him. I fucked up, ruining my life.

Yet, I wanted to run after him. I wanted to punch him in the face. But most of all, I wanted to tell him how sorry I was. But I couldn't. My feet were glued to the damn floor with a few dozen eyes on me.

"Mia," Momma coaxed, standing in front of me. "Oh my God! Is it true? You're pregnant?"

I stood there frozen in place, not knowing how to make it better.

"I didn't even know you had a boyfriend? And now this? What were you thinking? You got yourself wrapped up with an MC? How old is that guy? He has to be in his late twenties."

Her eyes filled with tears as she brought her shaking hand up to her mouth. My father stood there with rage in his eyes, hands in fists at his side. His friends ready to hold him back, from me. My glossy eyes wandered around the room, mortified, overwhelmed not knowing what to say.

"It's not his. It's his younger brother's. I'm so sorry, Momma," I found myself saying, running out the back door. I needed to get out of there, I needed some fresh air. The walls were caving in on me.

I ran all the way to my special spot on the other side of the lake. Hunching over by the willow tree, emptying out the contents of my stomach. Which wasn't anything new as of late. Looking over to the water, I tried to calm my nerves, picturing one of the happiest days of my life with him. Here on this lake. Thinking about where I went wrong since then. Going from innocent Mia to a fifteen-year-old knocked up and alone.

Wiping the corners of my mouth with the back of my hand, I took my phone out. Calling the only person, I knew that would be on my side.

"Hey babe, what's up?"

"Giselle, I need you to come get me," I cried into the receiver.

"Are you alright? What happened? Where are you?"

"Please, just hurry. I'm over by Uncle Austin's. The far side of the lake by the willow tree. I just need to get out of here."

"Mia, you're scaring me. What's wrong? Why aren't you inside with everyone for the christening party? I was just on my way there," she rambled.

"Giselle! Please!" I broke down, sobbing. My emotions taking over.

"Stay put, I'll be there in fifteen minutes."

I hung up the phone not saying another word. Sitting on the rope swing, rubbing my nonexistent belly, blankly staring at the ripples in the water from my tears. Wondering what the hell I was going to do.

Giselle pulled down the dirt road minutes later. I dried my tears the best I could, walking over to her car, opening the passenger door and getting in. She instantly pulled me over the center console hugging me tight.

"Why are you crying? What's going on?" she questioned, pulling back, looking me in the face.

I just shook my head, as more tears ran down my cheeks.

"Oh my God." Her hand went to her chest. "It's Mason? Did something happen to him?"

My brother re-enlisted for another two years in the Army, much to her dismay. I think they were now taking a break, whatever that meant.

I shook my head no, unable to speak.

"Mia Ryder! You almost gave me a heart attack."

"I'm so sorry. Can you take me home please?" I leaned against the window welcoming the cool sensation from the air conditioning.

"Not till you tell me what's going on."

"I don't want to talk about it!" I snapped, the hormones in my body on overdrive.

"Okay, okay..." She put her hands out in front of her. "You know you can talk to me, right?"

"I know," I whispered, still staring out the window. "You'll find out soon enough," I said to myself. As she drove off.

By the time we pulled up to my house, my parents' and my uncle's cars were all parked in the driveway. I walked inside like I was walking to my execution. The second I opened the door, I could hear them all arguing. Going back and forth on what was going on, how to handle me, and what would happen next. Like they were the ones to decide my fate.

"What's going on?" Giselle questioned, going in first.

I shut the door behind me, following close behind her. Everyone stopped talking and all eyes fell on me, once we walked into the room. Momma was sitting on the couch, looking like she hadn't stopped crying since the truth was thrown in her face. Aunt Lily was sitting beside her, rubbing her back. Dad was standing by the far wall seething, even more pissed than he was before I left Uncle Austin's.

All of my uncles stood around the room. Giselle went over to her dad, Uncle Dylan, with a confused expression on her face, mouthing, 'What was going on?'

I took a deep breath, sitting on the step that divided the foyer and living room.

"I know you're all disappointed in me, but I swear I never meant for this to happen. It was my first time. You know me... I'm not this girl. We used protection. I guess it just broke."

Giselle's mouth dropped open, her eyes widening in shock.

"The girl I know. The baby girl I raised would have never spread her legs open for some piece of shit on a motorcycle," Dad snapped, speaking to me in a way he never had before.

Giselle's jaw hit the floor, knowing exactly whom my father was referring to.

"Lucas..." Mom coaxed, shooting him a warning glare. Aunt Lily shook her head, knowing where this was leading.

"What, Alex? You're going to excuse your daughter for getting knocked up at fifteen? Who do you think is going to raise that baby? Huh? Who's going to help her? We are! Forgive me if I'm not babying my kid for her reckless irresponsibility that's going to fuck up her entire future and ours! What the fuck were you thinking, Mia?"

Maybe it was the hormones.

Maybe it was the lack of sleep I experienced since I found out I was pregnant three days ago.

Or maybe it was just not giving a shit anymore.

It couldn't get any worse.

"Now, you're not going to baby me? That's a first. You think I wanted this? You think I'm ready to be a teenage mom? Are you for real, Dad? All you've done in my almost sixteen years of life is treat me like I'm still five-years-old. I can't go here! I can't go there! I can't do this! I can't do that! I'm surprised you let me go to school and not have Mom homeschool me so I don't ever leave the house!"

He stepped toward me, but Uncle Dylan placed his arm out in front of him, stopping him. "You're blaming this on me? For protecting you?!"

"For suffocating me!" I stood, striding over to him, not giving a shit if I was about to cross the line. "Mason messed up all the time! How about the time you found weed in his truck? How many times did he come home drunk before he even turned sixteen? How many times did the school call you because he skipped or got suspended? How many times, how many times, how many times... the list could go on and on and on. Did he ever get punished? No! What did you do... Nothing! He got a slap on the wrist. Why? Because 'boys will be boys,' right? Isn't that what you said? Bo does whatever he wants. He's never even had a curfew! You even let girls in his room! Wonder what he's up to in there, Dad!" I paused to let my words sink in. "Me, on the other hand, I get straight A's, barely ever missed a day of school, and can never leave the house! What did you expect would happen?!" I screamed, stomping my foot. Needing to have my voice heard for the first time.

"You have never given me the chance to make mistakes! You never let me learn on my own! It's not fair! Yes! I messed up. I know that. I'm sorry! But I'm a good kid, I'm a good daughter." My eyes watered with fresh tears, my voice breaking. "You making me feel like a bigger asshole than I already feel like isn't going to change the fact that I'm pregnant. I have a baby growing inside of me," I cried, wiping them away. "And no, I'm not crying for you to feel bad for me. I'm crying because I can't stop crying! I can't stop throwing up! I can't stop feeling like shit! I can't sleep! Trust me, I'm feeling every last bit of the consequences for spreading my legs, Daddy. You can't punish me any more than my body, mind, and heart, already have and will continue to do for the next nine months!"

No one said anything for the longest time. I sat back down on the step, the nauseous feeling returning again with a vengeance. I placed my head in my lap, trying to breathe through the queasy feeling. Hoping it would go away fast, I didn't want to throw up again. I hated it.

I felt someone sit beside me moments later, rubbing my back, trying to make me feel better. I turned my head to the side to see who it was. Never expecting it to be my mother. Sitting there with a look of disappointment, hurt, and remorse all at once. Making me feel like a bigger piece of shit.

"Deep breaths, Mia, it will subside," she coaxed, pulling my hair off my back, keeping me cool.

Aunt Lily sat on the other side of me, handing me a glass of water, telling me to take slow sips. I knew it was far from over by any means, but it meant so much to me that my mom and aunt were at least trying to make me feel better. Silently praying that maybe they understood.

"Who is he?" Dad demanded in a hard tone. Shaking Uncle Dylan off.

I looked back up, taking in his expression I'd never seen before. He eyed me up and down as if he hated to see me hurting, but the disappointment was too much for him to overlook.

"It doesn't matter," I simply stated. "It's not Creed's, okay? Not the guy who showed up at Uncle Austin's. It's his younger brother's. I know it doesn't make this any better, but it was an accident. It's my mistake. It will be my responsibility."

Dad narrowed his eyes at me. "So he gets you pregnant and the little shit won't take responsibility for his own kid? What's his name, Mia?"

"I'm not telling you. You're just going to go over there. You don't know who you are dealing with, Dad. Who his friends and family are."

"Mia, is his whole family bikers? Is that your concern?" Mom inquired, trying to connect the pieces together.

"I don't know…"

"What do you mean you don't know? We need to talk to his parents'. They need to know what's going on. It's not as simple as you saying you're pregnant, end of story. The boy needs to—"

"I don't even know him," I blurted, interrupting her. Regretting my words immediately.

"You don't know him?" Dad repeated, taking a long hard look at me. "What do you mean you don't know him, Mia? He's not your boyfriend?"

My heart was beating so fast, I thought it was going to fall out of my chest as I looked around the room. Giselle's face filled with worry and guilt. I wanted to scream "This isn't your fault!" but I didn't want to call her out. She was the only person who had been there for me. This had nothing to do with her.

So I said the only thing to be true. "I went to a party…"

My father closed his eyes like he knew what I was about to say next.

"One thing led to another. He was nice. I don't know what else you want me to say."

I didn't want to go into more detail than that. If I mentioned the drinking then they would think he took advantage of me, which couldn't be further from the truth.

"I'm sorry. I know that doesn't make anything better. I just wanted one night to feel like a normal teenager. I know what my decision has cost me. I get it, okay? I can't change the past. I wish I could, but it happened. I'm pregnant. Nothing is going to change that. He didn't do anything wrong. It was all me. I take full responsibility for it. So, please... just drop it."

"Does he know, Mia?" Aunt Lily asked.

I nodded. "I told him, but I don't want him to be a part of anything. I just told him because it was the right thing to do," I lied, already knowing what my father wanted to do.

I could see it in his eyes, everything I was saying was pointless. It wasn't going to end here. That was for sure.

"Giselle," Dad said, turning to face her. "Do you know who it is?"

She shook her head no.

"Do you know who Creed is?" he followed, cocking his head to the side.

She looked back at me for a sign of what to say. I pleaded with her through my eyes. Begging her not to tell him.

"What's his last name?" Uncle Dylan broke in, looking down at his daughter.

If she gave him a last name, he could find him, he was a detective. All he needed was a last name.

"Giselle," he warned in a stern tone.

She frowned, mouthing, "I'm sorry," to me. Slowly peering up at her father and said, "Jameson."

I lost the battle.

Now bringing the war to Creed.

I stormed into Ma's house looking for Noah. He was nowhere to be found at the clubhouse, I waited for him all afternoon. He never showed up.

"Noah!" I shouted, barreling my way into his room. Slamming the door open, finding him sitting on the edge of his bed with his head resting in his hands.

"Jesus, honey, what is going on?" Ma announced, walking into the room behind me.

"Ma know? Did you tell her?"

He glared up at me. "Obviously not. How do you know?"

"You left your partyin' gift in my trash."

His eyes glazed over, opening his mouth to say something but quickly shutting it. Looking back over to our mother.

"Oh, no… Noah… please tell me, you didn't?" she pondered, her intuition kicking in.

"I used a condom. I don't know how this happened," he exclaimed and it took everything inside me not to knock him the fuck out.

"Please… tell me it wasn't one of the club whores. I will kill your father."

"No, Ma. She's the farthest thing from that," he replied.

"How did—"

"You little shit!" someone interrupted her, banging on the front door. Echoing in through the open windows. "Come out here, you piece of shit! You think you can knock up my daughter! Use her! Get out here and talk to me man to man!"

"Fuck…" I rasped, pushing Noah back. "Stay," I ordered him, my hand still placed on his chest.

I left before he could answer. Pulling out my gun and leaving it in my room. The last thing I wanted was to go head to head with Pippin's father, so I left my gun behind. If we were fighting, it would be with our fists. Even though I didn't want to disrespect him more than I already had. Allowing my anger to get the best of me.

With him and especially with Mia.

I couldn't blame him for showing up here. I would've done the same if it was my baby girl.

"I'm not here for you!" he roared, when I opened the door. "Where is he? Where's your brother?"

I was shocked when my mother pulled back the door, standing beside me.

"I know you're upset, sir," she calmly stated. "I'm his mother, Diane. I just learned of the news myself, seconds before you showed up actually. I'm not happy about it either, but how about you come inside and we talk like adults." She stepped aside, gesturing for them to come in.

I eyed her warily as she walked past me with everyone in tow, flashing me a reassuring smile. Although it wasn't under the best circumstances, I felt a sense of pride wash over me. Finally realizing how far she'd truly come.

"Would you like something to drink? Can I get you anything?" she asked, nodding to them.

They shook their heads no.

"Where's your son?" her dad demanded not wasting any time.

"Lucas," one of his boys with long blond hair, tied back in a ponytail coaxed.

I knew it was Giselle's dad, the detective. I recognized him from the pictures in her apartment. Also from some of the run-ins he had with the club when I was a kid. He eyed me when he saw I was checking out his holstered gun, quickly peering right over the Vice Prez on my cut.

"I'm not here for a pleasant conversation, I want to talk to your boy. Now, where the hell is he?" her dad snapped, bringing my attention back to him.

"Listen, man, I feel ya, I know he fucked up. But it takes two to tango. She's just as much to blame as he is," I proclaimed, even though it killed me to think of Mia as anything other than pure and innocent.

My Pippin.

He was over to me in three strides, getting right up in my face. His boys immediately came over, getting ready to hold him back.

I stood taller, not backing down.

"She's my baby girl!" he seethed, shoving them off. "That little shit knocked up my only daughter! If he's man enough to get her pregnant then he needs to step out here and man the fuck up! Instead of sending his big brother. Tell him to get his ass out here or better yet." He tried to sidestep me. "I'll go back there and drag him out!"

"The hell you are!" I pushed him back, regretting it was already coming to this. "Gonna have to go through me."

I learned right then that Mia's old man didn't fuck around. We had more in common than I ever would have thought.

He stumbled a little, catching himself on one of his boys. "Not a problem!" Charging me, he rammed his shoulder into my torso and slammed me back against the wall.

I instantly fought back, grabbing ahold of his shirt, trying to wrestle him to the ground. Both of us trying to gain the upper hand until his boys stepped in, yanking us apart. Holding us back while we tried to break free. Ma stood there and screamed the entire time for us to stop. Car tires screeched outside, bringing our attention to the front window, seeing a car slamming on the brakes. I watched Mia get out of the car before it even fully stopped. Running up to the door with Giselle not far behind her.

I shoved them off of me, opening the door for them before they knocked. Mia instantly looked around the room with a worried expression written clear across her face, knowing exactly what just went down between me and her old man.

"Please... Don't do this," she pleaded, running to stand in front of her father. Placing her hand on his chest, hoping to calm him.

"Mia, what are you doing here?" he questioned, breaking the silence.

"You can't do this! It's not going to change anything! Please... it's not Creed's fault!"

"It's not your fault either, Mia," Noah announced, walking into the room. Never fucking listening to a word I said.

"This him?"

Mia nodded, holding her father back.

"I'm Noah," he added, glancing over at Mia who had a surprised expression on her face. "Sir, I take full responsibility for my actions. You want a man, here I am." Rendering him speechless and everyone else for that matter.

Her dad eyed him up and down, taking in his tattoos, his cut, and the way he was standing. Then back at me, looking at me the exact same way with nothing but hatred and rage in his glare.

"How old are you?" he sneered through a clenched jaw.

Fuck, I knew where this was going...

"Eighteen, sir," Noah replied, eyeing me. Knowing what he was insinuating.

"You little shit! I'm going to have you arrested! She's fifteen!" He lunged at Noah as I stepped in front of him, but he was quickly halted by the detective grabbing ahold of him at the last second.

Stating, "Can't do shit, Lucas. In the state of North Carolina, it's not statuary rape if they're within four years of age from each other. She's also almost sixteen. It's the legal age of consent here, too."

I jerked back, caught off guard by the information. I never knew that. Her dad just shook his head, backing away. Grabbing Mia and pulling her with him. Taking one last look at us and turned to leave.

Mia and I locked eyes the entire time.

Both of us thinking the exact same thing.

Her sweet sixteen was only two weeks away.

I lay in the grass near the old train tracks with one hand supporting my head and the other resting on my belly. Looking up in the sky, watching the fluffy white clouds pass, blocking the warm sun. Thinking how my life had changed and what was yet to come.

I turned sixteen two weeks ago, and I was ten weeks pregnant and counting. My parents' were still pissed beyond belief, but my mom started coming around. At least we were on speaking terms, and she was willingly helping me. My dad, on the other hand, I was lucky if he looked in my direction. I steered clear of him on most days, not wanting to endure anymore of his disappointment. They made the decision to pull me out of school for the duration of my pregnancy. Mom started homeschooling me even though she had a restaurant to run.

Bo wasn't happy when I told him either, but mostly because he was my big brother, being protective over me. Wanting to know who knocked me up and when could he lay the boy out. Making me laugh. Mason hadn't called. He was deployed overseas again, and there was no knowing when he'd be in touch. So, I sent him a letter letting him know he was going to be an uncle and breaking the news it was Creed's brother's baby.

I'd hate to be the soldiers around when he read it.

My parents' let me get my driver's license, which was a complete shock to me. I guess they were trying to let go a little. Seeing it for what it was. Not sure if it was from being pregnant or what, but maybe my baby made them realize I wasn't a little girl anymore. Plus, I'd need a way to get around with the baby.

Mom took me to the OBGYN a few days after they found out I was pregnant, and the doctor only confirmed what I already knew. She cried, I cried, I felt like I never stopped crying. Dad didn't say a word as he stood there, but Mom said he would eventually come around. He was just being stubborn and bullheaded, and I would always be his baby girl no matter what. It would take him time to warm up to the idea that his baby was having a baby.

I hated being the reason that there was so much tension in my house again. Which was why I started spending more time at the beach or at the train tracks. I would come here from time to time, riding my bike when things were at their worst in life. I'd picture myself hopping on a train and never looking back. Getting away from it all. Sort of like I envisioned doing right now. Disappearing for a minute. For a moment. My life couldn't get any more complicated if I tried.

The rumbling of a motorcycle pulled me away from my thoughts. I sat up, looking behind me, watching Creed pull onto the grass close by. I hadn't seen him since the day my dad tried to raise hell at his house, three weeks ago. Thank God, Giselle knew where he lived, or who knows what else would have happened. He leaned his bike on the kickstand, took off his helmet, and looked down, locking eyes with me. Shooting an intense glare that left me speechless. His gaze speaking volumes without saying a word as he sat there on his bike, the two of us staring intently at each other.

For the first time, it pained me to have him look at me the way he was as if he was seeing me with different eyes. No longer the baby girl he thought I was but the woman who was carrying his brother's child. I knew this would change things between us and I hated that more than anything. For the last month, I thought about how our first encounter would go down. What I would say, what he would reply, what would come of our conversation. I didn't want a fight. I just wanted him to understand.

Never imagining it would be this hard.

When his stare shifted to my hand that was still on my belly, I swear I saw a glimmer of hope in his eyes, like he was contemplating things he felt he shouldn't.

262

"I didn't do it on purpose," I whispered loud enough for him to hear, focusing on my belly. Needing to get it out. "I didn't even know where we were going until my friend, Jill, pulled up to the clubhouse. As soon as I saw the men wearing the same cut as yours"—nodding to it—"I thought you might be there. It was part of the reason I got out of the car."

He didn't make a sound, listening to every word I was saying.

"We walked inside, instantly getting sucked into the chaos. One minute, Jill was next to me, the next she was gone. I'm sure you know what it's like. Those parties. I couldn't stop thinking about you, wishing you were there with me. Showing me your world. I was uncomfortable and I wanted to leave, but I left my phone in Jill's car. I tried to find her everywhere and I ended up drifting into the basement. This guy, Jigsaw came onto me…"

He narrowed his eyes at me, holding back his temper for what I just said. His hands white-knuckling his handlebar.

"I guess you can say your brother saved me. He was nice. I felt comfortable and safe with him. Why do you think that is, Creed?" I paused, looking up at him. "He's a part of you. I didn't know it then, but he's your brother and there was something about him that was so familiar, even though I'd never met him before. I guess that's why I told him he could call me Pippin because I wanted to maybe pretend it was you. I know that sounds so stupid and immature, but I missed you…" I explained, my voice breaking.

Dreading the next part of what I was about to say, knowing it would only further his pain. Hurting him more than I already had.

"He kept me away from the madness, we went out to his truck and drank way more than I should have. I just wanted to stop thinking about you. I just wanted to forget. I just wanted one night where I could be a normal teenager doing what everyone else does. I know I took it too far, but as much as I hate to admit this, I thought maybe if I wasn't a virgin anymore you'd want me," I breathed out, blinking away the tears. "One thing led to another, and we ended up in your room. He didn't know I was a virgin until…" Shaking away the memory, I took a deep breath. "He was good to me, but none of that matters because I couldn't stop thinking about you. Wishing it was you. Even after you pushed me away—rejecting me, being cruel—I still wanted it to be you."

He was the first to break our connection, staring out in front of him, staggered by my confession. Opening his mouth but quickly shutting it, struggling with what he needed to say. Biting his tongue with what he wanted to say. He took a deep breath, reaching into his cut and pulling out his cigarettes. Lighting one up, bringing it to his lips, inhaling half of it into his lungs before letting it slowly seep out of his nose and mouth.

"You're no better than the club whores," he blew out. "Sleepin' with a man to get somethin' in return. You got somethin' aiight, and it wasn't *me*. How's it feel to be knocked up and fuckin' alone?"

I cringed, my heart visibly breaking in front of him. Subconsciously placing my hand on my chest, I stood up on wobbly legs. His words cutting into my skin like tiny knives all over, in ways I didn't think were possible. After pouring my soul out, after everything I just told him, that was his response. If that wasn't a slap in the damn face, then I don't know what was.

I stepped back, away from him, shaking my head with wide eyes, my mouth open. I couldn't stand the sight of him for another second.

He wasn't the man I knew.

The man I thought.

I immediately turned to leave, not making it three steps until he caught me by the wrist and spinning me around to face him again.

"We ain't done. Don't ever walk away from me. You understand me?"

"Fuck you! Let go!" I struggled to get away from him, but he wasn't having it. He grabbed my other wrist, tugging me forward, making me lose my footing. Slamming me into his hard chest.

Our crazed stares never wavered from one another.

"That's what ya want, yeah? Fuckin' provokin' me. This what gets you wet? Me manhandlin' you?"

"No!" I lied, knowing he knew me all too well.

He snidely grinned. "Did my brother even make you come, Pippin? Did he even know how to touch your sinful fuckin' body? Your temptin' little pussy?" he growled close to my mouth.

"You're an asshole!"

"Call it like I see it, sweetheart."

I cocked my head to the side, looking deep into his eyes. Not faltering. "Yeah, Creed. He made me come. So. Damn. Hard… at least one of you has the balls to finish what he starts."

His eyes dilated, gripping onto the back of my neck he crashed his mouth onto mine. Clutching onto the side of my face with his other hand and biting my bottom lip, exactly the way I had fantasized him doing since our encounter in the guest bedroom. His hands fell to my ass, gripping me tight, picking me up in one swift motion, and causing my dress to ride up my thighs. Making me straddle his waist, he walked us backward.

My senses heightened, taking in the scent of cigarettes and whiskey as he plunged his rough tongue into my mouth. Suddenly realizing he had been drinking, but I didn't care.

The taste of him was all around me.

The memory of him didn't even compare to real life.

He straddled his bike with me now on his lap, yanking me closer, molding us into one person and kissing me as if his life depended on it. I moaned into his mouth, he groaned into mine as he fisted my hair by the nook of my neck. His other hand glided down the side of my breast to the seam of my panties.

"Please," I begged against his lips.

He roughly jerked my hair back to look into my eyes. He was fighting an internal battle I wanted to win so fucking bad.

I rocked my hips, pleading with him through my lust-filled glare. Baiting him. Tempting him. Doing whatever I could for him to touch me. When I felt his fingers slide my panties over, gliding them into my wet folds.

I swallowed hard.

"Fuck, you're so wet. I did this to you. Me," he growled, continuing to work my clit.

I leaned into kiss him again, but he tore my hair back harder, wanting me to stay right where I was, spread wide open for him.

Only him.

It was then I realized he wanted to watch me fall over the edge, and I swear I could have come from the intense, predatory, loving way he was staring at me, alone.

Feeling him deep within my core.

He rubbed me back and forth, and my body shuddered. I wanted to come so bad. Knowing it wasn't just what his skilled fingers were doing against my heat, but because it was him.

I was with Creed.

The man I'd loved since I was nine-years-old.

He became firmer and more demanding, pushing two fingers into my opening, causing a shameless moan to escape my mouth. His lips parted like he was feeling everything I was when all he was doing was watching me come apart for him. His fingers working me over, finding a spot inside of me, creating this longing, this intensity, this mind-blowing explosion all over my body. Every last inch of my skin felt what he was creating, especially my heart.

"Feels good, yeah?" he raspingly urged as I continued to try to keep my fluttering eyes open.

"Yes," I finally whimpered.

Completely at his mercy.

"Here?" he taunted, pushing harder against my g-spot.

My back arched over the gas tank, my dress riding up, exposing his sweet torture. Allowing him to go faster and harder. I felt warm all over with the uncontrollable need for something to happen that would take away this ache that he was building.

Higher and higher.

When I felt his thumb manipulate my nub as his fingers continued to rub my sweet spot, I thought I was going to die.

Right then and there.

"Come on my fingers, Mia. Wanna feel your tight, sweet fuckin' pussy."

That was my undoing.

My body erupted in a fit of spasms, my eyes rolled to the back of my head, and my breathing hitched. Panting out his name. He pulled me close, wrapping my arms around his neck and kissing me. Drowning out the loud, foreign sounds coming out of my mouth.

Biting on my bottom lip again, he ordered, "Eyes on me."

I opened my hooded gaze, trying to catch my bearings.

He took a long, hard look at me and spoke with conviction, "Only I can make you fuckin' come like that. And now I'm gonna make you come on my cock."

My eyes widened as he leaned back, unbuckled his belt, unzipped his pants, watching only me as his cock sprung free.

I slightly gasped.

He grinned, taking in the look on my face. "Don't worry, darlin', I'll start off slow."

He grabbed my hips, lifting me up, positioning himself at my opening. "Say the word, Mia. Gonna let me in? Cuz once I start, I won't fuckin' stop." Nudging the head of his dick in a little further, almost making me come undone from the skin-on-skin contact, savoring in the feeling only he could ever give me.

"Yes..." I panted.

That was all the convincing he needed. He eased me down on his shaft, letting out a groan when he was balls deep inside me. Allowing me to get used to the size of his cock.

Holding what was now *his* between his hands, he placed his forehead on mine.

"Fuck, Mia. So fuckin' tight, baby girl."

His hands made their way down to my hips once again, guiding my movements. Finding a rhythm as he drove his cock in and out of me. I couldn't take it anymore. I leaned back, relishing in what was happening between us. Overpowered by the feelings he stirred all around me. It was all I ever wanted, needed, finally feeling complete. Allowing the familiar ache to take over. He grabbed the sides of my face, bringing his lips back over to mine, kissing me with so much passion.

So much love.

So much everything.

He. Wanted. Me.

"No more bullshit between us. You want to be kissed, touched, fucked," he groaned against my lips. "Then *I* fuck you. I'm claimin' you, Pippin. You're fuckin' mine."

And I was.

I always had been.

She smiled, looking up at me with mischievous eyes as I helped her off my bike. Tucking my cock back into my jeans, I buckled up and adjusted myself on the seat.

"Why you smilin'?" I asked, arching an eyebrow, knowing all too well why she was.

She threw her arms around my neck, softly kissing my mouth again. Murmuring, "I love you."

"Pippin—"

"I know you love me," she interrupted. "I'm not expecting you to say it back. As much as I wanted this to happen between us, Creed, and you know I did, more than anything." Looking at me with so much worry in her eyes. "I'm carrying your brother's child, and I don't ever want you to think of you and me or what just happened between us as a mistake. It wasn't. Even though Noah and I were never a couple, we don't even know each other, it was an accident... I just can't help feeling bad. You know I'm not this girl... right? Please tell me you know I'm not one of those club whores."

I placed her face between my hands, peering at her adoringly, the way I had wanted to since the moment I gave her that first kiss. Mia had always been mine. From the second I watched her jump out of her mom's car, pigtails and all.

She was mine.

"You're the furthest fuckin' thing from those whores. Trust me, darlin', can't even come close to you. Shit happens. I know that more than anyone. Can't keep pushin' you away. Look what it cost me." I nodded toward her stomach. "I fucked up. Won't do that again. I know who you are, Mia Ryder. From the second I saw you, and I've loved ya every day since for it."

She beamed, tears falling down her sweet face.

"I lost one woman cuz I thought I was doin' right by her. Shit... I almost lost you. Not makin' the same mistake twice. Want you on the back of my bike, Pippin, ya feel me?"

She nodded.

And I meant every word.

Three hits of the gavel sounded, bringing church into session.

"As you know, Sinner's Rejoice's Prez and I have called a truce. It's taken over seven fuckin' years to get to this point, but we've come to an agreement. They stay out of our territory, and we'll stay out of theirs. They're no longer a threat," Pops declared, glancing all around the room.

"Just like that?" I replied, narrowing my eyes at him.

"You callin' me a liar?"

"Been gone a long time, old man. And up until I was discharged, shit was still goin' down. Find it shockin' is all."

"I take care of my club. Have been since before you even left my cock, Creed. I know what I'm doin'. You let me worry about our alliances."

"I'm Vice Prez, if you remember correctly. Got a right to voice my goddamn opinion, and I will," I rasped, leaning into the table. Resting my elbows on the wood. "Unless I'm put to ground. Then and only then, I'll be shit outta luck."

The air was so thick between us. It had been since the day I told him I was enlisting in the Army, but even more so now that I was back. The Prez didn't scare me any more than my old man ever did. I'd been through too much shit to give a damn about him any longer.

"Yeah?" I mocked, leaning back in my chair.

"Anyone else got anythin' to say? Speak now, or shut the fuck up," he added, knowing damn well no one would cross him. "That's what I thought."

The meeting carried on for the next half hour while regular business was handled. After Pops sounded the gavel, dismissing us, I walked back to my room to grab my phone. As I walked in, I heard it buzzing on the counter, grabbing it never expecting who the message would be from.

Unknown number, I swiped open the text.

You obviously haven't seen any of the files I gave you. Get your head out of your ass, son. I'll do you a favor this one time, but next time I hand you a golden fucking ticket, you better cash it in.

My phone vibrated again, indicating I had another text message.

"The fuck?" I whispered to myself, looking at a photo of my mother when she was younger, sitting in the arms of a man who wasn't my father.

"You headed over to your ma's?" Diesel asked from the doorway, bringing my attention back to him.

I clicked off the screen, placing my cell phone in my back pocket. Walking out of the room with him following behind me. "Naw, gonna see her tomorrow. Just got back, I'm fuckin' exhausted."

Pops had me traveling all over for the club, much like before. I'd been over in the Arizona chapter for the last three weeks.

"Oh, you're not goin' to the dinner?"

"Dinner?" I repeated, confused.

"Yeah. Rebel was sayin' some shit earlier that your ma invited his girl over for dinner."

"His girl?" I jerked back.

"Yeah. His baby mama. She's like five months along now, right?"

I shook my head, swearing under my breath, pissed as shit no one told me what was going on, especially Mia. She knew I was coming back today.

"Why you lookin' at me like that? You haven't fuckin' mentioned her. I figured you were over it. Don't fuckin' shoot the messenger!" he yelled out behind me.

I hauled ass out the door, jumping on my bike and getting the hell out of there. Speeding home to find out what the hell was going on. Why neither one of them felt the need to mention dinner. It didn't take me long until I pulled into the driveway, seeing Mia's black Jeep parked on the road out front.

I took off my helmet, peering into the house through the screen door from where I was parked. I sat there on my bike just watching Mia for a few minutes. I couldn't take my eyes off of her. I missed her so fucking much. She was wearing a long flowy dress, like the ones she wore all the time now. You couldn't even tell she was five months along unless she showed you her barely-there baby bump. Her dark, wavy, long hair cascaded along the sides of her face and down her back.

She was glowing.

Her pregnancy had been smooth sailing thus far. Growing fucking beautifully with each passing day. I already loved that baby living inside of her, even though it wasn't technically mine.

It was still a part of me, and that was good enough.

Ma walked into the room, fucking beaming, bringing her in for a hug. The excitement for something was written clear across her face, causing Mia to smile, hugging her tighter. She pulled away, handing Ma what looked like a picture. It wasn't until Noah came into view, throwing his arm around Mia and tugging her into his side like they were a fucking couple that lit a fire under my ass to get off my bike.

All eyes turned on me when I swung the door open, stepping inside.

"Creed, honey, what are you doing here?" Ma greeted.

"Since when do I need an invitation to come home? I interruptin' somethin', Noah?" I remarked, staring at my brother's arm which was still wrapped around *my* girl.

Mia followed my glare, shyly smiling at me before casually stepping aside from Noah. Trying to gauge my reaction as to how to act.

"Of course you don't. I just assumed you'd be at the club, honey, since you just got back this afternoon. Oh, you have to see this!" she celebrated, rushing over to me. "Mia brought this over with her. Look, honey! It's a girl! We're having a girl!" she beamed.

I grabbed the photo out of her hand, looking down at the baby girl in my grasp. There were no words that could describe what I felt holding a piece of Mia, a piece of my fucking heart in my hand at that moment. My eyes scanned the picture, taking in the tiny being's profile—arms, legs, hands and feet. Pouty lips like her momma.

She was already fucking perfect.

Peering back up at Mia, I asked, "Your phone broke, Pippin? Was workin' last night when you told me you missed me. Funny how those things work, yeah?"

Her smile quickly faded, not expecting that response. Taking baby girl's first photo out of my hand.

"Bro, don't see the reason why she has to call ya. You ain't the father," Noah snidely replied.

As much as I hated to give Noah props, he tried to get his ass to every doctor's appointment, much to her father's dismay and *mine*. He was stepping up, doing the right thing for his baby. Which also meant he was spending a lot of his free time with Mia, both of them getting to know each other. Figuring out how they were going to make this work before the baby came into the world in a few short months.

I was traveling so fucking much for the club, and I hated leaving her behind, but there wasn't much I could do about that. It's not like I could take her with me. It was too fucking dangerous, and she was quite pregnant, not to mention her daddy wouldn't have that. She was always on my mind, though. No matter where I was or what I was doing, my thoughts always drifted to her. We talked on the phone often, but it wasn't the same. Not even fucking close.

Our relationship was fucking complicated, to say the least.

"Boys..." Ma warned, looking back and forth between us. "Mia came over with some great news. You both check your testosterone at the door. You hear me? Not tonight. Dinner's going to be a while. Behave. I'm going to call Stacey and Laura and tell them we're having a girl."

Giving us both a stern face before she walked back into the kitchen. Noah's phone rang as soon as she left, breaking the silence between us.

"Yeah," he answered, walking out of the room.

I was hoping it was one of the brothers, ordering him to go be their bitch so I could spend the rest of the night alone with Mia. Actually fucking contemplating on calling one of them myself to make him go on a run. I grabbed Mia's hand instead, taking her by surprise, bringing her into my room. Shutting the door behind me, I leaned up against it and folded my arms over my chest.

She took a seat on my bed, preparing for my wrath. She knew I was fucking pissed.

"Creed…"

I put my hand up stopping her, cocking my head to the side. "You got one minute to fuckin' explain what the fuck that was." I pointed to the door behind me. "Before I lose my shit. Don't got any patience left for fuckin' bullshit tonight, Pippin. Fuckin' exhausted, been on my bike all goddamn day to come home to you. Only to find you at my ma's house with my brother's arm around you like you're his fuckin' property. When you're mine," I gritted out, emphasizing the last word.

She kicked off her sandals, sitting up on her knees in the center of the bed. Gazing up at me through her lashes, biting her bottom lip. She picked up the sides of her dress, swaying it side-to-side. Giving me that look I knew all too fucking well.

"Do you like my dress? It's new…" She smiled, batting her lashes. "I bought it just for you, babe. I know how you love the color white on me."

"Is that right?" I grinned, pushing off the door. Walking over to her.

She fervently nodded with mischief in her eyes. "Do you have any idea how hard it is to find a dress that's still small but will fit my…" Gliding her fingers along the tops of her tits that were popping at the seam. "They're huge, right?" She leaned forward slightly pushing them together, baiting me.

I sat on the edge of the bed, reaching over and gently bringing her to straddle my lap. Pecking her lips down her neck and to her breasts that doubled in size since I'd seen her last. Taking my time, running my tongue along of seam of her white dress. Her head fell back, and a soft moan escaped her lips.

"Pippin?" I said between kisses. "As much as I'd like to titty fuck you and come on these right now, asked ya a question, expectin' a fuckin' answer." I pulled away, laying back on the bed with my hands under my head.

Leaving her wanting more.

"Didn't you miss me?" She pouted, grinding her hips on my hard cock, causing me to chuckle. She wasn't going to give up, so fucking relentless.

"Creed? Mia? What the fuck are you doin'?" Noah knocked on the door.

"Fuck off! We're busy!"

Shaking her head, she leaned in to kiss me, but I stopped her, putting my index finger to her lips. "Not gonna ask again, Mia."

She sighed, finally giving in. "Noah was just excited about finding out we're having a girl. He got carried away. It doesn't matter. Don't you trust me?"

In one swift movement, I laid her on the bed, easing myself on top of her. Closing her in with my arms, supporting all my weight.

"How often does that little shit get carried away? I saw him eyein' your tits. He get carried away with them, too? Don't fuckin' like it."

"It's not like that. I love you."

"You love me so fuckin' much, I'm the last to find out you're havin' a baby girl?"

"That's not fair. My appointment was this afternoon. I knew you were riding home. Not like you could have come... Besides, you wouldn't have heard my call anyway."

"Phone's always on vibrate. Try again."

She sighed again. "I don't know how all this works, Creed. It's new territory for me, too. I want my baby to have a father, and Noah has been there for all my appointments, he knows everything that's going on. He seems invested in being a part of helping me raise her. We're just getting to know each other so we can be the best parents to our baby. That's all."

"I respect the hell out of both of ya for that. But I'm gonna be just as much, if not more, a part of this baby girl's life as he is. Ya feel me?"

She nodded, and a sense of uncertainty passed through her expression. "I know you said you're claiming me, but I don't entirely understand what that means. Are you my boyfriend? Are we together?"

I kissed along her lips. "Not fuckin' anyone else, Pippin. Haven't in a while. Who's my girl?"

"I want to hear you say it. Not going to ask again, Creed," she mocked, making me smile as I ran my nose from her chin to her collarbone, kissing all over her breasts.

"How you smell so fuckin' good all the time? You're my girl," I reassured her, pulling down the front of her dress. "I lov—"

"Oh my God, babe! She just kicked," Mia cut me off. "Give me your hand. You need to feel this." She took ahold of my hand, placing it on her stomach. "Say something, I think she likes your voice."

Out of the corner of my eye, I saw something move. I immediately looked up, catching the reflection of a man outside through the black TV screen. "Fuck!" I roared.

Sounds of open fire shattered the glass windows and ricocheted off the walls, surrounding my entire room. I sprang into action, rolling Mia and I off my bed, tucking her head against my chest and trying to break our fall as I threw her onto the wood floor. Shielding her body with mine within seconds.

The air filled with rapid shots throughout the house, bullet casings falling all around us. Mia started to scream and cry in what sounded like pain. Shaking so fucking bad in my arms. My mother's screams could be heard in the distance, somewhere else in the house.

This was my worst fucking nightmare.

I kicked the tall wooden dresser over, knocking it to the ground, covering Mia's body as best I could. I pulled out my gun from the back of my jeans, sitting up on my knees without a second thought. Returning fire, shooting one of the motherfuckers right in the head.

When I looked back down, Mia was recoiling in pain, clutching onto her stomach.

"Fuck! Baby, you okay?" Pure panic assaulted my core, thinking she might have been hit.

"Creed, I can't… she's… it hurts…" she whimpered, barely speaking through the pain.

Noah came barreling into the room with a Glock in each hand, breaking my train of thought. I could still hear sounds of fire at the front of the house.

"Boys are coming! Ma's in the steel pantry, she's safe! Give her to me, Creed! I'll take her to the basement!"

"The fuck you will! Cover me!" I picked her up off the floor, cradling her in my arms. She cringed from the sudden movement.

Violence had always been a part of our fucking lives, but this time it felt personal. Something wasn't right, coming to our home. Bringing it here. Made no fucking sense. Especially while there were bullets spraying all over the goddamn walls. I hurried across the hall and into the office, nodding to Noah to pull up the carpet and wood door that led to the basement. Pops made sure there was always a way we could get out safely. Rigging several places in the house to hide, just in case shit like this ever went down.

I gently laid Mia on the ground in the back corner, hiding her behind the boxes of Luke's stuff.

The irony was not fucking lost on me.

"I'll be right back. Do not move!" I demanded in a harsher tone than I intended. Fucking panicking on the inside that I was leaving her alone in the first place.

"Creed... please..." she bellowed, not sure if it was from the pain or being scared fucking shitless. "Don't leave me...please...please, I need you!" she begged.

The terrified expression on her face was one I wish I never had to see.

Not from her.

Never from fucking her.

"Mia, you need to stay here. Protect our little girl, alright," Noah chimed in, pissing me off even more.

"Promise, baby. Be right back." I kissed her forehead, letting my lips linger there for a minute.

Hating that she was in pain and I had to leave her there to suffer. Standing back up, I listened, hearing more rounds go off.

The motherfuckers weren't done yet.

"Stay with Mia—"

"Fuck you! You're not goin' up there alone. We can take them all out. The boys are on their way. Won't be long."

"Noah—"

"Wasting fuckin' time! Let's go!"

I took one last look at Mia, needing to see her beautiful face before returning to the fucking chaos that had always been my life.

Grabbing more clips from the gun safe in the basement, I followed Noah back up the stairs. We sprinted down the narrow hall, hauling ass through the house, to take out the remainder of the motherfuckers. Immediately opening fire as soon as we stepped foot in the living room. Lacing bullets in the directions they were coming from outside. Two men wearing black bandanas covering their faces appeared to our left, unleashing several rounds from the side of the house, one hitting me in the leg.

"Shit, Creed! You've been hit!"

"Fuck it! I'm fine!"

An endless stream of bullets kept coming at us. Ducking, dodging, knocking over furniture, or whatever we could find to shield ourselves, shooting back when it was clear. Reloading our guns over and over again. Adrenaline coursed through my veins, throbbing through my bloodstream as we took turns taking out one fucker after another. Needing to finish this off to get back to Mia, to get her to the fucking hospital before she lost our baby girl. My heart pounded against my chest, taking over every last inch of my body.

Blood was seeping through my jeans. Shot after shot erupted from our hands. It felt like fucking forever until I heard the rumbling engines of Harleys coming down the street. Causing all fire to cease and the pussy-ass motherfuckers to get the hell out of here.

"Get Ma!" I ordered Noah, running so fucking fast down the hall, ignoring the sharp pain in my leg and the blood I was losing in the process. Rushing back toward the office.

"Pippin! I'm comin', baby!" I yelled, throwing off the carpet and makeshift door, making my way down the stairs to the far corner of the basement where I left her. "Mia!" I called out again, desperately waiting to hear her voice, assuring me she was okay. Terrified when I realized the basement was silent.

No screaming.

No crying.

Blood.

"The fuck..."

I thought I had experienced every loss I could have in my life. Felt every pain, every agony, and every hurt known to fucking man. But nothing could compare to the moment when I walked back to where I left my girl safely.

Where I left Mia...

And she wasn't fucking there.

TO BE CONTINUED...

Don't hate me.
I won't make you wait long. <3

Made in the USA
Columbia, SC
11 July 2017